The Bible True; or, The Cosmogony of Moses Compared with the Facts of Science

Anatiposi

Elijah M. Fly

The Bible True; or, The Cosmogony of Moses Compared with the Facts of Science

Reprint of the original, first published in 1871.

1st Edition 2023 | ISBN: 978-3-38211-984-3

Anatiposi Verlag is an imprint of Outlook Verlagsgesellschaft mbH.

Verlag (Publisher): Outlook Verlag GmbH, Zeilweg 44, 60439 Frankfurt, Deutschland
Vertretungsberechtigt (Authorized to represent): E. Roepke, Zeilweg 44, 60439 Frankfurt, Deutschland
Druck (Print): Books on Demand GmbH, In de Tarpen 42, 22848 Norderstedt, Deutschland

THE

BIBLE TRUE;

OR,

THE COSMOGONY OF MOSES COMPARED WITH THE FACTS OF SCIENCE.

CONTAINING

THE ORIGIN AND CORRELATIVE POSITION OF THE DIFFERENT RACES OF MEN, AND A DESCRIPTION OF OUR EARTH AS IT WAS, AS IT IS, AND AS IT MUST BE.

BY

ELIJAH M. FLY,
OF GONZALES, TEXAS.

PHILADELPHIA:
CLAXTON, REMSEN & HAFFELFINGER,
819 & 821 MARKET STREET.
1871.

STEREOTYPED BY J. FAGAN & SON. PRINTED BY MOORE BROS.

Dedication.

TO THE LOVED ONES AT HOME,
WHO MINISTERED TO MY WANTS AND CHEERED ME
IN THE HOURS OF MY AFFLICTION:

TO THE HONEST CHRISTIAN,

REV. P. S. HENSON, D. D.,
OF PHILADELPHIA:

TO THE BOLD AND INDEPENDENT THINKER OF THE NINETEENTH CENTURY EVERYWHERE, WHO DARES INVESTIGATE AND REASON UNFETTERED BY THE BONDS OF PREJUDICE: THIS WORK, IN THE HOPE THAT IT WILL PROVE OF LASTING BENEFIT TO THE EARNEST INQUIRER AFTER TRUTH, IS

Affectionately Dedicated

BY

THE AUTHOR.

PREFACE.

TO no one is the arduous difficulty of this self-imposed task so apparent as to the author.

There is a large class of Christians who consider it unnecessary to adduce evidence to substantiate the claims of the Bible, arguing that the proof is *prima facie* and self-evident, and therefore to all who read the Holy Word the conviction of its divine authenticity will certainly come with overwhelming power.

Experience proves this to be a mistake.

Others demand for the inquirer a rationalistic answer to all questions, arguing that the mind must have everything fully and clearly demonstrated before it can be convinced.

This is also an error.

Two and two added together make four must be accepted by the reason. "God is love" is accepted by the heart.

There are truths in the Divine code not demonstrable. Where they occur, the mind and heart both enter into the investigation. There are truths everywhere we cannot demonstrate, yet they are none the less true.

Yet the rationalistic tendency of the age requires from the Christian deeper investigation and more catholicity of spirit.

Infidelity, like a simoon, is sweeping the field of religious investigation, and he who would escape its withering influence, must — as the individual in the caravan on the desert — independently of all others, labor for his safety.

The seeming contradictions and inconsistencies in the Bible, so harped upon by those who disbelieve, are apparent to every one who carefully reads the Scriptures.

They are not denied, not explained; and the honest mind is often driven into infidelity.

We must have a "living reason" for our faith, and not conclude, because the evidence of a fact is convincing to our mind, it is necessarily so to others.

Christians should be able and willing to accept the invitation of the skeptic, "Come now, let us reason together," with the full confidence of success which a thorough knowledge of our subject always inspires.

The earnest investigator begins with the firm conviction that the Bible is true, and meeting these, to him, inexplicable passages, seeks the professed believer, and to him looks for a solution of his honest doubts.

Unfortunately for him, frequently too, unfortunately for both, the only answer to his inquiry is, "It is so because the Bible says so."

This does not, will not satisfy the vigorous and independent mind of the nineteenth century.

The idea that it is sacrilegious to attempt the elucidation of the so-called "hidden mysteries" belongs to the past.

The Bible is true; and its truths, adapted to the wants of the human race for all ages, are in their nature progressive; hence their revelation will keep pace with mental and moral progress so long as time shall last.

We must "search the Scriptures" in this age of rationality.

To those who reject them, we would say a truth is none the less a truth because we do not accept it.

To the honest thinker, we would say, investigate fearlessly the word of God — but be thorough. Be independent, patient, but above all, not easily discouraged.

We were made to labor.

Our minds were given us for use.

Our earth is to us the primary school of heaven, and there intellect is free.

JOHN HENRY KERN.

WILLOWBROOK, GONZALES CO., TEXAS.

CONTENTS.

CHAPTER V.

CHAPTER VI.

CHAPTER VII.

CHAPTER VIII.

CHAPTER IX.

CHAPTER X.

CHAPTER XI.

CHAPTER XII.

CHAPTER XIII.

CHAPTER XIV.

CHAPTER XV.

CHAPTER XVI.

CHAPTER XVII.

CHAPTER XXVII.

CHAPTER XXVIII.

CHAPTER XXIX.

CHAPTER XXX.

CHAPTER XXXI.

CHAPTER XXXII.

CHAPTER XXXIII.

THE BIBLE TRUE.

INTRODUCTORY.

IN the investigation of any subject, there can be but little chance of arriving at the truth, if we approach it with our minds trammelled by preconceived ideas, so stubborn as to amount to ineradicable prejudices. Yet how few are there in this, or have been in the former ages, who have not, by this means, been prevented from attaining to that height in the development of the laws of mind and of matter which is within the reach of the human intellect. Reason is bestowed upon man for wise and noble purposes; but if those aspirations for knowledge which are essential to superior intelligence, are to be forever repressed by the dogmata of schoolmen, then is the power of thought, of investigation, given to us in vain; and our thirst for knowledge, instead of being our greatest blessing, is an unmitigated curse.

The bane of Christianity, in all ages, is the absurd and bigoted manner in which its professors frown down investigation. Good men, but men with narrow minds and prejudiced views, have had their theories, their standards of orthodoxy, and all thought must be squared by their rule; and woe be to him who dares to think outside of and beyond the tread-mill circle prescribed by the commentators. How much more honoring to the word of truth to invite investigation with a manly, ay, with a Christian confidence that the Bible will prove true, though the heavens fall, because it was given to us by the very God of truth, for the purpose of leading us when blind, and without any sufficient guide, into the contemplation of the glory of his works and the perfection of his attributes.

If, in the future pages of this work, any good man should think that we are disposed to make bold comments on the Scriptures, let him be assured that we do not so in a spirit of rashness; for we tell him now, that his reverence for the sacred record is not greater than our own; and if he will reflect that he may not be in possession of the whole of the truth, he may be disposed to give us a patient hearing; when, if he is able to overthrow our position by fair, logical deductions, we will admit that he and the fathers may possibly be right, and that we are wrong; otherwise, as an honest man, he must concede that there are truths attainable by profound thought and patient investigation, not yet dreamed of in his or our philosophy. We feel the necessity of deprecating the flings of scientific men, not less than the anathemas of theologians; for, strange as the assertion may at first appear, we believe the former to be more imperiously dogmatical than the latter.

We hope, however, that no one will conclude that we despise the learning of the one, or the opinions of the other. On the contrary, we reverence learning; we bow to the minds which have thought, and gladly adopt the truths which they have eliminated. We only claim for ourselves the same liberty of thought which they enjoyed; and we will not be restrained in our investigations now, or at any time, by the foolish charge of infidelity, or any other ugly epithets which may be applied to us by the ignorant and the silly; for such persons not only "wrest the Scriptures to their own destruction," but they are the votaries of error and enemies to truth at all times. "There is more hope of a fool than of a man that is wise in his own conceit."

When shut in from the outside world, and prevented, by

the disease of our eyes, from conversing with those who had thought and written before, our mind began to investigate that most sublime of all prayers, which was taught us by Him "who spake as never man spake." Especially was our mind directed to the petition, "Thy kingdom come; thy will be done on earth as it is in heaven." If prayer be the sincere desire of the heart, directed to a superior being, then, to use the words of a prayer without comprehending their import, seems very much like solemn mockery. A petitioner to an earthly tribunal always knows what he wants before offering his petition; and should we not have some conception of the things contained in the prayers which we offer up to the Majesty of the heavens? Do we use the Lord's prayer because the desires of our hearts are more energetically expressed by this than by any other form of words, or do we repeat it merely as a duty?

"When ye pray, say, Thy kingdom come; thy will be done on earth as it is in heaven." This was given to us as a form of prayer by Him who knows all things; therefore, it is our privilege to use the petition; but, when we do so, it is certainly our duty to endeavor to understand for what we are asking. The language of this prayer may have an individual and a universal application. Individual obligations and responsibilities are abundantly insisted on by the preachers; but the enlarged view of the subject, the principal idea presented in the petition under consideration, which, indeed, involves the other, or minor view, is not deemed by them to be of sufficient importance to practical piety to demand their attention; and, therefore, we consider that to be a subject open to our investigation. Can we obtain no insight into what the kingdom of God will be on earth, and how his will must be done here? If it be our duty, both to offer up these petitions, and to desire their accomplishment with all the vigor of the soul, then, certainly, we should try to understand their meaning. *Since God is immutable, so far as we may go in comprehending what was his original design in regard to the government of the world, so far will we proceed in establishing a rational view of what it will be in the end.* Our subject opens up a vast field of thought, and we intend to take so wide a range in our investigations, that we will enter freely into every path of learning which may promise to lead us into light, hoping that they will all converge in the very temple of the truth.

In the olden time, Moses veiled his face when he had been with his God, because the children of Israel could not bear the light of the truth; yet the revelation which he made was intended to be understood at some time, and was given for our instruction. Then, is it not strange that expounders of the Christian religion, even at this late day, should persistently shut out the light contained in the writings of the inspired philosopher, by declaring that the subjects of which he treats are "the hidden mysteries" of God, and are not therefore to be understood? Our Saviour spoke to the Jews in parables, lest they should understand, *but it was given to the disciples to know the truth.* "All Scriptures are given by inspiration," and are intended "for our instruction;" wherefore we boldly take the ground that at some time they must be understood, else were they written in vain.

In the effort to eliminate the truth, the mind must be free; for if we are trammelled by the dogmata of others, there is but little chance for progress of a decided character, and much less of the thorough eradication of error. We are impatient of restraint in our civil rights and physical actions; and yet, strange paradox, we are the willing, obsequious intellectual slaves of those who have thought and written in other ages. The original thinkers of former times were under no greater obligations to think than we are, nor are their researches entitled to any higher consideration than our own. On the contrary, aided as we are by the results of their investigations, the modern thinker ought certainly to be able to go farther, rise higher, and bring out truth in a clearer light, than those who lived and thought in the dark, the middle, or any of the former ages. If the conclusions to which they came are correct, we ought to receive them gladly; but, if they will not bear the test of reason, they ought to be rejected; for it is absurd slavery in us to be influenced by them.

That philosophy, as taught in our schools, is not what it ought to be — a satisfactory elucidation of the laws of mind and matter, an explanation of the causes of the effects with which we are acquainted — cannot be denied; and yet, theologians and philosophers are agreed in repressing investigation in the fields beyond themselves, by the assumption that *those things cannot be understood;* and no rational attempt to ascertain the real cause of human depravity and of the warring elements in nature is allowed. The one frowns, the other sneers, but we shall disregard them both; for we are in search of TRUTH. Many things now thoroughly comprehended, even by the ignorant and unlearned, were in the olden times classed by the most profound philosophers among "the hidden mysteries of God." Why then should it be deemed presumptuous in those, even of our humble pretensions, to brave the authority of the great thinkers of bygone days, and endeavor to ascend the higher heights, which Locke and Bacon and Newton and Franklin — the church-fathers and philosophers of other ages — have not been able to scale? They were but men as we are, and had no more right to trammel our investigations than we have to prescribe limits to the thoughts of those who shall come after us.

The dogmatical rules and traditions of the fathers have, at times, wellnigh driven the world into infidelity; and that the proscriptive tyranny of the friends of Christianity has not utterly destroyed the entire system with all thinking men, is a powerful argument in favor of its divine authenticity. Is it not passing strange that we should be required to stand in awe of the wisdom of the philosophers who cannot answer satisfactorily our plainest and simplest questions? They cannot tell us what gravitation is, or why matter is attracted by matter; what light or heat is; how water is evaporated; how rain is formed: in a word, the learning of the philosophers, instead of satisfying our desire to know, only leads us into the thick mazes of mysticism, and then they attempt to crush out the spirit of inquiry, by declaring that *what they do not teach, is beyond the comprehension of the human mind.* So much may not be written in their books, yet the idea is so successfully inculcated, that the declaration that this or that is one of the things which can never be known, is as often in the mouths of the blind disciples of the philosophers as of the unthinking advocates of the infallibility of the church fathers—the *ne plus ultra* of modern commentators. Nothing human is perfected yet, and the vast fields of unexplored wisdom still lie out before us.

We do not claim perfection, and willingly concede to others the right of free and full investigation, while claiming the same privilege for ourselves, so long as our thoughts run not contrary to the laws of God, as manifested to us in the great volumes of Revelation and of Nature. The book of nature is complete in itself; but owing to its seeming inconsistencies, which arise from the imperfections of our minds, and from the palpable warfare in nature itself, a revelation was absolutely necessary; and in our opinion these two volumes are so intimately blended, that to separate them is to mar the beauty of a symmetrical whole, and to preclude the possibility of arriving at the truth.

We can but pity those would-be philosophers who assume to themselves the ability to unravel and elucidate the laws of nature without the aid of revelation — who see no necessity for such divine direction, and therefore very unphilosophically reject the Scriptures as a cunningly devised fable. Such an assumption on the part of men who evidently think, most strongly proves the utter perversity of human nature; and the imbecility of their attempts to unveil the truth is an unanswerable argument in favor of the absolute necessity of a revelation from the universal intelligence, such as that given us in the Bible. Another class of persons, who unconsciously and ignorantly labor to shut out the light of truth from the world, are those who read the revealed word, but scorn or pass by unheeded the profound lessons of wisdom written by the finger of God in the great book of nature. The dogmatical folly of the one, and the stupid bigotry of the other, are the mental tyrants of the age, and equal obstacles to every effort to rise into the regions of intellectual eminence. If, however, we will throw off the one or the other of these humiliating yokes, whichever we have the misfortune to wear, and honestly apply our minds to the investigation of the wisdom of the ages, in an independent, yet not in a licentious spirit; if we will embrace the truths which may be so richly drawn from the storehouse of nature; if we shall drink in the floods of light poured down upon us from the glowing pages of inspiration — then will we be in the way where truth may be found; then will we be in the path which leads up to an intellectual elevation, whence we may obtain a rational view of the laws of mind and matter.

Notwithstanding our indifference to the querulous carpings of fault-finding critics, yet, in order to save them much labor and precious time, we will advertise them in advance that in the earlier part of this work we will use the technicalities of other systems of science, and keep the old ideas before the reader; because we do not think that we can better develop our own views than by an exhibition of the process of ratiocination by which we have arrived at the conclusions here given to the world. Indeed, we should scarcely expect a hearing should we announce the opinions which we entertain of the laws of mind and matter, of God, and nature, fully, and at once, without explaining to some extent the process by which our own mind has reached them. When this is done, when we have gone step by step through the entire train of thought, we expect that what will stand the test of right reason will be accepted by the wise; and we hope that whatever does not come up to this standard will be unconditionally rejected.

It may be safely laid down as a rule, that whosoever tears down a building not his own, is under weighty obligations to erect in its room what he considers to be a better one; and we are willing to be tried by this rule in all that we may say in these pages. The Romans were ages in developing the arts and sciences, which the Goths and Vandals destroyed in a few days. An insane barbarian, by the simple application of a torch to the library at Alexandria, blotted out the very footprints of the grand procession of ideas there collected from the wisdom of the mighty past. God requires a thousand years for the perfection of the strength of the giant oak, and yet the veriest fool may destroy it in an hour. It were cruel to destroy any part of the Christian's hope without offering a substitute for it; and it were reckless to annihilate a science or scientific theory without giving something which is believed to be better than its predecessor.

If, in the course of this work, we shall come in conflict with this theory or that, if we shall appear wantonly to attack the professors of one system of science or of another, let no one therefore conclude that we aim to rise upon the downfall of others, or that we are actuated by the small ambition to shine only as a demolisher of the edifices of other men; for our endeavor shall be to batter down and clear away so much only of their rubbish as to make room for our own structure. Should the building, when erected, not be squared by the rules of right reason, let it follow in the track of ruin made by theories which have perished before; yet we do insist that no man shall attempt to tear down our, or any other system, unless he can build up a better—shall not discard our theory of the laws of nature, and of nature's God, unless he can offer something more rational as a substitute.

A fact is believed only after the evidences of its truth have been presented and carefully weighed in the scales of the understanding; then, to say that we believe this or that to be true, without previous thorough investigation, is puerile, not to say idiotic. Absolute certainty is not attainable in our present mode of existence; but a rational belief, that is, an opinion formed upon the subjects before us, after thorough investigation, is a duty which every man owes to himself, his kind, and his God. Should any one be disposed to charge us with being theoretical in our views, let him consider that in the very nature of the subjects before us, rational theorizing is indispensable in making inquiries after the truth. Sir Isaac Newton was the greatest theorizer of his age; Dr. Franklin, too, was a great theorizer; and every other philosopher, from the sages of Greece down to the present time, have formed their theories and built their systems: then let it not be thought strange if, in our humble way, we also should have our theories and should build up our system.

Had the learning of the past ages, collected in the grand old library of Alexandria, been preserved to us, how different would have been the condition of the world! The learning in that noble collection, in all probability, would have placed the world as far in the march of mind then as it was in the days of Sir Isaac Newton, or possibly up to the present standard; and it may be that truths perished in those barbarous flames which even yet have not been reproduced.

It is quite evident that the knowledge of the magi of the East, and of the priesthood of Egypt, is lost to us. They were secret orders, whose time was spent in the study of the laws of nature and of God; but by the conditions of their organization, their learning was confined to themselves, while they invented a system of teaching for the people, as different from the truth as held by themselves as night is from day. We can only conjecture what would have been the state of learning now, had these ancient philosophers thrown the accumulated wisdom of their colleges upon the world. Unfortunately, they were bound to secrecy by such obligations, that no one ever had the temerity fully to lift the veil and show the populace what they knew and what they believed.

Moses, the great Hebrew lawgiver and philosopher, was taught in all the wisdom of the Egyptians; and although he could not release himself from the obligations not to reveal it to the world, yet, under the power of inspiration, he uttered the words of wisdom, which, when properly understood, places us on the highest pinnacle of knowledge ever attained by the intellect of fallen man. He spoke to the Israelites with a veil upon his face, because they could not then bear the light of the truth; and until this day the priests are unwilling that the veil should be removed from his writings. The first part of Genesis is either covered still, or it means nothing; it is a grand exposition of the penetralia of nature and of the purposes of God in creation, or it is a jargon of meaningless words.

We once heard a poor old preacher say, that when he came to a hard place in the Bible, he "just called it Jacob and went on;" and he is far from being singular in this respect. If, however, the Spirit of God indited the matter Moses wrote, it must be the very truth; and it is our bounden duty to try to unveil the mystery, and bring out clearly and fully its real and glorious meaning.

To gain a clear understanding of a kingdom, we must study its laws and its constitution; and this is not less true of the Divine government than of any other. We have already said that the laws of God are made manifest in the book of revelation and of nature. The constitution of His government is contained in the eternal principles of justice, mercy, and truth, the inalienable attributes of Him who rules in the heavens. Revelation is the acknowledged law of God, but it is no more so, than are the so-called laws of nature. God is unchangeable, and his laws must form a perfect system, unique and indivisible; wherefore, no more dignity or importance can be properly attached to one of His laws than to another.

That which cannot be discovered by reason, has been revealed to us. "Thou shalt not kill" was not enacted on Mount Sinai, but simply promulgated there; the principle contained in it being as old as the laws governing the motions of the heavenly bodies,—ay, as old as is the very truth of God. Whoso thrusteth his hand into the fire shall suffer pain, is upon the same platform, of equal dignity and binding force, with the above or any other revealed declaration in the law. If these laws be of equal authority, why, it may be asked, is the one set forth upon the pages of inspiration, and the other not mentioned there? The plain and sufficient answer is, that the latter could be discovered by the light of experience, and as God never does a superfluous work, it was not given to us by inspiration. Where the ability of reason fails, there the light of revelation begins to shine upon the darkness of our understanding.

To a perfect human intellect, as was that of Adam prior to his fall, the laws of nature and of nature's God were plain, or could be thoroughly comprehended by patient investigation; and when our intellect becomes perverted by the transgression of a fundamental law, His mercy revealed all that is necessary to restore us to the condition of perfectability. The thorough understanding of the laws of physics is as necessary to our happiness as is the moral law; and yet theologians ignore the former as unworthy of their attention, and are utterly astonished that all men do not devote themselves exclusively to the study of the revealed code; while the views of the philosophers are equally absurd in regard to the investigation of the physical laws.

It is our purpose to look into these laws, not attaching more dignity to the one than to the other; but treating all as emanating from the infinite mind. We are led to adopt this course with the greater assurance, because reason teaches us that the moral and physical laws are parts of the same universal code; and because, according to our understanding of the subject, the revelation contained in the first part of the book of Genesis is intended to be an exposition of the physical laws, and to show how intimately they are interwoven with the moral laws, if indeed it be not intended to teach us that they form an unique system; and because they all flow from the immutable God, we conclude that the sole difference between them is, that one controls mind, and the other governs matter.

The great first cause, the Infinite Intelligence, through all his vast dominions, effects spiritual ends by the employment of spiritual agencies, and accomplishes physical results by the use of physical means. There can be no departure from these fundamental principles; hence, matter acts on matter, spirit on spirit. Spiritual existence, therefore, must be governed by the laws of mind; the material worlds by the laws of matter. In a compound being, where the union of intelligence and materiality is so intimate as it is in man, it is impossible to understand the mode of his government, without a thorough acquaintance with both branches of the law.

We have inherited imperfection from our fallen first parents; and it has been positively declared by inspiration that "man by reason knew not God." Many have thought that to understand the physical laws is of little or no importance in the performance of our whole duty; but it is clear that this cannot be true, since man is a physical as well as an intellectual being; and since the inspired lawgiver devoted so much of his attention to hygienic regulations and the physical well-being of his people, we conclude that our duty requires us to study the physical as well as the spiritual laws. Was the Son of God incarnated to save the soul alone, or did he come to purify the spirit, to heal the physical maladies, to secure the resurrection of the body, and to save eternally both soul and body? If the latter were the mission of our Saviour on earth, then the spiritualist is as far wrong as the materialist, and the labors of both, in all probability, would scarcely discharge the obligations of one good man.

In these pages we shall endeavor to take a rational view of the laws of mind and of matter; and since whatever has been written by inspiration is intended for our instruction, and, as we believe, must at some time be understood, we will try now to comprehend what Moses, the philosopher, and the prophets have taught us in regard to the physical and intellectual laws. Our object is the investigation of truth, and if we shall succeed in throwing light upon our subject, or of giving impetus to thought in the right direction, we shall be satisfied, in spite of the vain carpings of querulous critics and offended sectarians.

We will here premise, that all the attributes of the Mighty

God are perfection, and his design the same, "yesterday, to-day, and forever." The puny arm of man, ay, the combined energies of all the creatures in the universe, cannot cope with the strength of Jehovah. He is immutable, and his designs cannot be thwarted; therefore beyond doubt, what the Almighty first purposed to do, he will most surely accomplish. "For I say unto you that the heavens and the earth may pass away, but not one jot, nor one tittle, shall pass from the law until all be fulfilled." Hence, *so much as we may ascertain of what was the original design of Infinite Wisdom in regard to the government of the world, so much may we know of its future destinies.* Unless we can form some conception of the material and intellectual condition of the world prior to the cataclysm and to the fall of Adam, it is useless for us to attempt to obtain anything like a rational view of what it will be after the ecpyrosis and the restoration of all things. And we request the careful reader to bear in mind these three fundamental propositions: God uses physical means for the accomplishment of physical results. God uses spiritual agencies to accomplish spiritual designs. God has said the law of reproduction is the law of death.

CHAPTER I.

EXPLANATION OF "IN THE BEGINNING" — MATTER NOT ETERNAL — TIME AND ETERNITY EXPLAINED — ETERNITY OF GOD — FIRST ACT OF SPECIAL CREATION — ORGANIZATION OF WORLDS — THREE HEAVENS — REGULAR GRADATION IN NATURE.

IN the introduction to the inspired code of laws which Moses gave for the government of the Israelites, he gives a succinct representation of the character of God, and of the manner in which he made and governs the worlds. Although we may not be able to comprehend all the grand machinery of nature, and the munificence of nature's God, in all the plenitude of the wisdom of Moses, yet we may climb with him to Pisgah's top, and gaze upon those sublime objects which he points out. He tells us that "In the beginning God created the heavens and the earth." What are we to understand by this terse and comprehensive assertion made by inspiration? It means something or nothing. It is a mere introduction to what follows, or it is intended to convey in itself a world of meaning, a universe of thought. From the design and pithy style of the writings of Moses, we are forced to reject the former and adopt the latter conclusion.

It is not asserted that God existed from all eternity, because that great truth is patent to our reason; but in order to assure us that matter is not eternal, it is stated positively that "In the beginning God *created* the heavens and the earth." By this declaration we are to understand, not that the worlds were then organized and arranged in the order and harmony which now pervade the spheres, but that matter was then spoken into existence, and was made to fill the immensity of space, as high as infinity, as deep as universality, as vast in extent as the boundless power of God. Here is a resting-place for the fatigued intellect of the laborious investigator of the physical laws. The finite must rest at that point where it is clearly ascertained that the Infinite Mind began to act. Reason might lead to the conclusion that universal matter, as well as the Infinite Intelligence, is eternal, were it not for this inspired declaration; but now all doubt is removed from the subject, and it is rendered absolutely certain that matter was spoken into existence, and that God is not only the constructor, but the absolute creator of all things.

Eternity is without beginning or end; therefore the beginning here spoken of must be that of time. No note, however, was made as yet of the passage of time, for the simple reason that there was no means of marking the periods of duration; because the worlds had not then been formed, and time could not be indicated by their revolutions.

Eternity is duration without events to mark its progress. Time is a section of eternity, whose duration is pointed out by the succession of events. From the beginning until the first act of organization, duration was neither time nor eternity. It was not time, because no recurring events marked its passage; it was not eternity, because it was the beginning, and ended when the work of creation indicated time by the succession of events. It would therefore be in vain to speculate in regard to the length of duration from that point in eternity when matter was called into existence to the first act of special creation. It may have been moments; it may have been, by our present mode of computation, innumerable cycles of ages. Finite reason has no grounds upon which to stand here, and revelation makes known to us no facts from which we would be able to enter upon such an investigation.

"And the earth was without form, and void; and darkness was upon the face of the deep." All the simple elements of universal matter were in existence, but in a confused, chaotic state. The materials of which worlds might be organized had been created, but all was without form, and void, and darkness covered the face of the infinite deep. "And God said, Let there be light: and there was light." This was the first act of special creation; and yet it must not be supposed that light was at that time originally created; for if light be matter, or the result of material action, then must it or its cause have been made to exist prior to this, and in the beginning, when all matter, or the heavens and the earth, were created. How grand, how glorious, how bewilderingly sublime the thought here evoked! The great God, who inhabiteth eternity, who sitteth upon the majestic heights of infinity, with a voice which reverberated through the darkest recesses of the boundless abysm, said, "Let there be light, and there was light."

The Almighty uses adequate means for the accomplishment of all his designs; but light was made to flash through the darkness on the first, and not until the fourth day of the creative week were the sun, moon, and stars created; therefore it is unavoidable for him who is in search of the truth to inquire into the means by which God caused the light to shine out of darkness. We will inquire at present, concerning the apparent and immediate cause of light, and reserve for some future part of the work a thorough investigation of the subject.

With infinite wisdom, power, and skill, the vast, unbounded universe, filled with the rich material which he had called into existence, and unconfined eternity in which to do his work, the Grand Architect of worlds could at pleasure select the purest, the brightest, and the best particles from his rich and exhaustless laboratory, of which to form a grand world, to be the centre of all other worlds. When this vast imperial world was created, when the great centre of all worlds was established, and when the eternal throne was erected there, then the mighty Builder ascended his high empyrean, and, surveying the works of his hands, pronounced it "good," and "very good."

After he had created the great central luminary, which, according to the teachings of the philosophers, must have contained much more matter and a vastly wider area of surface than all the countless millions of worlds in the broad creation, and when the effulgent rays of light corruscated from every pore of that glorious world, we may be allowed to conjecture that the Almighty gathered up the next purest and brightest material from his exhaustless treasury, and formed the myriads of suns, to which he prescribed certain fixed orbits around the grand central sun. Then collecting the residuum of refined material, he created the countless suns in the second degree of remove from the central sun, and assigned to them their orbits around the suns in the first degree of remove. Of the remaining matter in all the wide fields of space, God created the myriads of millions and countless billions of opaque worlds, which are in darkness, unless shone upon by some of the luminous worlds which are the centres of systems and the depositories of light.

When God had finished the suns in this order, called in the Bible, as we suppose, the first, second, and third heavens, he peopled those bright abodes with pure, spiritual beings, who serve him continually; who bask in his smiles and the rapturous joys of the heavens; who were the witnesses of his power, and participants in the work of the creation of world after world, and vast systems of worlds. If it were His will to make the heavens in different degrees, and to people them with beings of different orders and capacities, should this be a cause of discontent among his creatures? Should the angel repine because he is not made an archangel, or the tallest archangel because he is not equal with God? Certainly the potter has power over the clay, to make of the same lump one vessel unto honor, and another unto dishonor; nor has the thing made, any right to say, Why hast thou made me thus.

It seems that the law of regular gradation has been strictly observed in all the works of creation, from the resplendent heaven of heavens, down to the dark cold earth on which we live, and still down to the meanest atom of crude matter in existence. So, in created intelligence, there is a regular descent from the brightest archangel nearest the throne of God, down to the lowest order of animal instinct — one unbroken chain, with links gradually and regularly decreasing in length, from the highest degree of intellectual existence to the lowest grade of sentient beings. Who will find fault with the order which heaven has ordained? The angels who rebelled against the authority of their God, and attempted to destroy the order which he had established, most fearfully and terribly lost their first estate. Then how vainly absurd and wickedly presumptuous for weak, puny, ephemeral man to arraign the Omnipotent, and deliberately set about breaking down the subordination which He has ordained!

CHAPTER II.

MOVING UPON THE FACE OF THE WATERS — ROTARY MOTION FIRST ASSIGNED — EXPLANATION OF "EVENING AND MORNING WERE THE FIRST DAY" — LENGTH OF CREATIVE DAY.

TO return to our author: He says that "the earth was without form and void, and darkness was upon the face of the deep." All the matter of the universe, earth, air, fire, and water, were in a mixed and confused state, and darkness was upon the face of the deep—not the ocean, because there was no ocean then, nor land to bound its limits; but reference is evidently made to the vast deep of infinite space. Universal matter was without form and void, for what was true of the earth at this time, or in the beginning, was true of the whole creation. "And the Spirit of God moved upon the face of the waters." What is meant by the Spirit of God moving, will be reserved for another part of this work. The grand chaotic universe is called the face of the waters, because the liquid state in which all matter then was, bore a nearer resemblance to water than to anything else with which we are acquainted.

"And God said, Let there be light: and there was light." We have indicated how the light is collected in the heavens or suns, and is transmitted from one to another, until it reaches the most distant worlds. "And God divided the light from the darkness." When the countless suns which revolve immediately around the great central sun were formed, the All-wise assigned them a rotary motion upon their own axes; a similar rotary motion being assigned to the satellite heavens, of which our sun is one—the same being true of the planets and their satellites; and since it is clear, from every point of view, that motion is the condition of pleasure, therefore we may conclude that when God created the infinite centre, which was to govern the motions of all other worlds, he caused it to revolve upon its own axis. By the revolutions of the planets upon their axes the light is divided from the darkness.

"And the evening and the morning were the first day." It is evident that the day here spoken of does not mean one of our days, marked by the revolution of our earth upon its axis, because the earth was without form and void, and had no rotation; because the sun, moon, and stars, which mark our time, were not created until the fourth day of the creative week; therefore the day spoken of was marked by the revolution of some other body; and we will assume that it was the most important body, or central sun, which indicated by its axial revolutions the days of the creative week. This great centre being the primary depository of light, there can be no night there, but one eternal day. Then, at that point of time when it had completed one of its revolutions and had begun another, it might be said with propriety that "the evening and the morning were the first day." We cannot use the last sentence with reference to one of our days, because it begins with the morning and ends with the evening, the night intervening between two days; nor should we charge Moses with this misuse of language, this confusion of ideas, unless it were unavoidable.

After the suns and systems of suns were created and arranged in the grand order of heavenly harmony, the primary suns each being assigned, with its thousand of satellites or attendant suns, to a prescribed orbit around the sublime centre—all these worlds of light combining to illuminate the vast universe, yet casting but an uncertain and confused light upon the far-distant matter, not yet wrought into worlds—the Spirit of God, still moving through the boundless space of infinity, divided matter into sections, giving to each of these bisections a rotary motion, and thereby dividing the light from darkness.

As we have noticed, God separated the refined and luminous matter of the universe from the gross. Of the former he created the heavens and the heaven of heavens, or the great central sun, and the vast system and involved systems of suns which revolve around it. Of the gross matter he created the countless millions of planets and secondary planets which revolve around their respective centres, in a similar manner to our solar system. These planets were not all placed in their orbits when first created, but revolved upon their axes, in the distant fields of space, moving along their weary tracks around the vast system of suns. How long they continued in this exterior condition, without light, except the blended rays from all the suns which reached their remote situation, or whether all the worlds, even up to this time, have been marshalled in their proper orbits around their own centres, we may not certainly know; but we do know, from the inspired philosopher, that our earth was not introduced into the solar system until the fourth day of the creative week. But more on this point farther on. This much we will say here: "A thousand years with the Lord is as a day, and a day as a thousand years." "In the day thou eatest thereof thou shalt surely die." The Eternal made this declaration, yet Adam lived nine hundred and thirty years. Is this not proof positive that the day spoken of in the first chapter of Genesis is at least one thousand of our years?

CHAPTER III.

ORDER THE FIRST GREAT LAW OF NATURE — THE PROVINCE OF REVELATION — THE LOCALITY OF HEAVEN.

WE have assumed that the suns are the heavens, and that the central sun is the heaven of heavens. Since this proposition is not a self-evident truth, if true at all, it must be susceptible of proof, not by mathematical demonstration, but by analogical deduction. Order is the first great law of nature. Regular gradation is observed through all the works of creation with which we are acquainted; wherefore we conclude that whatever is true in regard to the works of God which come within the purview of our limited observation, must also be true in regard to the whole creation.

In the mineral kingdom we observe a regular scale of gradation, from the grossest and most crude to the purest and most refined of the metals, from the dull clod to the brightest gem. How beautifully is this subject illustrated in the vegetable world! When we consider that nature, by no violent leaps, but gently, step by step, through all the flowery paths of the green earth, ascends from the ephemeral mushroom, the moss upon the rock, or the lichen on the wall, to the majestic oak, in his own broad forest towering; or the tall fir-tree, on his native mountain, waving his glorious plumes to the passing breezes, or gracefully bowing to the raging storm — then may we appreciate and admire the perfect and harmonious order in the gradation of nature.

Again, when we observe animate nature, we see in this wide field that no two creatures were made alike; but the regular gradation, from the sponge in its briny bed at the bottom of the deep, up to man, made to be the lord and sovereign of this lower world, the endless variety and perfect order in creation fill us with unbounded admiration for the wondrous gradation which God has ordained. Have we not the authority of inspiration for saying that this law of regular gradation ascends from earth to heaven? for it is written that man is but a little lower than the angels are. If the law of gradation connects the beings of this earth with the spiritual existences of the heavens, without doing violence to the rules of analogical reasoning we may conclude that the law of gradation, which certainly holds in this world, from the grossest earth to the most brilliant gem, is continued, by a like ascending scale, from ours up to the world next above us. What must be the purity and brightness of that world whose grossest material is equal to refined gold!

How glorious must that world be! How transcendently happy must be its inhabitants! Yet, according to the law of regular gradation, as much as that world excels ours, so much is it exceeded in glory by the worlds next in order above it; and that, again, by the great central world which controls the nations and gives light and life to all the worlds and systems of worlds throughout the vast universe. How inexpressibly grand, how unutterably glorious that world of worlds, that exalted centre of all worlds! Is this not the heaven of heavens, the third heaven into which Paul was caught up? and are not the primary and secondary suns the first and second heavens? Thus we have our sun the first heaven, the sun around which the solar system revolves the second heaven, and the great central sun the third heaven, called also the heaven of heavens, because it controls and so far exceeds in glory all the others. "When I consider thy heavens, the work of thy fingers, the moon and the stars which thou hast ordained, what is man, that thou art mindful of him, or the son of man, that thou visitest him?"

We might rest here, as having made out a probable case, and thrown the *onus probandi* upon those who may undertake to controvert our theory; but we will proceed to fortify our position by additional analogical reasons. When God showed to Moses in the mount the pattern of the tabernacle, it was in three compartments: the outer court, the inner court, and the sanctuary, where the ark of the covenant and the cherubim were. When Solomon built the temple at Jerusalem, which was done under divine direction, and which, when completed, was accepted and honored by the Almighty, the same order was observed. There was the porch, where the people assembled; the holy place, where the daily sacrifice was offered; and there was the holy of holies, with the ark of the covenant, the shew-bread, the two cherubim, with outspread wings, touching in the centre, and stretching from wall to wall; where the golden altar and the mercy-seat were placed. Into this apartment no one entered except the high-priest alone, and he but once a year, to make an offering for himself and for all the people. Is it not legitimate to conclude that this oft-inspired pattern for the structure of places of worship is intended as a type of that great temple whose maker and builder is God?

Revelation is intended to unfold great truths which man's imperfect reason could not discover. Since God particularly reveals the pattern of the earthly sanctuary in which he would deign to fix his name, it must have been intended to represent the structure of the heavens; hence they should be in three degrees or compartments, the outer court or first heavens, the holy place or second heavens, and the most holy place or third heaven; and we have, as before, the suns around which the planets revolve for the first heavens, the centres about which these suns with their systems revolved for the second heavens, and the grand central sun around which all the suns and involved systems of worlds revolve, the third heaven, the heaven of heavens, the *sanctum sanctorum*, where the mercy-seat is established; where the altar is erected which can be approached by none, but by the great High-Priest alone, and that but once, and for the sins of the whole world. What a field for thought! How gloriously the worlds rise in grand gradation from the secondary planets, or lowest order, up, and still up, through the intricate involutions of systems, to the sublime height of the heaven of heavens!

Many persons may be unwilling to receive this as the correct theory of the heavens. With such we will reason a little further on the subject. You believe that there are heavens; but where are they? Have they no locality; and have the angels, the justified spirits and resurrected bodies of men, no fixed habitation? You assert that heaven is the place where God is. This is true, if you mean by the expression that God is in the heavens; but if you intend to say that heaven is wherever God is, you make a direct issue with the inspired psalmist, who declares, "If I make my bed in hell, lo, God is there." Heaven and hell cannot be in the same place, because they are antipodal ideas; neither can heaven be located now on this earth, because wickedness and misery, and crime, and death can never enter into the realms of the blest, and heaven is now in existence; therefore it is not in hell, nor on this sin-stained earth.

Then where is it? Perhaps you may say that heaven is in some undefinable locality, but where, it is not for us to know. Then for what purpose were the suns, conjectured by the philosophers to be such magnificent worlds, created? You answer, to give light upon the earth, and to garnish the heavens or the canopy of the earth, and for no other purpose. One moment's reflection, it would seem, ought to dissipate such an error. Can you believe that this little earth is the most important of the works of creation; and that all else was made solely for its pleasure and garnishment? The theory greatly magnifies the importance of our world, and of its inhabitants; but oh! how disparaging to God and his glorious creation. It is an error of the dark ages, and never once looks at the revelations which science has made.

We know that this is a small world in the solar system, to which near a hundred similar worlds are known to belong; and the sun is said by the philosophers to be greater in extent and amount of matter than they all are. The sun must be composed of very different material, and have very different surroundings, from the earth. It is the fountain of light and life to our world, which, without his influences, would be a mass of cold, lifeless matter. Now, since the sun is so great a world, his influences so benign, and his surroundings so delightful, and since nothing is done in vain, he must not only be inhabitable, but his inhabitants, revelling in all the beatitudes of original and ever-enduring light, must be happy beyond our conception.

What place in the solar system so suitable for the abode of its Ruler as its centre? Thence the great King, seated upon his high empyrean, sends forth his ready ministers to Mercury, Venus, Earth, Mars, Jupiter, Saturn, Uranus, the Asteroids, the various satellites, and the known and undiscovered planets of the system; commanding what he will, and enforcing obedience to his laws. But if this be true, it follows by easy deduction that the centre around which the solar system revolves, with all similar systems belonging to him, is the second heaven, which far exceeds in glory, grandeur, and majesty the first heaven; because there is located the power which gives laws and executes the government of all the solar systems revolving around that exalted centre. One step farther, and we come to the third heaven, the centre around which the universe revolves, and there the great God sits upon his resplendent throne forever.

CHAPTER IV.

Description of the Firmament — God uses Adequate Means to Accomplish all his Designs — Attraction, when first began to operate — Formation of Beds of Rivers — Circulation of the Waters — Waters Gathered into one Place.

"AND God said, Let there be a firmament in the midst of the heavens, to divide the waters from the waters.... And it was so. And the evening and morning were the second day." The firmament means the blue vault which arches above and around our earth, which sits upon the rivers and the seas, which bears the clouds and vaporous exhalations upon its crest, which is the medium of the transmission of light; and is therefore nothing more nor other than the circumambient air which we breathe, in which we "live, move, and have our being." In what sense did God call the atmosphere or firmament into being on the second day? He had created all matter in the beginning; but on the second day, He arranged the component gases and clothed the earth with the winds as a virgin is arrayed in her bridal robes; thus preparing the world for her approaching union with the sun, whose benign influences should cause her to yield her fruits in their season.

God uses adequate means for the accomplishment of all his works; then let us inquire what were the means used for the performance of the labor of the second day in the week of creation. We must remember that by no possibility could the days here spoken of, be marked by the axial revolutions of the earth. We might as well suppose that time was measured by the movements of any other of the planets as our own. But time in the Divine computation, must be marked, as before attempted to be shown, by the movements of the most important, and therefore the central world of the universe. What that time is has not yet been ascertained, although it may be within the reach of future scientific researches to develop it with tolerable accuracy. The day in the chronology of creation, does not certainly mean less than a thousand years; and for reasons which we will hereafter render, we will assume now, that the day in the week of creation indicates a period of fifty thousand years.

In the beginning, God spake the matter of the whole universe into existence. He then formed the worlds of light and set them in order around their grand centre; but the far-off distant matter of the universe was still void, and darkness was upon the face of the deep. It was, however, still approaching toward the system of suns; and when arrived near enough for the purpose, the spirit of God moved upon the face of the waters, and God said, Let there be light, and there was light. When all the materials of nature were in a confused and liquid state, and the blended rays from all the worlds of light met no surface to reflect them or effectually impede their progress, they permeated the whole mass, and thus the light was mixed with darkness.

When matter was sufficiently condensed by closing in upon the circle of the heavens, the great God divided it into sections, and gave to each a rotary motion upon its own axis; and then and in that manner the light was divided from the darkness. And the evening and the morning were the first day—or the close of the first period of the fifty thousand years in creative time. If it be remembered that there is no night in heavenly or superior time, and that when the evening ends the morning begins, we will the more readily comprehend the great operations of nature now under consideration.

So soon as the matter composing our world was separated from the great external mass, the principles of attraction became active between its particles, and the tendency was to the consolidation of all its materials into a body, more solid than the granite, more obdurate than adamant. To prevent this result, however, the Omniscient caused the world to revolve upon its axis; which not only divided the darkness from the light, but, tending to throw off matter from the centre of motion, prevented the too great consolidation of its solids, and brought all the various gases in a commingled state to the surface. When God said, Let there be a firmament, then the forces became active between the gases by which they were arranged in the skilful proportions of water and air. The water covered the face of the whole earth, and the atmosphere, having much less specific gravity, rose above it.

The principal gases driven to the surface of the earth were oxygen, hydrogen, and nitrogen. The air is composed of oxygen and nitrogen, in the proportions of 21 of the former to 79 of the latter. Water is composed of 1 part oxygen to 8 of hydrogen. When these gases arose to the surface, they were in a mixed and confused state, forming neither water nor air; but "God said, Let there be a firmament in the midst of the waters, and let it divide the waters from the waters. And God made the firmament, and divided the waters which were under the firmament from the waters which were above the firmament." After the particles of air had been arranged, by reason of its great elasticity and want of specific gravity it sprang up above the water; but it appears that the atmosphere also bore water upon its crest. Let us inquire how this could be.

One of the component gases, namely oxygen, is common to both water and air; but hydrogen, the other constituent of water, is the lightest ponderable body in nature, its specific gravity being only 0.0694; that of air being 1.00. In consequence of its extreme lightness, all its particles not held in the water on the surface of the earth, would ascend with the speed of light to empty space above the air; hence the oxygen in the upper air and the hydrogen upon its bosom is the water above the firmament. Because, whenever, by electricity or other disintegrating cause, any superfluous oxygen is released from combination in air, instantly, by reason of the extraordinary chemical affinity between it and hydrogen, they will rush together, and water will be formed. Hence the superabundance of oxygen in the atmosphere and the hydrogen above it, though not combined, are called the waters above the firmament. Who but the mighty God, with infinite wisdom, power, and skill, could have controlled the gases, and combined them in the delectable and useful proportions of water and air? And who but he could have devised immutable laws to prevent the decomposition of those two necessary elements, and yet be forever disintegrating and recompounding their constituents in a way to afford fresh supplies of water and air to the needy earth? What an inexhaustible source of reflection? And here, too, is an almost unexplored field for philosophical investigation.

"And God said, Let the waters under the heavens be gathered together unto one place, and let the dry land appear; and it was so." So soon as the atmosphere arose above the waters, superinduced by the rotary motion of the earth and other influences established in the beginning for the government of the tides, the waters began to ebb and flow with that restless, never-ceasing agitation which alone could have prevented stagnation and putrefaction. Who has stood upon the rock-bound coast of the ocean, and beheld its mighty billows heaving, and angry wave after wave, with foamy crest, surging up against its granite walls, and shaking the solid earth, until the voice of command has come, "Peace, be still," and the storm has ceased, the fury of the deep has subsided, the angry roar of the ocean has sullenly fallen back and lingeringly died in the distance, and a great calm has succeeded; or who has witnessed the ever-restless deep, even in its most placid moments, and could refrain from admiring, with all the energies of his soul, the wisdom which devised the laws of unceasing motion in the waters?

We must bear in mind that, after the atmosphere was made, the waters covered the surface of the entire earth. The tidal currents would remove the earth from one portion of the terraqueous globe and deposit it in another. From the time when water and air were separated, to the time when the dry land was commanded to appear, was one whole day of creative time, or an entire period of fifty thousand of our years. During all this time the waters were at work, scooping out the beds of the ocean, the rivers, and interior ducts, and depositing the removed earth upon the shoals then and in this manner forming; and in the morning of the third day the Omnipotent prescribed limits to the ever-restless ocean, and commanded her, "Thus far shalt thou come, and here thy proud waves shall be stayed."

God in his wisdom provided for the internal, as well as for the external circulation of the waters. What the blood is to the animal, water is to the earth. The heavings of the ocean, like the throbbings of the heart, force the water into the subterranean ducts, or the earth's arteries, whence it is propelled out to the surface, where it is collected into creeks and rivers, or veins of the earth, by which it is conveyed back to the ocean, or heart of the earth, and is impelled forward through the same channels—thus keeping up a continual circulation of the waters, or earth's blood.

The dry land appeared when God commanded; not instantly, according to our understanding of time, but at first the tops of the tallest mountains cropped out from the waters, and gradually they loomed up more and more, and, after the lapse of many years, the mountains, like giants, sat in solitary grandeur on the bosom of the watery waste. Then the hills and higher plains appear, and the waters, subsiding with the lapse of rolling years, fell, in obedience to the laws by which they are governed, from the higher to the lower places, excavating in their course the beds of rivulets and rivers, thus forming the earth's veins, through which her vital fluid might flow forever to her great heart. Let the ocean cease to heave, let the waters stagnate in the interior ducts or external channels, and it would be as certain destruction to the globe as it would be to a man should his heart cease to beat, and his blood congeal in his arteries and his veins.

After the dry land had appeared, and the watery circulation had been perfectly established, the earth was approximating to the condition of a habitable globe. There was nought upon it, however, to sustain animal life; wherefore, God said, "Let the earth bring forth grass, the herb yielding seed after his kind, and the fruit-tree yielding fruit after his kind, whose seed is in itself upon the earth: and it was so." When the heaving waters had dug the beds of the ocean, and had built up the mountains and the hills, then the waters were collected into one place, and the dry land appeared. The mountains were bleak, the hills were bare, the valleys were desert wastes. God made the grass, and herbs, and trees, in all their endless variety, by commanding the earth to bring them forth: and it was done. A crop of grass and herbs sprang from the bosom of the young earth, grew to maturity, and produced fruit, which, when ripe, was cast to the earth, germinated in an improving soil, and grew and brought forth fruit again. Then, and not until then, could it be said that the command which had been given to the earth to bring forth the vegetable kingdom had been accomplished.

It must have required thousands of years after the first vegetation grew upon the earth, before it could have arrived at a condition suitable for the support of animal life; because some plants are known not to yield their fruits until a hundred years have added vigor to their strength. God never exerts violent, extraordinary, nor miraculous means to accomplish those objects which may be as well effected by the operation of the laws which he has ordained for the government of the works of nature. When the dry land first arose from its watery bed, instead of being in a condition to produce a rich crop of grass, and herbs, and trees, we know that there was, there could be no soil or compound earth, such as is absolutely necessary to the growth of any except the lowest grade of vegetable existence. The mushrooms, and the mosses, and the ferns, and the lichens, in their order, could alone flourish upon the hitherto unproducing earth. When crop after crop of this kind of vegetation had matured, decayed, and returned to the earth from which it had sprung, a vegetable mould was thus begun, and a soil commenced forming, capable of supporting some of the poorer grasses and herbs. These growing, maturing, and decaying, added still more to the soil; and after the revolution of many ages, when many crops of vegetable matter had sufficiently enriched the soil, the trees sprang forth which formed the first forests in the world. Annually casting their leaves, they increased the richness of the soil from which they drew their own support, thus the better enabling them to bring forth fruit, and to mature the seeds which were to perpetuate their different varieties. Let us look at the world analogically as a huge animal, with bone, and flesh, and muscle—her great heart forcing the watery fluid through her arteries, or interior ducts, whence it is impelled out to the earth's crust, where it is taken up by the smaller arteries and carried to the surface, where, forming into rivulets and rivers, or veins, it is carried back again, to be loaded with the minerals necessary for the health of the world. As there are ten thousand small ducts branching off from the arteries, to carry the nutriment of the blood to bone and muscles, and lymph to the flesh of the animal, so there are millions of capillary tubes conveying the minerals of the ocean to every part of the mundane body.

As the more perfect animals, or those of a higher order, are almost all clothed with an hirsute covering, so the earth is covered with grass, and herbs, and trees. The water, loaded with stimulating substances, borne from the ocean through the interior ducts to the exterior channels, loses in its passage its salts and minerals. These are taken up by the capillary tubes and deposited in the earth's crust, thus enriching every part of her surface. When by this means the water is thoroughly distilled, it is prepared for the use of man and beast; and for this latter purpose, in ten thousand rills, rivulets, and rivers, at convenient intervals, and in all directions, it courses back to the ocean. This circulation of water loaded with minerals in solution, brings them in contact with the roots of vegetation. By the individual vitality of the tree it is thrown up through its body to its leaves, and as it rises through the arteries of the tree, the fatty particles brought from the ocean and the vegetable mould at its roots are deposited; and being thoroughly impoverished, the water returns to the earth: thence by deflexion and evaporation it finds its way back to the great reservoir.

When God surveyed the earth—with a delectable circumambient air, bearing upon its crest the constituent gases of water, which when necessary might be compounded and descend to the thirsty earth, to invigorate its soil and stimulate the growth of vegetation; with the dry land variegated by mountain, hill, and vale, and clothed with the green robes which he had ordained; with the water gathered into one place, throbbing with the regularity of a mighty heart, and diffusing by its grand pulsations vitality and energy to the whole body of the earth; with the grass, the herb, the tree, growing to maturity, producing seeds after their kind, then decaying and growing again, thus furnishing the earth with a soil and vegetation capable of supporting its future inhabitants—He saw that it was good. Another cycle of time of fifty thousand years, or one day according to the heavenly reckoning, had now passed, and Moses says, the evening and the morning were the third day.

CHAPTER V.

SIX-DAY THEORY CONSIDERED — MOTION THE LAW OF BEING — GRAVITATION CONVERTED INTO COHESION — COMMENCEMENT OF VEGETATION — WHAT KIND FIRST APPEARED.

AND God said, Let there be lights in the firmament of the heaven to divide the day from the night; and let them be for signs and for seasons and for days and years; and it was so. He made the stars also — and the evening and the morning were the fourth day. The greater light was made to rule the day, the lesser light to rule the night; the sun being the greater and the moon the lesser light; then, how is it possible that the previous days of the week of creation could have been marked by the course of the sun or by the axial revolutions of the earth? Such an hypothesis is wholly gratuitous, and, we maintain, utterly untenable, irrational, and unnecessary, and therefore inconsistent with the revealed character of the mighty Maker.

It is the business of those who may differ with us to reconcile the seeming absurdities and contradictions which oppose you at every turn in their system, before they can consistently attack ours. But, are not the attributes of Deity equal? Is He not the same, yesterday, to-day, and forever; unchanging in his character, filling with his presence eternity as well as infinity? According to your theory, God began to exert his creative power only about six thousand years ago; but his goodness, power, and wisdom are coexistent with his being: why then should these attributes have been in abeyance to within so recent a period? Is it not more honoring to the great God to understand in the beginning to mean so deep down in the rolling ages of eternity, that the finite mind of man staggers back from the mighty weight of its incomprehensibility? We know that the present works of nature have not been from eternity, because the great truth is revealed to us, that *in the beginning, God created* the heavens and the earth.

Some one says that the power of God is equal to the task of creating matter, and from it of organizing the heavens and the earth, in one hundred and forty-four hours, according to their theory of creative time. Certainly so. "Then, why," it is asked, "do you not adopt the theory?" Because it is absurd and inconsistent with the known laws of God; it is not revealed in the word of truth; it implies that the Eternal is in a strait for time; that He is compelled to hurry the completion of his task, by some stern, overruling necessity; and therefore, that he is not God supreme.

The Omnipotent could certainly have spoken the heavens and the earth into existence, in a perfect state of organism, at a word, but He did not so chose to act; for your theory claims that He took one hundred and forty-four hours in which to perfect the works of creation. Let us ask, if God inhabiteth eternity, could he not have taken one hundred and forty-four million of years as well as one hundred and forty-four hours? A thousand years is as a day with the Lord; then who are you that will assume to limit the time of the mighty God in the works of his creation to a few of our short hours? You cannot, you must not so circumscribe the time of the Eternal, unless it be so revealed in his written word or in his works. In the Book we cannot find it so written; and it is contradicted in all his works.

Ask the philosopher in what language he is addressed, he will answer you that the years are written by thousands on fossil remains, and on the granite rocks. He will tell you to count the annular rings in the gnarled oak, and learn that God has taken a thousand years to perfect the strength of a single tree. He will bid you look around on mountains, valleys, rocks, and hills: on all the objects of nature it is written, Time is old, and God, its author, is unchanging and eternal. The child is born and grows up to maturity; even the first man's body was made, and afterward the breath of life was breathed into his nostrils, and he became a living soul. The only begotten Son of His love was conceived by the Virgin of the Holy Ghost; was born in due course of nature, grew in stature and knowledge, — ay, remained in a state of pupilage for thirty long years. All the known works of nature proceed in like manner, step by step.

In the face of these facts, who will insist that the Eternal must, of necessity, perfect the works of creation in six of our days, or one hundred and forty-four hours? — and so destroy the independence or immutability of His character. But the laws of God are unchanging; therefore it required as much time for the germination and growth of trees when the earth first began to exert her functions, as now; and hence the greater works of nature were perfected in time proportionate to their grandeur, and the necessities of their organism, so as fully to meet the designs of their creation. One plant is an annual, and another is the growth of a thousand years. The laws of the Omniscient are perfect, and most wonderfully adapted to the accomplishment of his purposes. Then we hope that the want of time will present no further obstacle in the investigation of the truth, as revealed to us in the word of God, and in the developments of science.

And God said, "Let there be lights in the firmament of the heaven;" which we think may safely be understood to mean that the earth was at that time introduced into the solar system, and commanded to run its unending race around the sun. Let us suppose that in a space which to finite comprehension is infinite, God created the pure ethereal matter of which he would form the heavens and the heaven of heavens; and that outside of this vast circle, or rather sphere, He spoke into being the crude matter of which he would make the worlds which should attend and do homage to the suns in their grand procession around the central sun. It is rational also to suppose that of the matter thus created, he would form the mighty world which was to be the centre of gravitation to all worlds; and that then he created the glorious orbs which revolve around that centre, and afterward the suns which revolve around these glorious worlds and attend them in their unceasing course around the great centre.

When matter was first spoken into existence throughout space, had all its particles been equally endued with the power of attraction, there would not, there could not have been any motion in the universe, without some counteracting force, which would necessarily have been diametrically antipodal to the law of attraction. All the atoms of matter exercising equal force upon each other, there must have been universal rest; but as motion is the law of being, and as all nature is impelled forward in grand and glorious action, therefore, since God is infinite, so when the creative fiat went forth, all space was filled with matter; and hence the central atoms were of a different character, possessed greater affinity and more energetic attraction for outside matter than existed anywhere else in space. This centre, in obedience to universal law, began to agglomerate when Almighty power gave to the vast mass rotary motion, to prevent the too great consolidation of its particles. When this first stupendous world was formed, the hollow sphere of inorganic matter, in obedience to the law of gravitation, moved from all points toward the centre.

By this means the particles of matter, converging more and more, were rapidly gaining a proximity in which gravitation was being converted into cohesion. This was in the beginning of which Moses writes, deep in the unfathomable abyss of eternity, millions on millions of accumulated ages prior to the time when God said, "Let there be light," and the bright rays shot in upon the matter of our earth, and illuminated its hitherto utter darkness.

When the material sphere had approximated sufficiently near, Omnipotence separated the approaching mass, giving to each a rotary motion upon its own axis, and assigning to each a prescribed orbit around the immeasurable centre. Although the universe of matter had twice been bisected, and a vast system of glory worlds had been constructed, and multiplied thousands of our short years had been numbered, still the hollow sphere of matter in the far-off distance shone with the brightness of light reflected back to the worlds of light from whence it had first corruscated. This heavenly horizon, however, more brightly shone by its own inherent light, giving unmistakable evidence that the atoms of the distant mass were luminous in themselves, and kindred to those of which had been constructed the heavens and the heaven of heavens.

All space outside of the circle, made void by the concentration of the bright matter of which the heavens had been constructed, was filled with opaque matter; and it was approaching the heavens with a velocity accelerated in the inverse proportion to the square of its distance. As the dark mass neared the luminous system, God said, Let there be light, and the blended rays from all the suns penetrated the material horizon, which up to this time was without form and void, and darkness was upon the face of the deep. The Spirit of God, however, moving upon the face of the waters, God said, Let there be light, and there was light, and God divided the darkness from the light, by separating the rapidly proximating and consolidating surface of the material sphere into sections, and giving to each of them a rotary motion upon its own axis.

When these worlds approached the confines of the heavens, they began to be influenced by the contending forces of gravitation, and entered the system in much more eccentric paths than those pursued by the luminous bodies last created; because the latter were so many additional points of attraction to the approaching bodies. These new worlds flew through the heavens, tending first toward one star and then another; apparently governed by no law, and wandering at pleasure in their erratic course, but in reality urged on and still onward by the inevitable laws of gravitation, until their mighty career is arrested by the same great law and their orbits are fixed around those stars or suns to which they have approached near enough for the purpose. Sometimes, when a small body is attracted or passes in its wanderings sufficiently near to one of the primary planets, the former is caught by the influence of the latter, and revolves about it as a centre, thus becoming a secondary planet, as our moon and the satellites of Jupiter and Saturn. The creation had doubtless been going on for vast cycles of ages, before our world was rolled up from the vast deep of infinite space.

Many worlds had been previously set in order about their respective centres, myriads of new arrivals were threading the intricacies of the heavenly labyrinth in search of their prescribed orbits. At last, the first creative day, as applied to our earth, was ushered in. Infinite wisdom arranged the dimensions of ours and of all the innumerable horizontal worlds then coming up from the deeps of infinity, and caused the blended rays from all the worlds of light to flash into the heterogeneous mass. This was done in the morning of the first creative day, as applied to our world; and yet the grand hollow sphere for near a full period of time, or fifty thousand years, was constructing and condensing, as it approached the circle of the heavens, before it was divided into sections and received the rotary motion, by which means the light was divided from the darkness; for this was the last act of creation on that day.

Up to this period, on account of the rarity of the matter, the light and heat from all the suns had been sufficient to prevent the too rapid consolidation of the atoms of the new worlds; but at this point the tendency to fly off from their centre became necessary, and the axillary impetus was applied to them. When another period of fifty thousand years had passed, the materials of the earth were condensed, and the gases, by reason of their elasticity, were forced out and arranged above the surface of the earth according to their specific gravity. The firmament was then made, and the waters were divided from the waters. After this, when probably a half-cycle or twenty-five thousand years had rolled back into eternity, when the unceasing heavings of the waters had scooped out the ocean's bed, had piled the hills upon the plains, and erected the mountains in the valleys, God commanded the waters to be gathered together in one place and the dry land to appear; and it was so.

When the earth had sufficiently dried off, He commanded the earth to bring forth the grass, the herb, and the tree, each in its order; first that which required the least support, and so on by regular gradation up to that which requires the greatest amount of nutrition from the earth. Here the question may arise, how came the earth to bring forth vegetation without a sun or regularly returning seasons? It is evident, from the manner in which the earth had received its motion, that is, by the gravitation of the conglomerated system of suns and worlds, to which it was hastening, that there was no inclination of the earth's axis, and therefore a continuous direct concentration of all the light and heat which reached it, from pole to pole, would be enough to support vegetable life, though the earth were at an immeasurable distance from the system of suns.

Nothing is created in vain, but all is made good and for some useful purpose. Every world inhabited by creatures having soul and life and blood, must have a great central light, for signs and seasons, and for days and years. The comets have no such centres—therefore they cannot be inhabited; and hence they would appear to be useless and disturbing elements in the empire of God. If, however, His creative energies are unimpaired, if his spirit yet moves upon unorganized matter, and if he still repeats the command, Let worlds be formed, and be governed by the laws which control all my works—then must we not suppose that the comets are these new worlds, ever arriving, and moving with more than mathematical precision, through the labyrinthine system of worlds, to their destined centres and prescribed orbits?

It has been conjectured that the diffusive condition or want of density in the comets, is caused solely by the excessive heat to which they have been exposed. This cannot be the case, for if the comet were a solid body, and should come near enough to one of the suns to be melted with fervent heat and be diffused as they are when passing through a system, it would appear that it would be fastened upon by that sun as a centre, or that its rarefied matter would be attracted to and agglomerated with the sun to which it has so nearly approached. Then we are brought back to our original conjecture, namely that the comets are new worlds, just brought up from the deep abyss of space by gravitation, and in obedience to which they are hurried on until they shall find their proper place in the vast system of organized worlds.

The attraction between the particles of matter of which the comet is composed has not yet combined them into a solid mass; and therefore it will not readily yield to the gravitation of the bodies near which it passes. So soon, however, as gravitation between its atoms is converted into cohesion, it will present a point for concentrated gravitation, and its erratic course must be speedily arrested by some one of the heavenly bodies, around which henceforth it must necessarily revolve in a prescribed orbit. For illustration, take a quantity of down and a bit of lead of exactly the same weight, and let them go at the same time: the down will float in the air, while the lead will descend rapidly to the earth. Gravity acts upon both bodies with equal force, and in vacuo it is true that they would reach the earth's surface at the same instant. The matter of which the comet is composed is so widely diffused, and presents points of attraction to so many other bodies than that to which it has most nearly approached, that the attraction of the former more effectually resists that of the latter than the atmosphere does the falling of the down.

"He made the stars also." Moses does not say that the stars were made on the fourth day of the earth's creative week, but clearly leaves the inference to be made that the stars existed, even for our earth, from the time when it received its axillary motion, and when it first entered the system of the organized worlds. In the beginning, God spake universal matter into existence, and then He formed the heavens and the heaven of heavens; and after millions upon millions of our short years had been rolled back into vast eternity, and the heavens, according to our ideas of time, were immeasurably old, then God began the creation of the primary and secondary planets, and to arrange them in order about their centres in prescribed orbits. At last, the matter of our world was called up from the "vasty deep," and the evening and the morning were the first day; and after rolling on in its erratic course through the grand system of the worlds for more than a hundred and fifty thousand years, it was finally organized and introduced into the solar system, and with its satellite became an orderly world. "And the evening and the morning were the fourth day." What infinite wisdom and power are manifested in the grand concatenation of creation, and the continuous addition of new worlds to the already perfect and glorious system of God's universal empire! How unbounded the work of nature, how incomprehensible the attributes of nature's God!

CHAPTER VI.

CREATION OF FISH AND FOWL — NECESSITY OF DEATH AMONG PRE-ADAMIC BEINGS — BIRDS OF AQUATIC ORIGIN — EXISTENCE OF PRE-ADAMIC CARNIVORA.

"AND God said, Let the waters bring forth abundantly the moving creature that hath life, and fowl that may fly above the earth in the open firmament of heaven." How beautifully the works of creation proceeded, and how consistent with what an erudite philosopher might conclude would have been the case! The earth was taken from the great store-house of infinity; it was then organized and furnished with water and air; and afterward it began to produce vegetation; but being without a soil, its productions must have been quite meagre.

After the revolution of vast cycles of ages, when numberless crops of vegetation had grown and decayed, and a rich soil had in this way been formed, and when the earth was producing large crops of grass and seeds and fruits, then God created great whales, and every living thing that moveth, which the waters brought forth abundantly after their kind, and every winged fowl after his kind. Although the earth was doubtless producing vast amounts of vegetation, yet the Omniscient created only the fishes of the sea and the fowl of the air, or that kind of animal life which is least destructive to vegetation.

The cattle, the four-footed beast, and the creeping thing were not then created, because even then they would have been too destructive to vegetation. Submarine vegetation, however, is not nor can it be supported by compact earth, but merely fastens to the rocks or clay, and feeds upon the fatty substances with which the waters are so richly fraught. The waters, therefore, were abundantly supplied with nutriment for every living thing which moveth in them; and God created them all at this time, and commanded them to be fruitful and multiply and fill the waters in the sea. He made great whales, and Behemoth, and Leviathan, and all the finny monsters of the briny deep, and beautiful fish of a thousand varieties; and he made them all after their kind.

With the peculiar physical structure of the shark, could he ever have been other than a ravenous, carnivorous animal? His anatomical structure, his physical organism, forbids the idea that he ever lived upon other than the animal food which now sustains his being. Can we not perceive how admirably all this was done — what consummate wisdom designed, what wonderful skill accomplished the work of filling the waters with teeming life? So soon on the morning of the fifth day as the command was given to the waters to bring forth, the animalculæ were formed, and began to multiply notwithstanding their extreme diminutiveness, (for thirty thousand of them have been counted in a single drop of water,) yet the time of fecundation with them does not exceed a few moments; then what would have been the condition of the waters at this time, had no means been prepared for their destruction?

Next in order were made the fishes, which feed upon vegetation. Can it be supposed that all the graminivorous fishes, or those which now live on succulents and animalculæ, had there been no death among them, and had they, in obedience to the command of God, been multiplying till now, could be contained in the oceans and the rivers? Suppose that each female of all these different varieties of fishes should spawn once in a year, and take the number of eggs which Leuwenshoek counted in a cod of moderate size, namely, 9,384,000, as an average, and the seas would have been solidified with fish in less than a thousand years. But God, who beautifully regulates all his works, created many varieties of carnivorous fishes, to prey upon the former kind and upon the spawn and the young of each other; so as to keep all in such bounds that they may obtain a sufficient support from the waters in which they live.

At the same time when the fishes were created, God commanded the waters also to bring forth abundantly the fowl which fly in the air; hence it appears, contrary to the commonly received idea, that the birds in all their varieties are of aquatic origin; many of them are adapted to living on the seeds of grass and herbs and the fruits of trees; and some of them we know to be remarkable for fecundity. Had none of them died until a period of fifty thousand years, or a day in the creative week, had passed, when God had designed the creation of other inhabitants for our world, the whole face of the earth would have been covered with their countless numbers; the grass, the herb, and the trees would have been consumed by their unappeased voracity, and nought would have remained to support their own, much less the life of other animals.

God, however, does all things well, and he created birds of rapacity, with talons sharp and strong, adapted to seizing and holding their prey, and with beaks proper for the dissection of their unfortunate victims. The carnivorous birds are accommodated with no gizzards, and therefore are not prepared for living on a purely vegetable diet. That the vulture, the hawk, the eagle, and the carnivorous fishes ever lived on other than animal food, is a question which, it would seem, ought never to have been raised, when Moses so positively asserts that God made every variety of birds and fishes after his kind. Could it be said that this was so, if the carnivorous birds and fishes were made to live on vegetation? "And the evening and the morning were the fifth day."

CHAPTER VII.

CREATION OF ANIMALS — HIGHEST LINK OF ANIMAL CREATION — LAW OF HYBRIDITY — PLURALITY OF RACES CONSIDERED.

"AND God said, Let the earth bring forth the living creature after his kind, cattle and creeping thing, and beast of the earth after his kind; and it was so." Five successive periods, or, according to our estimate, 300,000 of our years, had now passed since the first special act of creation was directed to our earth. "God said, Let there be light, and there was light," was that first act of special creation, and it was performed in the beginning of the first day of our creative week; and it is separate and distinct from the duration indicated by "In the beginning," when universal matter was created, and the heavens and all the worlds were formed and wheeled into their proper spheres in the sublime system of the universe, while our earth was still in chaotic darkness.

After the first and second periods, or 100,000 years had passed, and the water and the air had been formed, and the earth had become solid, then she was commanded to bring forth the grass, the herb, and the trees; and it was so. On the next creative day she was joined by the moon, and assigned her place in the solar system. On the fifth day, when vegetation had been growing, maturing, and decaying, and growing again, for some 250,000 years, and a rich soil had been formed, and its productiveness indicated the fact that animal life might be sustained without damage to vegetation, then the fowl were created, and the aliment of the seas was so abundant that every living creature which moveth in the waters was then called into being.

Another day, or period of 50,000 years past: and although the fowl had been living and multiplying on the superfluous grass and seeds and fruits produced in each successive year, yet such had been the abundance of the crops returned to the earth, and such had become the exuberance of her soil, that the Omniscient, on the sixth and last day or period in the creative week, made the cattle, the four-footed beasts, and the creeping thing, in all their endless varieties. He made them after their kind; first the cattle, or all the different species of graminivorous animals, and commanded them to be fruitful, to multiply and fill the earth; and afterward, lest they should increase to such an extent as to crowd each other and destroy vegetation, he created all manner of four-footed or rapacious beasts, with capacities and instincts for seizing and living upon animal food alone. Then he created the reptiles, with poisonous fangs for self-defence, and with lungs suitable for inhaling and absorbing the noxious gases which must be eliminated from the heavy decay of the exuberant crops of vegetation. He also made thousands of insects to live on vegetation, to prevent its too luxuriant growth and the malaria which must be consequent upon its annual decomposition; and he made thousands of others with instincts leading them to live on the blood of animals, for the purpose of preventing too great plethora in the latter, and of stinging them into activity when not disposed to take enough of exercise for their vigorous health.

It will be observed that the first living creatures were made of watery substance, because the waters were commanded to bring forth the fish and the fowl; and the last from the earth, because the mandate was given, Let the earth bring forth cattle, four-footed beast, and creeping thing; and it was so. We should learn from this the fact which has been already intimated, that God created all things consistently with those great laws which he instituted in the beginning, which are still in force, and which we call the laws of nature. When the waters had produced a supply of food sufficient for the support of animal life, every creature which moves in the waters was created of the richness of that element; and at the same time, of the same material, he created the birds, with necessities demanding comparatively but little vegetable food for their sustenance.

They were endowed with appetites leading them to feed principally upon seeds and fruit, and with instincts inducing them to consume the superfluous crops, while the vegetation itself was left to decompose and go to enriching the soil. When another period of 50,000 years had passed, and as many crops of decaying vegetation had rendered the soil productive, and the grass and the herb luxuriant, while the tall forests of the growth of 100,000 years spread out their boughs and offered shelter and inviting shades to the teeming millions of happy singing-birds, then God created the cattle, which includes all the graminivorous animals, from the little squirrel, or the smallest animal that lives on grass or fruit, up to the huge elephant, and possibly to still larger species now extinct; and from the lowest order of instinct up to the highest degree of animal intelligence short of governing qualities.

As no question of importance arises in regard to the minimum of this regularly ascending scale of beings, we may turn our attention to ascertaining the maximum, or what animal possessed sufficient intelligence to entitle him to the place next in order below the man who was made in the evening of the sixth day of the creative week. If we begin with the highest species of the genus homo, and descend to the lowest order of monkey, we shall find the nicely graduated scale to be complete — the concatenation of being perfect. As we find the distinct varieties, so must they have been created; for Moses emphatically states that God created all animals after their kind; that is, each should propagate their own, but no other species.

This point may receive additional proof and satisfactory illustration by looking into the working of the laws of nature. In the genus horse there are many species; each may propagate their own, and may even produce a single cross on one of the other species; but the law of hybridity is there interposed to prevent the further and permanent violation of the law that like must produce its like, or that God made every creature after its kind. This great law, without which all order in the animal kingdom would long since have been banished from the world, not only prohibits the intermingling of different orders of animals, but also of the various species of the same genus. It further implies clearly that the physical structure of the first created pair of every living thing must be transmitted, without the least shade of anatomical difference, to their latest offspring. The ancillary law of hybridity fully preserves that great law of order in the brute creation, and to some extent in the higher class of animals, or those capable of having a law addressed to their understanding.

Let it be remembered that all the works of nature are performed on a regular scale of gradation. The equine, the bovine, the feline, the canine, embrace many species in each genus; ascending from the lowest order of graminivorous and carnivorous animals, up to the glorious horse, the stately ox, the noble mastiff, and the lordly lion. Although there is a vast difference between the highest and lowest of each of these classes of animals, yet if the various species of each of these be brought together and properly classified, how beautiful the gradation! how wonderful the skill which created the numerous species of these various concatenations of beings, so nearly resembling one another, yet perfectly distinct in all their varieties!

The genus monkey, in all its various species, is included among the four-footed beasts; but when we trace the rising scale, step by step, we cannot readily tell where it ends, or what particular order is at the maximum of the scale. Does the orang-outang, or the stupid old man, or the gorilla, complete the concatenation? and does the genus homo stand by itself, or, like the truncated section of a huge mountain, was it hurled into the ocean of time in violation of the universal law of gradation? And by his isolation was he intended by his Maker to be the author of confusion—an element of discord in the harmonious workings of the laws of nature?

We repeat, all things are in a regularly graduated scale. We contemplate the moon, or the smallest of the satellites; we ascend to the primary planets, thence to the sun; we go on to the centre around which the solar system revolves, and then we rise up to the grand centre of the universe. There is a vast difference between the glory of the moon and of the sun; but when Mercury, Venus, the Earth, Mars, Jupiter, in a word, all the planets, are set in order between them, we can readily perceive how beautifully the yawning, the apparently impassable gulf, is paved over by the rising scale of magnifying worlds. They increase in splendor in proportion to their dimensions, from the complete opacity of the moon to the semi-luminous character of some of the exterior planets.

The rise from the lowest up to the most glorious world of our system is nowhere violent, but so gradual that we are scarcely sensible how or when we accomplish the grand ascent. The sun so far exceeds all others in dimensions, the brilliancy of its materiels and its surroundings, as to make it the source of light and the governing centre of the whole system. The same law of gradation which exists between the particles of matter which compose the earth is observed in the order of the heavenly bodies. The vegetables grow in similar degrees of resemblance, but distinct forms; and the same regular, almost imperceptible, yet beautiful rising scale of intelligence is observed, from the lowest animal instinct to the highest order of monkey shrewdness. Here we are lost in the mists of traditional prejudices. Could this Cimmerian darkness be lifted up from our minds, so that we might view the subject in the true light of revelation and philosophy, how transcendently beautiful, regular, and immutable would appear all the ways of Him who made and rules in the heavens.

The point lies just here: a false and a very strange construction, at an early and a dark age, was given to the inspired history of the creation of the heavens and the earth. Were the book of Genesis submitted to a well-informed man, whose mind had not been warped by traditional prejudices, who, in a word, had never heard or known of the existence of such a work — can it be believed that such a one would ever think of placing the construction upon it which is enforced on us as a test of orthodox Christian faith? Could that unprejudiced philosopher suppose that a man of the profound erudition of Moses, even leaving his inspired character out of the question for the moment, could have been guilty of the absurdity of computing time through three creative days by the motion of the heavenly bodies, and afterward, in the same chapter, of telling us that the sun and moon were made on the fourth day, for signs and for seasons, for *days* and for years?

Who, that is not wilfully self-deluded, and perversely blinded by traditional prejudices, can earnestly read the account of the creation, and, because Moses did not particularly enumerate all the varieties of monkeys, and on up to (the) Adam, will believe that he intended to assert that all the animals called man are descended from the same parent? As well might we conclude that all the fishes having scales and fins are derived from a single pair; that from one couple sprang all the graminivorous animals, and from another pair descended all the carnivora. This would not go further toward throwing suspicion upon the truth of what Moses writes, than the strange, yet, in Christian countries, almost universal dogma, that all the animals called man are derived from Adam and Eve.

Moses and the prophets have asserted no such facts; but the honest inquirer after truth must conclude that they teach the very reverse. The law of semi-hybridity, the history of all ages, the observation of philosophers, psychological incompatibilities, anatomical differences, physical incongruities and antipathies, nature's mighty voice in tones of thunder, all, all are continually reasserting the really beautiful, but to perverted man the terrible truth, that God made all his creatures after their kind.

In order to believe that the different races or types of men sprang from a single pair, we must disregard the plain indications of reason, the inspired teachings of Moses, and the sure instincts of nature. In the different concatenations of being, there are animals almost identical in structure and habits, to superficial observation, but really of different species. They may graze the plains, or roam the forests in intimate companionship for generation after generation, yet the law that each shall multiply after his kind will forever prevent any cross between them. But for the interference of man, there would be no such an animal as a mule. He may go so far as to cause a single cross, but here the law of hybridity is interposed, and every mule must be produced by the same management of man.

Sheep and goats, between whom there is much less anatomical and physical difference than between some of the types of men, have herded together from the earliest ages; and although the goat is the most lascivious of all the graminivorous animals, yet we dare say that in no instance has a cross ever been produced between them of their own pleasure; and the same assertion is also true of the horse and the ass. This instinct or antipathy between the different animals, together with the law of hybridity, is the means used to prevent man from destroying that order which God has established among his non-intellectual creatures.

The naturalist can pursue the regularly graduated ascending scale, from the lowest order of monkey to the highest type of man, and he will not hesitate to tell you that they all belong to the same genus; and that the link between the highest species of baboon and the lowest of man is as regular as any other in this chain of being. If the plurality of races be taught by the Bible, asserted by nature, and approved by reason, will we still cling to the wicked and absurd tradition that Adam is the father of them all? There never was, there never can be any natural instinct leading to an honest matrimonial connection between individuals of different races; then is it not strange that men should insist upon the dogma of the unity of the races, and consequent miscegenation, an error which sprang from the father of lies, and is utterly subversive of the laws of our being.

Good men contend with extraordinary zeal for this doctrine. They assert that Moses informs us that Adam was the first man, and that Eve was the mother of all living; and therefore they conclude that the various species in the genus homo are derived from that single pair. Moses, without doubt, speaks the truth, and no suspicion must be cast upon what he writes, because he wields the pen of inspiration, and his declarations are the words of the God of truth. It is your duty and ours to read his books, and, as honest inquirers after truth, thoroughly impressed with the majesty, the purity, the perfection of the God of inspiration, and the vileness and imperfection of our nature, we ought to search for the meaning of what Moses says; and if we differ in opinion on the subjects contained in his writings, let us not so far disagree as to blind our reason, for we are no infidel, neither are you a fool, but we are rational men, responsible to God for the right use of the faculties which he has given us, and for the manner in which we understand his word.

Moses tells us that God created everything after his kind; and when he comes to speak of Adam, he introduces him as the father of that race whose history he proposed to write. He asserts, it is true, that Eve is the mother of all living; but this can only mean that she is the mother of her own race. It will not do to say more, for the baboon and the horse are living creatures, as well as the individuals of the different races of men.

Our author does not undertake to write a natural history, nor of any other races of men than that of Adam. He does not mention the great elephant, the huge mastodon, the beautiful horse, nor the man-like gorilla; is there any more reason why he should, in this connection, have spoken of any other races of men than those with which he immediately had to deal? In the terse and pithy style in which he wrote, it would have been wholly out of place for him to have done so; and it was enough for him to speak of particular animals and of the other races of men, as they became incidentally interwoven in his subject.

CHAPTER VIII.

CREATION OF THE GOVERNING RACE—CREATION OF "THE PRINCE OF THE POWER OF THE AIR"—HIS LOCALITY AND INDIVIDUALITY.

THE cattle, the four-footed beast, and the creeping thing went on multiplying after their kind, and living according to the laws of their being, because guided by the sure instincts of the nature given to them by their Creator. We will assume for the present, as rendered at least probable from what has already been said, that some of the four-footed beasts were endowed with the power of speech, and were therefore superior to all others; in other words, that the genus simia had culminated in a species which possessed the power of speech and was then the highest order of intelligence on the earth, yet not endowed with capacity for government.

This condition of things might be well suited to the earlier ages, when the animals were few in numbers, and the wide and luxuriant world was before them; but when they should have multiplied and replenished the earth, in the absence of a governing intelligence, it would have been a condition of confusion and misery.

Wherefore, near the end of the animal period, or in the evening of the sixth creative day, "God said, Let us make (a) man in our image, after our likeness; and let them have dominion over the fish of the sea, and over the fowl of the air, and over the cattle, and over all the earth, and over every creeping thing that creepeth upon the earth." When this man was made in the image of God, that is, with the capacity to govern, the concatenation of animal being and intelligence was complete; and the world was fully prepared for sustaining the vast amount of animal life and happiness for which it had been designed. "And God saw everything that he had made; and behold, it was very good."

We have heretofore intimated that, since God is immutable, is the same yesterday, to-day, and forever, and since we know that he has created, therefore he now creates, and will create forever. We must also logically conclude that he did create from all eternity; for otherwise we would assign to him at one period the character of an active, creating, sustaining, governing intelligence, and at another period we would give to Him simply the character of self-existence. Material creation, however, is not from eternity, because the inspired philosopher declares that "*In the beginning* God created the heavens and the earth," and that a part, of which he was to write, namely the earth, and by synecdoche, universal matter, was in a state of chaos, hence matter was created in the beginning. Since God is eternal and immutable, he must have created before the beginning; and since the former creations were not material, they must have been spiritual.

It was then — may we not suppose? — that He made the angels, and the archangels, the cherubim, and the seraphim, placing one in authority over another, in all the spirit-worlds which he created, and surrounding his spiritual throne with the ministers of his pleasure. We might also suppose that this spiritual system of spiritual worlds, and their spiritual inhabitants, still existed in a separate and distinct locality, outside of the vast system of the heavens, and their involved systems of worlds; but we are led by analogical deductions to the conclusion that the Almighty erected in that most transcendently bright, pure, and holy heaven, the centre and concentration of the glory of the universe, the majestic throne of his power, and that to his faithful ministers, whom he had created in his image and likeness, he gave the dominions and principalities which he established in the primary and secondary heavens, which revolve in angelic grandeur around the exalted throne of the high majesty of the mighty God. We are induced to imagine in that section of vast eternity which had rolled back before the beginning, that the mighty angel who had been first created was nearest the throne, and the best beloved of his God, the exalted seraph who had seen the beginning of all the beings in the universe, except only that of himself and his God, and had been associated in the creation of all, and since when he first awoke to the consciousness of his own existence and that of his God, there appeared no evidence of the prior existence of the latter, therefore he reasoned that he was the equal of God, and when the creation of material heavens and worlds began, that mighty angel formed the resolution and actually aspired to the dominion of the new creation.

The mighty King would not stoop to contend with even this, the mightiest creature in the universe; but, clothing his faithful minister, Michael, with the prerogatives and power which had been forfeited by the defection of the tallest son of the morning, he sent him forth, with all the loyal hosts of heaven, to purge that pure, holy, and immaculate realm of the horrid crime of rebellion. The dragon, and the rebellious spirits which followed his standard, fought, and Michael and his angels fought; and, favored by their God, the latter mightily prevailed, and drove out the hosts of the rebellion from the immaculate presence of their Almighty Sovereign.

This, we suppose, may have occurred in the spiritual heaven which was before the beginning, or at the time when the material heavens were in process of creation. Sin had now entered that holy place, and there was no offering which could be made for the sin of spirits in a spirit-land; and no blood with which to purify the place; therefore, at the command of Omnipotence, the old heavens passed away, and the new heavens were created, wherein there is no sin or stain of rebellion.

To the great central glory world, where is concentrated the light, and the power to illuminate and govern the universal fabric of creation, was transferred the exalted throne of the Eternal Majesty, where he sits and governs the vast system of worlds which he has created and now creates. We have supposed that around this great centre revolve thousands and millions of bright worlds, which are the heavens in the first degree of remove from the heaven of heavens; and around these revolve myriads of glorious worlds similar to our sun, among which he is numbered.

The incommunicable glory and power of God are concentred in the heaven of heavens—the *sanctum sanctorum* of the universe. There, it may be, that no creature has ever entered; that angels and the tallest archangels have desired to look into the secret designs of the Omniscient, and to approach the ineffable glory of his unrevealed majesty; but the radiant brightness of his throne, the exalted grandeur of his presence, have awed them back, and none but the great High-Priest, the incarnate Son, can approach the throne of the Father.

The seraphic legions are enthroned in the primary revolving suns, as the executive deputies of the mighty God, and the cherubic hosts reign in the secondary suns, or more distant provinces, under the supervision of their seraphic superiors. Should Gabriel, if it be he whose seat of power is in the sun, and whose dominion extends to the remotest bounds of the solar system, be dissatisfied and murmur because he is not the peer of that tall seraph around whose blazing throne the solar system revolves? or should he envy the exaltation of the envoy nearest the throne of God? He who made them certainly had the right to establish the order and subordination among them which might seem good to him, and none must say, Why hast thou done it? nor, Why hast thou made me thus? Even the first and greatest created being, aspiring to be equal with God, and attempting to break down the order of heaven, fearfully lost his first estate; and he drew after him the third part, or all the disaffected spirits, into the same condemnation with himself.

No atom of matter can ever be destroyed, though it may be caused to undergo a thousand different changes; but pure celestial spirit is subject to one only change, which is from purity to sin. This change was effected by the son of the morning, and the angels who with him rebelled against the subordination which had been established in the celestial empire.

Had Lucifer not attempted to subvert the order of the heavens, he, no doubt, would have been appointed to the highest place of honor; ay, had possibly been inducted into the dominion of the first great glory world, which was ever to revolve nearest to the grand centre and dazzling throne of God. It is possible that in the heaven over which he presided was the scene of the conflict between him and Michael, described by John; and that although he was dethroned and driven out from the heaven originally designed for him, yet, having been polluted by the sin of rebellion, the almighty fiat went forth that no heaven in the second degree of remove, and, consequently, that no solar system, should ever revolve around that great centre — that in solitary grandeur it should forever move around and nearest to the heaven of heavens, without the hope of a nearer approach to the eternal throne.

As there are no suns, or solar systems, moving about that fearfully grand hell for a centre, so there can be no system of hells answering to the glorious system of the heavens. If there be any subordinate hells, however, analogically we must suppose that the inferior planet, or that which revolves nearest the heaven or sun of the system in which sin is committed, must be its hell. We know that sin has been committed in our solar system; hence, upon this hypothesis, we would conclude that Mercury was its hell, and that there the wicked of this world and of the other planets, if any of them be so unfortunate as to have fallen, will be confined, in that intermediate hell, with a fearful looking forward to final judgment, when the devil and all his angels will be bound in adamantine chains forever, and cast into that terrible hell which revolves immediately around the burning throne of God.

CHAPTER IX.

Plurality of Races Established — Description of the Primitive Earth — The Fossil Remains of *supposed* Extinct Species Accounted for — The Meaning of the Command "Subdue the Earth."

AND God said, Let us make man in our image, and in our likeness." We have seen how regularly and how beautifully the genus simia rises from the lowest species up to the gorilla. Who will contend that the Australian, who lives in dens or builds his nest in the hollow of trees, yet makes some uncouth guttural sounds in communicating his crude ideas to his fellows, is not the link in the same genus above the gorilla? Or who will presume to assert that the one possesses a living soul, and that the other does not? Is the difference between the Hottentot, whose highest ambition is to wear for a crown or covering a putrid mass of carrion, so far superior to his neighbor the ape, that, while the latter is allowed to be a separate creation, the former must be descended from him who was created in the image and likeness of his God?

Every anatomist who has studied the structure of the various species of the genus simia and the different races of men, knows that there are no physical reasons why the baboon tribes should be sprung from different pairs, while all the races of men are descended from a single pair. If we will further test this subject in the light of external physical and internal psychological reasons, we must perceive clearly that the claim to be descended from Adam is but slightly better for the Australian than it is for the ape.

Who can behold the red skin, the long, straight black hair, the keen black eye, the erect form, the proud and lordly mien, the majestic bearing, the self-reliant air of the American Indian, and then view the savage of Africa, with bowed legs, misshapen feet, long, ungainly arms, thick lips, flat nose, goggle eyes, ebon skin, woolly head, "an apish forehead villanous low," in a word, with every feature distorted, and in comparison with the other races apparently bestowed in derision, with instincts leading him not only to submit to the superior races, but even to worship them as gods — who can attentively consider these physical differences and psychological incompatibilities, and then seriously believe that the Indian and the negro are descended from the same parents? It does appear that no one in the full exercise of right reason could ever heartily indorse such an incongruous absurdity.

Then, how has such a wide-spread impression favoring this

view of the subject been fastened upon the public mind in Christian countries? The advocates of the doctrine of the unity of the races will answer at once that it is taught by Moses and the prophets, in the account of the creation and the history of man. How strange the perversion, how incomprehensible the misconception of Holy Writ! Heroditus and Sallust are not so construed. We can account for the delusion upon no other grounds than this: that the times of this gross ignorance is winked at, and that, for our persistent wickedness, "God has given us over to hardness of heart and reprobacy of mind, to believe a lie, that we may be damned."

Except for the judicial blindness with which we and our fathers have been smitten, it would be utterly beyond the reach of conjecture why such an absurd gloss should ever have been given to the writings of Moses. Does he not say, time and again, that God commanded all his creatures to multiply after their kind, and that *it was so?* There is no change of time, of place, of circumstances, with God; therefore, the laws which he put into operation in the beginning are still unaltered and unalterable.

If the Indian and the negro sprang from the same origin, they should have appeared in the first family; and to maintain inviolate the immutability of the law, negro pickaninnies and Indian papooses should have appeared indiscriminately in all their families down to the present time. On the contrary, however, the red and the black man have never been found indigenous to the same country; and wherever they have met, the latter have invariably submitted to the dominion of their lordly superiors.

One of the laws of animal being, ordained for the preservation of order and for the perpetuation of the different species, is the want of sexual desires, the natural antipathies between them. These natural antipathies are destroyed only by perverted reason, or the wicked will of man. The Indian and negro meeting in any part of the globe, will fall into their normal relations of master and slave, and, unbiased by the white man, there would be no cross between them in a thousand years; no more than between the horse and the ass, or the sheep and the goat. "Let every creature multiply after his kind," is a law never violated, except at the instance and through the contrivance of the white man.

What abhorrence is manifested by the Indians whom we have known, spoiled as they were by the vices of the whites, at the idea of amalgamation with the negro! When the Indian is with his tribe, though the negro is his slave, yet you never meet with a cross between them, effectually restrained as they are by the sure instincts and strong antipathies of nature. It is made manifest by the concatenation of being, it is proven by the unmistakable instincts of nature, it is established by the laws of reason, it is written in burning characters in the book of inspiration that the negro and the Indian are distinct animals, not made so by chance, the accidents of climate, nor the skill of man; but on the sixth day God created them, and commanded them to multiply each after his kind, and it was so.

On the last creative day, God made the cattle, the four-footed beast, and the creeping thing. It is evident that the monkey, the ape, the orang-outang, the gorilla, are embraced among the four-footed beasts; and that, according to the law of gradation, which is violated nowhere in nature, the lowest race of man must be next in order to the highest species of baboon. We have it in proof that the red and black man cannot be sprung from the same parents; hence we must conclude that the inferior races of men were created, and merely mentioned as four-footed beasts, which was sufficient, as they were not the subjects of the succinct history which

Moses was writing of a different race. And God saw that it was good.

After all of the living beings which He had created had multiplied for thousands of years, the negro being superior to all other animals then in existence, yet incapable of governing the world; when age upon age had added a rich accretion of vegetable mould to the earth's surface, and luxuriance to its crops of fruits and grass, when the fishes were multiplied in the sea, and the fowl in the air, and the living creature on the earth; and there were none able to take the government upon their shoulders, then God said, Let us make (a) man in our image and in our likeness — and let them have dominion over all the earth.

The six days of the creative week were now ended; the works of creation were perfected, and God rested on the seventh day. We must bear in mind that these days were cycles of time, each embracing 50,000 of our years; and that the earth, in the morning of the Grand Sabbath, had existed, since light had first flashed in upon its chaotic mass, three hundred thousand years, and that the happy period of vast cycles of ages of animal ease and prosperity, and unalloyed happiness, was now before it. God blessed the seventh day, and set it apart as a day of rest through perpetual generations. If it were so important in the divine economy for the seventh to be observed as a day of rest, that God should impress it upon us by example as well as by solemn command, how recklessly daring indeed must he be who wilfully violates its sanctity!

The day of the creative week is a period of 50,000 years; therefore, as the command to bring forth the grass, the herb, and the tree was given to the earth on the third day, the process of vegetable growth, maturity, and decay had been going on for 150,000 years. If we bear in mind that there was no washing rain nor deportation of soil through all these mighty ages, we may form some idea of the richness of the soil, the luxuriance of vegetation, and the perfect ease with which every want of animal existence could be satisfied through all the grand period of the divine Sabbath.

It is a law in physics that a body will move in a direct line with the motive power. At the time of which we are speaking, there was no disturbing cause, no conflict in nature; therefore the earth revolved on its axis in a right line, or perpendicularly to the plain of its orbit, and hence the days and nights were equal through all the year. The sun shining daily upon the earth from pole to pole, and in its annual revolution around the sun, there could be only a little increase of the heat at the perigee, and a slight diminution at the apogee, so that the year round was a happy blending of vernal flowers and autumnal fruits.

The benign influences of the sun were exerted by day, the gentle dews descended upon the happy earth by night; then how bountifully productive must have been the primitive earth! Crop after crop, through the vast ages of the vegetable period, was added to the soil; while no washing rains nor accumulating waters rushed over the surface of the earth, down the hill-slopes, and through the valleys, sweeping the rich compost earth into the ocean. Where the vegetable grew, there it decayed and was mingled with the soil which had given it life.

The mountains, hills, and valleys were equally rich. No deep scars had been cut in the mountain-sides, no dark ravines in the vales below, and no ugly gulches were excavated among the hills. How magnificently luxuriant and gloriously beautiful must the world have been before the curse of sin had come, or ere the angry tornado had swept in violence over the plain, or the furious blast had driven the black thunder-cloud across the hills and against the mountain-sides, which, by their discharged burdens deflowered the earth of her virgin soil. There were no vicissitudes of seasons then, no autumnal frosts, no summer's heat, nor wintry blast; no burning equatorial sun, nor polar snows; but the whole earth was superlatively lovely and blessed; it was a paradise. How delightful for all kinds of animals to live in such a world! where there were no extremes of heat and cold, of wet and dry; no change of climate nor of soil; no scarcity of food, but with abundance in endless variety covering the entire earth from pole to pole, and through all the year; the grass so rich, the herb so succulent, the fruit so luscious, that the imagination itself staggers under the weight of conception of the beatific conditions of such a world. Oh, it was a paradise!

Animal life was joyous then, and their physical development perfect; and their fecundity and longevity must have been very great. There was no necessity for them to search for food, and they exercised only in sportive gambols induced by the wanton instincts of buoyant and happy vitality. The horse must have been perfect in beauty and form, beyond the conception of the most enthusiastic connoisseur of to-day.

The difference in the variety of this animal at the present is very great; yet the anatomical identity of structure proves them evidently to have sprung from the same origin. The race-horse, the Conestoga, and the Shetland pony are living monuments of the sad havoc which want and suffering from the vicissitudes of climate have effected upon the animal economy of the world. Almost inconceivable differences have been effected by these changes. Here might be found, in all probability, a satisfactory explanation of the huge fossil remains which are the puzzle of the world and the subject of curious investigation with learned geologists.

If we will bear in mind that the earth is many many thousands of years old, and how immensely rich and productive the soil must have been in the primitive ages, much of the difficulty in regard to the mammoth and other such fossil animals, will disappear, and we will be able to perceive that many, if not all of the species of animals, hastily decided by geologists, on account of their enormous size, to be extinct, are not so in fact; but they have been so contorted in form, so diminished in size, by hunger and exposure to the inclemencies of the seasons of a cursed world, that they are not recognized by being compared with the bones of their happy progenitors, or rather the latter are not known from their dwarfed and ungainly offspring.

The Shetland pony, which will probably weigh from seventy-five to one hundred pounds, and the Fleming horse, which weighs from fifteen hundred to two thousand pounds, both sprung from the same origin, are living proofs of the power of dietetic and climatic influences, in increasing and diminishing the size, and marring the beauty of animals. The latter horse is some twenty or thirty times as large as the former; then what must have been the size, and beauty, and symmetry of this noble animal in the pristine ages, when there was no lack of rich and suitable food, and no suffering from change of seasons or of temperature, and therefore no disease? The horse then must have been grand in his proportions, and beautiful beyond conception.

An immense change can be made in the breed of hogs, by close attention to their comfort for a few generations; then how different must have been this gluttonous animal, filled to satiety with the richest and most nourishing food through all the vast cycles of the pre-Adamic ages? His gross appetites and sensual tastes lead him to feed with equal avidity upon succulents, grass, grain, fruits, and flesh; and though he crowd his maw to repletion, his wonderful powers of digestion never cry "Hold, enough!" nor refuse to appropriate to his use whatever, in excessive quantities, his voracity may bring into that extraordinary animal laboratory, the stomach of the hog. In the primitive condition of the world, when he had but to reach forth and take what his taste prompted, he must have been a very large, yes, an enormous, monster beast. The Siberian mammoth released from the icebergs in the present century, had "black bristles as large as a goose-quill, and a foot long, with flexible hair, and a woolly covering underneath." If there were no anatomical incompatibilities, would it be an unreasonable tax upon the credulity of the thinking geologist, to ask him to inquire if this huge animal might not have been the progenitor of the wild boar?

However nice the taste or particular the appetite of the animal, it could be satisfied without laborious effort; and, therefore, whether graminivorous, granivorous, or carnivorous, with just exercise enough to give zest to the appetite and vigor to the digestion, the wants of all sorts of animals could be gratified; and hence they must have grown to an enormous size and wonderful beauty and perfection, in comparison with their starved and degenerate offspring. The races of men in those ages must have been grand and noble in stature and beauty in proportion to other animals.

Then let the geologist pursue his investigations in view of the wonderful changes wrought by dietetic and climatic agencies, and he will discover that many of the fossils of huge animals considered to be extinct, are the bones of the mighty progenitors of pigmy species of animals now extant, and well known to the naturalist, and his labors will prove much more agreeable, and the results much more satisfactory and promotive of the truth of science.

In order that the chain of being may be preserved unbroken, and the ascent be without any violent steps, there should be an animal so nearly resembling man in appearance and intelligence, and a race of men so inferior, that the transition would scarcely be perceptible. We actually find this close resemblance between the orang-outang and the negro of Africa, or between the gorilla and the aborigines of New South Wales. Their physical conformation is nearly identical; the one chatters, the other mutters a gibberish language; indeed, they are as much alike as the proximate links in any rising series of graduated nature. It is patent to unprejudiced reason that the negro is superior to the animals and inferior to the other races of men.

The animals were all made after their kind, or with the power of propagating their own, but no other order of beings. Many animals resemble each other physically and psychologically much nearer than the negro does the white man. All allow the diverse origin of the former. Then why will we obstinately close our eyes to the light of nature and the truth of revelation, and blindly insist on so gross a natural and biblical absurdity as is the doctrine of the unity of the races? This wide-spread error can be accounted for in no other way than that it is a delusion of the devil, introduced into the world for the purpose of ruining the races and destroying the order which God has established. He made everything not only good, but very good; and order was preserved throughout all his works. Wicked man, however, has studied out many inventions, perverted the ways of truth, and with vile, unbridled passions, has violated this great law of his being; and, still urged on by unnatural lusts, the little creature man rises in rebellion against his God, and demands of him, Why hast thou established this order? Why hast thou made me thus? or, Why were not the animals, especially those called men, made all equal?

If the Omniscient saw fit to create animals of various kinds, who will find fault, and say that it is not well done? He created many varieties of the monkey, and commanded each to multiply after his kind; but had he made one pair only, and left them to introduce all the varieties, they would have been not merely progenitors, but makers, and would have been to the creatures who had derived their being from them in the place of God. If Noah was the father of three distinct races of men, he must be the creator of at least two of them; for the universal, invariable, inexorable law of animal being is, that they shall multiply each after his kind, or like shall beget like, in all their generations.

There is as great a difference in the races of men as exists between the proximate links anywhere in the graduated chain of animal being; and the black, red, and white men, with their anatomical differences and psychological antipathies, without impugning the immutability of the character of God, cannot be said to have sprung from the same great ancestor. If the white man be like Adam, then it is evident that the black and red men are not like him; therefore he could not have been their father; and hence they were separate creations. In the evening of the sixth creative day, God said, Let us make (a) man in our image — that is, with goodness, and justice, and truth; and in our likeness — that is, with judgment, and discretion, and the power to rule. Let this high intelligence, this ruling spirit, be incorporated in flesh, and indued with animal life, that they may be able to sympathize with and govern properly the present and future teeming millions of living creatures which move upon the face of the earth.

So "God made man in his image, in the image of God made he him;" that is, clothed him with the attributes of sovereignty, the capacity for governing the world in wisdom, justice, mercy, and truth; "male and female made he them." "And God blessed them, and said unto them, Be fruitful and multiply and replenish the earth, and subdue it." The blessing was that they should multiply until the earth was filled with their race. He was commanded to subdue the earth; and he was promised the dominion over the fishes of the sea, the fowl of the air, and over every living thing which moveth upon the earth.

The race was to be prolific, warlike, and to live by the chase. The word "subdue" is the strongest that could have been used in the language, and has a meaning, though it be generally passed over as a sounding brass and a tinkling cymbal. The meaning of the word as here used requires explanation; for it carries in it the idea of resistance, conflict, and subjugation, by the intelligent use of physical force. The fishes of the sea, the fowl of the air, the animals of the chase could offer no resistance requiring a war; and when the man desired them for food, it would afford him a pleasant pastime to take them; therefore, the word "subdue" could not have been used in regard to them.

The animals have been multiplied after their kind; therefore there were ferocious wild beasts then, just as there are now. They were created with carnivorous instincts that they might prevent too great an increase of the graminivorous animals; otherwise they might have become so numerous as to have destroyed even the enormous vegetable productions of the world, and thus have produced misery and want inconsistent with the then existing order of things. It was the duty of the governing man to destroy the wild beasts when the general welfare of the world required a reduction of their numbers. The animal economy was thus nicely regulated with checks and balances; but to kill or destroy is not to subdue.

The lion, the tiger, the hyena may be caged, and man may hold the dominion over them, but they retain their ferocious character still, while the noble horse and the faithful dog are subdued. Can it be believed that God created a man in his image and likeness, whose highest ambition should be to become a queller of wild beasts, to follow through all his generations the occupation of Van Amberg? The generous earth could not require the amount of labor for its cultivation which would justify the use of so strong a term as to subdue is. Then what will we do with the command to subdue the earth?

If, in the morning of the sixth day, God made an intelligent race of beings, endowed with the power of speech, but not with discretion or governing capacity, in time, by concert of action, if not restrained, they might destroy entire species of animals, if indeed they should not turn *felo de se* and by internal discord destroy their own race. They had been upon the earth for many years, and having become numerous and dangerous to the animal economy of the world, a governing race was rendered necessary; and then God said, Let us make (a) man in our image and in our likeness, and let him subdue the earth and have dominion over it.

Is there any such race of men as here supposed? Let us look at the African negro, and can we find a single community, ay, or one individual of the pure blood of that race, with the capacity for forming social relations, and of administering civil government, or of protecting the wild beasts from destruction by themselves, although from that source they draw almost their entire support. When their chiefs die they sacrifice whole hecatombs of their young men, the most athletic of their tribes, to the manes of the dead old men.

Close, intimate association with the highest order of American civilization for two hundred years, and a very considerable admixture with the superior race, has effected but little for the negro; so little, indeed, that, if left to himself, twenty-five or thirty years would place him again on a level with his African brother. Had there never been any other race of men, what would have been their own and the condition of the world? It is clear that the negro is a distinct animal from all other men, because it is an inflexible law of nature that like shall beget like, and because he has always been what he now is; and no sane man can believe a thousand consecutive generations in the future can produce any perceptible change in his physical or psychological peculiarities. "Can the Ethiopian change his skin?" The negro certainly has no capacity for government, much less for scientific investigations. Does the question arise here in the minds of any, why the negro was made thus? why was he not endowed with the capacity to subdue and govern the world? With equal propriety, we might ask why the lion, the horse, the elephant, or any other animal was not made the last in the series, and imbued with the highest order of intelligence?

The sufficient answer to all such questions is that the Omniscient did not so design it; and we should be content with the order of nature which he has ordained. It is no offence that the angels are not the equals of the archangels, nor that the latter are not the peers of the Almighty; neither do any find fault because the highest order of men were made a little lower than the angels. No one thinks it strange or unjust that the negro should have been made superior to all the animals, physically and intellectually — that he should be gifted with the power of speech which was denied to them; then why is it such a rock of offence, if, in carrying out the design of a perfectly graduated scale of being, God saw proper to put other orders of intelligences between the negro and the angels?

The distance between the negro and the lowest order of angels is too great for the latter, a pure intelligence, to have been the immediate ruler of the former, or to fill the requirements of the gradation so strictly observed in all things else. It ought to be a source of gratitude that a material being superior to the negro, endued with the capacity for governing, and responsible to God for the manner in which he executed his trust, was created, and that the dominion of the world was laid upon his shoulder. The poor negro would have been utterly crushed by the weight of such a responsibility. It will be well for him if he shall be able to make a favorable report to his God in regard to his responsibilities as an individual.

It will be remembered that the animals were created in the sixth day or geological period of fifty thousand years; that many ages had passed away, and that the beasts of prey had become numerous. Following the instincts of their nature, they were in the way, even at this period, of destroying some of the species necessary to the gradation in the economy of nature. The indolent and thoughtless negro then, as now, cared for none of those things. He was perfectly satisfied to devour the animals which he could entrap, to fill himself with the esculents and luscious fruits everywhere around him, to drink the pure waters which gurgled through the veins of an uncontaminated earth, and bask in the glorious sunshine of a happy world. He would not raise an arm except in the defence of his own person, and the youngest of his offspring, to which he was compelled by natural instinct.

A superior governing man having become necessary, he was made in the evening of the sixth day, and was commanded to subdue the earth. We would suppose that they would use the means and pursue the course by which their task could be most easily accomplished. If they did so, they first subdued the race of men whom they found in the world, and used them in destroying the supernumerary beasts of prey, and of driving the balance into coverts and secret places, whence they issued in the darkness of the night, in search of their food — a mode of life for which nature had admirably adapted them.

The authority thus established by the governing man

over the negro, instead of being grievous, was honoring to him, and indeed the only way in which the race could have been rendered prosperous and happy. Without this superior intelligence, a continual state of warfare must have existed between the negro and the ferocious wild beasts, until the former might possibly have become extinct. The relationship of governor and governed, of protection and willing service and unlimited trust, it would seem, is the normal condition of these two races; so that the same subordination is observed among animate beings on the earth which exists between the angels in the hierarchy of the heavens.

The concatenation of government, from the high imperial sovereignty of the universe down through the archangelic powers of the second, and the angelic authorities of the first heavens, is perfected by the creation of a material being, with godlike capacities, upon whose shoulders was laid the government of the world. The government thus early ordained was not questioned through all the vast cycles of the pristine ages, the governing not being more benefited by the relationship than was the governed race.

When the earth was young, her capillary tubes were open, and the insensible perspiration, if we may be allowed the use of the expression, was full, free, and healthy. In youth the head of man is covered with rich glossy curls in wanton profusion; but when he is old, the pores of the scalp are closed up, the vital fluid is cut off, the scalp becomes dry, the hair is harsh and dead, and, finally, if not supported by the application of pomades, must fall off, and leave the head bald and the scalp without energy ever to reproduce its last covering. Were the man always perfectly healthy, were he never exposed to the extremes of heat and cold, of wet and dry, with no hunger, no thirst, but always richly supplied with healthy food and pure water, with no violent exercise of mind or body, he must live out his appointed time in strength and vigor, and his hirsute covering would become more luxuriant and glorious with the lapse of years. The world, with similar happy conditions, would have gone on increasing in productiveness until her mission had been accomplished.

In such a healthy and vigorous state, the earth continued to sustain the teeming millions of her children through all the vast ages, until she was cursed on account of the transgression, on account of the sins of their sovereign and federal representative. There was no sin, no pain, no suffering then, except what was ended by immediate death.

So God created the ruling race, male and female created he them; and blessed them, and commanded them to be fruitful and multiply and replenish the earth, and subdue it, and have dominion over the fish of the sea, the fowl of the air, and over every living thing that moveth upon the earth; and through all the peaceful ages of the divine sabbath, or geological period of fifty thousand years, they held the happy rule of all the earth.

CHAPTER X.

The Influence of the Moon upon the Seasons — Superior Chronology — The Age of the Earth — The Condition of the Pre-Adamic Races — The Negro the Servant of the Red or Governing Race — Necessity of Creating the White Race.

THUS the heavens and the earth were finished, and all the host of them. And on the seventh day God ended all his works which he had made; and he rested on the seventh day." The Septuagint, the Syriac, the Samaritan have "the sixth day" in the first clause, which is no doubt the correct reading, and removes all obscurity from the text. By the heavens, as used here, we are to understand the sun, moon, and stars. The sun and the moon were given to the earth for signs and for seasons, and for days, and for years—the unchanging sun for the certain, fixed return of days and of years, the fickle moon for the uncertain signs and seasons. It requires no research whatever to show that the day is under the control of the sun; and philosophy has demonstrated the fact that the year also is governed by the same luminary; or, more accurately speaking, the axial motion of the earth causes the day, while a complete revolution in its orbit around the sun makes the year. The elucidation of these facts in modern times has been effected with philosophical investigation; and the result shows how perfectly Moses understood the relationship which existed between the earth and the sun.

The learning of the wise, in these latter times, lead them to scoff at all signs and seasons, and derisively to ignore the moon as a ruler of the night, except so far as she gives light upon the earth, and her revolutions around the earth, dividing the year into thirteen equal seasons, or months. These months, and the harvest, and other apparently conventional periods fixed in the Jewish economy, are, without doubt, and we believe without controversy, the seasons to which the inspired philosopher alludes. The moon shines at night, but one-half of the time; therefore, if this were her only office, she is evidently a ruler of the night, only one-half of every month, and one half of the year. But, if she is also set in the heavens for signs to the earth, though apparently ever so fickle, yet is she constantly enthroned, and, no doubt, governs the signs as well as the seasons, by laws as certain as those by which the sun rules the days and the years.

Let the would-be philosopher cease to sneer at what he is

pleased to consider the ludicrous credulity of the ignorant, until the true philosopher shall have investigated the laws by which the moon governs the signs—lest the old woman's instincts, the personal observations of the ignorant, and the traditions which have been crudely handed down to them from the learning of the past, should prove a better guide to truth than all his boasted philosophy, and thus the bitter jest be bitterly turned against him. After thorough investigation in the light of reason, we may reject or embrace any theory submitted to us; but to do so before testing the subject in the light of our own rationality, merely because it is sneered at by one or embraced by another, is derogatory to the manhood of our race, pernicious to the advancement of civilization and truth, and insulting to the God who gave us reason, and made each responsible for its proper use. We tell you, there are more things in heaven and earth than are dreamed of in your philosophy.

The sun is placed in the heavens for days and for years to us; but David and Peter inform us that a day is as a thousand years with the Lord. Since the sun rules the year as well as the day, and since three hundred and sixty-five days make one year, therefore we would conclude that a year in the superior chronology, or the computation of Adamic time, must be 365,000 of our years. The laws and designs of the Almighty are perfect, and what he first intends to do he will surely accomplish in the end. One week, two weeks, or any number of these seasons marked by the changeable moon, less than fifty or a year, as indicated by the sun, is not a perfect cycle of time. All the works of nature are performed in rounded periods; therefore the world, it would appear, must exist at least one complete cycle of 365,000 years.

Would the great earth be created and accommodated with all her beautiful paraphernalia for a single year's existence?

Reason answers no; and revelation, from Sinai's burning crest, and from Calvary's bloody brow, in tones of thunder and the wails of agony, proclaims, in accents unmistakable, that the world was made for grander periods, for a more extensive and perfect history.

It is written in the plains of Siberia and on Himalayan heights, in the deserts of Africa and on Alpine peaks, in the broad valley of the Mississippi and on Andesian rocks, in the eternal icebergs of the poles and in the Western prairies of America, that this world is vastly old, and that God, who made and sustained it, is unchangeable. He is the same yesterday, to-day, and forever. He effects all his purposes by the operation of certain fixed laws; yet he is not the slave even of his own perfection, but doeth whatsoever seemeth good unto Him. He can set aside or reverse the laws of nature, but when he does so a miracle is wrought. It would be absurd to suppose that he had created the heavens and the earth and all that therein are, in opposition to the laws which since have governed their being.

"In the beginning God created the heavens and the earth," that is, he spoke universal matter into existence, and established the great law of gravitation, by which he made the worlds. Who can explain this wonderful agency? Is there any reason why one particle of inert matter should attract and be attracted by another similar particle? The only solution to the question is that the law of attraction, which governs in spiritual or intellectual as well as in physical being, is the active power, the vital energy of God, by which all things are created and sustained. "In the beginning was the Word, and the Word was with God, and the Word was God. All things were made by him, and without him was not anything made that was made."

The laws of nature are but the power of God to create and sustain all material existence; and, *mutatis mutandis*, the same may be said of all spiritual existence; therefore they must be unchangeable, and hence as much time must have been necessary for the growth and maturity of the first animal bodies and the first trees as is employed at the present time to effect the same purposes. If we observe these laws in following the retroceding foot-prints of time, we are soon lost in the misty cycles of the vast ages of the past. All external things declare that the world is old.

The geologist reads in the old red sandstone the revolution of mighty ages. In the fossil remains, he reads of powerful generations long since passed away. In the excavation made for the gas-pit in New Orleans, two subterranean cypress forests were discovered, which, with the one now growing upon the surface, show that the Mississippi River has been making alluvial deposits there for 54,000 years. The foot-prints of time are evident upon the continents and the islands; everywhere the evidences are abundant that the ages have been multiplied by ages, and that thousands and tens of thousands of years have passed away since our earth began to be a world.

Science may read the handwriting of God as plainly upon the granite rock as Moses could read the decalogue upon the tables of stone delivered to him in the mount. The researches of the geologist prove that the earth is old enough to be near the close of a grand astronomical year; and the prophets indicate clearly that we are in the last day of the Adamic week. The commentators are all agreed that at the end of this week the Christian dispensation must be perfected; and most of them believe that it will culminate in a sabbath measured by prophetic time, or Messiah's reign on earth of a thousand years.

The chronologists show us that this is the end, or near the end, or that it has been about six thousand years since Adam was expelled from Paradise. If this were the first after the creative week, it also appears from the whole tenor of sacred writ that it is the last of the world's present mode of existence; for the prophets, and Christ and his apostles, all speak of the end of time, or the end of the week of sin, as being now at hand, and the thousand years' rest about to be ushered in, during which the Lord God Omnipotent shall reign, and his will shall be done on earth as it is done in heaven.

It would appear, then, that not only the end of the week, but the end of the last day of the week, is upon us. Whatever God does, is not only done perfectly, but in perfect cycles of time. Thus he wrought in creation by whole days, and rested one entire day. He established the same order for the observance of man in all ages. Every seventh was the sabbatic year with the Jews; the forty-ninth, however, was not the year of jubilee, because the week of weeks was not completed until the forty-nine years had passed, and the next succeeding, or fiftieth year, was the time appointed for giving freedom to the slave and liberty to the oppressed. Hence we learn that God operates in perfect or full periods. Since, in the emblematic system of the Jews, six years are appointed for labor, and the seventh is a sabbatic year — since God made the heavens and the earth in six days, and rested on the seventh — since all his works are done in perfect cycles of not less than seven days, and since it is made known to us by inspiration that one of these days, as applied to the history of our race, is a thousand years, therefore we conclude that the Adamic race must exist in labor and sin six thousand years, and then will follow a thousand years of rest, in which God will be served on earth as he is in heaven.

We would impress it upon the reader that two kinds of time are brought to view by the prophets. In the first place, our day is made to represent a thousand years, when reference is made to the history of the Adamic race; and, in the second place, that each day in this thousand years may mean a year in superior or astronomical time.

If Adam were created on the first day of the last week of the astronomical year, and if the first governing man was made, as Moses tells us he was, on the last day of the first week, then fifty thousand years had supervened from his first appearance until the advent of Adam, and through all these vast ages that man had exercised dominion over the world. Here, however, we are told that the man made in the image and likeness of God and Adam are one and the same. This brings up the most momentous question that has ever engaged the attention of philosophers or theologians, and one with which we intend to deal fully and fairly, in the light of reason and revelation.

It is true that, as the first man here spoken of was made in the image and likeness of God, and clothed with the dominion of the world, he was then the greatest of earthly beings. He was made to be not only a queller of wild beasts, fully invested with the power of life and death over them, but, as we have already seen, he was also a ruler of men. Every green herb, and the fruits of every tree, were given to him for meat. He was commanded to *subdue* the earth, and to have dominion over the fishes of the sea, the fowl of the air, and over every living creature which moveth upon the earth. He was, therefore, a man of war, and lived by the chase, and from the spontaneous productions of the earth. How nearly do his descendants, the American Indians, resemble this picture, even at this distant day!

This man, who was created male and female, in the evening of the sixth day of the creative week, was commanded to be fruitful, to multiply, and to replenish the earth. He was made perfect, and no restraint whatever was imposed upon him, but he was permitted to follow freely the promptings of his natural instincts and inclinations; for he was governed in this respect by the great law of being, just as all other animals.

After this man had been created on the sixth day, and after the seventh, the day of rest, of fifty thousand years, had passed—after all this, Moses says God had not yet caused it to rain, and there was not a man to till, or who would till the ground. "And the Lord God formed (a) man of the dust of the ground, and breathed into his nostrils the breath of life, and man became a living soul. And God planted a garden eastward in Eden, and there he put the man whom he had formed, to dress the garden, and to keep it. And the Lord God commanded (this) man, saying, Of every tree of the garden thou mayest freely eat; but of the tree of the knowledge of good and evil, thou shalt not eat of it; for in the day that thou eatest thereof thou shalt surely die."

How widely different the two characters here brought to view! God made the first in the evening of the sixth day, male and female created he them; and blessed them, and said unto them, Be fruitful and multiply, and replenish the earth, and subdue it, and have dominion over it. No restraining command was given to him; no particular locality was assigned to him; but he was left to roam at large, a denizen of the world; and the destination of his race was to fill all the ends of the earth. The fish, the fowl, and every living creature, were given to him, as well as every green herb, and the fruit of *every* tree for meat. The second, or Adam, was made after the sabbath of divine rest, when the world had been divided off into different countries; for he was placed in a garden planted in one of them, called Eden. He was made a single man, and placed in that garden, to dress it and to keep it; and he was commanded to eat of all the trees of the garden except that which is called the tree of the knowledge of good and evil. The first was to be a fishing, fowling, hunting freeman, at liberty to roam the wide world over; the other was doomed from the beginning to a local habitation, and, consequently, to the arts of civilization and scientific investigations.

These two characters, as portrayed by the pen of Moses, are as different as we see them between the natural and the civilized man of to-day, or between the noble native of the North American forest and the philosopher of the American or European city. Is it possible for the two characters described by Moses in the first and second chapters of Genesis to be applied to one and the same individual? As well might you attempt to confound the character of the lordly Powhatan with the lofty, intellectual, and scientific character of Sir Isaac Newton, as to blend the character of the man who was made to roam the forest, the lord of his own presence, and the ruler of those about him, who was made to follow all the instincts of his nature, and to multiply and fill the whole earth, with that of the man into whose nostrils God breathed the breath of life, and he became a living soul or intellectual being, capable at once of appreciating a high state of civilization. That Adam was made thus is evidenced from the fact that the trees of the garden were selected with a view to their fruits being pleasing to a delicate taste, and that they were arranged in the order which would be gratifying to a refined eye.

The earth in its primitive condition, and especially at the time of the advent of Adam, with the accumulated compost soil made by the decay of the vegetable and animal matter, must have been inconceivably rich and luxuriant. For we must remember that in all this time no washing rains had fallen, but where the vegetable grew, there it decayed, and there the compost earth remained; so that the mountain-peaks and steep hill-sides were equally as rich as the valleys. What an immense crop of vegetation must the earth have been capable of producing then! We will also recollect that the poles of the earth were then erect, and that she then revolved upon her axis perpendicularly to the plane of her orbit, and the sun beamed upon her from pole to pole, through all the year, so that it was impossible for her anywhere to bear the extremes of heat and cold. Her veins and arteries were all open, her capillary attraction was perfect, and the gentle dews of heaven nightly descended to water the face of the ground. With all these favorable conditions, the mind cannot comprehend, the imagination fails to depict the exuberant fertility of the soil, the vast abundance of vegetable productions, the immense quantity of luscious fruits, or the happy contentment of the teeming millions of animate beings then upon the earth, with every want gratified, and all things moving on in the harmonious order which God himself had established.

There was no sin, there could be no transgression in the primitive world, because man as well as beast had but to follow the promptings of his nature, the instincts of his being, and all was well. Then, when the laws of nature were unperverted, with the highest order of intelligence, as with the inferior animals now, the great good consisted in the speedy gratification of every desire. Oh, what a world of peace and joy and happiness was this earth when Adam came! No sin, no sorrow, no suffering, no pain; and death came in such a guise, that he was no more dreaded than the gentle sleep of each returning night. The lower animals passed off the stage of action without reflection and without more than a spasmodic struggle; and man knew that his spirit was in the hands of the Father of spirits, and therefore all was well with him.

The negro, who has no more capacity for government, in and of himself, than many of the other animals, we have supposed was made when the four-footed beasts were; and the Indian, whose proud, unyielding spirit, and lordly bearing even now, points him out as the descendant of that pair who were made for dominion in the evening of the sixth day, were the two races of men on the earth from the creative week down to the advent of Adam. The red men were the ruling race, and the black men were their servants. God made every animal after his kind; and before sin entered into the world, there was no more desire for the amalgamation of the races of men, than there now is among the lower animals to mix their species, and thus overturn the first great law of God, and destroy the order which he has established.

Let us indulge for a few moments in conjectures relative to the governmental and social relations of the primitive world, in the light of analogical reasoning. The man who was created in the image and likeness of God held the sovereignty of the whole earth, for it was given to him by the earth's Creator. Although, at that early period, the production of the earth was comparatively small, and the beasts of the field were comparatively few in number, yet there was enough of vegetable and animal life to satisfy all his simple wants, and to give scope and exercise to his limited desires for dominion.

The same law of increase which obtained in regard to the vegetable and animal kingdoms, also held in regard to the first governing man. The numerous family which the first pair reared were all equals, and one was entitled to govern as much as another. While they were growing up, the animals, including the inferior race of men, were increasing, so that their father could retain his own authority and yet give a similar government to each of his sons. Their reverence and love for their father would induce them to govern under his direction, so that he would continue in fact to be the ruler of the whole earth, until death removed him from the stage of action.

When there was no longer a federal head, all of the sons of the first governing man, being equals, became the patriarchs of their respective families. In this way, after the lapse of time, the families grew into tribes; but there were no chiefs among them; for in the governing race, in a state of innocency, every adult man who had a family was equally entitled to dominion with all others of the same race. Their desires were, however, limited, and each was satisfied with the exercise of absolute authority over whatever was immediately about him. The inferior race of men never thought of rebelling against the dominion of him whom God had given for a ruler and protector.

There was no jealousy, no covetousness, no envying the one of another, therefore no efforts by one to injure another, and consequently no combinations to repel wrong. This form of government, or of social order, so long indulged in by this race, is yet that most loved by them. The Indian is not ambitious of extensive authority, though imperious above all others in what he deems his own prerogatives. He is so impatient of restraint, that he will readily die rather than be a slave. He is kind to the negro as his servant, but spurns the idea of social equality and intermarriage relations between his own and the inferior race, with all the abhorrence of natural instinct still active in the red man's soul.

He readily acknowledges the superiority of the white man's intellect, but never submits to his authority. He meets the man of his own race as his equal, but admits of no superior. The forest is his home, where "he sees God in the clouds or hears him in the wind." He never soils his lordly hands with husbandry. He scorns manual labor as derogatory to his manhood. His occupation is to subdue the earth, and to have dominion over the fish of the sea, the fowl of the air, and over the beast of the field. He subsists on every green herb and the fruit of every tree, and whatever he can take on the war-path and in the chase.

Remove the wicked influences of the white man from him, ay, contemplate him as he was when Columbus discovered America, and does he not bear a wonderful resemblance to the man described by Moses in the first chapter of Genesis? That man, the noble, the imperious, the self-willed, reigned in the earth during vast ages of the world's existence, with none to question his right to dominion, none to oppose his will, none to resist his authority. He was then, as the red man is now, exact in scrupulous regard for the rights of his brother, or every man of his own race. He looked on the blacks under his control and all the animals as his own, and, as their heaven-appointed protector, he administered to their wants, and in every respect treated them kindly.

Thus the world went on producing increasing crops of luxuriant vegetation, with rapidly increasing numbers of animals and of both the black and red races of men, until, in the end of all the happy ages, they became so incomprehensibly numerous, that, notwithstanding the astonishing productiveness of the earth, yet it had become so crowded with teeming animal life, that it was about to fail to produce vegetation enough fully to supply all their wants; wherefore it became necessary for the earth to be cultivated. With the roving disposition and independent character given to him when he was created, the untrammelled mode of life and the free instincts which had been transmitted to him through a hundred thousand generations, to have cultivated, or even to have superintended the cultivation of the soil, would have been to the Indian, not only disagreeable. but torture itself; therefore Moses declares that there was not a man to till the ground; and hence the necessity for the advent into the world of a being with instincts leading to husbandry and the arts of civilization.

This necessity demanded a being with an intellectuality not only capable of developing the productiveness of the soil to the utmost of its capacity, but a bent of mind which would render him best contented when thus employed. He must have patience to search after, and ingenuity to develop the secret resources of nature. He must possess the mental power which would enable him to compel the objects in nature to be the ministers of his will — to annihilate time and space, and bring together all the ends of the earth. He must have a mind which could analyze water and air, and ascertain their component gases — which could enchain the subtle fire of heaven, and compel it to do his bidding. He must possess the high attributes of sovereignty in so eminent a degree that he could wield the sole sceptre of the world, and compel a willing obedience from every creature. He must be a teacher who could lead the minds of his subjects through the material blessings which surrounded them to the contemplation of the Giver of all good, and his glorious works — to adore Him who upholds the life of the sparrow, and who has created and sustains the heavens and the heaven of heavens, and all the hosts of their attendant worlds. He must have the qualities of goodness, mercy, and truth, and a jealous, uncompromising desire for sole sovereignty, that he might be fully qualified to be the world's universal king; so that he may never grow weary in the discharge of the high duties, and would be miserable without the grand prerogatives of his exalted position.

No such being was in the world, for the existing races had each multiplied after his kind, and as the father, so was the son, through all their generations, in moral disposition and in mental capacity. From our knowledge of the Indian character, we know that, left to himself, he never could have become a civilized man, and he would have embraced death more willingly than universal sovereignty. He is equally averse to manual labor and to long-continued intellectual effort; therefore he could never be brought to develop the rich productiveness of the soil by cultivation, nor the secret wealth contained in the bowels of the earth, in the bosom of the ocean, by the mental and physical effort necessary for the purpose.

God, however, uses adequate means to accomplish all his designs. Physical agencies effect physical results; spiritual means accomplish spiritual ends. There were, no doubt, many lofty spirits in the heavens, who would have been intellectually equal to the task of assuming the government, and of wielding the sceptre of the world in its then condition of innocency, and of preparing it for the future intended for it; but mighty physical results were to be wrought out, which, requiring a material agent, would have necessitated the incarnation of the Spirit before he could have accomplished the grand physical results which were designed.

God for no purpose will clothe the pure, free, unconfined spirits which he created of old, in the habiliments of clay. Such a state of being would be as wretched to the angel as the requirements of civilization would be to the Indian. In effecting the purposes of infinite wisdom, the physical resources of the world must be developed; mind must triumph over matter; universal submission to one will, representative of the majesty of the heavens, must be effectually taught and clearly exemplified in practice. Unlimited goodness and mercy would not, even to effect these great objects, impose restraint upon a holy spirit which had served him faithfully in the courts of heaven, nor yet upon a man of the race to whom he had given instincts unconquerably averse to manual labor and to continuous mental effort. Hence the absolute necessity for the creation of a new body into which the mighty Sovereign of the universe might infuse a higher order of his own image and likeness.

Wherefore God formed (a) man of the dust of the ground, and breathed into his nostrils the breath of life, and he became a living soul. He was made so much like God, in the attributes of goodness, mercy, and truth, that he would not unnecessarily injure nor restrain the rights and pleasures of the least or meanest creature ; yet so jealous of his own high prerogatives, that he could no more bear corrivalry in the sole sovereignty of the earth, than God would admit a divided authority in the hierarchy of the heavens. He would spurn the surveillance of any being whatever, save that of his Father alone, to whom he would bow with high filial affection and the profound adoration of a creature.

CHAPTER XI.

LABOR A SOURCE OF PLEASURE TO ADAM—REVERENCE FOR A HIGHER RACE A NATURAL INSTINCT IN THE NEGRO.

"AND the Lord God planted a garden eastward in Eden, and there he put the man whom he had formed."

He to whom the supreme sway over the whole earth was given should possess the attributes of justice, mercy, truth, wisdom, and power so blended in him, that he might resemble the Supreme Ruler of the universe, to the end that he might govern the world as the Eternal Majesty rules everywhere. As God is a jealous God, and as he will brook no divided authority, or allow of any rivalry in all his wide dominions, so his vicegerent on earth must be constituted with a mind which can admit of no corrivalry or partnership in his throne. Made in the express image of his Father, he bore the godlike attributes of sole sovereignty, and the coveted government was laid upon his shoulder.

The weight of universal empire was no burden to him, because for this very purpose he was created and admirably adapted; and the high aspirations with which he came into the world could be satisfied with nothing less than the absolute sovereignty of all the earth. He was also imbued with the godlike desire to create, and therefore, in order to be happy, he must ever be engaged in planning those changes in the material of which his world was made, and in superintending their execution, which would tend to the increase of the happiness of his subjects, and the beautifying and adorning of the world. This same desire would lead him to the cultivation of the earth, in order to induce her to yield her whole strength for the support of animal life, and especially the life of the multiplied millions of the black and red races of men then covering the face of the whole earth. He bore the power and exercised the providence of his God. His care was extended to the meanest as well as to the most exalted of the animals, in the proportion of their intelligence. He overlooked not the weak and defenceless, nor permitted their species to become extinct, nor the strong to suffer for food.

He made use of the red man, who had always held the dominion over animate nature, still in that capacity, but subject to his supreme authority. The garden in Eden, with all its beauty and loveliness, with all its glory and magnificence, that Paradise into which Adam sprang from the hands of his Creator, was the model by which the whole world was to be perfected. For we may well conjecture that when Adam had been clothed with sovereignty, and placed in the garden, to dress it, and keep it in the perfect state in which he found it, the injunction was laid upon him to put the face of the whole earth in the same condition; and may we not suggest that the command given to Moses on another occasion, with the necessary change, was given also to Adam? See that thou do it according to the pattern shown thee in this garden.

Labor is a curse when imposed upon those having strong natural antipathies thereto; but, in moderation, it is the normal state, and, therefore, the condition of the greatest happiness to many of the animals, as well as to the semi-intellectual black man. The horse, the ox, the ass, and probably some other animals, are much better developed physically when under the hand of intelligent man than when in an unreclaimed state. They exhibit much more beauty and symmetry of form, and far more of strength and vigor and buoyancy of animal life. And all intelligent persons know that gentle, moderate exercise is absolutely necessary to the rearing of a perfect animal.

The horse, the pet of man, has been more thoroughly studied than any of the animals, and therefore his habitudes are best understood. All know that this noble animal is capable of astonishing improvement under proper care and attention. Let him be taken when a colt, and housed, and blanketed, and thus let him be thoroughly protected from all disagreeable changes and inclemencies of the weather; let him never know what hunger and thirst are, and let him have no exercise except an occasional play in the lot, and now and then a little run around his keeper. Such treatment not only disqualifies him for the rough changes of the out-door climate, but his beauty is not brought out, his muscles are not developed, his bones acquire no strength; there is in him no pride, no courage. Because he has been injudiciously cared for, and the great law of physical being, which requires proper exercise, has been violated, he is far more wretched than if the care of man had not been extended to him.

The other extreme, or too much use, is equally pernicious to the perfection of the horse. He is unnaturally developed in the muscles most severely taxed, and thus his beauty and symmetry are destroyed. He is dwarfed by hunger and thirst, by the keen wintry blast and cold drenching rains, and by the fierce rays of the fervid suns of summer. Under such circumstances, with such tyrannical treatment, he can never attain to beauty of form, to symmetry of proportion. His spirits are broken; his courage is dispelled; his disposition is rendered vicious; he experiences no ebullition of animal spirits; he doggedly performs the drudgery imposed upon him; he drags on his miserable existence until friendly death comes to his relief.

"He hath given the horse strength. He hath clothed his neck with thunder. The horse cannot be made afraid as the grasshopper; the glory of his nostrils is terrible. He paweth in the valley, and rejoiceth in his strength; he goeth on to meet the armed man. He mocketh at fear and is not affrighted; neither goeth he back from the sword. The quiver rattleth against him, the glittering spear and the shield. He swalloweth the ground with fierceness and rage; neither believeth he that it is the sound of the trumpet. He saith among the trumpets, Ha, ha! and he smelleth the battle afar off, the thunder of the captains and the shouting." This is, indeed, the description of a glorious animal, and shows that in the time of Job, as well as now, his perfections must be developed by the use and care of man. Take the finest specimen of the wild horse, and will he at all compare with this description? This proves that the normal condition of the horse, and therefore his greatest happiness, is in the service and protection of man.

This conclusion obtains with equal force in regard to all the domestic animals; but is it true of any race of men? Those who know the negro as well as we do, will readily answer this question in the affirmative. He was made with great powers of physical endurance, yet with a soul so sluggish that he is perfectly incapable of arousing himself to systematic physical action. Exercise is just as necessary to the full development of his form and symmetry, and therefore to securing his complete physical happiness, as to almost any other animal; and although he so far surpasses them in mental capacity, yet he is so indolently constituted as to be incapable of making any effort whatever, either physical or intellectual, except what is absolutely necessary to satisfy some immediate, pressing want.

With all his mental powers, (and they are considerable,) if left entirely to himself he is but slightly superior to the baboon tribes around him. All the animals were made to multiply *after their kind;* therefore, as we find the negro disposed, in his native wilds, at the present day, so he was made; and so, left to himself, he would continue to the end of the world, unless his race sooner became extinct. In the primitive ages, when he had but to reach forth and take what he wanted, to eat, and to lie down, and slake his thirst with sweet water from the sparkling brook, what were his habits, if left to himself? Did he not eat, drink, and sleep; and eat and drink and sleep again? Under such circumstances he certainly would have been one of the most completely dormant animals in nature.

His physical nature would have so suffered for the want of healthy exercise, that, instead of being happy, as the state of innocence in which the world then was required every creature to be, he would have been miserable; or, at best, his mode of life would have resembled that of a vegetable rather than that of a sentient being. He also was created without any intellectual aspirations or pride of individuality, so that in him, physically and psychologically, there is no motive power whatever, except what is common to the lower animals, and in many of them in a higher degree than in him.

Instinct is the guide to the brute, as reason is to more elevated beings. Instinct is more clear and certain in the lower animals, growing less so as we ascend the scale of being, until we arrive at the grade of man, where it is almost totally lost in the effulgent light of rationality. Some of the higher order of animals are possessed of intelligence enough to obstruct the sure workings of instinct, and not enough to guide them in the way of their greatest physical good; and hence the necessity, in the beginning, for the creation of a being who should exercise dominion over them. The negro, however, is endowed with superior intellectual capacities to any of these, by which means his instinct is blinded to a greater extent than any of theirs; and since no intellectual motive power or incentive to thought was bestowed upon him by his Creator, therefore, without a ruler, protector, and guide, he of all beings is most miserably situated.

In the plenitude of his goodness and mercy, God made ample provision for the comfort and happiness of all his creatures. He implanted in the negro unbounded reverence for superiority, whether intellectual or material, and this quality leads him willingly to submit to men of a superior race, as they do to God alone. As the negro is the lowest of intellectual beings, so also he is the highest of the imitative animals. He is therefore so constituted that he cannot elevate himself by the powers of his own intellect, neither can he secure a high degree of physical happiness by following the dim light of his instincts; hence he must have been unhappy without a superior intelligence, upon whom he could rely for protection, and to whom he could look for guidance and support.

So long as such superior retain the image and likeness of his God, that is, with power and justice mingled with mercy and goodness, the negro would be aroused from his lethargic state by the benevolent administration of his superior. All his imitative powers would be called forth in his efforts to be like his lord; and he would proceed with alacrity in the performance of the behests of the being who to him was in the place of God. Thus the black man, with beclouded instincts, and with no certain light from the lamp of reason to guide him, who seemed to be without the hope of either physical or psychological enjoyment, when the red man appeared upon the stage of action, was drawn to the latter by the strong impulse of admiration for his noble person, and devotionally followed him as his superior. He served the red man to gain his good will and protection. He executed the wishes of his chosen lord with alacrity, and, rapidly assimilating to him by reason of his wonderful powers of imitation, was greatly elevated and rendered joyous in perfect animal felicity beyond all others.

We conclude then, as we have concluded before, that the rising scale of animal life in the first creation, that is, in the morning of the sixth creative day, culminated in the formation of the black man. He was not made in the image and likeness of God, did not have the capacity for self-government, much less for the government of the world; hence the necessity for making the governing man in the evening of that day, whose noble qualitities of head and heart, and perfect adaptation to the duties of his station, are not even yet wholly lost in his just, imperious, self-reliant, but unambitious descendants, the red men of North America. Those who have known the slaveholding Indians in the United States can form a fair conception of the happy condition of the negro in the pre-Adamic ages. No oppressive exactions were made upon him for labor, no restraint was laid upon him which was at all grievous to be borne. He was treated with kindness and the consideration due to an inferior; but if he attempted to cross the natural barrier between him and his superior, it was so promptly repressed that it would not be tried a second time. The relation of master and slave between the Indian and negro, as we have seen it, is most admirable, conferring, if there were any difference, the greater amount of happiness on the negro. So, no doubt, it was through all the primitive ages.

The red men held the absolute dominion over the world through all those vast cycles, and still they were a multiplying race. Every man among them was the equal of every other ; yet they had no desire whatever to infringe upon the rights of each other, so that notwithstanding the authority was in multiplied thousands of hands, yet it was peaceful and harmonious.

This happy state of things might have continued, but the earth failing by spontaneous production to satisfy all the wants of the teeming life upon it, and since there was not a man to till the ground, and since it would appear that God designed, in order that the law of gradation might be still observed, that the government of the world before the end should be assimilated to that of the hierarchy of the heavens, therefore a man must be found with capacities and aptitudes for universal sway. Such a one there was not in all the earth ; nor yet was there a being in the heavens who could take upon him the sovereignty of the earth ; hence the necessity for the creation of the third or white man, into whose nostrils God breathed the breath of life, and he became a living soul, fully capacitated with all the exalted qualifications for the performance of the high duties intended to be assigned to him.

He resembled God in the attributes of justice, mercy, and truth, nor could he admit of rivalry or divided authority. He might employ the red man as his minister, he might delegate authority to him, and through him govern the black man and the world, but all must bow to him. The red men, who were all equals, might submit to the authority of a being evidently superior physically and intellectually to all others, though they could never be induced to unite in obeying any one individual of their own race. Although their king came to them indued with intellectual perfection, and all the lofty attributes of sovereignty, to be in the place of God, and although they must submit to his authority, yet we may surmise that the proud, haughty, imperious disposition which had been given to their first parents in the day in which they were created, and had been transmitted from father to son through all the generations of the mighty past, notwithstanding their state of innocency, would cause them occasionally to chafe even at the order which God had established; and the wish, unbidden, would rise, that no superior had been given them.

CHAPTER XII.

THE DIFFERENT PERIODS OF TIME IN WHICH THE RACES WERE CREATED — "NOT A MAN TO TILL THE GROUND" EXPLAINED — DESIRE FOR UNIVERSAL SOVEREIGNTY INHERENT IN THE WHITE RACE.

LET us inquire further at what period of the world Adam was created; then we may remark upon the length of time he reigned, the character of his government, and the manner of his fall. From what has already been said, we may assume for the present that he was the third created man, and in the proper place we will endeavor to prove the fact to a logical certainty.

We will remind the reader here, that, according to our

theory, the negro was made in the morning of the sixth day, and that he was so constituted as to make his happiness depend upon a superior; and since none existed then, the necessity arose for a further creation; and, hence, in the evening of that day the red man was made, in the image and likeness of God; and he was appointed to be the ruler of the black man, and of the whole earth. As this governing man was made to be a multiplying race, therefore the government must necessarily be divided indefinitely; but, since God is a universal sovereign, it was necessary for the government of the world, which is a province in his grand dominions, to be brought to assimilate to the universal monarchy; hence it became necessary for a third man to be made, with the high attributes which would qualify him for sole sovereignty.

If he became the progenitor of a race in obedience to the law, "Let every creature multiply after his kind," his descendants, like himself, must ever aspire to the highest place in the government of the world. Is there a race of men who do and have ever exhibited such unbounded ambition for exalted rule? The history of the Caucasian race is but a recital of vaulting ambition and bloody efforts to rise to the loftiest eminence in government — to the pinnacle of earthly fame. The first chapter of post-diluvian history begins with the building of towers, the founding of cities, the erection of monuments, the creation and consolidation of principalities and powers and dominions; and, from that time to the present, like the restless ocean, the ambitious race has been raging and surging up against the granite cliffs of God's will, chafing to leap over the bounds which he has appointed by the command, "Thus far shalt thou come, and here thy proud waves shall be stayed."

Belus erected the great tower of Babel, and Ninus Nineveh. Semiramis led forth her conquering armies, and brought into subjection to her sway the surrounding countries. She built the great city of Babylon, and erected other monuments to secure for herself the crown of lasting fame. Macedonia's warlike son, as a god, aspired to universal sway — maddened by the grand desire, he led his rough warriors from country and from home, and, like an infuriated deity, overturning thrones and tearing down kingdoms, swept over the then known world, and left a broad, charred desert behind his devastating army. But not content with this vast sovereignty, he aspired to be a god, and died a miserable wretch. Cæsar's vaulting ambition led him into the high dominion of the Roman world; but ambition in Cassius and in Brutus induced them to strike him dead at the foot of Pompey's statue. Ambition drew the Saracen, with fire and sword, into the heart of Europe; and this same love of fame, this desire for the eminent place among men, drove back on the surging tide of war the mailed knights of Europe to the Holy Sepulchre and to the walls of Jerusalem. The ambition to be the world's imperial sire steeped Napoleon's hands in human gore, made him death to millions of his race, and the apparent incarnate prince of the power of this world, "raging hot from hell." It was the love of pre-eminence which brought on the late war in the United States, resulting in the destruction of the fairest heritage of man on earth, laying waste the comfortable homes and devastating the rich fields of the South, baptizing in fraternal blood this hitherto peaceful land, and making eternal enemies of the kindred people of the North and South. But why, even had we the space, should we particularize, when the entire history of the race, from the first murder in Eden down to the assassination of Lincoln by the aspiring hand of Booth, is nought but a continuous black record of crime and suffering and cruel death inflicted by one upon another of the race, in the pursuit of that desire for sole distinction, for universal sovereignty, which was, for the noblest purposes, inspired into Adam when he became a living soul.

The desire for distinction is the tormenting thorn in the flesh of every born son of Adam's race. All struggle by their own efforts to clothe themselves with immortality. Each torments himself with the raging, consuming passion to grasp the hissing, flaming bauble honor, which, when apprehended, will burn all goodness from the heart, and pierce the immortal soul with the very flames of hell. Ambition cannot be wholly eradicated from our nature. It may be crushed and repressed for a time, but it will patiently contend with all sorts of difficulties, whenever the least opportunity offers. In fits of desperation, it will fly at impossibilities, and in the ravings of the maniac, swear —

> "By heaven, methinks it were an easy task
> To pluck bright honor from the pale-faced moon;
> To dive into the bottom of the deep,
> Where fathom line could never touch the ground
> And pluck up drowned honor by the locks;
> So he, that doth redeem her thence, might wear
> Without corrival, all her dignities:
> Out upon this half-faced fellowship!"

Although this passion for pre-eminence, this desire for sole sovereignty, this jealousy of rivalry, has been the cause of the destruction of the peace and happiness of mankind, the cause of all the misery with which the world is cursed, yet it was bestowed upon Adam as a blessing, ay, the crowning gift by which his likeness to God was rendered complete. By it, he was fully prepared to reign in the theocratic government of the whole world, which it was his mission to establish upon the existing democracy, and to maintain the position of universal autocrat, until he should render back the sceptre to the God who had given it to him.

We have seen that the descendants of the man made in

the image and likeness of God, on the evening of the sixth creative day, are the red men; and since the law is inexorable that all things must increase after their kind, therefore that man could not have been Adam, or that he is not the progenitor of the white race. God rested on the seventh day, which, we must bear in mind, was a period of fifty thousand years; but if it were but twenty-four hours, still the entire day was past. After this, Moses says that it had not rained upon the earth, and there was not a civilized man, or a man to till the ground.

This does not assert, as many have supposed, that there was no man in all the earth, but simply, that there was not a man with the capacity to develop the resources of nature. On the contrary, what follows would seem to show that the world was not only populous when Adam was created, but that it was also divided into countries, with metes and bounds and local names. "And God planted a garden eastward in Eden." If this country was so named after the garden was planted eastward, why does not Moses say so? it would have been as easy as to say that it was planted in Eden.

Eastward and westward are relative terms, and indicate the direction from the speaker or writer, or from some standpoint well fixed in the minds of all as neither east nor west, but the point from which longitude is reckoned, as the city of Washington, in the United States, or the town of Greenwich in England. As, however, in the days of Moses, the world had no established basis of longitudinal reckoning, we must understand him to mean that the garden was planted in a country, at that time called Eden, which lay to the east of some other important country of the ante-Adamic ages, and also of Palestine.

All that we wish to establish in this place is the fact that the world was then divided into different countries, with fixed boundaries, and specially named, as Eden and the land of Nod. Therefore Eden was not the name of the garden, but it was the Paradise of God, planted in an eastern country of the pre-Adamic world, called then and before the land of Eden; hence we conclude, as heretofore, that the world must have been inhabited prior to the advent of Adam.

God governs the universe by the use of adequate means; and the agencies by which he works out natural results may be understood by all those who take delight in them, and will patiently investigate the laws of nature. These things have been given to us and to our children. How, then, was the garden planted in Eden? It was, as must be admitted by all, a physical work, and performed after the world was clothed in hirsute covering of grass and herbs and trees. It was necessary, then, that the ground be cleared off, that the spontaneous vegetation be removed, and that the trees which were pleasant to the eye, and which would bear fruit good for food, should be transplanted into that favored spot.

If there were men then, as there must have been, God would perform that work by their hands. As we have seen that the red man will not soil his lordly hands with labor even now, then we must not suppose that they would work in the days of their innocency; nor would God, unless in punishment for crime, enforce any, and especially the highest order of earthly beings, to do that which would cause physical suffering and mental anguish. Then may we not suppose that God selected a red man, the chief, it may be, to whom he communicated the plan and charged with the planting of the garden, as Noah was afterward chosen for the building of the Ark? May we not also suppose that he executed the work by the hands of his dependants, the black men, who were the connecting link between the lower animals and the governing red man, and whose greatest pleasure consisted in following their superior and in executing his will?

In this way the garden may have been prepared for the reception of the representative of God and the king of all the earth. The trees selected, under the divine direction, may have been transplanted by them; or, the ground having been first prepared, the chief may have caused his servants to gather the chosen fruits and bring them to the garden, where he could see that the seeds were planted in the order indicated to him by Infinite Wisdom. To the latter hypothesis we are inclined, because God is never hurried or in a strait for time, and could as well take a thousand years as one day for the preparation of Paradise. As Noah was one hundred and twenty years in the building of the ark, that space of time may have been sufficient for the planting and perfection of the garden in Eden.

Geology informs us that thousands upon thousands of years are written upon the surface and in the bowels of the earth; yet it has been but six thousand years, or one week of the world's year, since the fall of Adam. The account of Moses does not state the time that he held the government of the world prior to his fall. He certainly had been inducted into his office of sole sovereignty, when all living creatures were caused to pass in review before him, in order that they might receive the names by which he would call them, and learn what disposition he would make of them; therefore he was in office for some space of time.

Adam was made perfect, with a high order of intellect, capable of grasping almost by intuition the most difficult problems in government or science which might come up for solution. Yet he was not omniscient, for this would make him equal with God; therefore what he knew he must learn, as all other creatures do in heaven and in earth. The means of learning, with him, as with us, were by precept, by observation, by investigation, and by reflection.

CHAPTER XIII.

COMPUTATION OF TIME — SCIENCE VS. MOSES — THE FIRST DEMOCRATIC GOVERNMENT — FIRST MONARCHY — CREATION OF EVE.

IN the Jewish economy, we have the week of days, the week of years, and the week of weeks of years; every seventh day was a day of rest; the seventh year was the sabbatic, or year of rest; and when seven times seven years were completed, the next, or fiftieth, was the year of jubilee. That was a year of rejoicing and doing good, when the debtor was released from his obligations, the homes of the poor were restored to them, the bondmen were set at liberty, and the prison doors were thrown open and the prisoners went out free. It was a settlement of all abuses, a quieting of all old disputes, a time of general good feeling, when the oppressor must lay his oppression upon the altar of his God; and thus the whole nation must again begin the world aright on every fiftieth year or year of jubilee.

If this institution of the Jews, as all believe, was typical, may it not have represented some great truths in the history of the world? A week of weeks of superior time, as applied to the operations of nature in our earth, would be 49,000 years, and the next succeeding period of 1000 years would be the grand jubilee. In this view of the case, every fiftieth period would be a complete geological period, or one astronomical day. We have assumed heretofore, from the fact that fifty-two weeks are reckoned to one of our years, that 52,000 years would therefore make one astronomical day, or a perfect geological period; but from an examination of the rules for the construction of prophetic time, it will appear that 30 days are allowed for a month, and 360 days for a year, which would make fifty-one and a fraction of weeks in a year.

This, it would seem, should give us the true geological period; but since all the operations of nature are accomplished in perfect cycles, therefore, without doubt, there must be an error in such a basis of computation, which we have no means of correcting except through the medium of revelation. From the Jewish institution of the year of jubilee, we think that we may obtain the true rule and possibly the exact geological period or astronomical day.

Let us take 1000 years, as indicated by the sacred writings, to be the superior or Adamic day; then 7000 years will be the Adamic week. The square of this mystic or sacred number is 49,000. This is the perfect number, and we would therefore have supposed that the 49th would have been the year of jubilee in the Jewish economy; yet we find that Moses, under divine guidance, appointed the 50th year to be the year of jubilee, or the beginning of a new era. Upon reflection, we must perceive that this is the true rational arrangement; because the 49th is an ordinary sabbatic year, and is necessary to close up the old order of things, to complete the grand square of 7 times 7; wherefore that could not be the year of jubilee, which is the beginning of a new era; hence 50 years were necessary to make a full or round period of time in the Jewish economy.

If we take a day in the Jewish week of weeks for 1000 years, we obtain 49,000 years; when, by adding the fiftieth day of 1000 years, we shall have 50,000 years for a full period of time, a geological epoch or astronomical day; and since 360 days in prophetic time are reckoned for a year, therefore we have 360 multiplied by 50,000, equal to 18,000,000 of our years, for a complete astronomical period of time.

"Besides turning on its axis, the sun, attended by its

planets, moves at the rate of 8 miles a second, in a circular path round a centre far off in the fields of space. So vast is this path that it will take the sun 18,200,000 years to get once completely round it." (Astronomy.) By our deductions from revelation we obtain 18,000,000 years for the astronomical period, while the mathematical calculation makes it 18,200,000; hence here, as everywhere, true science and revelation, rightly construed, corroborate each other, and unite to pour down a flood of light upon the rational view of the laws of mind and of matter.

Since six geological periods or astronomical days had well-nigh passed before the man was made in the image and likeness of God, therefore the world was near 300,000 years old when the first governing man came upon the stage of action. Then God rested one whole astronomical day or geological period of 50,000 years before Adam made his advent into this world. But if he were ushered in at the beginning of the second astronomical week, and just at the beginning of the first inferior geological day of 1000 years, it must have been the fiftieth sabbath of the world and the beginning of the first grand jubilee. The full climactic time of the old order of things was now completed, and, the grand jubilee coming on, it was the time for the introduction of the new constitution and the establishment of the mighty theocracy over all the earth.

When the first governing or red man was made, he was commanded to be *fruitful, to multiply, and to replenish the earth.* We here lay down the broad proposition that whatever reproduces must die. When the corn has yielded its fruit, the object of its life is accomplished, and it straightway must die. The tree may produce many crops and then live, yet the effort is such a tax upon its vitality, that each returning crop proclaims the fact that the tree must die. It is written in every page of the history of nature, that whatever animal produces young must surely die. The red man was made a fruitful animal, therefore he was made mortal, and as he was, so must those be who are sprung from him; for he was to multiply after his kind, that is, reproduce exact copies of himself. These multiplied men were to subdue the earth, and to have the very same dominion over it which had been given to and exercised by their first parents. All the men of this race, as the individuals of all other races of beings, are born equal. The innate sense of justice of the red men would in their state of innocency ever prevent one from infringing in the least upon the rights of another; or if such a thing had occurred in the geological jubilee, during which time they had the dominion, all the others would have united to compel the others to restore his rights to the injured party. Hence arose a great democratic government, as extensive as were the races of men and animals.

The governing race were all equal in power; equal in intelligence; equal in justice; equal in jealousy of individual rights; equal in the love of truth;—and the inferior race were on equality with each other, and found exuberant happiness in performing the behests of their merciful masters and kind protectors of the superior race. The only form of government which could possibly exist under such circumstances was a democracy.

We would be inclined to the conclusion, since the government of the whole world was the same, and since democracy must have existed everywhere, that, therefore, there would have been no political or geographical divisions of the earth; but, from what Moses says on the subject, we are forced to a different conclusion. Before Adam made his advent into the world, the garden was planted in an eastern country, called Eden; and when but two men had been born of the race of Adam, and one of them had slain the other, and when the first was driven out before the Lord, he went into another country, then called the land of Nod. Hence, it would appear to be evident that the world was divided into different countries, with metes and bounds marking tribal territories. As Palestine was divided into twelve parts, and as everything in connection with the Jewish history is typical, so we would conclude that the primitive earth consisted of twelve grand divisions, which, with all their numerous subdivisions, were regarded as sacred by all the tribes.

Much insight may be gained in regard to the governmental and geographical condition of the primitive world, by studying the character, customs, religion, and government of the aborigines of North America, whom we suppose to be the pure descendants of the original governing race. Our space, however, will not permit us to pursue the subject in detail, and we must leave it, with a passing notice, for the investigation of others.

When, in the lapse of rolling ages, these red men, like the children of Israel, asked of God a king who should administer universal and uniform justice, we may suppose that he authorized them to select one of their own number, a man of their own race, to be their representative; or it may be, that the Almighty chose this individual, as he did Samuel. It was the duty of this representative to prepare a place for the coming sovereign, to receive him when he came, and to submit to his authority for all the race: the man whom they selected may have been the chief of the tribe which inhabited Eden; that, probably, being the identical locality where the first red man was made, and ever since had been held by the right of primogeniture; hence, the chief of Eden, the oldest country on earth, could with propriety be selected as the common representative of the race.

The chief of Eden, whom they had all chosen as their wisest man, to whom Infinite Wisdom had intrusted the preparation of the garden, who, as the representative agent to receive the king, and act for them in establishing the new government, this elevated character, we may suppose, he would take nearest to himself, in the capacity of premier or grand vizier of the world.

Thus the democracies or tribal governments were united in one great and glorious monarchy, and placed under the authority of an earthly sovereign, who was so transcendently perfect, both in body and mind, that he was in the government in the place of God to the aboriginal inhabitants. This mighty ruler was incorporated with flesh and blood, that he might be able to enter into the views and sympathize with the feelings and passions of his subjects. He was made perfect and beautiful in body, and endowed with those lofty attributes which rendered him worthy to represent God on earth, and so far superior in intellectual qualities, that even the haughty red man could bow to his supremacy without doing violence to his excessive pride. We must bear in mind that pride in the red man then was no sin, for thus his God had made him.

Although the empire had been established from the rivers to the ends of the earth, the change was so little in the working of the present government from the past, that the people were sensible of the change chiefly on account of the benefits of the present. Let us repeat, that in computation of time, the day period, where it alludes to the history of man, is a thousand years; where it refers alone to the great operations of nature, it is a period of fifty thousand years; and the day of twenty-four hours; so that the sacred number of three is observed here, as in all the works of God; that is, the natural day, the human superior day, and the astronomical day.

If Adam ascended the throne, as we suppose, in the morning of the eighth jubilee, there were before him a thousand years of rest, of peace, and of quiet happiness, during which time, in solitary glory, he might rule as god over the whole earth. The people could but be happy under such a government, and would voluntarily offer more than its necessities required. Emulous in the service of their beneficent king, all rejoiced in the glory of his reign. Like the merciful God, whose vicegerent he was, he dispensed blessings on every living creature; for all kinds of animals, as well as both races of men, were the subjects of his government and the objects of his care. In this way, Adam reigned in all probability for hundreds of years, with instincts and intellectual endowments so perfect that he was "a law unto himself," and did whatsoever seemed good to him. Thus, in fact, he was a god on earth, yet did nought except with the full approbation of his Heavenly Father.

During this happy period, Adam bore the same relation to his Father and his God that Jesus did through all his pilgrimage on earth. He was the only son of his Father, and bore the express image of his person. He and his Father were one, because his mind was under the complete control of the Divine Will; his every thought was by the inspiration of God. He was such, we may suppose, as Peter and James and John saw Christ in his transfiguration on the mount.

So perfect a being, the sole sovereign of the earth, seated upon his earthly empyrean, his will done on earth as that of his Father is done in heaven, basking in the light of God's countenance, and enjoying familiar converse with the lofty One who inhabiteth eternity—it would appear that such a one should be perfectly happy. So, no doubt, he was; yet he was a solitary being, without companionship, without an equal, and, consequently, without complete sympathy in all the universe. In heaven he had no fellows, for he was clothed in flesh, and there all is unincumbered intelligence. He was so transcendently superior, physically, morally, and intellectually, to his subjects, the red men, not to speak of their black servitors, that there was not in the earth one being with whom he could associate on terms of equality. His days were spent in ameliorating the condition of his subjects, the improvement of his world; his evening in contemplating the glories of God and the perfection of his works. His mind was employed, and he was content.

Though perfectly happy, his was a quiet, profound, unvarying contentment, which flowed from the gratification of all his desires, and an abiding sense of the discharge of every duty; yet, being without a companion with whom to associate, although he knew no sorrow, he could know no joy. The poet says:

> "The world was sad, the garden was a wild,
> And man the hermit sigh'd till woman smiled."

"And God said, It is not good that the man (or Adam) should be alone; I will make him a help meet for him. And the Lord God caused a deep sleep to fall upon Adam, and he slept; and God took one of his ribs, and closed up the flesh instead thereof; and out of the rib which the Lord God had taken from man, made he a woman, and brought her unto the man." She was made to be a help suitable for him, a companion, the partner of his throne, the equal participant in his glory and power. This being was the last of God's earthly creations—the adornment, the crowning glory of creation — made for the pleasure of the world's great king, and, therefore, more beautiful than the king himself, more lovely far than all the works of God.

While Adam was in his first transport of joy, the warning voice of their Heavenly Father repeated the command, "Of every tree of the garden ye may freely eat; but of the tree of the knowledge of good and evil, ye shall not eat of it; for in the day that ye eat thereof ye shall surely die." The excess of joy in Adam was immediately tempered down into rational happiness and quiet contentment. Adam was made, inaugurated, and reigned in solitary majesty until God, of his infinite goodness, made and presented to him a help suitable for him — a companion who could sympathize with him in his intellectual labors, and in the honors of vast dominion; and all this occurred during the historic jubilee, as applied to the old races, and the first superior day, or period of one thousand years, as applied to Adam.

CHAPTER XIV.

THE MEANS GOD USES IN THE ACCOMPLISHMENT OF HIS DESIGNS — THE TRINITY IN UNITY — SPIRITUAL RESULTS ARE EFFECTED BY SPIRITUAL AGENCIES — PHYSICAL RESULTS ARE EFFECTED BY PHYSICAL MEANS — THE CONNECTING LINK BETWEEN MIND AND MATTER — GOD'S MEDIUM OF COMMUNICATING WITH MAN — INSTANCES — PROOF.

HERE let us pause for a time in the investigation of our main idea, to examine into the manner in which the animals were created. And, in the first place, it becomes necessary to inquire somewhat into the attributes of God, and the means by which he accomplishes his designs, both of a material and of an immaterial character. We would approach this subject with that reverence and deep humility which is due from a sinful son of father Adam to the almighty Maker and Sustainer, whose purity is such that he cannot look upon sin with the least degree of allowance.

The fact of the existence of God is nowhere revealed in the Bible, because, by the power of ratiocination, the fact can easily be deduced from the grandeur of his works and the necessities of the case. Nothing is made known to us by revelation except what cannot be discovered by patient thought and profound research. Up to the time of Moses the existence of a God had never been doubted; but, for reasons which we will hereafter have occasion more particularly to notice, the prevailing error in that day was in the other direction; for "they had lords many and gods many."

The Greek philosophers discovered, by the light of unaided reason, the existence of the great First Cause, and erected in Athens an altar to him as the unknown god. It remained, however, for the apostle, in the light of revelation, to remove their doubts by saying to them, "Whom ye ignorantly worship, Him declare I unto you." It is true that in David's time the *fool* in his heart had said there is no God; but if any such unfortunate existed in the time of Moses, he was too insignificant to excite even a passing notice from the inspired writer. He boldly assumes the existence of God, and, in the very first sentence which he writes, reveals the tremendous truth that, "In the beginning God *created* the heavens and the earth," or universal matter. Were it not for this declaration, the philosopher might be led by logical deduction to the conclusion that matter is eternal.

And the Spirit of God moved upon the face of the waters, or of chaotic matter, and "God said, Let there be light, and there was light." Here we have a revelation of the triune character of God. In the beginning God created matter; then the Spirit of God moved through chaos, and the Word said, Let there be light. God the pure intellectuality, the *Nous;* God the thought, the product of the mind, and yet the mind itself, the *Logos* or Word. "In the beginning was the Word, and the Word was with God, and the Word was God. All things were made by him, and without him was not anything made that was made." Further, there is the principle of energy, which is the Spirit. The Spirit of God moved upon the face of the waters. Man by wisdom could not know this mystery of three persons in one God, therefore the important truth so essential to the proper understanding of the character and attributes of Deity, and the great plan of the world's redemption, is mercifully revealed to us.

We know that man is endowed with intellect, because he can lay down premises, and, reasoning therefrom, can arrive at logical, or, still more accurately, at mathematical conclusions. We infer the existence of mind from its operations, for there can be no effect without a cause, and conversely there can be no active cause without effect. Therefore there can be no thought without mind; no more can there be mind without thought. Thought is the product of mind, and they are so inseparably connected that they are one; and we have the mind the Father, the thought the Son.

Without language there can be no thought. All conclusions arrived at without the mental use of language are the result of mere animal instinct. Mind does not move instinctively, but rationally; therefore thought is language fitly used, and hence the Infinite Thought is called the "Word of God."

When the Spirit moved in chaos, God said, let there be light; that is, when the Eternal Mind had educed thought into a purpose, almighty power went forth to its accomplishment, and when the word was spoken the deed was performed. The physical strength of a man is the result of physical energy or effort; and yet this strength is so intimately connected with the body, that it is one with the body. The energy which attends the delivery of an oral address, but is lost in the written document, is the spirit, the living energy of the mind, which cannot be transmitted through the gross media of ink and paper. Hence the spirit of a man is the result of mind and thought, and yet it is one with them. There can be no mind without thought, and no thought without energy or spirit.

The great truth of the existence of the Mind, the Thought, the Spirit, three persons, yet only one Inhabiter of eternity, has been revealed to us. No man can see the mind of God; the Thought or Word has been made flesh, and dwelt among us, and the Spirit, the energy, the power of God is known to us by his works.

Here we will observe that the Almighty accomplishes all his designs by the use of adequate means. Spiritual results are effected by spiritual means; physical ends are attained by the use of physical agencies. God, who has established this great law, is a Spirit without body or parts; then how, let us inquire, does he act upon the gross and the more refined material of which this and the universal system of worlds are composed? The answer, in short, is that He accomplishes all things by the use of adequate means, which it is our business now in hand to examine into and illustrate.

When matter was created, it was in different degrees of purity, or rather in different degrees of grossness. It rises gradually from inert dull earth to the rich ingot of gold; from the rough opaque sandstone to the brilliant diamond; from the almost non-elastic oxygen, up through all the etherial gases to the divine element of electricity. This last is the highest form of materiality; then if the law of gradation be observed here as elsewhere, may we not conclude that it is the lowest form of spirit, or, in other words, that it is the connecting link between mind and matter, and the consecrated medium by which God effects all his purposes in the material universe? On account of its extreme subtlety and wonderful energy, some have thought it to be spirit; but spirit cannot be seen, neither is it appreciable by the physical sense of touch; and since electricity is both seen and felt, therefore it must be material, and the mighty agent which He spoke into existence in the beginning: "And said, Let there be light, and there was light."

Whatever is created is not God; and is it not true that whatever is uncreated must be God, or appurtenant to him in such a manner as to be essential to his being? Goodness, wisdom, truth, and power are the attributes of Deity; and, may we not also add, ubiquity and eternal existence? But what were ubiquity without extension, and what eternal existence without eternity? Extension and duration could not be created, therefore we must conclude that they are not independent of, but attributes of, or essential to the being of God.

To every creature He gives time and space, and when these are taken away the creature ceases to exist. Without the little space which our body occupies, and the few days of our life, we could never have been a man. It is impossible to conceive of existence, material or immaterial, without duration and space; but God is an immaterial being, therefore extension and duration are prerequisite necessities of his existence, and hence they are uncreated. God could not create these pre-existing conditions of his own being; but since whatever is uncreated is God, as before we conclude that eternity and extension are attributes or essentials to the being of God. Electricity is not absolutely necessary to spiritual existence, and though it be the mighty agency by which God effects all his purposes in the material universe, yet it was created by him.

In all the works of creation the law of gradation seems to be universal and uniform in its application. There is no exception to this, unless the link in the chain which should connect the material with the immaterial be wanting. If such a connecting link do exist, it must be a pure, ethereal, subtle element, which can pervade the most compact material substance, affect the most gross, and yet constitute the medium of intelligence between spirit and spirit. Such should be its characteristics that it would be difficult to determine whether it were a material substance or an immaterial principle or element.

Electricity actually fills these conditions, and is therefore the connecting link between mind and matter. Now let us see if this is the instrumentality by which the great I Am effects all physical results.

When Moses was upon the mount feeding his flocks, he beheld a bush in flames which was not consumed, and when he turned aside to see the wonderful sight, God spoke to him from the midst of the bush. It is evident that God in this instance manifested himself to Moses through the medium of electricity.

The philosophers tell us that every object pertaining to our earth contains latent heat, called caloric, which, educed by friction or violent concussion, results in fire. If the rays of the sun be concentrated with a lens the result is fire. If a current of electricity come in contact with combustible matter the effect is fire. Similar results are produced by similar causes; and if the same effect is obtained from dissimilar causes, we must conclude that the dissimilarity is only apparent, and though with different modifications and surroundings, yet the cause is one and the same.

On a clear night the gentle dews descend and water the ground. At noon the black clouds cover the heavens, the sun is darkened, the rain descends in torrents, and again the earth is watered. The restless ocean, by its mighty heavings, forces the waters through the internal ducts or arteries of the world, to external channels or veins, and by capillary attraction the liquid is diffused through the surface of the low valley and the high mountain, so that the earth literally sweats at every pore, and the ground again is watered. How different the processes, yet the result is the same; and we know, without a syllogism, that the cause is the same — that is, the ground in each case is moistened by the application of that compound of oxygen and hydrogen called water.

So fire is obtained from caloric, from the rays of the sun, and from the flashes of lightning; therefore, though under different modifications, caloric, the rays of the sun, and the lightning are one and the same. But lightning is known to be electricity; hence caloric, the ordinary light of the sun, and all supposed agents which will produce fire, are electricity.

May we not assume the fact as not only susceptible of proof, but abundantly proven, that through the medium of fire alone God communicates with material beings? "God, out of Christ, is a consuming fire." "No man can see God and live." Should the spirit of the immaculate God come in direct contact with the sin-stained soul of man, he must surely die! By the intervention of a Mediator, and by the use of the subtle element of electricity, which so perfectly connects spirit with matter that it is difficult to determine whether it is the one or the other, the Almighty establishes intercourse between himself and his creature man.

A man's head may be compared to a telegraphic office, the brain the apparatus, the soul or intellectuality the operator. He may occasionally transmit a message of his own, but ordinarily he is engaged in receiving and despatching the thoughts of others. The operator recognizes the operator with whom he converses, by the various calls of the different offices with whom he is in communication. If God addresses himself to man's intelligence through the medium of electricity, and if, by permission, it be possible for man to communicate with other spirits, and they with him, yet he certainly should be able to recognize the call and communication which comes from his Maker.

"The prince of the power of the air" makes himself to

appear as an angel of light to the sons of men; it will not do, then, to answer and rely upon every call that comes clothed in light to us; but if the operator will send up an earnest petition to the throne of his Heavenly Father, he will be certainly notified when God or his angels speak, or if the call be from the devil or evil spirits.

If God acts upon the mind of man only through the medium of electricity, because the mind is connected with materiality, much more will he not move gross matter itself without the use of this subtle and powerful agency to effect his purposes.

The chariot which bore Elijah from earth to heaven was a chariot of fire. When this same devout man had made an issue with the four hundred prophets of Baal, and had stated the proposition to the people, that if "Baal be God, serve him, but if the Lord be God, serve him," then he brought the question to arbitrament by saying, Whoever answers by fire, let him be God; and the Lord answered Elijah by fire, in a most wonderful manner. The electricity or a flash of lightning from heaven fell upon the offering, and not only consumed the sacrifice with the wood, but also the rocks of which the altar was built, and even licked up the water in the trenches round about. When Abraham had divided his offerings in twain, and had laid them upon the altar, a flash of electricity or fire passed between the parts and consumed them. But why multiply instances of this kind? For under the old dispensation, God ever answered his servants by fire.

The Tabernacle was consecrated, the altar was made holy by heavenly fire; and the Urim and the Thummim ever glowed with electricity when God was pleased with his people, but the bright flame was wanting when he was displeased. When Solomon had erected the great temple at Jerusalem and consecrated it in solemn prayer to his God, then the lambent flames of electricity flashed through all its recesses, played upon the cherubim in the holy of holies, fell upon the altar of burnt offerings, and consumed the hecatombs of lambs and bullocks which Solomon had sacrificed on that grand occasion.

"O Lord, how great are thy works, and thy thoughts are very deep." "Great and marvellous are thy works, Lord God Almighty; just and true are thy ways, thou King of saints." "The works of the Lord are great, sought out of all them that have pleasure therein." "I will praise thee; for I am fearfully and wonderfully made; marvellous are thy works, and that my soul knoweth right well." "O Lord our God, thou who makest thine angels spirits, thy ministers a flaming fire," guide us to speak aright of thee and of thy laws.

CHAPTER XV.

Electricity the Means used in Creating — The same Means used in Governing the Creation.

IT was by electricity, as we have seen, that oxygen and hydrogen in water were united; and with it God combined nitrogen and oxygen, and thus made the firmament, by which the waters on the earth are divided from the waters which are attracted by electricity above the firmament. By this same agency, He gathered the waters together into one place, and caused the dry land to appear. By electricity, the water was evaporated, the earth was warmed and energized, and vegetation, at the command of God, was brought forth. In the fulness of time, when Omnipotence spake the command to the waters to bring forth the fishes and the fowls, and to the earth to bring forth cattle, four-footed beasts, and creeping things, it was electricity which energized the water and the earth, and compelled inert matter to obey the high command.

We cannot believe, as stated in another place, that the small fishes, and the great whales, and Leviathan, and all the monsters of the briny deep, and the little birds, and the swan, and the pelican, and the ospray, and the ostrich, and all the feathered tribes, were created instantly, in a state of full maturity; because they were commanded to multiply after their kind, which we understand to mean, not only that the offspring were to be like their parents, but also that they were to come into being and to maturity like the first pairs. Since we cannot conceive of the idea that the Eternal God could be hurried in His work, we can by no means suppose that less time was taken for perfecting the bodies of the first animals than is now allowed them for procreation and maturity. Not because the Omnipotent could not speak them into existence, but because he chooses to accomplish all his designs by the use of adequate means. Being immutable, He effects His objects by the same means yesterday, to-day, and forever; therefore, if it require five, ten, fifteen, or twenty years for the procreation and maturity of an animal now, we may with propriety conclude that He would take at least as much time in which to fecundate the waters and the earth, and cause them to bring forth living creatures, as is required now to perfect their bodies.

Electricity, then, is the agency by which the Almighty is pleased to sustain all nature, both animate and inanimate; but, since He is immutable, the means by which He now sustains are the same by which He created; hence, when the waters were commanded to bring forth abundantly the living thing which moveth in the waters, and the fowl which fly in the air, energized and fructified by the sun's electricity, they brought forth in obedience to the sovereign command. So, also, when the earth was at first commanded to bring forth the grass, the herb, and the tree, and afterward the cattle, the four-footed beasts, and creeping thing, fecundity was imparted by this agency, and she brought forth whatever the wisdom of God had designed.

The fishes deposit their spawn in a shallow part of the water, and they are energized into life by the sun's electricity; then, by this fecundating agency, we may suppose that God caused the waters to bring forth the fishes in the first place without the spawn. By the same vivifying influence, and at the same time, the waters brought forth abundantly the fowls which fly in the air.

As previously stated, vegetation, in all its endless variety, did not instantly spring into mature existence, because this would have been contrary to the natural laws of production. There could be no necessity for hurrying the creation; and God never works miracles unless it be for the purpose of carrying out some special design. The earth, when first fecundated by solar electricity, having no soil, brought forth ephemeral fungus growths; and then the mosses, and the lichens, growing, maturing, and decaying, returned to the earth, and so a vegetable mould began to be formed. By this means an annual increase was added to the capacity of the earth to produce; and in due time, the poorer grasses and the lighter kind of herbs, and so on, until finally all kinds of vegetation, up to the lofty pine and the giant oak, by the subtile and powerful agency of electricity, were brought forth from the bleak and barren bosom of the earth.

In the primitive ages, there was no rain to wash off the forming soil, so that the mountain-tops and steep hill-sides were equally as rich as the valleys below. The placid electricity of the sun, by means of the relay batteries formed in our air, decomposed the water by day, and, being removed by night, the constituent gases were recompounded, and the gentle dews descended and watered the whole face of the ground. Thus with electricity the earth was warmed by day, and watered by night.

After thousands of years had added richness to the soil and abundance to its production, the fishes and the fowls, being the least destructive to vegetation, were energized by electricity into life. After another astronomical or creative day of fifty thousand years, when immense richness had been added to the soil, and astonishing luxuriance to its crops of vegetation, at the command of God the *vis vitæ* energized into being the cattle, the four-footed beast, and the creeping thing. Lastly, by the same energizing power, he created man, in his own image and likeness — male and female created he them; and blessed them, and commanded them to be fruitful, and multiply, and replenish the earth, and to subdue it, and to have dominion over it.

We intend to prove, before we have done, that this man was not Adam. But before entering more fully upon the task than we have already done, we earnestly deprecate the prejudices of theologians, and solicit all earnest inquirers after truth to investigate the subject, and severely test our views by the rules of right reason. We must, right here, however, add something further in answer to the question, How did God, who is a spirit, form the first animal bodies?

When the Infinite Mind designed the creation of worlds, his spirit moved upon chaos, and, electricity flashing through the mass, it was bisected, and the worlds were made. By the same instrumentality the earth brought forth vegetation in all its thousand varieties; and since the earth, in obedience to the same command, brought forth all living creatures, was it not done by the same means? The cabbage-head and the broad-spreading top of the oak are supported by the earth through the stem upon which they grow.

If the animal bodies were vegetated into life, after the sap had freely circulated through them for ten, fifteen, twenty, or a hundred years, is it not rational to suppose that the vegetable fibre may have been consolidated into the strength of bone and muscle, that the pulpy substance was converted into animal flesh, and the internal bark into skin. The electricity from the sun to-day energizes the spawn of fishes into life, and brings forth the half-vegetable, half-animal sea-nettles, sponges, and the like. The earth, then, fecundated by the same generous means, must have brought forth the first animal bodies.

To say that this is "a hidden mystery," and that it is therefore beyond man's comprehension, is not only false, but a mean evasion of the question under consideration. It was made a subject of revelation, and ought to be investigated, and at some time will be clearly understood; if not, the revelation amounts to nothing. The earth was commanded to bring forth vegetation, and she obeyed. Afterward, in the same words, she was required to bring forth the living creature, and she did so; and if the process had not been the same, would not the inspired writer have given us some clue to the fact? We are told that Moses in another place declares that God made every living creature of the dust of the ground; and this, instead of controverting, helps to establish our views.

Whatever means the Almighty uses in upholding nature, we may safely conclude are the same which he used to create. It is understood how the fœtus is formed, and how it is supported by the life-blood of the mother. In the beginning there were no mothers; but God commanded the earth to bring forth abundantly, as the universal mother of all flesh.

According to the plain rules of analogical reasoning, we must conclude that the first animals were supported by the circulation of the earth, through a similar channel and by similar propulsion to that by which the fœtus is supported in the mother's womb.

The young animal body is supported by infusion through the navel cord until perfectly formed; and yet it breathes not until it is separated from the mother. Since the earth could not be a nursing mother, it was necessary for the first created animal bodies, especially those whose young are now dependent on the nursing care of the mother, to have continued their connection with and drawn their support directly from the earth, through the original channel, until the body was not only perfectly formed as at birth, but until the body had ripened into full maturity.

At that time it became so thoroughly permeated with electricity that the unconscious vegetable body, at the command of God, was converted into a living, breathing, sentient animal. Where is the difficulty in the creation of a living animal upon this hypothesis, when art can apply electricity to a dead body and cause it to exhibit all the external signs of vitality, even to the deep breathing of profound sleep.

"The works of the Lord are great, sought out of all them that have pleasure therein." Then, if you have pleasure in the works of God, you must not say that these are mysteries which are not intended to be understood; and especially when the work, as in the case in hand, is the subject of revelation. Man is endowed with the power of ratiocination, to the end that he may be able to comprehend the sublime works of nature, and through them to look up to and worship that Infinite Mind which has planned and executed the vast designs of the complicated system of worlds, and the endless variety of vegetable life, and of all sentient beings.

Then, with us, look into the works of nature, and through them up to nature's God.

It is a fixed law of nature, that nothing shall be done without the use of adequate means; spiritual objects must be attained by spiritual means; material ends are accomplished by material agencies. The Author of Nature established this law, and it would not only be inconsistent, but dishonoring to the exalted immutability of his character to suppose that he created universal nature in direct opposition to, and in gross violation of, this great law of universal application. But if nature was created under law, you must conclude with us that the means by which it is sustained are the same by which it was created.

We have seen that through the instrumentality of electricity the world is sustained and was created; that all the influence from the sun is electricity; and yet this influence is now the only support of vitality on the earth. We have seen how vegetation and animal life might have been brought forth by this same agency; then why suppose that any other means were employed, or, still more, that they were called into being, without the use of means, in contravention to the universal law above refered to?

By the rays of the sun, which are electricity, the earth was impregnated, energized, and, at the command of God, brought forth first the grass, the herb, and the tree, in their order; and then the living creature in all the vast concatenation of animal life.

CHAPTER XVI.

REPRODUCTION IS DEATH—MOSES WRITING ONLY THE HISTORY OF THE ADAMIC OR WHITE RACE—THE USE OF REVELATION.

WE have already observed that all nature, which was originally commanded to multiply after its kind, was, without any design of inflicting punishment, intended to die. The grass, the herb, and the tree, which bear seed for the reproduction of themselves, are subject to decay and death. Every kind of insect, and all kinds of animals, according to the law of their being, multiply after their kind; and when old, and life becomes a burden, they die, to make room for their more vigorous offspring.

The governing man or Indian, as well as the animal man or negro, were subject to the law of increase or propagation; and, therefore, also subject to the universal law of decay and death. The love of life is common to all animals; and He who made them, gave to each the instincts and capacities necessary for their self-preservation, to a certain extent. However, lest the world should become overburdened with living creatures to such an extent that the earth, even when most exuberant in her productiveness, could not yield a sufficient supply of vegetation for the support of all, the Omniscient created the shark of the seas, the eagle of the mountains, the lion of the forests; in a word, He created the carnivorous animals, to feed upon and to keep the graminivorous animals in due bounds.

Lastly, lest the monsters of the deep, the mightiest of the birds, the terrible monarchs of the forests should exterminate the feebler animals in their respective elements, therefore God said, Let us make man in our image and likeness, and let them have dominion over the fishes of the sea, the fowl of the air, and the living creature that moveth upon the face of the earth; that is, this man, by his superior intellect, should have the power, as well as the wisdom and the justice, to take the lives of those animals alone which shall be necessary to his own comfort, and which should threaten other varieties of animals with extinction. It was his duty to preserve the order in animal being which God had established.

To this governing man, the animal man, on account of his helplessness, was an object of peculiar care; while the animal man, in return, was a most faithful servitor and adorer of his protector. This governing man, however, was averse to labor, intellectual and physical, and therefore disqualified in his very organism, constitution, and in all his instincts for forcing the earth to yield her fruits more abundantly by cultivation; hence, after the government of the world had been in his hands for vast ages, when the world was old and densely populated, and though rich in soil and exuberant in productiveness beyond our conceptions, yet the teeming millions of men and beasts demanded the cultivation of the ground, in order fully to meet and satisfy the multiplying wants of its numerous denizens. The governing man would not, could not work, or even plan agricultural labor for the animal man; wherefore Moses says, "And there was not a man to till the ground." On this account, and that the government of the world might be assimilated to the hierarchy of the heavens, God formed the body of a man out of the dust of the ground, as he had originally formed the bodies of all the other animals, and "he breathed into his nostrils the breath of life, and he became a living soul."

In the very nature of things and in the necessities of the case, this man was formed to be a king, the supreme ruler of the whole world; and therefore he was not, as all other animals, as the animal man and as the first governing man, made male and female. The single body of this man was formed, so different from all others, so superior, so transcendently beautiful and majestic, that even the proud, imperious Indian, with all his high instincts of personal dignity, could but bow in admiration of this glorious personage. When the divine afflatus was breathed upon Adam, and godlike intelligence beamed forth from his every feature, the lordly governors of the earth, as Peter and James and John at the scene of the transfiguration on the mount, involuntarily prostrated themselves at the feet of his majesty, and acknowledged Adam to be the representative of God and the sole ruler of all the earth.

"And God planted a garden eastward in Eden, and put Adam therein, to dress it and to keep it." The garden was watered by a river which was there parted into four heads, or rivers described as running out from thence in as many different directions. That no such geographical locality exists on the face of the earth accessible to man is evident, or it would long since have been pointed out by Biblical antiquarians. If such topography ever was in the world, where men now dwell or travel, it is clear that it was so utterly destroyed when the fountains of the great deep were broken up, and the internal waters were forced to the surface, as to remove every vestige of hope that it can ever be identified. We know, however, that this garden was a locality, for Adam was a material being, and therefore required for his convenience and happiness a local, material habitation.

For reasons which we shall hereafter render, we suppose that the scene of Adam's majestic and paradisian happiness was situated high in those beatific hyperborean regions the traditional remembrance of which has been handed down even to our own times through the poetic literature of the Greeks.

We will observe, however, at present, that although this description may and certainly does have a literal signification, it is also allegorical, and without doubt the information principally intended to be conveyed to us is from this latter sense.

If we will take a work on anatomy, and look at the inverted rivers delineated in a cut of the human body, we shall have presented before us such a topography as that which Moses describes as the garden of Eden. If the heart be taken for a river, it parts into four heads, and runs off as four great rivers, or the arteries which run through the arms and the legs, and branching off into every part of the human body, it is moistened by that vital fluid. As seen in the cut, there is one great river, the aorta, parting into four rivers delineated in full form, and flowing in appearance up stream, or from their mouths to their sources. This map will answer the description given by Moses, unless we shall consider it as a representation of the whole earth, when the garden would be situated near the one sea of the whole earth, which possibly was somewhere in the present Atlantic Ocean.

Then if, in a literal sense, we should understand the whole earth to be Adam's Paradise — in the figurative sense, being that with which we are here more particularly interested, the garden of Eden certainly was intended to represent his own body, in which God planted all manner of desires, instincts, and inclinations, the gratification of which would bring pleasure to their possessor. Among the chief of these desires was that represented as the tree of life, or devotion to the God who had made him, and that called the tree of the knowledge of good and evil, which represented the passion growing out of his virility. The latter was the only instinct or passion in his whole nature which it was unlawful for him to gratify.

Why, it will be asked, did God plant this desire, or the

capacity out of which the passion might grow, in Adam, and then prohibit its indulgence; and especially since no such prohibition had been imposed upon the animals, nor upon the inferior men? A sufficient answer would be, because it so pleased the Author of all things; and he certainly has the right to dispose of and impose whatever conditions and laws upon his creatures and all his works which he may deem proper. Since he has condescended, through the works of nature and by his prophets, to reveal his reasons for what he does in the world, and especially for the course which he has pursued in regard to our first parents, therefore it is both reasonable and right that we should attempt to justify his ways, even in the eyes of his rebellious creatures, and show how the miseries, the sufferings of the whole earth sprang from the wilful disobedience of man.

Let it be borne in mind that, according to our theory, when Adam made his advent into the world he found it full to overflowing with teeming life—animals and men being more numerous then than at any time since the fall—and that his mission here was to be a king, the universal monarch of all the earth. This theory we have builded upon what we consider a fair and rational construction of the account of the creation by Moses. In view of the handwriting of God in the works of nature, the vast ages in which the mountains have stood, the rocks have matured, the strata of the earth have been formed, the fossil remains have been deposited—in view of all these cumulative proofs, the world was certainly old, very old, when Adam came, or at least when he was driven out of Paradise, six thousand years ago.

When the earth was commanded to bring forth the body of Adam, he sprang from the earth in a manner similar to that in which the bodies of the other animals had been formed. It was superior to them all in beauty and perfection; and when God had breathed into his nostrils the breath of life, through the instrumentality of electricity, he became a living soul—that is, he was endowed with an intelligence far superior to all earthly beings, which was but a little lower than the angels. Notwithstanding his great perfection, yet his body was material, and therefore subject to the laws which govern materiality—that is, the same cause which produced decay and death in other animals would also produce the same results in his body.

The law of reproduction is the law of decay and death. The grass, the herb, the tree, which produce seed, are therefore subject to the law of decay and death. The living creature which procreates must, from that cause alone, as certainly die. The strength of the earth thrown into the vegetable increases its healthy growth, until it begins the work of forming and maturing fruit, when its vitality is chiefly directed to this object, whereby the vigor of the plant is materially affected; and this recurring year after year, the plant sooner or later, in proportion to the substantiality of its structure, must decay and die.

Animal life is produced and sustained by the same instrumentality which produces and sustains vegetable life. That agency is electricity; and any means by which the normal quantity of the *vis vitæ* is lessened or diverted from its appropriate mission of supporting the individual vegetable or animal, whether the diminution or diversion be by violent disorganization or by a process less active, yet the effect must be the same in the animal as in the vegetable. The vitality which should go to the support and invigoration of the parent animal is diverted from this object, and goes to the procreation of a new body like itself.

The mind controls the electricity of the body to a certain extent, and with it controls the body. When the mind wills that the body move from one point to another, immediately it throws a sufficient quantity of the electric energy into the lower extremities, and the required motion is produced. Whatever movements of the hands or other parts of the body are required by the mind, are effected in the same way; and so soon as this object is accomplished, the extraordinary concentration of electricity, being no longer necessary in that particular part of the body, in obedience to the will returns to the brain, which is the palace of the soul or intelligence.

If any contusion, fracture, or violent aperture be made in the body, the mind directs unusual energies to that point for the purpose of repairing the injury. By the extraordinary and lasting concentration of electricity in that particular part, the balance of the body, neglected, suffers for its usual supply of electricity; or, as it is commonly expressed, the whole body, through sympathy, suffers with the afflicted member.

The vitality of the vegetable, or of the animal, not only has a special direction in the act of procreation, but is exhausted, or escapes, never to return to the parent stalk, or to the control and invigoration of the parent animal; therefore every act of procreation is a sure blow aimed at the life of the procreating animal; and death must inevitably follow, sooner or later, in proportion to the frequency of the tax on the vital energy and vigor of the constitution of the procreators. Death will as certainly result from procreation as from a pistol-shot or the guillotine.

The animals, which God made and commanded to multiply after their kind, had no restraining law imposed upon them, and can therefore have no fear of the judgment, and, do what they will, can have no consciousness of having infracted a law of their being. Although they have the love of life and the instinct of self-preservation, yet death to them is not that terrible monster which he appears to the guilty infractors of the known moral laws.

The animal only sees danger when it confronts him. The instinct of self-preservation arms him for resistance. A conflict ensues, an effort, a struggle, and death closes the scene. The herd or flock to which the victim belongs either flee or overcome the danger, and straightway forget their late companion and death. To such, death is shorn of his terrors. The negro in Africa, and the nobler Indian of America, are in this category.

The hare is timid, the lion is brave, yet death is no more terrible to one than the other; in other words, neither of them is afraid of death, but fears impending danger, and acts upon the instincts or promptings of the laws of self-preservation. When an African chief dies, whole hecatombs of the young and robust are immolated upon his tomb. This practice to us seems horrible, yet to the African it appears all right. The African is a timid animal, and will shrink and flee from that danger which the white man, with the fear of death ever before his eyes, will sternly brave. It is abundantly apparent that it is not death, but danger, which the negro fears. If he is quietly led to the block or stake, not a nerve in his system will be disturbed, but he dies without a single fear or regret; yet he is thrown into immense trepidation and terror by the report of a cannon or the bursting of a shell. He meet deaths as a natural consequence; he fears danger from instinct.

The nobler and more intellectual Indian, whose bravery exceeds that of the impetuous lion, which sells his life to the hunter only at the most extravagant price, yet the fierce son of the forest has no overweaning love of life or great fear of death. Previous to contact with and contamination by the white man, no Indian, who had forfeited his life to the laws of this tribe, was ever known to save it by fighting, because he confidently expects to pass from this stage of action to the more pleasant hunting-grounds beyond the western hills. He sees his tribe melting rapidly away without more than a passing pang for those who have died, while the enduring grief, that reaches the very core of his existence, is for the young and vigorous warriors who should have been born to his tribe.

Death is therefore as much the normal condition of all procreating animals as life and health. If any unprejudiced reader will take the account of the creation as given by Moses—indeed, if he will read everything in the Bible bearing on this subject, he will be astonished that the idea of Adam's transgression having brought death upon all animals should ever have obtained such a hold upon the Christian mind. To such a one, that other general absurdity, that all the different species of men are derived from the same pair, will appear in all its native ugliness.

Moses sets out with the design of writing the history of the race of Adam; then we could scarcely expect of him an extended work on zoology. Were you to undertake to write a history of the United States, would you feel bound to enter into a detailed account of the inhabitants of Mozambique, the qualities and appearance of the Bengal tiger, the intelligence and enormous proportions of the elephant, the ferocious strength and majestic grandeur of the lion? Rather would you not confine yourself to American history, and make mention of outside men and things only as they became interwoven in the subject under consideration? If mention should be made of the horse, it is because it is necessary to the full development of the American character. If the Indians or Chinese are brought forward in your work, it is for the purpose of illustrating American character as exhibited in connection with those people.

This is the natural, the only way in which any other historian than Moses is expected to write. Why should he not have the same privilege, or, rather, be bound by this universal rule of the historian, and especially as he was giving only a synopsis, or at most a very succinct and comprehensive account of the times of which he wrote. Indeed, he only speaks of the creation apparently for the purpose of showing that God is the author of all things; that he made everything very good, and that Adam by wilful transgression brought death upon himself and all his posterity; that, notwithstanding the voluntary wickedness of the race, His goodness induced him to plan the redemption of the race from the bondage of sin and death.

When Moses had said enough to introduce his subject properly — to show that God is infinite in goodness, power and wisdom — that man, who was made good and just and holy, rebelled against the law of his being, and thereby incurred the penalty of death — and after mentioning a few prominent facts for the purpose of impressing these truths upon the mind, he proceeds directly into his subject, which is the history of the Jews, or of Abraham and his posterity. In such a work could we rationally expect the author to give a detailed history of the horse, of the gorilla, or indeed of any other animal or man, than of him from whom sprang the subjects of his work, and of others incidentally, as they might become connected with and involved in the history of those concerning whom he wrote?

We certainly ought not to look for a special account, or even the incidental notice of the creation of any race of men not directly or indirectly connected with the fall of Adam nor involved in its consequences, any more than we should expect a particular account of the creation and subsequent history of any other animal. For information, however, the inspired writer does mention the fact that God created all things, the vegetables and every living creature, and that he commanded them all, except Adam alone, to multiply after their kind.

We think that we will be abundantly sustained by reason in the conclusion that all the animals which were originally intended to multiply or procreate, were also intended to die. In this view, and this alone, can we understand the Mosaic account of the creation, and the succeeding early history of the world, as restored to us by inspiration, and reconcile it with the handwriting of God as plainly seen in the fossil remains of animals deeply imbedded in the bosom of the earth long anterior to the advent of Adam.

It is not to be doubted that Adam was made to be immortal, nor that by transgression he brought death upon himself and upon his posterity. "The wages of sin is death," and when he violated the law he justly obtained this reward, and therefore died; but by the sin of Adam the sentence of death passed upon all his race. Wherefore might this be? Was the heinousness of the offence so great, in a moral point of view, that the offended justice of God must pursue with unrelenting rigor the unborn millions of his race, and that judicial punishment for this first offence must be inflicted upon them to the end of time? Or was the act of Adam, in its legitimate consequences, such a complete subversion of law and order that the incarnation, suffering, and death of the second Adam became necessary to restore the world to its former condition? After Adam's fall, do not his descendants die in the due course of nature, just as all other animals?

"Wherefore, as by one man sin entered into the world, and death by sin; and so death passed upon all men, for that all have sinned." We see from this passage that the transgression of Adam was a representative act, which affects all his race; but how, let us ask, could it, in the sight of infinite justice, reach and impose penalties upon the denizens of the ocean, of the air, and of the forest? If God had intended to inflict direst punishment upon all sentient beings, would he not have declared the fact? It is true, that incidentally and unavoidably, all do suffer with him, inasmuch as the earth was cursed for his sake; but it cannot be that they were arbitrarily punished to the extent of the loss of immortality, and such an important fact not be mentioned by Moses.

Even upon the serpent and upon his seed, though the wrath of the Almighty was kindled hotly against him for the part which he had taken in bringing about the fall of Adam, yet the sentence of death was not passed, for the simple reason that by the very law of his being he was already subject to death. Upon Adam himself, God did not denounce the judgment of death, but cursed the earth for his sake, and declared the evils of the life he should henceforth live, until he should return to the earth, as the legitimate result of the act by which he had violated the law of immortality.

Whatever is important for us to know may be discovered by the investigation of the works of nature; otherwise it has been made a subject of revelation, and may be ascertained from the Scriptures. When both the book of nature and the inspired volume are silent on any question, it is not only safe to pronounce against it, but it is wholly absurd and irrational to contend for it.

Throughout all the vegetable kingdom, decay is written upon every object that lives. The same law is enstamped in unmistakable characters, that whatever is born or comes into the world by procreation must die. Yet the Scriptures only speak of man who is born of a woman, being but of 'a few days and full of trouble,' although it is equally true that the days of the animals are also few and soon ended.

The book of nature makes the fact clear, beyond a doubt, that the laws of reproduction and of decay and death are as inseparably connected as light and heat, as cause and effect. The immortality of Adam, which was directly in opposition to this well-known universal law of animal as well as of vegetable being, would not be discovered by the light of reason; hence, that all might see the justice and goodness of God, the fact was made known by revelation. The primitive happiness of Adam may be inferred from the light of reason; but his original immortality, and the fact that by his own voluntary act he brought misery and death upon himself and all his race, and produced by his rebellion all the ills of earth, could not be so discovered, and was therefore made the subject of direct revelation.

Man is found to be a reproducing animal; but it is plainly written on all the works of nature that whatever reproduces must die; therefore to reveal that fact would have been unnecessary. Since man is now a procreating, and consequently a dying animal, if he were ever a different being it could be known in no other way than by direct revelation.

The converse of the proposition, that whatever reproduces must die, is that whatever does not reproduce cannot die. Spirit does not reproduce, therefore spirit is immortal. Matter may be changed into a thousand different forms, yet matter is indestructible. Certain forms of matter may be increased, but the quantity of matter is not increased; hence, it appears that, because matter does not reproduce, it cannot die. The law of reproduction and death is universal, and, like all the laws of God, is without exception. Then when he declares to us that Adam was made to be immortal, we must conclude that the condition of immortality must have been the only one of which we can have any conception, that is, that he should not be a procreator. Had there been any other death-producing cause, since it was of such vast importance to us, it certainly would have been revealed; but since there are no two causes in the universe which will produce the same result, and since the anomally is not revealed to us, therefore we arrive clearly at the conclusion that reproduction is the sole cause of death, and that Adam died not, nor would ever have died, had he not become a procreator.

We are here met with the assertion that sin is the cause of death. Ay, that is the very thing which we were saying; but sin is the violation of the law. Reproduction is the law of death, and conversely, non-reproduction is the law of immortality; hence, as before, the condition of Adam's immortality was that he should not procreate. By reason we can discover no other cause adequate to the subversion of the original designs of the Almighty in regard to Adam; therefore, had there been some other, it surely would have been revealed to us; hence, from every stand-point, it abundantly appears that the act of procreation was the cause of the fall and death of Adam.

CHAPTER XVII.

Adam and Eve could not have been both Immortal and Procreative — Location of Eden, both Figurative and Literal.

IN the last chapter, we have seen that the cause of death in all nature is reproduction, and besides this we fail to discover, either by the light of reason or of revelation, any other cause adequate to this result; and that, therefore, Adam, who was made to be immortal, was designed to be a non-producing being. It is our purpose at present to inquire into other reasons by which we think the condition of the immortality of our first parents will be further elucidated.

If Adam and Eve were made to be both immortal and

procreating, what would have been the condition of themselves, of their offspring, of the world, at this time? Let us allow twenty-five years as the time for procreation, and then run back only two hundred and fifty years, and our ancestors number one thousand and twenty-four. Allowing each of these to have married into other families than their own kindred, and then each being the parent of five children, and it is apparent that each of us have had 9,765,625 blood relatives descended from the same pair, in the short space of two hundred and fifty years. This basis of calculation will admit of the death of the race at thirty-five years of age. Let the calculation be run back through six thousand years, and it will appear through what untold millions of ancestors each individual has derived his being; and it will appear that whole volumes would be necessary to set down in figures the number of his collateral relatives, or the entire number of the descendants of Adam and Eve.

When they were made, however, they were pure and good and perfect, and since they were immortals, had it been designed that in that state they should have procreated, they certainly would have multiplied after their kind, or reproduced immortal beings just like themselves. Again, had they reproduced at all, they certainly would have been as prolific as their diseased, dying descendants; and since they must have remained youthful forever, therefore had they been intended to be procreative beings in the first place, they must have continued so to the end.

From every point of view, from reasons *a posteriori* and *a priori*, from analogical deductions, from all the works of nature, and from revelation, we must conclude that the immortal man was a non-procreating man, and that, when he became a procreator, then and by that act he brought himself under the general law by which all reproducing creatures are governed, and hence became subject to the law of decay and death.

The man who, on the last day of the creative week, was made in the image and likeness of God, was made male and female; and "God blessed them, and said unto them, Be fruitful, and multiply, and replenish the earth." He, then, was made to be a procreative being, therefore subject to the law of decay and death, and hence, by no possibility, could be identical with that immortal being known to us as Adam, who, by the transgression of the law of immortality, brought death upon himself.

In that first man, to whom the government of the world was intrusted, were implanted instincts and capacities which, followed and developed, were all that was necessary to render happy and contented the nomadic race in the primitive abundance and delightful condition of the world. If we will look at the blessing bestowed upon him, we will be convinced that his descendants were intended to be a nomadic people, and to a wonderful extent this natural disposition has been transmitted to his pure descendants, the Indians of North America.

To this man was not given the capacity or the desire for extensive, much less for universal sovereignty, nor any inclination whatever to develop the dormant resources of the earth by manual labor; wherefore, when God designed to assimilate the government of the world to the hierarchy of the heavens, and when it became necessary for the comfort of the millions of men and beasts that the earth's production should be stimulated by skilful labor, then it was said, "And there was not a man to till the ground."

"And the Lord God formed (a) man of the dust of the ground, and breathed into his nostrils the breath of life, and he became a living soul." He was placed in the garden of Eden, to dress it and to keep it; and the beasts of the field and the fowls of the air were brought to him, to see what he would call them; and whatever Adam called every living creature, that was the name thereof."

The man who was made in the image and likeness of God was commanded to *subdue* the earth, and to have dominion over the fish, the fowl, and the beast; but this man was placed in the garden to dress it and to keep it; and sitting there as the supreme ruler of the earth, without any effort on his part which would be necessary to subdue any animal, all the living creatures voluntarily presented themselves to acknowledge their entire submission to his sovereign will. The first man was evidently intended to be a follower of the chase, and to live by the spontaneous productions of the earth; but Adam was as clearly designed to live by horticulture, and by reason of his superior intellect and the majesty of his person, that all living creatures should voluntarily bow to his authority.

It would appear to be difficult to reconcile these two characters, as belonging to one and the same individual, in the condition in which the world must have been before the fall; therefore, we again conclude that the man of the second chapter and the man of the first chapter of Genesis are not identical, but very different characters.

In another part of this work, we have seen that the world must have been at least 350,000 years old when Adam was made. The first man had been multiplying for more than one geological period, or astronomical day of 50,000 years; and, therefore, the world must have been vastly more populous than it were possible for it to have been since the cateclysm. With these facts remembered, a rational view of the subject before us will be much clearer, and more easily obtained.

In the garden where Adam was placed was every tree bearing fruit pleasant to the sight and good for food, and in the midst of the garden were the trees of the knowledge of good and evil and of life. Adam was permitted to use at will the fruit of the trees of the garden, except the tree of the knowledge of good and evil: he was forewarned that "in the day that thou eatest thereof, thou shalt surely die."

The idea conveyed to us by the description of the garden is literal, but without doubt is also highly figurative. In the latter view alone are we to extract the high moral truths which the writer intends to inculcate. If we consider the subject as literal only, what great principle is established, except that God has a right to give laws, and that it is the duty of his creature to obey? It would represent the Almighty as imposing an arbitrary law, merely to show His authority and the dependence of man.

Taken figuratively, however, as no doubt it was intended to be understood, and it illustrates the goodness of God, as well as the right to create and govern in whatever way seems good to him. It shows that man was not only made perfect and good and immortal, but that he was made the guardian of his own attributes, and that when he fell, he alone was responsible for the fall.

In the first place, taking a literal view of the description given by Moses, it becomes important to inquire where the garden of Eden was located. It will not do to look at the present map of the world, and expect to find the locality on this continent or on that, because the whole face of the earth, as is abundantly proven, by new formations of rocks and fossil remains, has been completely subverted by mighty upheavals and depressions.

On the highest mountains, as well as in the lowest valleys, over much the largest part of the present dry land, it is written in unmistakable characters that here once rolled the waves of the briny ocean. Deep in the bowels of the earth are found primitive rocks, primitive trees, and the bones of primitive animals. High on the top of the loftiest barren peaks of mountains, where no foot-print of the deer or antelope or of the bear or panther is seen, and where the aspiring eagle scarcely ever extends his royal flight, there are found those shells and petrified bones which in life must have belonged to animate beings in the bottom of the sea. It is evident, therefore, that the whole face of the earth has been changed, radically changed, since it first was made.

In Europe, in Asia, in Africa, in America, in the isles of the sea, everywhere the handwriting is seen—The waters have been here. Yet it is not universally so; for here and there we find a spot of primitive soil, where salt water never flowed, and where, but for the curse of an incensed God, would grow in primitive luxuriance every tree bearing fruit good for food and pleasant to the sight. This primitive soil, though rich and blessed with a suitable climate, will not produce, like made soil of inferior quality, cotton, hemp, flax, and whatever is used for purposes of clothing; but yields much more abundantly grains, fruits, grasses, whatever is used as aliment for the support of animal life. This fact proves, if further proof were necessary, that man was once in a very different situation from that in which he now is; that the world is now used for very different purposes, and has vastly different capacities from those which it originally possessed.

The account which Moses gives of the goodness and perfectibility of the earth and its inhabitants, and the lapse of its supreme ruler, and the ruin which followed, if rightly construed, gives a satisfactory explanation of our present surroundings. The ingenuity of man fails in any other way to account for the good and the evil; for the perfection and corruption; for the love of life and peace, and for the existence of wars and of death; for the love and hate which we bear our race; for the wretchedness of life, and the fear of death, and the dread forebodings concerning the future state;

for the dissatisfaction with the present, and the feverish desire to look into that which is to come; for the unwillingness to be governed, and the universal desire to rule; for the ignorance of our race, and their thirst for knowledge; for the perversion of our nature, and the purity of our conceptions; for the fertility of the valleys and the hills, for the barrenness of the mountains and the plains; for the fevers of the equator and the icebergs of the poles; for the wintry blast and summer's heat; for parching droughts and excessive rains; for the warring elements in ourselves, in earth, in water, in air, in fire, in everything pertaining to this world. All, all proclaim, in language clear and unmistakable, that God did not create things as they are.

Reason as well as revelation proclaims man to be the lord of the world; wherefore it is not irrational to conclude that the perversities of our natures, and the cursed, unhappy condition of the world, must have been brought about by him who possessed the superior intellect and the capacity to govern. Men of the highest order of genius are those with the most glaring weaknesses. The most frank and generous are those who sink most surely into the grave of dissipation. Those who have the highest moral and religious instincts frequently become the most desperately wicked and dangerous of men.

The worst of infidels are the most superstitious of mankind. The man who will deride Moses and the prophets, and scoff at the immaculate Son of God and his apostles, has great confidence in his own knowledge of the future through the medium of his dreams, "sees portents dire" in an unexpected flash of light, reads of fearful wars, of pestilence, famine, and death in every extraordinary phenomenon in nature. It is strange, yet it is true, that the man who will fearlessly curse God at high twelve, in the stilly night will tremble at a flitting shadow, or the low moaning of the gentle winds. Do not these inconsistencies in the workings of the human mind prove its abnormal condition?

Did the world and all things come by chance? Reason and nature answer, No. Did a good and merciful Being make them as they are? Nature and reason answer, No. How, then, is it that all nature is at war with itself, and that man is the worst enemy of man? The answer is contained in Moses and the prophets, and without revelation reason wholly fails to solve the difficult problem.

But to return. The handwriting of God upon rocks and hills declares the fact that the present map of the world gives no idea of its primitive geography. The key thereto was lost to us, but restored again by Moses, who informs us that God gathered the waters together into one place, and that the dry land then appeared. Consequently the map of the ancient world would exhibit no continents, no islands, no lakes, no seas; but a globe with the waters all in one place, and the remainder of its surface dry land.

Paradise is literally the garden of pleasure; but the whole earth was then as it was made, pure and right and good, and was, therefore, a world of pleasure. Adam was made to be the supreme ruler and federal representative of all the earth; therefore, a rational view of the subject would indicate that his palatial residence, his seat of power, should be a miniature representation of his entire dominion.

We have already supposed that Moses, in describing the garden of Eden, must have had reference to the anatomical structure of the body of Adam. If this be true, may we not suppose that the best idea of the map of the primitive world may be drawn from the delineation of a perfect human body?

Our experience, our knowledge of geography, of hydraulics, are to the effect that rivers are formed by the agglomeration of water from a thousand springs and brooks and rivulets flowing into a common channel, one after another, and finally in a body disemboguing into the ocean, the common receptacle of the water of the whole earth.

That it was not always thus, or that the laws of the circulation of the waters through the body of the earth was not always as it is now, may be very clearly inferred from the fact stated by Moses, namely, that in all the primitive ages God had never caused it to rain, but all evaporation was of that regular and moderate character which produces dews. Taking the garden of Eden, or of pleasure, by synecdoche, to represent the whole earth, then we shall have the one great eternal channel running from the great sea and parting into four heads, which ran out in different directions to the extremities of the earth, in continually branching off and diminishing streams, like the arteries of the human body. The water was then taken up by innumerable small ducts running out and coming together like the veins in the human body, as we see the rills and rivulets now forming our creeks and rivers, and by these the water was conveyed back to the sea.

A map of this one sea and the internal circulation of the waters, we have seen, is most fitly represented by a drawing of the arterial circulation of the human body. The aorta is the great river which parts into four heads, and runs off in four different directions — the profound deep of the sea, the heart, and its surface, the lungs, where the blood of the earth is exposed to the atmosphere. If we add to this a map of the venous circulation of the human body, with all its beautiful external delineations, we shall obtain a more perfect idea of what the primitive earth was than it were possible to obtain in any other way. The whole globe was represented by the human body, the gathering together of the waters into one place, called the seas, is represented by the heart; the river which parted into four heads is illustrated by the aorta parted into four arteries, running through the arms and legs, and dividing off into innumerable branches, by which the whole mass of the earth was moistened; and the impoverished water was then taken up by the veins, and conveyed back to the sea or great laboratory of the waters.

It were preposterous to suppose that anything like the present extent of the earth's surface was originally covered with water; because the design of its creation must have been to support as large an amount of animal life as possible. Since this is sustained by vegetation, and since vegetation is produced on the dry land, therefore no more of the earth's surface was covered with water than was absolutely necessary for the comfort of the fishes of the sea, the fowl of the air, and every living thing which moveth upon the face of the earth. It is evident that by increasing the depth of one great sea, whole gulfs and seas and oceans, with a healthy circulation of the waters through the body of the earth, might be converted into dry land, richly productive of vegetation and supportive of animal life. Moses tells us emphatically that the waters were gathered into one place; which ought to be an end to the argument, for he wrote by inspiration.

If the earth be represented by the human body, the north pole would be the head; the south pole the feet; the gathering together of the waters, the heart; the river which went out of Eden, which parted into four heads to water the garden, and by synecdoche, the whole earth, the aorta and the four arteries into which it is parted. The river Pison would be that artery which runs out in the right arm; Gihon would be that in the left arm; Hiddekel would be that in the right leg; and Euphrates would be that in the left leg. The resemblance between the earth and the human body is established by the collection of the waters into one place, the ebbing and flowing of the tides exactly resembling the throbbings of the heart, and the flow of the blood through the arteries and veins. The water exposed to the atmosphere, or the surface of the one sea, we may suppose did not bear a greater proportion to the body of the earth than the lungs to the human body. As the amount of water could not possibly have been increased, how unfathomably deep must that one sea have been, representing at its surface the world's lungs, and extending down to the profound depths of her great heart!

The remaining surface of the earth was dry land, diversified with lofty mountain ranges, with broad valleys, with romantic hills, and lovely dells. From the fossil remains of animals found in the extreme northern part of Siberia, and from other geological specimens found there, we know that region to have been once the habitation of animals which could live only in a temperate climate, and that it was richly productive of vegetation which could grow only where no blighting wintry blast could come. This proves beyond a doubt that the present geographic and climatic condition of the earth is vastly different from what it once was.

If it be a fact, that the range of mountains running north and south across the American continent is the great barrier over which the floods have never passed; that most of the country east of that range is upheaved and new formation; that all beyond is primitive formation, which was never submerged in the briny deep — may not that belt of primitive earth indicate the locality of the river Pison, and may not California be the land of Havilah, where there was gold? If this be so, if the range of mountains which runs north and south across the American continent, was the great bulwark which resisted the western rolling of the proud-crested waves of the heaving ocean; then, the earth being represented as a human body, the Rocky Mountain range would be the right arm, and the Cordilleras and the Andes would be what remains of the right leg. Under these mountain ranges would run the rivers Pison and Hiddekel.

We have nothing on the Eastern continent to indicate so clearly the position of the other two internal rivers; but we would suggest that beneath the Ural Mountains flowed the Gihon, when that would be the left arm of the world, and the Euphrates would be that grand stream which flows through the Mediterranean Sea, and passes under the African continent, along the place indicated by the Mountains of the Moon; which, therefore, would be the left leg.

As the primitive ocean was in proportion to the earth as the heart to the human body, and as the heart is under the left arm, therefore we may suppose, and especially since the great internal stream still runs out therefrom, that the Mediterranean Sea was then covered with a crust, and was a part of that great artery of the world which passed in through the Straits of Gibraltar from her great heart in the breast of the figure, or where the Atlantic rolls between Europe and North America.

The investigations of scientific men have led to the conclusion that our Gulf Stream is the outflow of a mighty volume of water which passes from the Mediterranean Sea, under Africa and the Atlantic Ocean, and comes to the surface in the South Atlantic, or in the Caribbean Sea. Is this not a justification of our theory of the internal or arterial circulation of the waters through the body of the primitive earth?

It might be made interesting, possibly useful, should the geologist trace out as far as indicated by the fragmentary ranges of mountains and hills, the great internal, arterial, and venous channels of the primitive world, where pulsated, in obedience to the surging of the sea, vast volumes of salt water, by which means the whole earth was moistened, its surface was rendered productive, and from which flowed out the rivulets and rivers, or external veins. The water, when thrown out from the sea, was laden with salt and all kind of minerals in solution, which, filtering through the earth, deposited its fatness in the soil for the support of vegetation, and finally gushed out upon the surface, pure sweet water, fully prepared to slake the thirst of man and beast; when by many a tortuous winding, it flowed back to the universal reservoir of water, the great heart of the world.

How can we account for the fact that the hills and the mountains always run in ranges, unless we suppose that in the original plastic condition of the earth, her arterial waters, surging beneath the surface, threw up these ranges, which formerly, as broad arches, stood above the internal volumes of the flood. Now, however, those channels are for the most filled up, and, it may be, with the immeasurable treasures of the old world. What vast riches and inestimable wealth may we not suppose to be heaped up in that channel under the Rocky Mountains where once flowed the Pison, one of the earth's great internal rivers!

We might trace a further resemblance between the world and a human body by pointing out the rock formations in the former answering to the bones in the latter; and we feel confident that the analogy between the two would appear so striking that no one would hesitate to agree with us that the body of Adam was formed to be a representation of the world. We will not dwell here, however, hoping that enough has already been said on the subject to induce the intelligent reader to make the comparison for himself, and to deduce his own conclusions.

CHAPTER XVIII.

Locality of Eden Literally — The Hyperborean Regions of Orpheus.

WE understand the description given by Moses of the garden to be a prefiguration both of the world and of the body of Adam. Before discussing its application particularly to the body of Adam, it becomes necessary to the development of our plan here to inquire more fully as to the locality of the literal garden of Eden, in which Adam lived and reigned and sinned and was disgraced.

If the garden were established to represent the whole world and the body of Adam, then was it variegated with gently rising hills and lovely dells, like the graceful swells caused by the veins and muscles in a healthy human body. At a glance Adam could see the miniature representation of the vast dominion over which he reigned.

In such a representation, where else but at the head of the world would be located the power which should govern the world; therefore we conclude, as we have concluded, that the garden of Eden was at the north pole, or head of the world, and that the artery which is divided in the temples answers to the rivers which watered the garden. Like the rich curls on the head of youth, the trees and vines, loaded with luxuriant fruits and lovely flowers of many variegated hues, and redolent with a thousand sweet odors, formed a glorious canopy over the happy residence of the world's great king.

There were no extremes of heat and cold, no sun's fierce fervors, no wintry blasts, no burning heat, no biting frosts, no extremes of wet and drought; nature and nature's laws were perfect and in perfect harmony, and all things conspired to render the garden of Eden a Paradise, "where even a god might deign to dwell." The garden was a map and a miniature representation of the primitive condition of the whole earth. How vast must have been the climatic and meteorological differences in the world then and now!

What is it which produces the change of seasons, the extremes of heat and cold, of rain and drought, the fervors of the equator and the eternal frosts of the poles, the dead calms and furious storms, the unceasing change and universal confusion under which all nature labors?

It will be remembered that, according to a fixed law of motion, the earth should revolve in a right line to the motive power, and, therefore, that her axis should be perpendicular to the plane of her orbit, or at right angles to the current of electricity from the sun. This kind of revolution would produce equal days and nights from pole to pole, and, consequently, a temperate climate everywhere; but the most delightful spots, because there would be eternal light, would be at the poles.

The sense of touch goes out from the head, and conveys impressions to the brain from every part of the body; and yet this universal sense is divided at the head into the four senses of hearing, seeing, tasting, smelling. By the one river divided into four rivers the garden of Eden was watered and rendered fruitful—was made the glorious habitation of the lord and sovereign of all the earth, which without them would have been a barren waste. By the one universal sense of touch, divided off into the four specific senses, the brain is rendered active, fruitful of thought, the seat of the soul, the material organism through which divine intelligence may act; but cut off all these senses, and the brain is inert matter, incapable of thought, of impulse, and of action.

The garden of Eden, then, was located at the north pole,

or head of the world, and when she revolved upon her axis perpendicularly to the plane of her orbit, it was in perpetual light, without the possibility of any extremes of heat and cold, and of wet and dry. It was the head, and crowned with unending light; and the whole body of the earth was blessed with equal days and nights, through all the year, from pole to pole. On this account the seasons were always and everywhere the same, except only the slight difference produced by the distance from the sun, between the aphelion and the perihelion of the earth's orbit.

When the earth revolved upon her perpendicular axis, the atmosphere must have been greatly elevated at the equator and correspondingly depressed at the poles. This condition was lasting, because the motion which produced it was regular and continuous. The elevated atmosphere at the equator would necessarily soften the direct rays of the sun, and the depressed atmosphere or that of less elevation at the poles would admit the oblique rays of the sun to penetrate there with such freedom that the temperature must have been everywhere near the same, and perfectly delightful. There could be no cross currents of the atmosphere, no violent winds, no aerial commotions; but gentle breezes, redolent with balmy odors, from east to west, caused by the solid earth revolving more rapidly than the circumambient air, breathed delicious, even ecstatic joys on all the happy denizens of the earth.

There could be no sickness or protracted pain or misery in such a happy world; and man and beast, in perfect bliss, must have lived out their appointed time. The happy beasts, with every want gratified, parted life without a pang, and their bodies furnished food for the carnivora; which in turn becoming so numerous as to endanger the order of being which God had established in the world, with a quick, sharp blow from the men whom He had made in his image and likeness, were removed from the stage of action; and these last, at the call of their Maker, yielded up their happy lives without a murmur or regret. Happy denizens of a happy world!

Moses informs us that there was, in all the primitive earth, no rain; but a mist went up and watered the whole face of the ground. The electrical condition of the earth and air was uniform, and there could be no extraordinary evaporations, and no rain-clouds could be formed. The gentle evaporation which daily went on like the insensible perspiration of a healthy body, in a world where all was order and regularity, was nightly condensed, or more accurately, the gases, relieved from combination by the great electrical machine, the sun, were recombined.

The happy earth, by day, was slightly stimulated by the rays of the sun, which prepared a delightful anodyne for her at night; and thus she was rendered productive beyond our most extravagant conceptions; and no doubt the number of men and of beasts which then inhabited her surface would be astonishing to the most devout student of the laws of nature in this miserable age. We may form some idea of the richness of the soil and the luxuriance of vegetation, by remembering that there were no rains to wash off the soil; but where the vegetable grew and matured, there it decayed and went to enrich the earth.

In this happy state, thus perfect and populous, the world was, when Adam came to be her imperial lord. He came, not as the man who was created in the image and likeness of God, to subdue the earth, but to receive the voluntary submission of the world to his august authority. He came, not to people the earth, but to rule its numerous inhabitants, as God rules in the heavens. He came, not with his mate, as the other animals and men had done, but he came as the sole sovereign of the world.

An angel could not have governed the world, because its inhabitants were physical beings. No individual of the then governing race could be elevated above his brethren without humiliation and great violence to their feelings, even if one suitable to the task could have been found. The law was ever unchanging, that whatever procreates must multiply after his kind; therefore, since the first governing man was not endowed with the desire or capacity for empire, none of his descendants could possess these qualities; and hence the necessity for the creation of another man; a man whose physical beauty and perfection, and whose intellectual superiority should as far surpass that of the governing man as the latter excelled the animal man.

His body was made most perfect, most complete in loveliness, and beauty and nobility of appearance, and in refinement of its material, of any which had yet been made; and into this body was breathed the breath of life, and he became a living soul. To this man was given the passions, instincts, and desires of perfect manhood, else how could he be a fit ruler of men? He was endowed with intellectual capacities and powers inferior only to the high intelligences of heaven; for man is but a little lower than the angels.

The garden into which he was placed, as we have seen, was located at the north pole; and this we shall now proceed to make more clear, by reference to other facts than those already adduced. From revelation, and the necessities and aptitudes in the case, we have concluded that the garden in which Adam was placed was there; and if this were not so, whence were derived the traditions in regard to the hyperborean regions? They were not a pure invention, for if any man, however deep in the folds of antiquity, had possessed the temerity and unbounded powers of invention to have originated these traditions, he certainly would not have been forgotten; but would, in the affections of the ancients, have usurped the position of Apollo, and, as the president of the Muses, he would have been worshipped as the god who had come to them literally from beyond the north.

It is impossible to conjecture that the rude, uncultivated ancestors of the Greeks could have invented, without some facts to start with, the glowing description of the hyperborean regions, as given us by Orpheus and Pindar. They say of the inhabitants of that happy land, "On sweet and fragrant herbs they feed, amid verdant and grassy pastures, and drink ambrosial dew, divine potation; all resplendent alike in coeval youth, a placid serenity forever smiles on their brows and lightens in their eyes; the consequence of a just temperament of mind and disposition, both in the parents and in the sons, disposing them to do what is just and to speak what is wise. Neither diseases nor wasting old age infests this holy people; but, without labor, without war, they continue to live happily, and to escape the vengeance of the cruel Nemesis."

Is this not a traditional description of the Paradise which Moses describes? In the present condition of the world, by what train of reason, or by what kind of flight of fancy could the most poetic imagination have thought of placing the "happy regions of the blessed beyond where the north wind begins to blow?" Who could, in the wildest fancy, have dreamed of perpetual spring and unending grassy pastures at the north pole, when all experience and all reason would lead us to the conclusion that that locality must be bound up in the adamantine chains of unending ice? The poetic imaginings of the ancients must have been founded upon some tradition handed down to them from more antique times, and was an indistinct remembrance of a former and very different and far more happy condition of the world.

What that condition was, and how the vast change could have been brought about, was lost to mankind, and could not possibly be recovered except by a direct revelation. In infinite mercy this was given to Moses, by whom we are informed that the whole earth was as happily situated as these hyperborean regions are described to be by the poets, and that the world was cursed on account of the sin of the world's supreme ruler. A rational view of that account, and the necessity of the case, has already led us to the conclusion that the scene of the majesty and the fall of Adam was at the north pole, from which he was driven out, and which is guarded to this day by circumambient icebergs, like a flaming sword turning every way.

The tradition of the hyperborean regions proves the fact that an imperfect recollection of the primitive happy condition of our first parents was preserved through the cataclysm and the dispersion, even by the heathen; and it proves further that the seat of original happiness was at the north pole, or in the hyperborean regions. Therefore, Adam, as the great sole sovereign, was enthroned in the garden planted for him at the head of the world.

He was endowed with the lofty capacities for investigation and the comprehension of the physical and metaphysical laws, in order that he might reveal and put to use the vast resources of nature, which to the red man would forever have remained among "the hidden mysteries." He was clothed with the godlike attributes pertaining to a high order of intelligence, and an uncompromising desire for sole sovereignty; and hence being jealous of all rivalry in government and philosophical attainments, he was a suitable representative, the fit vicegerent of God on earth.

As such, all men and animals voluntarily offered their humble submission to him, and God commanded him to eat freely of the trees of the garden, except of the tree of the knowledge of good and evil; "for in the day thou eatest thereof thou shalt surely die." It is true that, had not this single restraint been laid upon him, he might have become arrogant in his self-sufficiency; but yet we must believe that this injunction was imposed upon him as a paternal warning rather than as an arbitrary threat; and no doubt Adam, with undarkened intellect, saw clearly the connection between the physical cause and the physical effect, between the inhibited indulgence and the result in death. Therefore, when he did violate the law, he was without excuse, and was himself the author of his own misfortunes and of his own misery.

CHAPTER XIX.

The Locality of Eden Figuratively Considered.

MANY commentators and expounders of the Bible are in the habit of spiritualizing everything in it, until, to say the least, they often make it appear a very silly book; yet, strangely enough, they seize upon the evident figures under consideration, and insist with all the tenacity of fanaticism in giving to this particular passage a literal construction. We will admit the description of the garden in Eden has a literal meaning—that the garden was a miniature representation of the whole earth; but the great lesson intended to be taught—the beauty of the passage—is contained in its metaphorical sense. The passions and instincts of the body, the desires and aspirations of the intellect, are the trees which God planted in the garden, which is the body of Adam. He might freely indulge and gratify to the fullest extent all the animal appetites and intellectual desires of his nature, one passion only excepted, which is represented by the tree of the knowledge of good and evil, which is in the midst of the garden.

God does not choose to govern the worlds or to deal with his creatures in an arbitrary manner, but works out all his designs by the use of adequate means. The death of the body is a physical result; therefore the question arises just here, What passion is that, which, if indulged, will of itself produce death?

We have already seen that, by the law of reproduction, decay and death will follow, or that whatever reproduces must die; hence it would appear that the only restraint imposed upon Adam was this: Thou shalt not procreate; for in the day thou dost indulge that passion, in conformity with the universal law of being, thou shalt surely die. This was not the threat of a tyrant, but the merciful injunction, or, rather, the kind admonition of a Father.

That he might be thoroughly qualified to fill the high position which he had been made to occupy, Adam was indued with the lofty ambition for sole sovereignty. He was created to be the king of all the earth, and in order that he might be well prepared to discharge the functions of his office, and that the position might ever continue one of pleasure to him, he was so constituted that, to be happy, he must rule the world; and he could no more bear rivalry in this, than the Universal King could permit a divided authority in the government of the heavens.

It is an inflexible law of being that whatever propagates its species *must multiply after its kind.* If Adam, the monarch of all the earth, should become the father of a race, his offspring, like himself, must be possessed of an ambition which could not be satisfied short of universal dominion. It therefore would appear, without argument, that there could be no place in the world for more than one such individual;

and Adam, with perfect and unclouded intellect, must have fully comprehended this truth. When he first came upon the stage of action, God mercifully informed him that he was made to be a sole sovereign, and that if he should procreate his species, the confusion which would thereby be introduced into the world would render it absolutely necessary that he should die.

We have already supposed that Adam understood and obeyed this injunction, and lived and reigned as the world's great king through one whole day of superior or Adamic time, or a thousand years of ordinary time. It is reasonable to suppose that this time was spent by him in the investigation of the laws of nature, the development of the resources of the earth, and the amelioration of the condition of his subjects, the primitive inhabitants of the world.

At the end of this period he had learned from experience, as well as from his own reflection, that whatever reproduces must die; and that like must beget like. Then, when he was thoroughly fortified against the only transgression which it was possible for him to commit against God and his own being, and when it was evident to him that there was in all the earth no being capable of entering fully into his views, of sympathizing in the joys and majesty of his reign, or of appreciating completely the physical improvements of the earth, and the discoveries in the arts and sciences which he was continually making — then "God said, It is not good for the man to be alone."

The want of such companionship was the only desire Adam could have which had not been gratified; therefore God determined to make a *helpmeet* for him — not a wife, but a companion, a friend; an individual who should be like him in physical perfection and beauty, and in intellectual endowments and high aspirations. He was now strongly fortified by experience against the violation of the law of his immortality.

In a thousand years of philosophic investigation and reflection, Adam had so schooled his animal desires that he felt no inclination to transgress in this direction; and hence, no doubt, his prayer to God was for a companion who could sympathize with him in the affairs of his government, and who, endowed with capacities similar to his own, could appreciate the discoveries which he was continually making in the arts and sciences. God heard his prayer, and gave to him a helpmeet, a suitable companion — one in every respect the exact counterpart of himself — more beautiful in form — with the intellectual capacity for comprehending all mental efforts, and a quick intuition and appreciation of the beautiful in nature and in art superior to his own.

Such was the companion, not the wife, whom God gave to be with Adam. To her he imparted the condition upon which their immortality and their happy reign over the whole earth depended. This companion was a female, and the natural desire of Adam might therefore be excited by continual intimate association; yet he was so fortified by faith in his God, and his experience of the operations of nature, and his knowledge of the relation between cause and effect, that his great enemy never once thought of attacking him directly, nor ever hoped thus to tempt him to his ruin.

The woman, his companion, however, who was new in the world, and therefore inexperienced, although she daily witnessed the intellectual labors of her lord in the investigation of nature and nature's laws, yet, inspired as she was with the same thirst for knowledge which elevated Adam so far above all other creatures — fortified as she was only by the advice and counsel of Adam — she was approached by the tempter. With subtlety superior to that of all the beasts of the field, well understanding her great thirst for knowledge, the serpent attacked her in this direction, because the passion which must not be gratified was represented by a tree called the tree of the knowledge of good and evil.

"Adam was not deceived: but the woman being deceived was in the transgression;" and when she had been seduced from the path of purity and innocence, went to the great sovereign of the world, and telling him what she had done, induced him, though fully aware of the terrible consequences, to partake also of the tree of the knowledge of good and evil.

Two questions come up here for investigation; namely, Why was Adam's helpmeet or companion made a female? and, Who was the serpent who tempted and beguiled Eve from the path of virtue and of life? These questions we will attempt to answer in their order, and as clearly as we may. We care not whether our solutions shall be according to the teachings of the commentators or not, provided they shall comport with truth and reason.

CHAPTER XX.

Why the "Helpmeet" God gave to Adam was a Female — The Fall.

HAD the companion of the world's great monarch been a man, he must have been equal to Adam; equal physically, equal intellectually, equal in capacities and in high aspirations. Adam was so constituted that he could not be happy without the sole, undisputed sovereignty of a world; and had another man, such as Adam, been created, he too must have possessed the same thirst for knowledge, and the same desire for universal authority; and, instead of being a helpmeet, this other man would necessarily have been thrown in opposition to Adam; and jealousy, envy, rivalry, and war must inevitably have resulted from the very constitution of the two monarchs. No more could the world remain at peace with two such beings as Adam in it, than a divided authority could be tolerated in the hierarchy of the heavens.

However, could not a man have been made as a companion for Adam without the desire for sovereignty, or any disposition which might lead him to interfere in the government of the world? If Adam was made to be a universal king, and if his happiness depended upon the possession of absolute dominion, how could any one be a helpmeet for him, who cared for none of these things? If such a being would have supplied the demand of his heart, the yearnings of his nature, there was no necessity whatever for a new creation; because such individuals were abundant among his subjects, the old governing race of the world.

It is utterly impossible for any one who cares nothing for authority himself, to sympathize with him who, to be happy, must wield the sceptre of universal authority. If we suppose that another man had been made without the ambition for sovereignty, but with the same intense desire for knowledge that distinguished Adam, do we not perceive that, while the latter was engaged in governmental affairs, the former would be pushing his philosophic researches, and in a short time would become much wiser than he who sat upon the throne. This would have introduced a condition of things which by no means could have been tolerated by the absolute and jealous lord of the whole earth.

It follows, then, that a man could not be so constituted as to meet the designs of the Almighty and the desires of Adam. A merciful God was so careful of the happiness of Adam, and of the peace and harmony of the world, that he would not create this man and his female at the same time, as he had done in the creation of all other animals and the first governing man; and this would certainly have been the case in this instance as well as in all others, had reproduction been the design of his being.

Moses tells us that the first governing man was created male and female, and God blessed them, and said unto them, Be fruitful, and multiply, and replenish the earth. When Adam was created, however, he was made as the other animals had been; that is, his body was brought forth by or sprang from the earth; and when fully matured, God caused the current of electricity to put the finely constructed organism into operation, and Adam became a living animal. Had it been intended that he should have been a reproducing animal, would not his female have been made then and in the same manner?

Since, however, Adam was designed to be the sole representative on earth of the wisdom, power, and majesty of God, he was endowed with a high order of intelligence, but a little lower than the angels are, and hence it is said that he became a living intelligence or soul. He was immediately installed into his high office, placed in his palatial residence in the garden of pleasure which had been prepared for him, and commanded to dress it and keep it. We have already seen that this command extended to the whole earth, for all the ends of the earth were given to him for a possession.

Afterward, but how long we can only conjecture from circumstances and from analogy, and which we have supposed to have been at least one superior day or a thousand years according to our reckoning, then God said, It is not good for the man to be alone. So he made a helpmeet or companion for him, who should be with him in his lonely and reflective hours; who should rejoice in his high governmental honors; who could fully appreciate without jealousy the vast improvements which he had made and was still making in the condition of the world; who could understand and admire the godlike ability with which he investigated and developed the laws of nature, by which not only this, but all the worlds and vast systems of worlds are governed.

This companion must of necessity have been like him in physical perfection and mental refinement, endowed with the ambition for universal dominion, and the desire for knowledge as keen and intense as these passions were in Adam himself, in order that this being might fully appreciate and heartily sympathize with him in all his schemes, in all his mighty mental efforts. Had such an individual been made a man, it is evident that the two jealous kings would in time have disagreed, and confusion and war would have ensued. God, in mercy, to prevent the possibility of any future variance between Adam and his helpmeet, made her a female.

Further, He would not even make her body directly from the earth, as the bodies of the females of all other animals had been made; but, causing a deep sleep to come upon Adam, God took one of his ribs and made of it a woman, whom He gave to be with Adam. Thus a great miracle was performed, the only one mentioned in the history of the entire creation, in order that Adam might have a companion, not similar, but the exact counterpart of himself; a distinct individuality, yet bone of his bone and flesh of his flesh, with instincts and ambitions as lofty as his own, yet life of his life and soul of his soul. He and his companion were two perfect and distinct individuals, yet — mystery of God! — they were but one. By this wise and merciful arrangement Adam obtained the desired help and companionship without the sole sovereignty and peace of the world being endangered, because the desire of the one was the ambition of the other; what was the pleasure of one was the pleasure of both. Under these auspicious circumstances, how glorious was the government of the world!—and but for the transgression of the law of immortality and of sole sovereignty, it might have so continued to the end of time.

The queen of all the earth, endowed with the lofty desires of her lord, with impulses much more intense, and fortified neither by long experience nor deep reflection, as her mind was not matured in regard to the immutable laws of nature, her faith in God was not rationally established; therefore, when caught alone, she was persuaded to believe that by the transgression of the law, all that wisdom which was obtained by Adam only by patient thought and philosophic research, would come to them by intuition. She was the more easily deceived because the passion which they were forbidden to indulge was represented by a tree in the midst of the garden, called the tree of the *knowledge* of good and evil.

We suppose that the tempter pointed out to her the indulgence of this passion by all living creatures except alone by her and Adam, and that death in no instance had ever followed the act; then why should it be so in their case only? All other creatures die because He has made them to do so; but you He made immortal, and therefore He knows that you can never die.

Thus our poor mother was deluded, when, joyous with the discovery that neither death nor any perceptible harm attended the act, she ran with the acquired knowledge, and persuaded Adam that all this while he had been duped by his God; "and he took the fruit which the woman offered, and did also eat."

As to the immediate results of the fall, as well as to its legitimate sequences, we have volume upon volume of spiritualizing; yet the subject has been so mystified, the word "Jacob" so frequently occurs, or is implied, that the inquirer after truth had best lay them all aside, and, in the fear of God, depend upon the light which Moses gives, and investigate for himself.

What is the natural and rational view in which we are to consider the fall of Adam and his helpmeet? If we are to understand that the eating of the fruit of the tree of the knowledge of good and evil is to be taken in a literal sense alone; if it was not the representation of a moral action, or the violation of an immutable law of being, one absolutely necessary to the accomplishment of the designs of God in the creation and government of the world, it must be confessed that what Moses says on the subject is dark and mysterious, instead of being, as it should be, an illumination of the subject to us, the most interesting, possibly the most important of all others.

How shall we account for the existence in the world of good and evil, of life and death; for the tenacity with which we cling to the one and the horror with which we dread the other; the shortness of the one, and the terrible certainty of the other; the strifes within, and the warrings without; the confusion of the elements; in a word, all nature unsettled and contending with itself? These have been questions which have agitated the minds of the thoughtful in all ages.

The Jew and the Gentile, the priest and the philosopher, the statesman and the soldier, the young and the old, are all agreed that He who is infinite in goodness as well as wisdom and power, could not have made things as they are — could not have constituted the world as a wretched stage, and then made the teeming millions of sentient beings to be the miserable actors in the terrible tragedy now being here enacted. As good a being as God must be could never take pleasure in erecting such a stage, on which lasting joy or permanent happiness cannot be represented, and in calling into being performers who are overwhelmed in pain and misery from their forced entrance to their fearful exit.

Deep and laborious have been the researches of the philosopher, in every age and in every clime, to discover why the world, planned by Omniscience and created by Omnipotence, should be so imperfect, and how the government of the same should pass from His hands. They, however, are unable to solve the mystery; but Moses, admitted to the councils of the Most High, tells us that the transgression of Adam brought death upon our race, and for his sake the earth was cursed.

The law is immutable and without exception, as every law of God must be, that all results, both spiritual and physical, must be accomplished by the use of adequate means. Geology, as we have already seen, declares that the present appearances of the earth have been produced by a vast revolution and universal upheaval of nature. It is proven by fossil remains that animals and vegetables, now found only near the equator, once flourished in much greater perfection as near the north pole as the philosopher has yet been able to push his discoveries. Moses tells us that the physical ruin, as well as the moral blight of the world, was effected by the sin of Adam. But what was the mighty means by which Adam could thwart the moral and physical designs of Almighty Power in regard to the world?

We are taught that Moses intends for us to understand him literally only when he tells us that Adam brought about all the vast ruin of the world by the mastication of an apple. With due deference to the wisdom of the theologically learned, let us ask, what connection can there possibly be between the eating of an apple and the pain and misery and death of his youngest son? You say that, although the slow poison of the apple did not kill Adam for near a thousand years, yet it is so powerful as to kill his descendants now at all ages, from birth to the age of threescore years and ten; but that this is by no means a literal, but a spiritual, figurative poison. If this be so, then it must have been a figurative poison which killed Adam.

Then you insist that a real, literal apple figuratively killed Adam, has killed all his race, and now, six thousand years after the eating, its figurative effects in killing is more powerful than ever before. A real cause produces real results; a figurative cause, if we may be allowed the expression, can effect only figurative ends. If, as you maintain, the forbidden fruit which Adam ate was a real, literal apple, its poison is literal, and therefore the conclusion is unavoidable that the death which it produced on Adam and his race is a real, literal death. If it were a figurative apple, then the poison is figurative, and the resultant death must be figurative. Hence it is a double absurdity to say that Adam drew from a literal apple a figurative poison, which produces real, literal death.

You teach us that the results of eating the apple are spiritual. The act of eating is wholly physical; then how could it produce spiritual results? You tell us that the tree, with its tempting, luscious fruits, was placed in the midst of the garden, and that Adam was forbidden to eat thereof merely as a test of obedience; that when he did eat of that tree, God was so incensed as to curse, not only Adam and his offspring, but also the entire animal and vegetable kingdoms, ay, the very inanimate earth upon which they dwelt. This kind of punishment would have been arbitrary in the extreme, such as a very passionate tyrant might be supposed to be capable of inflicting, if he should punish with death a whole nation because of the disobedience of his own son.

According, however, to our views, God, the creator and

upholder of all things, never acts arbitrarily, but works out all his designs by fixed and immutable laws; therefore, notwithstanding the offensiveness to the majesty of heaven of the transgression of Adam, yet God punished him not as a passionate man might have done, but, as a just judge, declared the law in the case, and at the same time, as a gracious, merciful father, gave promise of future hope and happiness to his guilty, offending children.

Hence death, all the moral and physical ills which have come upon Adam and all his race, the warring of the elements, the confusion in nature, are not the effects of the vengeful wrath of God, but the legitimate, ay, the inevitable results of the disobedience of him who had been appointed the universal representative and supreme ruler of the world. These mighty results, by no process of reasoning, can be deducible from the eating of an apple.

If Adam were made for sole sovereignty, and indued with a lofty ambition which could be satisfied only with undivided and world-wide supremacy, then, in a perfect state of happiness, there was in all the earth no place for another such being as he was. Should others like him, with instincts and aspirations for supreme authority, come into the world, it is evident that envy, jealousy, strife, confusion, and war must necessarily come with them. Had God originally designed a race of such beings, and yet made them immortal, would he not have been the author and builder of a pandemonium, from which there could have been no escape? And would not all have united in a petition to him to open the door of mercy, and permit friendly death to release them from the horrid scene of strife and confusion? God is not the author of confusion, but of peace, harmony, and happiness; therefore he could not design that there should be, in a perfect and peaceful world, more than one being with desires and capacities for supreme authority.

And hence he did not command Adam, as he did every other living creature, to multiply after his kind.

We have seen that whatever procreates, *ipso facto* must die — that is, the law of reproduction is the law of death; therefore, if Adam transgressed the law by the observance of which his Creator had declared that he might be immortal and a happy monarch forever, then it was by his own act that he brought death upon himself, and strife and confusion and misery upon the world. He voluntarily, and contrary to the law, procreated a race of beings, who, like himself, were ambitious of universal supremacy, thereby necessitating his own abdication of that throne, without which, from the very organization of his nature, he must be miserable. The beings whom he forced upon the stage of action in opposition to the will of God, from the fact that they must be like him, with his disposition to rebellion, with all his desires and instincts, must necessarily be born to an inheritance of envy, jealousy, disappointment, misery, and death.

Here we might rest the question, but yet we will again appeal to the record to fortify our opinion, after we have inquired who and what the tempter was.

CHAPTER XXI.

WHO THE TEMPTER WAS — "AND THEY SEWED FIG-LEAVES TOGETHER AND MADE THEMSELVES APRONS."

"THE serpent," or beguiler, who "was more subtle than all the beasts of the field, said, Yea has God said, Ye shall not eat of every tree of the garden?" We learn from this, not that the tempter was a beast, but that he was more intelligent than all the beasts of the field. The subtlety of his argument shows that he was a rational being, and the power of speech abundantly proves that he was a man; for no other animal possesses this faculty, which, indeed, is the distinctive evidence that an animal belongs to the genus homo. It matters not what degree of intelligence may be possessed by an animal, if he have not the faculty of speech he is not a man; in the converse, however mentally defective, if he possess this faculty he is therefore classed among men. Man alone, of all the animals, has the power of speech and of ratiocination; but the tempter not only spoke, but reasoned subtlely; hence the conclusion is unavoidable that the tempter was a man.

But what man was he? This is a question easily answered, if our position, that the man spoken of by Moses in the first chapter of Genesis, who had the capacity to govern the world for at least fifty thousand years, be correct. We must bear in mind that the world was in a perfect state; that, instead of the extremes of heat and cold, of wet and dry — instead of polar ice and equatorial fervors, whereby much of the little dry land which now appears above the watery waste is rendered uninhabitable to man and beast — it was a beautiful earth.

The waters were then gathered together into one place, and the dry land appeared from pole to pole; the axis of the earth being perpendicular to the plane of her orbit, the days and nights throughout the year were equal, and one eternal spring, with just change enough from the perihelion to the aphelion of her orbit, and back again, to prevent monotony, and to mark the earth's annual rounds. The whole earth, as it was then, is described in the portraiture of the garden of pleasure where Adam was placed. With this picture of the primitive earth before us, we may be able to form some faint idea of the vast population which the old world supported, even without cultivation.

During all the years, from the last day of the creative week, down to the advent of Adam, the man, who had been made male and female, had subdued the earth, and had dominion over the fishes of the sea, the fowl of the air, and over the beasts of the field. Through all the rolling ages, more than 50,000 years, this man, no doubt, in obedience to the instincts of his nature and the command of his Maker, had been fruitful and multiplied, and had replenished the earth from pole to pole, and all around the pleasant and luxuriant earth.

Would not Adam, who was made the king of this race, select from among them the most intelligent, to be his ministers, and to surround his royal court; and would he not impart to them much of the wisdom which he acquired during the thousand years of his happy reign? The chief of these, the minister of state — the man who was nearest the throne — might, with propriety, be said to be "more subtle than all the beasts of the field." This individual, we may suppose, was admitted to free converse, not only with the king, but also with the queen; and may we not identify such a one as the serpent who beguiled Eve? How much more rational to suppose the serpent to have been a noble specimen of the old governing race — a red man, or Indian, such as the aborigines of North America — than that he was a snake, a reptile, an orang-outang, or some other dumb brute!

Had a creature, who had never spoken before, addressed the woman, as the serpent did, what would have been her surprise, her amazement! Under her extreme astonishment, she certainly would have been in a poor frame of mind to listen to an ingenious argument, to give and receive intelligent answers, much less to be led away from the path of duty, and to be enticed into sin and ruin by this same dumb brute. Had Moses supposed the serpent to have been such a beast, would he not have said something in reference to the miraculous means by which he was not only enabled to speak, but to reason with that degree of subtlety which overcame the virtue of the world's great queen? We are informed by the commentators that this was the work of the devil.

If this were so, would the difficulty be removed? But can it be true? God, who created all things, gave to every animal such organs and adaptations as would answer the design of their creation. To the courageous he gave strength and the means of defence, to the timid he gave speed and acute sight and hearing. He made one animal ruminant, and another non-ruminant; but to all he gave the organs necessary to the proper mastication, and the healthy digestion of the kind of food which the instincts which he had implanted in them should lead them to select.

In like manner, He gave to each the organs requisite to enable them to utter such sounds as are necessary to express the thoughts which their degree of intelligence suggests to them. To man alone, he gave those organs which will produce articulate sounds. It is a physical, as well as a moral impossibility, for any other animal than man to utter conventional sounds by which ideas may be conveyed from one to another, except those of the simplest character. No other animal than man can think consecutively enough to use language, and therefore no other has the necessary organs of speech.

If the ox or the ass should speak, it would be contrary to the law of their being, in opposition to their physical organism; therefore it would be a miracle, and a violation of the law both of mind and of matter. Is it rational to suppose that the devil could have the power, in a perfect world, to have wrought such a double miracle, when he clearly has no such power now? Who can believe such an extreme proposition, unless it were distinctly revealed to us? Even had the spirit of evil been mighty enough to have accomplished the astonishing result of converting a dumb brute into a subtle debater, Eve must have been previously completely under his influence, or she certainly could not have been fascinated by the arguments of a creature which she had never heard speak before.

Those who tell us that the tempter was a dumb brute, also tell us that the only object which the devil had in view was to induce the woman, literally, to eat an apple from a certain tree. If this were all, if he could influence her so far as to hold calm discourse with a brute, why did he not impress her mind a little further, without the intervention of the beast, and thus lead her to the eating of the apple? This would have been the easier, and much less miraculous way, of accomplishing his object. The organs of speech were wanting in the animal, as well as reason; hence, nothing could possibly be gained by the use of such an instrument.

But if the procreative act was the forbidden indulgence, then can we see why the devil, who is a spirit, must use a physical agent to effect his design, and why that instrument must be a man. In this view of the fall of Adam, the account which Moses gives us seems plain enough; in any other light, all is uncertain, doubtful, and mysterious, beyond comprehension or rational belief. If the rational view of the subject be consistent with the inspired account of this momentous affair, how blindly absurd to insist upon a mysterious, not to say ridiculous exposition, which was never satisfactory to any one! Then we again conclude that the procreative act was the forbidden fruit, and that a man of the old governing race was the tempter.

As soon as the act violative of the law of God was performed, Adam and the woman knew that they were naked, and were ashamed; for they immediately made for themselves aprons of fig-leaves. It is not possible that Adam, who had lived for some time, as we have supposed, a thousand years at least, and, as we shall hereafter show, had profoundly investigated the laws of nature, and had possibly advanced the arts and sciences to a degree of perfection not reached by us — we say that it is utterly impossible for him not to have known himself to have been naked. Yet the discovery of his nakedness seems to be the great central, if not the only idea which he obtained by the transgression of the law.

If he were really so blind and unobservant as not to have known that he had on his body no artificial covering, nor that his beautiful body was in that perfect state in which God had formed it, yet why should he have been ashamed when he did finally discover that he had upon him no clothes? Must we believe that Adam by transgression became suddenly so wise, that his idea of beauty and perfection so far excelled the standard of the Almighty, that he was overwhelmed with shame and confusion because of the nudity of his own body, which had been made according to God's highest model of physical beauty and perfection? He who would exhibit a fine horse, will never think of covering up the body of the animal, even in robes of linen and of gold; but he glories in showing the magnificent proportions and beautiful symmetry which God has given the noble animal; no part of which it is thought necessary to be covered before he is brought into the presence of the admiring crowd. When was this, or any other, the most sagacious animal, ever known to be ashamed of any part or function of his body?

If Adam's body was made more perfect and beautiful than the body of any other animal, why should he be ashamed of it, or of its legitimate functions? It is clear that he was not so in the state of innocency, for it was the violation of law which made him ashamed of his own body, and it is made manifest by the putting on of the aprons of fig-leaves.

Had the mouth been the member which, by the mastication of an apple, had so fearfully offended against the law of God, against the law of their being, ought not that to have been the member of which they should have been ashamed, and ought they not to have covered their mouths with the fig-leaves? According to every rational view of the subject, we must perceive that they would be and were ashamed of the offending member of the body. That member is clearly indicated by the putting on of the aprons; but since no offence could possibly come from thence against the law of life, except the act of procreation, therefore we must conclude that this was the offence pointed out by the figure of the eating of the fruit of the *tree of the knowledge of good and evil, which grew in the midst of the garden.*

Is any other solution of the problem of the existence of good and evil in the world satisfactory or rational, except that given by Moses of the exaltation and fall of the world's great representative, the vicegerent of God on earth? Can any exposition of that account be given which is more rational than that which is here presented? If so, we will be the first to embrace it; but if this be the truth, let theologians cease to carp, and let them cease to prattle about the snake, or even the orang-outang theory. Our views are our own, and we would submit them to be tested by the severest scrutiny in the light of reason and of truth. Reject them not because of their novelty, for we believe that they are entertained and taught by Moses.

CHAPTER XXII.

The Effects of the Fall—Moral and Physical.

THE wilful, determined rebellion of Adam, and the foolish, daring fall of Eve, the favored children of their Father, and his representatives on earth, constituted an offence so provoking, that God, the Supreme Ruler, might have crushed the miserable sinners as a man does the crawling insect; yet He would not even pronounce the legitimate consequences of the violation of the previously promulgated law, until after examination and full confession of the act by themselves; so that they, and their descendants in all the future ages, must pronounce the sentence just.

To the serpent He granted no such consideration, but upon the testimony of the woman, without question or examination, "The Lord God said unto the serpent, Because thou hast done this thing, thou art cursed above all cattle, and above every beast of the field; upon thy belly shalt thou go, and dust shalt thou eat all the days of thy life. And I will put enmity between thee and the woman, and between thy seed and her seed; it shall bruise thy head, and thou shalt bruise his heel."

Here is evidence as strong as Holy Writ can make it, that the serpent was not only a man, but that he was of the household of Adam; in other words, that he was his constant attendant: for even after he had seduced the woman and brought ruin upon his lord, yet when the Almighty calls Adam and the woman from their hiding-place, the serpent, though unbidden, is present at the audience. Moreover, as the sin or first impulse thereto originated with him, God did not deign to ask him why he had done this thing, but immediately pronounced the above-mentioned terrible curse upon him. Nevertheless, even this was not vindictive justice, but the announcement to him of the legitimate and inevitable consequences of his wicked interference and premeditated intention to overturn the order which God had established.

To the serpent He said, You were made the governing being of all the earth, and when in the revolution of ages your race and all the varieties of animals became so numerous that the luxuriant earth could no longer support the teeming life upon it without cultivation, in mercy a saviour in the person of Adam was sent to be the gentle and beneficent ruler of the world. He was endowed with supereminent intelligence, leading him to become a philosopher, and by his scientific researches through the superior day, or a thousand years, of his solitary reign, he has developed to a high degree the resources of the earth, whereby the condition of all animate nature has been greatly ameliorated. These benefits have redounded chiefly to your good, as the principal and governing race; then wherefore should you envy the supremacy of Adam and of his helpmeet, and why have you lent yourself to the destruction of the head and heart and soul of the whole world?

Could you not perceive that, although one immortal Adam, whose supremacy there was none to dispute, was the greatest blessing ever bestowed upon this or any world, yet that two or more of such beings must prove an unmitigated curse, and especially to your race? It is not in your nature to care for extensive authority; but when the Adams are multiplied, with their ambition for sole sovereignty, and with all their superior intelligence, conflict, war, and terrible confusion must ensue, and woe be to your inferior race; for they will not only struggle with each other for the mastery, for sovereignty, but they will utterly crush out your race whenever it comes up in the pathway of their tempestuous march.

Your race held the entire dominion until Adam was sent to rule over all, as the vicegerent of God, and the world has been superlatively happy and prosperous under his benign and philosophic reign; but you, the individual of your race the most honored and trusted by the world's great king, have basely and wickedly betrayed your lord's companion, and then, through her, the king himself, who thereby has been dethroned. On this account enmity must ever exist between you and the woman. She hates you, and you hate her; and the enmity began here must continue between your rival races to the end. The war between you shall be waged with unmitigated rancor, but the superior descendants of the woman shall bruise thy head, while thy inferior race shall only be able to bruise his heel.

The curse inflicted on Adam, and on the earth, on Adam's account, as he is the head, shall be extended to all living creatures, but more especially shall it fall with grievous weight upon thee and upon thy proud race. The generous earth, which has heretofore been so genial, so productive, shall become inclement in its seasons, and its sterile soil shall no more bring forth spontaneously those fruits and vegetables which hitherto have afforded abundant supplies for thy race and the teeming millions of living creatures, all of which, until now, have acknowledged the dominion of the king and thine; but henceforth the few of them which by reason of the diminished production of the barren, cursed earth are left, will rebel against thy race.

They will fear you as their worst enemies, and when you shall need them to supply your increasing wants, you shall take them only by stratagem, or by going on the belly.

How humiliating to the proud race, whose nature is opposed to labor, now, when the earth more imperatively demanded it, to have not only the inferior animals to flee from them, but even to have the animal man, who had always served them faithfully, ay, worshipped them as gods, to fall off and leave them in their greatest time of need, to refuse to do them service willingly! When these results became apparent, it is perfectly natural that enmity should have existed between the foolish tempter and poor, deluded victim; and well might it be said that the proud serpent race should eat the dust of mortification and misery all the days of their lives.

The design of the red man in tempting the woman to sin, was to get rid of Adam as the king of the world. He believed that God had spoken truth when he said to Adam, "In the day thou eatest thereof, thou shalt surely die;" but, with many of the present time, confounding a diurnal revolution of the earth with a day in superior time, not knowing that a thousand years with the Lord is as one day, no doubt he confidently expected to see Adam and the woman expire immediately upon the accomplishment by them of the act violative of the law of God and of their immortality.

Then what must have been his astonishment, his horror, when the truth flashed upon his mind that the day in which Adam must die meant a thousand years, during which time he would propagate a whole race of Adams, all ambitious, like their father, and that, finally, from the woman should spring the second Adam, who should not only restore the world to its former condition, but, excelling the race of Adam far more than Adam did the old red race, the former would take the place in the restoration which had been occupied by the latter in the old kingdom; while the animal man, who had no agency in the fall, would only suffer with all the earth, and in the restoration would occupy his old place of servitude. He would follow, not the tempter or his race, but would serve the descendants of Adam, who would be the immediate subjects of the Great King.

"Thou art cursed above all cattle, and above every beast of the field; upon thy belly shalt thou go, and dust shalt thou eat all the days of thy life." In this fearful curse not one word is said to the tempter about the power of speech. It is beyond controversy, however, that he did then possess this faculty; and had it been intended to take it from him, most assuredly the fact would have been mentioned in the curse. Moreover, *nachash* was more subtle than all the beasts of the field, and he reasoned with the skill of an accomplished sophist. Had he been deprived of reason, would not that important fact have been mentioned? Hence it is logically true that the seed of the *nachash* is to-day in possession of a high order of intelligence and the faculty of speech.

Nachash, in one place in the Bible, at least, is translated "filthiness," meaning fornication. (Ezek. xvi. 36.) Between the seed of the *nachash* and the seed of the woman there should be enmity; but this could not be true if the tempter were an inferior animal; nor could the word, translated as it necessarily is in Ezekiel, have been applied to a dumb brute.

If we will place a fair, not to say liberal construction upon the curse imposed upon the beguiler, we may certainly learn that death was not inflicted on him because of the part which he had taken in the fall of Adam. Had this been the case, would not the momentous fact have been mentioned? It is evident that if death had been brought upon him by that transaction, the fact would have been mentioned, and death would have been set down in the catalogue of the ills which his crime had drawn down upon himself and his seed. Moses uses no word intimating such an idea; but, on the contrary, the *nachash* is addressed as being already a mortal, whose term of existence is made up of the short days of our earth. "Upon thy belly shalt thou go, and dust shalt thou eat *all the days of thy life*." In this announcement, not even a shortening of the days, or any hastening of the time of the departure of the fornicator, or *nachash*, is in the most remote manner indicated.

CHAPTER XXIII.

THE EFFECTS OF THE FALL, CONTINUED.

"Unto the woman he said, I will greatly multiply thy sorrow and thy conception; in sorrow thou shalt bring forth children, and thy desire shall be unto thy husband, and he shall rule over thee." "I will greatly multiply thy sorrow and thy conception." If we are not wilfully blind, we may see here that sorrow and conception are placed upon the same footing as to their inception and continuance. If it were possible for the woman to have conceived in her state of original purity, by what rule of construction is it possible for us to conclude otherwise than that she must also have sorrow in that state. All agree that sorrow could not enter Paradise—no more could the woman have conceived in that holy place.

Again: the word *multiply* used in this place, as in the first chapter of Genesis, has a more extensive meaning than is usually attached to it. In that place the word signifies to begin, and to increase greatly; we should therefore understand the above language to mean: Since, contrary to my declared will, you have determined to become a mother, therefore, as the legitimate consequence of your perversity and sin, I will begin and greatly increase thy sorrow and thy conception.

"In sorrow thou shalt bring forth children." Here the proof is still to the same point, and forces us irresistibly to the conclusion that the offence of Adam and the woman was the act of procreation. It is believed by many that the sorrow spoken of in this place is the physical pain and danger through which the female must pass in reproduction, and especially in parturition; but these difficulties, this labor, is common, to a greater or less extent, to the females of all animals. Can we believe that the females of all animals were cursed in reproduction because the woman had eaten an apple? Where is the connection between physical cause and effect? The idea is too absurd to be attributed to Him whose every act is governed by principle or his own immutable laws, and whose judgments are but the declaration of the consequences of the violation of those laws.

The labor of reproduction in the other animals is natural, was intended for their good, and cannot, therefore, rationally, be tortured into being a curse. An effort of nature is absolutely necessary for the throwing off the fœtus which has so long time remained with the mother—a relaxation of the muscles, and an extension of the bones; consequently there must be suffering under the law of animal existence. Were this not the case, were no drafts made upon the female constitution, in the support of the fœtus and in the labor of parturition, then might she have been immortal, while the very action of pleasure will certainly bring death to the male. The woman, who was made to be immortal, was commanded not to reproduce; and when she did so, in violation of law, instead of becoming a mighty goddess, to create immortals, she sank down to the level of other animals in sorrow or labor and sequent death, as well as in a vast multiplication of the ills of that coveted conception.

"And thy desire shall be unto thy husband, and he shall rule over thee." Still proof to the same point. And is it not strange that there should be doubt in the mind of any thinking man in regard to what that sin was which was represented by the fruit of the tree in the midst of the garden? The temptation was, that ye shall be as gods; ye shall procreate a race of beings like yourselves, and therefore superior to all the creatures of God. This was an argument of the tempter, which, addressing itself to the ambition of the woman, by it she was overcome, by it she lost her high estate, and by it she was plunged into the vortex of misery and shame.

After the commission of the act violative of law, she keenly felt her shame; and she and Adam were ashamed of the comely persons which God had made, and covered them with aprons of fig-leaves. When the woman had sinned, and not until then, she went unto her *husband;* by the transgression her sorrow and her conception were multiplied; from henceforth, and clearly not before, she should bring forth children; her desire should be unto her husband; and not until this affair was completed did Adam name her the mother of a race, or of all living. Previous to this time she had been the equal, the helpmeet, the companion of Adam; but after the fall she became his inferior, because of her sorrow, her child-bearing, and consequent desire unto her husband; and thereby she became subject to the authority of Adam, as the women of the old governing race had always been subject to their lords. How the offence which the woman committed could have been made plainer through the figurative Oriental language, it is difficult to imagine; and yet learned theologians do not so understand the sacred historian. That the commentators should teach us that a snake or a baboon delivered an ingenious harangue to Eve, thereby inducing her to eat an apple, and that they should insist that this is revealed truth, is strange beyond our comprehension: "But even unto this day, when Moses is read the veil is upon their heart."

"And unto Adam He said, Because thou hast hearkened unto the voice of thy wife, and hast eaten of the tree, of which I commanded thee, saying, Thou shalt not eat of it; cursed is the ground for thy sake; in sorrow shalt thou eat of it all the days of thy life; thorns also and thistles shall it bring forth to thee; and thou shalt eat the herb of the field; in the sweat of thy face thou shalt eat bread, till thou return unto the ground; for out of it wast thou taken: for dust thou art, and unto dust shalt thou return."

In the examination of this subject there are two propositions, which we must bear in mind, viz.: That Adam was made to be the immortal king of all the earth, and that in the wide universe no result either of a physical or spiritual character can be effected without the use of adequate means. If the earth was cursed for Adam's sake, cursed physically, there must have been some connection between that curse and Adam's transgression. If his were only a moral offence, how could it effect physical results? Is the connection apparent between an abstract act of disobedience on the part of Adam, and a cursed earth bringing forth thorns and thistles?

If the offence were a physical action, from it we might expect physical results. If the offence of Adam, the sole sovereign of all the earth, was in character both moral and physical, then could we rationally look for from it both moral and physical results, as extensive as were his vast dominions. Since we know that the moral and physical world is in a state of confusion, and since we are informed by the inspired writer that the world was cursed for Adam's sake, therefore his sin was an offence both against his moral and physical constitution.

Adam, in attempting to be like God by becoming the procreator of a race of highly intellectual beings, violated the law of sole sovereignty; when God in mercy drove him out of the garden and from the tree of life, to the end that the violated law of immortality might work out its legitimate results, lest he should be cursed with an eternity of misery on the earth; "for dust thou art, and unto dust shalt thou return."

"Cursed be the ground for thy sake," because thou art the king, and unto thee have I given the earth. I do not take back this gift, but leave it with you in the condition in which you have placed it by your transgression. The question here comes up, by what means did the sin of Adam effect such a material change in the condition of the world? Since, however, we have had this subject under consideration elsewhere, we will not stop to investigate it further in this place.

"Thorns also and thistles shall it bring forth to thee." Is it not here made clear that the laws called the laws of nature were as effectually under the control and dependent upon the moral conduct of Adam as that the consequence of his transgression should be followed by his physical death? "Cursed be the earth for thy sake. Thorns also and thistles shall it bring forth to thee." It is hence abundantly apparent that what are called the laws of nature and the moral laws are one and the same, or rather, that they are but branches of the same great system.

Still it is insisted upon that the transgression of Adam was only a moral offence. Let us see what is meant by moral action; for the use of words without a settled meaning, conveys no definite idea. Moral action, as in contradistinction to physical action, would seem to imply intellectual effort. All being is either mental or physical, therefore all action must be mental or physical, hence moral action must mean intellectual effort. Death is a physical result, therefore the action which produces physical death must be a physical action; hence it is absurd to say that Adam's was a moral transgression, and exclude the idea of physical offence.

The true statement would be that the mind of Adam having conceived an immoral idea, he wrought out a physical offence, which resulted to himself and his race in physical death. Adam was the sole sovereign of the world and its moral representative; therefore his intellect was that which controlled the physical condition of the world, and when he sinned against the law of his own being so that he must die, then the whole physical frame of the world, left without the control of a perfect intellect, rushed into wild disorder. Or rather, when the sole throne of the earth was abdicated by him who had been constituted universal king, the reins of the government were seized by that usurping spirit who had aspired to the throne of the heavens, and, balked in that lofty design, with his followers, had come to our earth with great wrath, and having secured the dominion thereof, erected his throne in our atmosphere, and has since been called the "prince of this world, and the prince of the power of the air."

Under the reign of Adam, as well as before he came, the pole of the earth was directed, as we have seen, toward its true centre, or toward that bright world around which our sun, with his system, revolves; but when Adam fell, then the earth lost its true polarity, and since has revolved upon its axis, at such inclination as is necessary from the obliquity of the position of that baleful world where the empyrean of the power of darkness is established. Then for the present we will conclude, as we have concluded, and as we think the facts fully justify us, that the transgression of Adam was a physical as well as a moral offence; that it was so great a sin against the physical constitution of himself and of his empire, the world, as not only to cause death to him and all his posterity, but also to produce all the disorders and confusion in nature. "Cursed be the earth, for thy sake."

"And thou shalt eat the herb of the field." What are we to understand by this, except that whereas the exuberant earth and the genial climate with which it was blessed caused the fruits which now flourish but poorly only in the tropics, then to grow in such perfection and in such profusion, that all the wants of its inhabitants were supplied to them by spontaneous production; and that now, under the curse inflicted upon it by the act of Adam, it would require laborious cultivation, and, even then, its condition was so changed that those fruits could not be produced, and therefore Adam must eat such herbs or vegetables as the cursed earth would be compelled to yield? Because it is said, "In the sweat of thy face shalt thou eat bread, till thou return to the ground; for out of it wast thou taken: for dust thou art, and unto dust shalt thou return." Hence, the sin of Adam was so tremendously physical, that it caused his death and the derangement of the natural laws of the whole earth.

"And Adam called his wife's name Eve, because she was the mother of all living." This is the second time that she was named by Adam. The first time, she was called "Woman," because she was taken out of man. Then, she was a helpmeet, or companion, for him. After the fall, however, she is presented to him in the character of a wife; and then he gives to her a new name, calling her "Eve," because she is the mother of all living. It appears from hence, that at first the woman was intended to be, and was actually, a companion merely for the man, and that, by the fall, their relationship was changed to that of husband and wife.

Some persons think that the new name of Eve proves, beyond controversy, the unity of the races. If we depend upon this for proof on this subject, shall we not find that it proves too much? The declaration is, that "she is the mother of all living." Is this not as good to prove that Eve is the mother of a gorilla, as that she is the mother of an Indian or a negro? We know that Eve is not the mother of all the animals, nor was it intended to attach any such meaning to the expression here referred to.

If, however, she was not the mother of all animals, of how many, and of what kinds, was she the mother? We are answered, that she is the mother of the entire genus homo; but we would ask, where does that genus homo begin, and where does it end? You tell us that it begins with the negro, and ends with the white man. We, much more rationally, as we think, contend that the genus begins with the lowest type of monkey, and ends with the highest order of man. If, as you say, the genus begins and ends with the races of men, and if these are all descended from the same parents, that is, are nothing more than varieties of the same family, do you not see the folly of talking of the genus in which there is but a single species? Eve is not the mother of the baboon, nor of the negro, nor yet of the Indian; but the language under consideration means, that, since the woman had violated the condition of immortality, she should therefore become a mother, and the mother of the race who should be descended from Adam.

"Unto Adam also, and to his wife, did the Lord God make coats of skins, and clothed them." These coats were, no doubt, intended to subserve the double purpose of covering from view their bodies, which had become mortal by transgression, and of which, on that account, they were ashamed, and of protecting them against the inclemencies of the weather, with which the world was cursed by their folly and their sin. If there had been no death among the animals up to the fall, as is supposed by some, whence came the skins of which these coats were made? The fact that they were made of skins, excited no surprise or comment whatever; yet, these skins must have been taken from dead animals; hence, the animals must have died before the fall, that is, death was common then, or, rather, was the normal condition of all animals, before as well as after the fall.

"And the Lord God said, Behold, the man is become as one of us, to know good and evil." Does any one believe, that his general intelligence or mental organism was improved by sin? If this were the case, then did not God intend to make man as perfect as he has made himself by the transgression of the law? And man's restoration would be his degradation, an hypothesis not for one moment to be entertained. Some learned theologians, who think that the sin of Adam brought death to all the animals, believe that the carnivora, contrary to their nature, contrary to all their physical adaptations, were compelled to live in the abnormal, and consequently the miserable condition, of subsisting on vegetation, when their whole being required — ay, yearned for — animal food.

If so great a blessing was conferred upon the carnivorous animals by Adam, and if he really made himself more wise, increased his general intelligence beyond what God gave him, then we must conclude that the fall was no curse, but a blessing to the world. Reason, however, shows us that the world is cursed, and revelation declares that the sin of Adam brought about all the ills of earth; therefore the theologians, though wise, are evidently wrong in regard to both these positions.

The offence of Adam, since he was the representative and sovereign of all the earth, affected the laws of nature, disorganized the condition of the world, brought on the vicissitudes of the seasons, with the concomitant barren soil and unhealthy atmosphere; yet certainly it brought death abstractly to none, in other words, subjected none to death but himself and his posterity. Whatever reproduces must die; and all the animals were commanded to multiply in the beginning; hence to die was as much their normal condition as to be born; and when Adam became a reproducing animal, he too became subject to death.

How then shall we understand the declaration, "that the man has become as one of us, to know good and evil?" and more especially when it is added, "and now lest he put forth his hand and take also of the tree of life, and eat and live forever; therefore the Lord God sent him forth from the garden of Eden, to till the ground from which he was taken?" It is quite clear that Adam had by the fall gained some knowledge which he did not before possess, and which made him like God. Since this was not general knowledge or intellectual perfectibility, we must conclude that it was the knowledge that he could procreate, without immediate death, beings like himself, who was the highest order of material intelligence.

Then "lest he should put forth his hand and take also of the tree of life, and live forever; therefore he was sent out of the garden." Now if this garden was a literal garden only, and if the trees therein were only literal trees, is it not exceedingly strange that Adam, who was made to be immortal, and was allowed the free use of the fruit of all the trees in the garden, except of the tree of the knowledge of good and evil; and since the tree of life was in the midst of the garden, we repeat it, is it not astonishingly strange, as is here plainly indicated, that he had never yet tasted of the fruit of the tree of life, which to us would appear to be the most important of all the trees in the garden?

We hope that we have before shown that the garden, although a local habitation, yet it referred figuratively to Adam's body; and that the trees of the garden were the passions and instincts of his body; that the tree of the knowledge of good and evil was the capacity to procreate; its fruit was the indulgence of the passion represented by this tree;—but what power of the body or capacity of the mind was adumbrated by the tree of life? We would answer that it was the capacity to submit to the will of God; and its fruit was repentance toward God. If, then, Adam had never eaten of the fruit of the tree of life, it was because he had no occasion for it. If he had never repented, it was because he had never sinned, and therefore had nothing for which to repent.

When Adam became a procreator of kings, or rather of would-be kings, beings like himself, who could not be happy without universal authority, then God drove him out of the pleasant garden, and put the passion which had been aroused by the inhibited indulgence to guard its gate; in other words, the passion which had been unlawfully evoked was permitted to rage with unrestrained ardor, and this effectually barred the gate to repentance.

Adam, having deliberately violated the law of immortality, must necessarily die; but since a representative man of the old governing race had seduced Eve, and was the instrument by whom Adam was dethroned, the unerring connection between cause and effect required, and the immutable justice of God demanded, that the intermeddler too should suffer the consequences of his crime. Hence it seemed good to the Almighty to respite Adam for a season, that he might become the father of a race between whom and the serpent race there must be enmity and war until the latter should be crushed out by the restless, grasping, usurping sons of Adam. "It shall bruise thy head."

"So God drove out the man, and he placed at the east of the garden of Eden cherubims, and a flaming sword which turned every way, to keep the way of the tree of life."

We have seen in a former chapter that the figurative meaning of this passage is that the tree of life is repentance, and that the Almighty suffered the unlawfully aroused passion to rage in his fallen creatures with such fury that it might well be likened to the cherubims or guardian angels who were to keep them from effectual repentance, which it would appear was possible; and that the raging desire which had been unlawfully called forth might in time be allayed, is intimated by the language, "and now lest he put forth his hand and take also of the tree of life, and eat, and live forever."

That the account here given of the expulsion of Adam from the garden of Eden has a literal and physical meaning, must be admitted by all who believe that the garden was a locality, and that the sin of Adam was the cause of his physical death. If Adam were really driven out of this real garden, unless we intend to consider Moses, writing as he was by inspiration, to be the author of a medley of absurd facts and foolish metaphor, it must be conceded that the flaming sword which turned every way was a literal and physical fact, as well as a moral, spiritual truth.

This flaming sword, as fondly supposed by some, is not placed in the hands of the cherubim, but is a separate and distinct feature in the picture. Had Moses declared that the flaming sword was to be wielded by the cherubim, then we would have been forced to receive the whole account as figurative only, which would be as fatal to the theory of the theologians as to our own. A sword is a material instrument, but the word *flaming;* as applied to it, is figurative; and the expression flaming sword conveys the idea of a bright, material weapon of offensive and defensive warfare; which could no more be wielded by the cherubim than it could be used against them.

It is not to be supposed that Moses would have been

guilty of placing one flaming sword in the hands of a host, or even of two cherubim. Evidently the author intended for us to understand the cherubim to be the spiritual guards representing the perverted passions, now placed so as to prevent repentance on the part of Adam, and the consequent return to his original spiritual condition. By the flaming sword we have further assurance that the garden of Eden was a locality, and that God had erected a physical barrier to prevent the return of Adam and his posterity to the scenes of his former grandeur and happiness, or rather these disabilities were created by the disobedience of Adam. We have already indicated how he did this, namely, that his act would introduce into the world another individual who could not be happy without sole sovereignty, and that therefore he brought about a state of warfare; and that it was a high act of mercy when God took from him and his posterity the possibility of immortal existence on this earth; and especially since the spiritual control of the world had passed temporarily into the power of that usurping spirit who is the father of lies and the author of all evil.

If, as we have supposed, the garden of Eden was situated at the head or north pole of the earth, and if, by the voluntary disobedience of the world's sovereign, its polarity was destroyed, so that it should move in its orbit around the sun, with an inclination of its axis of 23½° to the plane of its orbit, it is evident that very great changes must be wrought in the seasons. Notwithstanding the terrible curse which Adam by his voluntary act brought upon himself and the world, yet even then God of his infinite goodness and mercy promised a restoration of all things, inasmuch as he declared that the seed of the woman should bruise the serpent's head.

During the present century extraordinary expenditures of means and of human effort have been made to discover what lies concealed about the north pole, but the insurmountable wall of ice, like a flaming sword, which turns every way, has hitherto guarded the passage; and no mortal man has penetrated the mystery, has stood where Adam reigned in innocency; or if he has wandered through the rich ambrosial groves of Paradise, has slaked his thirst in the waters of the river which there parts into four heads, has plucked and eaten the luscious fruit of the tree of life, he has not been permitted to return and report to the miserable, aspiring sons of Adam the glories of the place, the beatitudes of the garden,—nor must he; but there, with Enoch and Moses and Elias, must bide the time when all things shall be restored to the status originally intended for them by the Mighty Builder of the heavens and of the earth.

Geology has already proven beyond a peradventure, as we have before shown, that a uniform temperature once surrounded the whole earth; at least, that the rich fruits, the tender plants and delicate animals which can now exist only in the torrid zones, have flourished much more perfectly as high up in the frozen regions of the north as the science of ambitious man has ever gone. Then, without further hesitancy, we think that we may challenge the logical reasoner to subscribe to our often-drawn conclusion, that we are taught by inspiration and by science that the north pole, or head of the world, was once the beatific residence of the thrice happy king and queen of the whole earth, who by transgression forfeited their high estate and became the authors of our wretched race; that Adam's fall in some way affected the laws governing the motions of the earth, so that its true polarity was destroyed; and that he, being forced out of Paradise, the circumambient fields of ice were drawn around its sacred precincts to prevent the entrance there by sinful man.

CHAPTER XXIV.

FIRST ACT OF RELIGIOUS DEVOTION — CAIN'S OFFERING CONSIDERED — THE ORIGIN OF THE MONGOLIAN RACE.

ABEL was a keeper of sheep, but Cain was a tiller of the ground. And in the process of time it came to pass that Cain brought of the fruit of the ground an offering unto the Lord. And Abel he also brought of the firstlings of his flock and of the fat thereof. And the Lord had respect unto Abel and to his offering; but unto Cain and his offering he had not respect; and Cain was very wroth, and his countenance fell. And the Lord said unto Cain, Why art thou wroth, and why is thy countenance fallen? If thou doest well, shalt thou not be accepted? and if thou doest not well, sin lieth at the door."

This first act of religious devotion is thus particularly noticed, not only for the purpose of introducing the catastrophe in which it culminated, that is, in the death of Abel, but also for the purpose of teaching other and high moral truths. What the moral intended to be taught is lost to us, unless we look at the subject and construe it rationally. It will not do to dismiss it by saying that the offering of Abel was made in faith, and that of Cain was not, and pass it over without further investigation; because in this way we only learn that a fratricide was committed by the first son of Adam, and the only idea of God extracted by this mode of disposing of it, is that he is the arbitrary ruler of the world and of men.

Can it be believed that Cain was punished for making a mistake in the kind of offering which he laid upon the altar of his God? He was a tiller of the ground, and of the first fruits of his labor he brought his gift. He could do nothing more. Abel was a keeper of sheep, and he from the firstlings of his flock made an offering unto the Lord; nor could he have done otherwise. Embracing the view of the theologians, that the offering of Abel was made in faith that the sins of the world should be atoned for by the shedding of blood,—if we regard the question here, it must be in the light that the sacrifices were offered with the view to ascertain from which of them should spring the seed which should bruise the serpent's head, or that eminent personage who should restore and occupy the station which Adam had possessed and lost. But let us right here inquire into other ideas which are presented.

Why should an offering, obtained from the earth by honest toil, be less acceptable to God, who had commanded Adam to gain a support in that way, than one taken from the flock? "The Lord had respect unto Abel and his offering; but unto Cain and his offering he had not respect." It cannot be that the kind of property offered made this difference, for both offered the best which they had. Then it would appear that we must search farther for the true explanation of the result here stated.

There is no past or future with God; therefore, as far as himself is concerned, it would be perfectly competent for him to punish an act in the future as though it had been already performed. But his creature man is a finite being, whose existence is marked by the recurrence of events, and whose conduct is influenced by circumstances, and hence could never, in time or eternity, be brought to see or acknowledge the justice of punishment inflicted for an act which had not been accomplished. Although God made known to Abraham the future wickedness of his descendants, yet Abraham was not punished therefor; nor have we an instance where sin not enacted was ever punished, unless it be in the case in hand, and, as some contend, in the case of Cainan, after the flood. As God is just and unchangeable, and all his laws are of universal application, we must conclude that he never inflicts punishment except for sins which have been actually committed, and these apparent exceptions are so only in the estimation of the unthinking, the bigoted, and the fanatical.

It is clearly intimated in the account of the offerings of Cain and of Abel, that there was something in the prior conduct of the former which had rendered him unacceptable to God; but what follows places it beyond doubt that he had transgressed law, had offended against the right, and therefore sin lay at his door. What was his offence? and what sin had he previously committed which could render him and his offering unacceptable to his God? When the fishes of the sea, the fowls of the air, the cattle, the four-footed beasts, and the creeping thing, ay, even the grass, the herb, and the tree were called into being, each was made after his kind, and everything which reproduces was commanded emphatically to multiply after his kind. So jealous was the great God of the order which he had established, that the law of hybridity was interposed to prevent its destruction among the lower or irrational animals; whereas, this law does not fully obtain among the rational animals called men, because they possess the intelligence to comprehend the enormity of miscegenation, can understand the import of the law, "Thou shalt not commit adultery."

From the subsequent history of Cain it is rendered morally certain that, previous to the time of making his offering, he had violated the order of nature by taking a wife of the daughters of the old governing man; for, when he went out from the presence of the Lord, he dwelt in the land of Nod, and in that same year in which he slew Abel, and in which he left Eden, his son Chanoch was born, and he built a city, and called it Chanoch, in honor of his son. Cain, at the time of these occurrences, was one hundred and twenty-eight years of age.

It is great folly to suppose that Cain would say that "every one who finds me will slay me," had there been no other man in the world except himself and his father. The land of Nod, as well as of Eden, were countries with metes and bounds and particular names; and that the former was at that time populous, is proven by the fact that there were people then and there to build a city, and certainly no sensible man would have built a city unless there had been a population to occupy it. That these were the red men, or old governing race, is abundantly apparent from the consideration that Cain, being a white man, would be so marked among the people where he dwelt that he should be readily known as soon as seen.

That he was superior to the people among whom he had cast his lot, is made manifest in this, that he immediately established himself as the head of the nationality, and gave the name of his son to its capital city; which, may we not ask, was transferred to the whole land of Nod, and has been transmitted through all the ages, from his own to the present time? Where is there a nation so ancient as Chanoch, or China? or a city which has stood longer than Cainton, or Canton? The Chinese claim that their nation has existed and has a history extending back for sixty thousand years. Are not the records of this people, whose customs and government are more stable than those of any others, entitled to as much confidence as the annals of any others? Then may we not conclude that Cain went, with the arts and sciences which he had learned of his father, and established the form of government and the civilization which has been handed down through all the generations of six thousand years to the present time?

It is in proof that Cain had done wrong, for God said to

him, while he was enraged at the result of his and his brother's offering, "If thou doest well, wilt thou not be accepted? and if thou doest not well, sin lieth at the door." Are not the evidences sufficiently convincing that the offence which he had committed was the taking of a wife of a different race from his own? for, although his own act had precluded him from the possibility of leaving the succession of his father's prerogatives to his son, yet the offence against God was so far forgiven that it was added, "And unto thee shall be his desire, and thou shalt rule over him." This was as much as to say, You shall possess the sovereignty of your father during your lifetime, and Abel will willingly submit to your authority.

Cain was not content, however, with this state of things, and in order that he might cut off the possibility of the succession passing from his own to the family of Abel, while they walked in the fields he rushed upon and slew his brother. "And the Lord said unto Cain, What hast thou done?... A fugitive and a vagabond shalt thou be in the earth." When Cain complained of the heaviness of his punishment, and expressed the fear of being slain by every one who should meet him, a distinct immunity from violent death was given to him; and if this promise extended no further than to himself individually, it would be exceedingly difficult to conjecture why the affair was at all alluded to by Moses; for it was a violation of the first commandment given through the same inspired writer for the government of the sons of Adam. "Whoso sheddeth man's blood, by man shall his blood be shed."

How, then, are we to understand it? If Cain had offended against the order of nature, by choosing as the mother of his children a woman of an inferior race, the Almighty would not depart from his own immutable laws so far as to make Cain's mixed descendants superior or even equal to the unadulterated sons of Adam. Like produces like, and as the parents, so must the children be. It would therefore have been in direct violation of the unchanging law of reproduction for the children of an inferior woman to have been made equal to the Adams of the pure blood.

However, we understand the promise given to Cain to mean that, notwithstanding his own conduct in taking a strange and inferior woman to wife had precluded the possibility of the succession of his children to the chief authority over the family of Adam, and although his crime in slaying his brother utterly forbade that he should remain in his father's house, or even in the land of his nativity, yet he might remove to the country from which he had taken his wife, and that there he might raise up the miscegenated family of whom he had chosen to become the father. "Therefore, whosoever slayeth Cain, vengeance shall be taken on him seven-fold."

That the offerings of the brothers had reference to the succession to their father's authority, it would seem should be rendered clear beyond a doubt, by the promise before quoted, "his desire shall be unto thee, and thou shalt have dominion over him;" but with any other interpretation this passage and the whole account is utterly and hopelessly obscure. Cain and Abel, like every pure descendant of Adam and Eve down to the present time, could not be happy without sovereign power; wherefore they both inquired by sacrifice who should succeed to the dignity and authority of Adam. Abel obtained the favorable response, because Cain had identified himself with an inferior race, and had thereby cut off the possibility of transmitting the throne to his son, who, to have been even equal to his subjects, must have had in his veins no taint of inferior blood.

Since the seed of the woman (Eve) should bruise the serpent's head, and since Cain had attempted to break down the enmity which God ordained by allying himself with the serpent race, therefore it was impossible that Shiloh, or the successor to the universal throne from which Adam had been expelled, could come from the mixed family of Cain.

When he went out to dwell among the red men, by reason of his superior physical beauty, the fairness of his complexion, the regularity of his features, the elevation of his intellectuality, and his vaulting ambition, he was a marked man. He was superior to his subjects not only in all these respects, but still more in longevity. If the life of the Indian then was what it is now, and that of Cain as protracted as the lives of Adam and his antediluvian descendants, he must have outlived many generations of his short-lived subjects; and, by frequent marriages with their daughters, might have lived to see a large community of his miscegenated descendants. May this not have been the origin of the Mongolian race? and may not Moses have introduced the short history of Cain for the purpose of giving us information of the origin of that apparent cross between the red and the white man?

It would seem that since Cain had committed offences against his own or the white race, and although he might not fear personal violence from the red men, yet he could but fear that the enmity which was established between the seed of the woman and the seed of the serpent might be extended to his own descendants, who would be sprung maternally from the latter race; and it is but reasonable to suppose that Cain not only understood the immunity to be granted to himself, but also to extend to his race. "Therefore, whosoever slayeth Cain, vengeance shall be taken on him seven-fold."

It is not a little remarkable that in all the bloody wars which make up the early history of the white man in that cradle from whence they spread out after the flood, that there was scarcely ever a conflict between the Caucasian and Mongolian peoples. Even Alexander, the Grecian thunderbolt of war, stopped short in his wild carnival of blood at the banks of the Indus. Cæsar's towering ambition, which led him to intrench his forces and fiercely fight beneath the shadow of the Pyramids, and to lead his hosts across the burning sands of Libya, and to invade and to subdue the western Asiatics, and to forage in the gore of Europe, never once induced him to conceive the idea of conquering kingdoms and subduing empires among the Mongolians. It was reserved for the moderns to seize on India, and open up the ports of China and of Japan. It has been within the last few years that the first Caucasian guns have thundered on Mongolian shores, that the first Caucasian steel has flashed in Mongolian streets and been bathed in Mongolian blood; and it remains yet to be seen whether Caucasian acquisitions will result in good to the conquerors. "Whosoever slayeth Cain, vengeance shall be taken on him seven-fold."

CHAPTER XXV.

PROOF OF CAIN'S MISCEGENATION — THE FIFTH KING OF THE LINE OF CAIN NOTICED — NAAMAH — THE APOTHEOSIS OF LAMECH — WHY CAIN WAS PERMITTED TO ESTABLISH THE MONGOLIAN RACE.

IN the succinct history of the six generations from the fall of Adam to the sons of Lamech, inclusive, is embraced, according to Archbishop Usher, and other distinguished chronological authorities, only one hundred and twenty-eight years. This would allow of about thirty years between each of the generations; which seems to prove two propositions, namely, that Cain reared a numerous offspring, previously to having made the offering mentioned, the murder of his brother, and his expulsion from Eden; and that the family of Cain was much more rapidly reproductive than that of Seth. Jared, the sixth from Adam of the latter, was not born until five hundred and sixty years after the expulsion, and three hundred and thirty years after the birth of Seth. Have we not, in this, incontrovertible testimony that the race of Cain was of a more prolific stock than the family of Seth, and, therefore, that they were more short-lived?

It is a rule laid down by naturalists, that animals which become soonest reproductive are soonest subject to decay and death; that the age of maturity, multiplied by three, gives the length of the lifetime. Now, if this be true, then the race of men who would become reproductive at twenty-five or thirty years, would certainly be much shorter lived than the race which was not matured until it arrived at one hundred and ten to one hundred and thirty years; therefore, we again conclude that the race of Seth was much longer lived than the race of Cain, and hence, that the latter were not of the pure Adamic blood. If Cain, however, lived through near a thousand years, as did the other antediluvian descendants of Adam, and if he continued to rear families from the short-lived daughters of the red men, then it is evident that a whole nation might be miscegenated by Cain, even during his lifetime; and in this way was established the Mongolian or Cainic race.

Why did Moses leave the legitimate subject in hand, to write such a history as that which he introduced of Cain? And why did he trace them through five or six generations, and then and there drop the race at once and forever? Had Cain or his descendants, at any time, been reintroduced to the readers of the Bible, either by Moses or any of his successors, the fact would certainly have been considered of sufficient importance to have demanded particular notice; yet, no such formal reintroduction is anywhere made.

The history of Cain was, without doubt, intended to convey a whole volume of information; and since its meaning has not been apprehended, and since it is intended for our instruction, therefore it is a legitimate subject of inquiry, and presents itself here for investigation.

Adam violated the law of his God, the law of his own immortality, by choosing to become the progenitor of a race of Adams, or of beings similar to himself; but the great mercy of God, his Maker, not only stayed the tide of decay in his vitiated blood, but even promised that his should be the ascendant race, and should finally triumph gloriously, in the full restoration of all things which had been lost or perverted by him. Cain chose to propagate a race inferior to that of Adam, because he selected as the mother of his children an inferior woman, a daughter of an inferior race. The natural aversion to labor of the children of Cain, inherited from their maternal ancestry, rendered them incapable of pursuing the calling of their father, which was that of tilling the soil, without great physical and mental anguish; and yet he had chosen to propagate this inferior race, and to curse them with necessities compelling them to pursuits wholly incompatible with the tastes and instincts of their maternal nomads. "When thou tillest the ground, it shall not henceforth yield unto thee her strength." This seems to indicate, that although the descendants of Cain would, for the most part, follow his vocation, yet they would be physically and mentally inadequate to the task of compelling the earth to yield her strength.

Notwithstanding Cain had chosen to become the progenitor of a mixed, and therefore of an inferior race, and thus, by his own voluntary act, had incapacitated himself and his descendants from ruling over the superior race, and especially had cut off, by his own act, the possibility that the successor to the lost throne of Adam should spring from him, yet he complains of the heaviness of his punishment, when the Almighty announced to him that his conduct would compel him to fly from his father's house, and wander among the ancient peoples of the world, from whose daughters he had taken his wife. However, sovereignty was promised to Cain, which he obtained in the land of Nod, to which he removed, and which, according to Moses, continued uninterrupted through five generations.

A great mistake is ordinarily made in the supposition that the mark which "the Lord set upon Cain, lest any finding him should kill him," was done after he had murdered his brother. It might be curious to inquire what kind of mark, under this supposition, was set upon Cain, in what way it was done, and, if he lived as long as his brethren, how all men everywhere were to know the mark and recognize the man as soon as seen; but as these absurdities do not come up in our theory, and it is no business of ours to endeavor to harmonize them with reason, we will not stop to examine them. It is palpable to reason that "Cain went out from the presence of the Lord and dwelt in the land of Nod, on the east of Eden," just such a man, physically, as he had ever been; but being the only white man there, and dwelling among Indians, or primitive red men, he was a marked man, and none seeing him there could fail, at a glance, to recognize him; and his descendants were as different from the people about them as the Chinaman of to-day from the aborigines of North America.

He evidently secured the love and respect of the tribes among whom he settled; for none who found him desired to kill him, and he reigned in the land of Nod before Abel could have ruled in Eden, and built a city there in the same year in which he had permanently cast his lot among them.

Having been convinced that, henceforth, all his hopes and fears were united with and dependent upon the red men of the land of Nod, he immediately seized upon the reins of government there, which the circumstances prove were willingly conceded to him, and, like a sensible man and prudent ruler, he began his administration by building a city, and by introducing among his subjects the arts and sciences of the civilization from which he had been expelled.

Four kings successively ascended the throne which Cain established in the land of Nod, without anything to mark their reigns of sufficient importance to render them a subject of special remark by Moses. Of the fifth king of the line, or the sixth including Cain, namely, Lamech, there is a curious little history, which but few try to understand, and it is so construed by them as to be made meaningless and wholly unintelligible.

"And Lamech took unto him two wives; the name of the one was Adah, and the name of the other Zillah." "And Lamech said unto his wives, Adah and Zillah, Hear my voice, ye wives of Lamech, hearken unto my speech; for (marginal reading) I would slay a man in my wound, and a young man in my hurt."

What is the meaning of this passionate speech of Lamech? Does he, as the commentators fondly explain the common version, simply intend to communicate to his wives the information that he had killed a man? or, according to the marginal reading, had he been grievously wronged or insulted, and was he thus formally and passionately expressing his desire or expectation of revenge? The first view will not do; for, upon the hypothesis that Lamech had committed crime, he declares that his was much greater than that of Cain's fratricide. How could this be, or how even could he think so, unless he had killed his own son? But had he done this, would not Moses have recorded the fact, especially as his sons had all just been mentioned? It could not have been his father who had been slain by Lamech; much less could it, as some suppose, have been Cain, his ancestor in the fifth remove, because, in his passionate speech, he speaks of a young man. Would Moses have made him so designate his own father? and still more, would he have so spoken of his grand ancestor, who was the first man of the Adamic race born into the world? We would conclude that Lamech had just become aware of a high crime and injury to himself, as far exceeding, in his estimation, the superseding of Cain by Abel in the government of the Adamic race as seventy and seven exceeds seven. "If Cain shall be avenged seven-fold, truly Lamech seventy and seven fold."

A rational exposition of the passage would seem to indicate that Lamech had outraged right and the laws of happiness far more than Cain had done when he slew his brother, and now that his crime had ripened into punishment, he claimed an immunity from the extreme results of his offence by pleading as a precedent the case of Cain; or, in other words, as Cain had killed a young man in his passion, and as he had resisted what he considered a much greater provocation to commit murder than that which had provoked Cain, that, therefore, the injury which had been done him rendered him so much more an object of compassion, and entitled him to so much more of revenge.

What was the high offence of Lamech thus brought to view? It is certainly stated by the inspired historian, else it would be difficult to assign a reason for the introduction in his work of this episode in Cain's history, after he had gone into the land of Nod.

When God made the first governing man, "male and female created he them," wherefore he evidently intended that they should be a dual animal, not merely because they were so created, but, because of the language used by Moses, it would appear that he so understood it. For much stronger reasons are we to believe that when Adam elected to become a propagating, was he to be a dual animal; or that no man should be at the same time the husband of more than one wife. Adam was not made male and female, but a sole being in the world. At his desire for companionship, God caused a deep sleep to come upon him, and, taking out one of his ribs, made of it a woman, for which cause, after they had fallen and become man and wife, since she is bone of his bone and flesh of his flesh, he must leave father and mother and cleave unto his wife. These conditions could not be complied with by any man who should be the husband of more than one wife; hence, we are confident in the conclusion that Moses intended to convey the idea that the man was intended to be the husband of one wife. His own example, also, proves the correctness of this view.

But, says one, there is no revealed law against bigamy, nor yet against polygamy. Neither is there any such law against a man thrusting his hand into the fire; because in the one case, as in the other, the existence of the laws are attainable by reason and experience, and nothing is revealed except what is beyond the power of man's reason. Bigamy is so clearly a violation of the natural law, is so intimately connected with, and so invariably carries its own punishment along with it, that revelation leaves it, as it undoubtedly should, with all other natural laws.

Abraham did not become the husband of Keturah until after the death of Sarah, satisfied fully with the experiment which he made in concubinage. At the earnest desire of his wife, he went in to her handmaid, Hagar; and, although he did this at the instance of Sarah, yet it caused such interruption in the family that Abraham, to secure quiet, was compelled to send away the handmaid and his young and helpless boy. Jacob was hoodwinked by his father-in-law into the folly of taking two sisters to be his wives, but their jealousy and contentions, which were transmitted to their sons, formed the great burden of his troubles through all of his long life. Moses and the prophets, and the patriarchs and apostles were the husbands of one wife. For a man to have two or more wives at the same time is an outrage against the law of order and of happiness, and carries with it such condign punishment that a revelation of the law, or any other infliction than that which the man suffers in the act, is wholly unnecessary.

If no true son of Adam and Eve could be satisfied with anything short of universal sovereignty, no more can any true daughter of the same race be content with a divided interest in the affections of the man to whom she commits her happiness as her husband. She is more jealous in this respect even than the man is of power and dominion. "Thy desire shall be unto thy husband" is so intensified, that any invasion of her rights in the man of her choice so outrages her peace of mind that she will surely bring misery upon him with usurious interest.

Lamech having been the first whose temerity led him to venture upon the experiment of introducing into his house two wives, even of the mixed race, the fact, with its dire consequences to his peace of mind, is mentioned by the sacred historian. The sons of Adah were Jabal and Jubal; and Zillah was the mother of Tubal-cain and of Naamah.

The troubles of Lamech, no doubt, began so soon as he brought himself under conjugal obligations to both of those women, each being jealous of the other, and continually annoying him with their bickerings and complaints, not only of partiality toward themselves, but much more toward their children. When these were grown up, the strife between the mothers gathered strength, and the children joined with their respective mothers, about the rights of succession; Adah and her sons claiming that it was due to them, while Zillah and her children as fiercely contended that the inheritance should be theirs. Who does not perceive how thoroughly miserable the old man must have been rendered by the jealous wrangling and unceasing contests of the two families in regard to the succession? How could he decide between them? Both were equally near and dear to him, and to have declared in favor of either would have driven the other outraged from him, and made those of his own household his implacable foes. He could therefore do nothing but suffer on, and waste his life in vain regrets over the folly of his youth, when he became the husband of two wives and the father of two families.

Moses gives us these facts in the history of Lamech, and indeed says all that is necessary of Cain and his descendants to point them out and identify them; then leaves us to learn from profane history what we wish to know more of them, as we do of the offspring of Ham and Japheth, as well as of Shem; since the subject of sacred history is the Hebrews, and all others are mentioned only incidentally, as their fortunes become involved with those of the peculiar people.

If, as we have supposed, the land of Nod is the country now known as China, then we must understand this short account of Lamech and his sons to be intended to show us that the ancient kingdom of Cain was torn into fragments by his descendants, the sons of Lamech. It would appear that the two families carried on their contests about the succession, without obtaining any decision of the question by Lamech, when finally they conspired together against the old imbecile, their father, and that, having seized upon, they divided his dominions among them.

When this result was accomplished, when the sceptre was

wrenched from his grasp, and it was imperative for the old man to remove from the land of his nativity and from his paternal throne, then, in the bitter anguish of his soul, he cried out, "Hear my voice, ye wives of Lamech, hearken unto my speech; for I would slay a man in my wound, and a young man in my hurt. If Cain shall be avenged seven-fold, truly Lamech seventy and seven fold."

The author of this work has but little doubt that if he had free access to the learning of the Chinese and of the Bramins of India, it could be satisfactorily shown how the land of Nod was divided among the children of Lamech. From what we do know, however, it appears to be sufficiently clear that Tartary is that portion of the great empire which lay eastward of Eden, that fell to the lot of Jabal. This is indicated by the habits and customs of that people, which are described in modern geographies, without the most remote reference to antiquity or the sacred writings, in the precise language used by Moses in describing the people over whom Jabal ruled. He says that "Jabal is the father (or prince) of all such as have cattle and dwell in tents." The modern geographers say of the Tartars that "the great body of the people live in tents, and roam from place to place with their horses, camels, and cattle." Is this not a remarkable coincidence, and are we not well sustained thereby in the conjecture that in the division of the empire of Lamech among his children, Tartary is the part which fell to Jabal and his nomadic followers? They are the same to-day that Moses described them to have been near six thousand years ago—a fact which can be true of Mongolians, but never of Caucasians.

Jubal obtained, as indicated by its name and by the refinement and civilization of the people, that portion of the ancient dominion now known as the empire of Japan. "And Jubal was the father (or chief) of all such as handle the harp and the organ." Tubal-cain seized and held the throne of China, and that country has continued to be an immense workshop even down to the present day. "And Tubal-cain was an instructor of every artificer in brass and in iron; and the sister of Tubal-cain was Naamah."

Female characters are not introduced by Moses in the pithy history which he was writing, except for a very pointed reason. But why was this daughter of the house of Cain mentioned in this connection? No such distinction is awarded to any daughter of Seth, even down to the time of the flood. We have seen why the two wives of Lamech were brought out in the narrative. But why was this girl introduced to the reader? There would have been fully as good reasons for mentioning the names of the daughters in any other family, in giving their genealogy, as this daughter of Lamech. Then, without doubt, the writer intended to present her as one of the prominent actors in the revolutions then and there transpiring.

Since Naamah is introduced as a political character, may we not suppose that in the division of the grand Mongolian empire, or the land of Nod, India and the surrounding countries were allotted to her? and that there she is worshipped as Bramah at the present time? May we not also with propriety conjecture that Lamech is worshipped in China and Thibet as the Grand Lama, and that his unfortunate name has thus been preserved, and that he has still been honored as a god in his native land, whence, by the conspiracy of his undutiful children, he was expelled, as being unworthy to reign as a mortal king?

The apotheosis of Lamech, if that be a fact, would seem to indicate that he left the throne of his fathers, not only in a sudden, but in a mysterious manner. The contests of his two families were evidently well known to his subjects. After he was dethroned by his children, as is clearly indicated by his speech to his wives, he followed the example of Cain, and fled his country and his kindred. It would be the interest and the inclination of the unnatural usurpers to cover up their own unfilial conduct, and hence they would unite in palming off a deception upon their subjects, in representing to the people that Lamech had parted his empire equitably among all his children, and then, bestowing his blessing upon them, in their presence, and in the presence of the priesthood, he was translated to heaven. Thus may have been inaugurated the worship of the Grand Lama.

While these events were transpiring in the land of his nativity and in the empire from which he had been expelled, he was wending his weary way to a far-distant country, from which he hoped never to be heard of at home, and where he would never hear from thence. We may be able to follow him in his hegira, if we take it for granted that he had learned wisdom by his past sad experience, and if he took with him but one wife.

When the Spaniards first visited Peru, they found the country with an organized government, and ruled by "Incas," or children of the sun. They had a tradition among them that a great while ago the Peruvians were savages, like those who then inhabited other parts of the continent and the islands; that they lived, like them, on that which was taken in the chase, and on the spontaneous productions of the earth; that they used no covering for their bodies; in a word, that they were savages in every respect, even to cannabalism, — when a white man and a white woman suddenly descended to them from the sun; that the man taught them to construct instruments of husbandry, to till the ground, to build houses, and to do many useful things; that his wife taught their women to spin, to manufacture cloth, and to do all manner of household work;

and, as the tradition goes, this man, whom they call Manco-Capac, and his wife, introduced the arts of civilization among them, established formal government there, and since that time the country has been ruled by the Incas, or descendants of Manco-Capac.

Whence came this man and woman? for we cannot suppose that the savage Indians could, in the first place, have invented such a story as this, and it must therefore have been circumstantially based. We know that this couple did not come from the sun. Then, who were they, and whence came they? It is clear that they were of the Caucasian or Adamic race, because they were white — unless we indulge in the violent supposition that they were a different creation from Adam. But the creation of another white man would have been a work of supererogation, and therefore this could not be indulged as a probable conjecture, for God never performs a superfluous work. It cannot be that this tradition was based upon the advent of Adam and Eve into the world, because, as we have seen, Peru could not, by any possibility, have been the site of Paradise, and because this tradition could not, in this way, have come down through the flood and left Adam's descendants reigning over the old race in the lovely plains of Paradise, especially since he certainly had no offspring while he was there.

It could not have been Cain, because we have traced him to the eastern part of Asia, and because, according to this tradition, both the man and the woman were white, and Cain only was thus marked when he went into the land of Nod. It would seem, therefore, that it would be reasonable to suppose Lamech and one of his wives — who proved true to him in adversity, and leaving the ill-gotten prosperity of her children, chose to cleave to her husband through all the days of his severe trial and wretchedness, and to follow his fortunes whithersoever he should go.

Again, there may be something in the name which may aid us in identifying the father of the Incas with Lamech. We are ignorant of the language of the aboriginal Peruvians, and consequently know nothing whatever of the surname of the first Inca. The translation of Manco might throw light on our subject, but the similarity between Lamech and Capac, in view of the difference in the languages of the Chinese and of the Peruvians, is sufficient, we think, to justify us in the conclusion that Lamech, who lived and reigned, and was dethroned and driven from his empire of China, is the same who came into Peru and erected it into an empire, where his descendants reigned until the last of the long line of kings was barbarously murdered by that bloody butcher, Pizarro.

The difficulty comes up here: Lamech, who was a Mongolian, was not a white man; but the man who made his advent into Peru was white. This difficulty is only apparent; for a Chinaman, among pure-blooded Indians, who then inhabited South America, is of so much fairer complexion that they would call him a white man. Because Lamech was a Mongolian, therefore, does not in the least vitiate our application of the remarkable tradition of the Peruvians to him.

Cain violated the order of nature by misecegenating with a race different and inferior to his own, and thereby precluded the possibility of leaving the dominion over his father's house to his adulterated children. By the same circumstance he lost all prospects of leaving the inheritance to the lost throne of Adam to his family. When this latter fact had no doubt been frequently a subject of conversation and controversy, they finally referred the contested point to the arbitrament of Heaven, and when it was decided in favor of Abel, then Cain was wroth and his countenance fell; and notwithstanding personal dominion was promised to him, yet he slew his brother, and thereby rendered it imperative for him to flee from home and country, and seek his fortune in a foreign land. Still, Cain was not only pardoned, but he was permitted to propagate and perpetuate as a permanent race the cross between himself and the inferior woman of his choice.

Lamech transgressed the law of order and happiness by taking to himself two wives; and although he suffered the consequence of his act of folly by the entire absence of domestic peace and quiet, and finally in being driven by his conspiring children from his throne and his home, yet he was guided by Providence to the distant land of Peru, where he established an empire, and left to the children of his one faithful wife, who had left all to follow him in his wanderings, the peaceable, quiet, and legitimate inheritance of his throne.

The question may here arise in the minds of some, if miscegenation be so great a crime in the sight of Heaven, that it cannot be looked upon with the least approximation toward approval, why was not Cain cut off before his offence ripened into the broad proportions which it attained before it resulted in the establishment of a permanent race of mixed blood? It is clear that ordinary offences against the natural laws are left to work out the punishment of the offender in their abnormal and always unhappy results. Cain's experience at an early period in the results of miscegenation were of a wretched character, and he was driven, in a fit of envy, to murder his brother, and then to flee his native land, and leave the more elevated race from which he was sprung at once and forever. His vagabond life was spared, and he was allowed to establish the Mongolian race, that the question might be forever at rest of the possibility of rearing a mixed race of men superior or even equal to the standard race of the red man, much less to that of the Adams. The Mongolians being a cross between Cain and the first and therefore the most perfect specimen, both physically and intellectually, of the race of Adam and the old or red race—and that race having the ability only to retain the civilization which was ages ago delivered to them, not to improve or invent anything whatever; hence no sickly, diseased, degenerate son of the Caucasian race need ever to expect anything but inferiority from such a cross.

CHAPTER XXVI.

IDEAS SUGGESTED BY THE HISTORY OF LAMECH—EVIDENCES OF ANTEDILUVIAN CIVILIZATION.

HAVING seen that the miscegenation of Cain was permitted, to show that if something of intellectuality might be added to the inferior race, much more is lost to the superior race, and that Lamech for the same reason was probably permitted to go out from the Mongolian and rear and leave a family of that blood among the pure red men of Peru, we will here revert to a state of things then in being and brought to view in the history of Lamech, which is wholly incompatible with the vulgar gloss of the history of Adam. According to the chronology in the margin of our Bibles, and the common interpretation, God created in a few hours the heavens and the earth, commanded the light into existence, formed the circumambient atmosphere, compounded the water, scooped out the bed of the ocean, and gathered the waters into one place, and made the dry land appear. He commanded the earth and she brought forth the grass, the herb, and the tree. He brought up and marshalled our world in the array of the solar system, ay, more, he created in twenty-four hours the sun, moon, and stars. He made in the like space of time the fishes also, and great whales, and all the birds which fly in the air; the cattle, the four-footed beast, and the creeping thing, the man in the image and likeness of God, who was created male and female. He made Adam out of the dust of the ground, breathed into his nostrils the breath of life, and he became a living soul, was placed in the garden to dress it and keep it; the animals all passed in review before him, and received their names; he became weary of his loneliness, and God caused him to sleep while one of his ribs was taken out and formed into a woman, who was given to him for a companion in a single short day. They lived in innocence, were tempted, overcome; they sinned, and fell from their eminence, were ashamed, disgraced, and driven out of the garden into a cursed world; and Cain was born; and all these grand, mighty, and wonderful events were crowded into one of our little years! Adam and Eve were parents at the age of one year. They were youthful, and, with only a few months' experience of life, must have been very badly prepared for taking charge of the rearing and education of a family.

The wonderful, incomprehensible, miraculous operation of the laws of mind and of matter do not stop here; for Moses, according to these same chronological authorities, tells us that one hundred and thirty years after Adam was expelled from the garden of Eden, "Jabal was the father" or leader "of all such as dwell in tents, and of such as have cattle;" that "Jubal was the father" or chief "of all such as handle the harp and the organ;" and that "Tubal-Cain was an instructor" or prince "of every artificer in brass and in iron."

These facts, as we conceive, were detailed by Moses, not only for the purpose of showing that Lamech was dethroned by his children, and that his empire was divided among them in the lifetime of their father, and that in this division Tubal-Cain was considered the more direct successor to the throne of Cain, but also to make known to us the fact that there was a civilization among this mixed, and therefore inferior people, even in the very first centuries of their existence.

Savages never have flocks and herds, but depend wholly upon the spontaneous productions of the earth, upon the snare and the chase, for the meagre supply of the few wants of their simple habits; but the followers of Jabal dwelt in tents, and had cattle; hence they were semi-civilized, their habits and customs being identical with those of the Tartars of the present time.

To handle the harp and the organ argues no mean proficiency in the arts and sciences, and in artistic skill; and much more are we assured of the advanced knowledge of the mechanic arts by their presupposed ability to construct those complicated musical instruments, the harp and the organ. We have no evidence whatever that the organs of our churches are an improvement on those upon which Jubal performed; and the splendid pianos of our parlors are nothing but that antique instrument, the harp, placed horizontally, and provided with keys with which to strike the strings, instead of causing the vibrations by the touch of the finger. None but the highly civilized have ever constructed or handled such complicated musical instruments as the harp and the organ.

To be an instructor of every artificer in brass and in iron indicates a degree of civilization, equal to that, at least, which prevails in China at this day. He who works in iron must have a furnace, bellows, anvil, tongs, hammers, vice, files, and grindstones. The construction of these appurtenances of a blacksmith-shop requires skill, and such skill as was never known to exist among any people who did not dwell in houses, and who did not possess the arts of agriculture and of commerce. Agriculture, manufactures, and commerce are the handmaids of the most elevated civilization; and the first two of these, at least, as we are assured by Moses, were possessed by those people.

Further, they were sufficiently advanced in the arts and sciences to be able to form, of the simples found in nature, skilfully artistic compounds. How many even intelligent men, in Europe and America, at this day, would be puzzled to extract iron from the ore, and then cut, weld, and form it into the various articles in use in agriculture and architecture? and how many more are utterly ignorant of the process of obtaining copper and zinc from the mines, of purifying them, and then of compounding them into brass? not to speak of the difficulty of working that compound metal into the various articles of ornament and of use for which it has always been employed.

The people who were skilled in civilized music, and those who were artificers in iron and in brass, without controversy must have lived in houses; for, ransack history as we may, no instance can be found anywhere of a people possessing these arts who have not possessed houses and lands. That the peoples over whom Jubal and Tubal-Cain had authority lived in houses, is settled by Moses himself, when he states the fact that the followers of Jabal dwelt in tents. The subjects of Jubal and of Tubal-Cain either lived in houses, or in the open air, like the beasts of the field. The latter hypothesis is barred by the facts which he states of their habits: therefore they lived in houses, and were a highly civilized people.

If the nationality of China has existed for sixty thousand years, as they claim, it is clear that they were not of the family of Adam, whose expulsion from the garden of Eden was not more than six thousand years ago. The arts and sciences could not be invented by the ancient race, for the unmixed red men have never been able to do anything of the kind. We will not rely on this fact, however, for the Chinese themselves inform us that their civilization was brought to them by a philosopher named Confutse. We have not the means of ascertaining correctly at what time this man flourished, but if it could be shown that he lived about six thousand years since, then might we trace the probability that the philosopher Confutse is the same as the vagabond Cain. We may possibly have something more to say on this subject in another place.

We will, however, add in this place, that no philosopher, in an ordinary lifetime, could have imparted the civilization of China to Chinamen, who, though they had the intelligence to receive, and have in a wonderful manner retained the learning, the arts, and the sciences once delivered to them, yet have made no improvements, no progress, no innovations, but are to-day what their fathers were thousands of years ago. We shall continue, then, to treat the subject upon the hypothesis that this empire was founded and its civilization was established by the labors of Cain, through the long lifetime enjoyed by the antediluvian descendants of Adam. We might as well in this place observe that the chronology, as applied to the history of Cain and his offspring, is of no value whatever, since Moses, the only authority on the subject, gives no data from which any calculation can be made. Cain must have lived and reigned in the land of Nod about eight hundred years; but after having fully established his authority, we may rationally suppose that he transferred the burdens of the administration to his son Chanoch, and made this position hereditary in his family.

Cain himself probably retained the supreme power in his

own hands, while Chanoch and his successors were viceroys or prime ministers to the king. Possibly, the division of the empire among the children of Lamech, and the expulsion of that unwise and therefore unfortunate individual, was the work of Cain. If this were the case, if Cain imposed the burdens of the government upon his short-lived descendants, while he retained in his own hands the chief authority, it must have been in order to devote himself to the impartation of knowledge and of fixing among his people the highest degree of civilization of which their capacity would admit.

We know that Cain was a tiller of the soil, and consequently he must have been acquainted with the arts necessary to the construction of the implements of husbandry. To slur over this point by saying that he cultivated in a rude manner, and had tools of the simplest and most imperfect kind, will not do, because his descendant Tubal-cain, while Cain was still a comparatively young man, was an instructor of every artificer in brass and in iron. It is much more rational to conclude that Cain's husbandry, which was taught him by Adam, and consequently his farming implements, were of the most perfect character.

During Adam's stay in Paradise, where he reigned in happiness and in conformity with the laws of his being, and which may have continued for hundreds or even for thousands of years, what could have been a more appropriate employment for the world's great sovereign and the vicegerent of God on earth, than the investigation of the laws of nature, and the development of the arts and sciences.

Is it not in proof that he was made to be the chief of all the earth, not only to rule over the men and animals, but also to govern the very laws of nature; to have the ground cultivated in the easiest and most efficient manner; to overcome the difficulties; and in a word, to bless the world, the old governing or red man, the animal or black man, and all the inferior animals, by rendering the earth most productive, and all things most convenient and agreeable for all animate beings? If the affirmative of these questions have been made to appear, let us inquire, with his perfect intellect and unrestrained intercourse with the Infinite Intelligence, and the vast resources of nature and the teeming millions of men then in the happy and richly productive earth at his command, what could he not do; and who can fix limits to what he actually did accomplish?

It is our opinion, that if the present mode of building is best, then Adam taught his people to build as we do; if our vehicles, our furniture, our implements of every kind are in the best and most convenient mode, then he had those of his people similarly constructed. If steam be the best agency for transportation and locomotion, then we should feel assured that a system of railroad and steamboat communication was by him perfected.

He must have possessed a much more thorough and intimate knowledge of the laws of nature than any philosopher has ever attained; and therefore he knew that electricity is the sole grand motive-power, is the agent with which the Almighty created and sustains worlds and involved systems in all their complicated and sometimes apparently eccentric orbs. Electricity is not only the force which both attracts and repels the worlds, but causes the winds to blow, the waters to flow; which scoops out the valleys and the mountain gorges; which heaps up the granite hills and makes the lofty mountains stand. It draws rich juices and subtle gases from earth and water and air, and forces them through the delicate ducts of vegetation; and, under the name of the odic fluid, it compels the blood from the heart by the arteries, and back to it by the veins; and is that which moves the hand or foot, and, when the mind wills, puts the whole body in motion.

Adam certainly knew all this, and far more in regard to the universal agent than has yet been discovered by the moderns; and he, being the ruler of the whole earth, how could he communicate his commands from pole to pole and around the globe's circumference so easily and so expeditiously as with the agency electricity?

From all the surroundings, from the facts which are made known to us, we must conclude that the profound philosopher and great king not only understood the powerful agency of electricity, but, since telegraphic communication was more pressingly necessary then than now or in any of the past ages, he must have environed the world in a network of electric conductors. Further, may we not suppose, since his wisdom was so great and his power was without limit, that the transportation and travel of the universal king and his subjects were accomplished on perfect tracks, belting the whole earth in its longitude and latitude; accommodated with machinery far more complete than has entered into the minds of the moderns to conceive; and driven by electricity with the speed of thought from pole to happy pole, and from the broad bright rivers to the rich ends of the earth?

With this kind of locomotion, the great king, with his glorious retinue, might visit and make actual personal observation upon every portion of the green and pleasant earth.

In this view of the mastery which Adam had acquired over the laws of nature, very many difficulties of the antiquarian may be removed. Every observer of the pyramids and obelisks of Egypt and other wonders of the Nile, must be forcibly impressed with the fact that the artificers of those grand old works must have been in possession of a knowledge of natural forces, and the skill to render them subservient to the will of men, not yet known to us. The lost art of embalming proves that their skill in pharmacy was so far in advance of the moderns, that no living man can scarcely hope to see its complete restoration.

In the days of Abraham, the Emperor of China ordered his two chief astronomers of state to be put to death, because they had failed to calculate correctly an eclipse of the sun. This, we must remember, was only some four or five hundred years after the flood, and yet it proves, positively, that science had advanced at that early day, in China, to a position not attained by Europeans until many ages afterward; the imperfect prognostication of Thales, which only amounted to the foretelling the year in which an eclipse would occur, was only about five hundred years before Christ, or one thousand years after a slight inaccuracy in the calculation of the Chinese astronomers cost them their lives.

The vast populations of that ancient country might have been equal to the task of erecting that wonder of Asia, the Chinese Wall; but would the design have been formed and the enterprise undertaken by an ephemeral prince, like one of the modern emperors, and who had no higher knowledge of the natural forces and their artistic application than the latter? It must have required ages, with the knowledge of the mechanic forces which they are generally supposed to have possessed, for them to have accomplished that stupendous work. It is said to have been built to prevent the irruptions of the Tartar hordes into the cultivated fields of China. Is it not clear that those fierce semi-barbarians would have interrupted the work from time to time, and protracted its completion almost indefinitely, or finally would have driven off the laborers, and prevented the finishing of the wall?

The wall was 1,500 miles in length, 30 feet high, and 30 feet thick: could such a structure have been made in the presence of such an enemy as the Tartars, with the appliances which are usually supposed to have been employed? The largest of the pyramids is four hundred and eighty-one feet high, and six hundred and fifty-three feet on the sides; its base covers eleven acres of ground. The stones are about sixty feet in length, and nearly two feet and a half thick. It is supposed to have been built about four thousand years ago, or immediately after the flood. How could 330,000, or any other number of men, without vastly superior knowledge to what is usually assigned to them, have elevated and placed those huge rocks?

It would appear to be the more rational view to suppose that, when the great wall of China was constructed, the knowledge of the mechanical forces was so far retained that that vast wall, in all its protracted length, and in its astonishing width and height and strength, was completed in a very short time. With fabulous expenditures of money, and the employment of the most powerful steam-engines, the enormous stones above described might be elevated to their places in the pyramids, but by no other known means; then is it not evident that the Egyptians, four thousand years ago, instead of being rude barbarians, were equal, if not superior, to the philosophers of the present age, in the knowledge and application of the mechanical forces?

That there was a civilization in the primitive days of the Adamic race, which has been lost and not yet fully recovered, is further proven by the few intellectual scintillations which have reached us from the ancient secret associations of the learned. The philosophers of China, the Brahmins of India, the magi of Assyria, the priesthood of Egypt, kept secret from the people of their own time the wisdom of their orders, by the most terrible obligations imposed upon all who were admitted into the mystic wonders of the learned. All that we have obtained from those rich depositories has been handed down to us by the Greek philosophers.

Who knows the deep extent of their secret lore? Who can tell what mathematical revelations were made by the Chinese, or what sublime astronomical observations were set down in the hidden records of the magi? Who, even at this day, would dare to declare the breadth and height and profound depth of the learning of the priests of Isis, of Osiris, of Orus, of Thoth? Or who now would undertake to unfold the unfathomable riches of the wisdom of the ancient, or even of the modern priesthood of the Grand Lama, of Trimurti, of Brahma, of Vishnu and Siva, of Varuna and Dhermarajah?

Had the library of Alexandria escaped the flames of the barbarous Omar Pasha, or had the secret books of the magi been saved from the cruel ravages of revolutions and the all-corroding march of time, and had they been handed down to us, much, evidently, of antediluvian and of the primeval learning of Adam, would be in our possession, which has not been transmitted through the channel of the Grecian philosophy; and, without doubt, many wonders of ancient lore would now be unfolded to the literati of Europe and America, by free access to the archives of the learned of China and of the priesthood of India.

The wisest and most renowned sages of Greece drank from the wells of the learning of Egypt, in order to perfect their philosophy. Had they not been tied down by obligations to the mystic colleges from which they drew much of their learning, (or if they were not bound as other members of those orders, it was because the penetralia of their wisdom was not unveiled to them,) how much more would have been given to us by those same philosophers than we have received from them!

Moses, the saint, sage, and philosopher, the leader and lawgiver of his people, the inspired prophet of God, was thoroughly learned in all the wisdom of the Egyptians; and yet even he, in view of the awful obligations which he had taken upon himself, revealed the deep mysteries of nature and of nature's God only with "a veil over his face." Had it been lawful for him to have elaborated fully the great truths which he reveals in the first part of the book of Genesis, together with all the profound philosophy of which he was perfect master, men, wicked and self-sufficient as they then were, and as they now are, scorning the humble teachings of religion, and rebelling against the authority of the God of the universe, they would, in their own strength, have aspired directly to the perfectibility of our nature, in contravention of the curse which Adam had drawn down upon himself and his race, and of the blessed restoration which a merciful God had designed for the world.

Then for the hardness of their hearts this great light was withheld from our fathers; "for until this day remaineth the same veil untaken away in the reading of the old testament; which veil is done away in Christ. But even unto this day, when Moses is read, the veil is upon their heart. Nevertheless, when it (the heart) shall turn to the Lord the veil shall be taken away." (2 Cor. iii.)

Have we not shown that there was a civilization in the primeval days of our race, equal, if not far in advance of the present progress? and that that civilization was built up by Adam while in innocence he reigned in Paradise? If these facts have been made sufficiently apparent, then it is easy to see how this knowledge of the arts and sciences was handed down by Adam to Cain, and by him to all the peoples over whom the sons of Lamech presided. By Adam, also, the wisdom which he had acquired before the fall was imparted to Seth and his other sons and daughters; for it is in proof that the sons and grandsons of Noah did possess the arts of architecture, and whatever it is necessary to know to build. The knowledge by which the ancient cities of Babylon and Nineveh, Thebes and Memphis, the obelisks, the Labyrinth, and the Pyramids, were constructed, must have been brought down from beyond the flood by Noah.

If the question of the existence of a high state of civilization in the time of Adam, and that, too, immediately after the fall, were tested by the rules of evidence as applied to any other fact, it would be manifest to a moral certainty that Adam brought through the fall an intimate knowledge of the arts and sciences, a large and expanded comprehension of the character and attributes of the Almighty Ruler, and of the laws by which he governs, in the greatest and the most minute; that he was such a philosopher as the world will never see until the second Adam come to restore all things to their primitive and normal condition.

The unprogressive descendants of Cain, the Mongolian race, have presented the best depository of the ancient learning of the world, and we would therefore expect to find among the learned of that race more of the sciences taught by Adam than anywhere else outside of the inspired volume. Had Cain stayed longer with his father, the Mongolians would have been taught by him more than they were. Let the records of the Chinese be examined, let the learning of the Brahmins be uncovered, and the learned world, without doubt, will be astonished at the revelations which will be made.

CHAPTER XXVII.

"THE SONS OF GOD SAW THE DAUGHTERS OF MEN" EXPLAINED —WHY "NOAH FOUND GRACE IN THE SIGHT OF THE LORD."

AND it came to pass, when men began to multiply on the face of the earth, and daughters were born unto them, that the sons of God saw the daughters of men, that they were fair, and they took them wives of all such as they chose. And the Lord said, My spirit shall not always strive with man, for that he also is flesh; yet his days shall be an hundred and twenty years. There were giants in those days; and also after that, when the sons of God came in unto the daughters of men, and they bare children unto them; the same became mighty men, which were of old men of renown."

Before remarking upon the above, it becomes necessary for us to revert in our minds to what has been said in the former part of this work in regard to the pre-Adamic condition of the world. We have said, and Moses has said, that the waters were all gathered together into one place, and that everywhere else the dry ground appeared. We have said that the whole earth, from pole to pole, and all around the circle of the globe, was more densely populated by two races of men, and by all of the present and many varieties of now extinct animals, than it were possible for it to sustain since the folly and fall of Adam. If the reader has been impressed with the rational view which we have taken, in the light held out to us by Moses, and which we have endeavored to present to him, and if he will keep that view before his mind, then will he be in a position to comprehend and appreciate the exposition of the meaning which we attach to the above-quoted revelation.

In it two distinct and different characters are brought before us — the sons of God, and the men who at that time began to multiply, and unto whom daughters were born. We are informed by the commentators that the righteous were called the sons of God, and that the unrighteous were those styled men. But will this gloss bear scrutiny? A little farther on it is said, that "God saw that the wickedness of man was great in the earth, and that every imagination of the thoughts of his heart was only evil continually," and he declared that "It repenteth me that I have made man;" and he determined to destroy man from the face of the earth.

Let us ask where were the righteous called the sons of God? On another occasion, "Abraham said to the Lord, Wilt thou also destroy the righteous with the wicked? That be far from thee to do after this manner—to slay the righteous with the wicked; and that the righteous should be as the wicked, that be far from thee: shall not the Judge of all the earth do right?" "And he said, I will not destroy it (Sodom) for ten's sake." Hence, since Noah alone "found grace in the eyes of the Lord," and of all the world he and his sons alone were saved, they must have been the only righteous upon the earth; and it follows that they had intermarried with the daughters of men; and that God destroyed every living creature from the face of the earth for the offence committed by those persons alone whom he saved from destruction. Will any seriously contend for such an interpretation? "Shall not the Judge of all the earth do right?"

Others again will tell us that the two classes referred to were the descendants of Cain and of Seth; but upon what grounds, to us is by no means apparent. If, however, this be the proper view, these expositors make an egregious error in claiming that the children of Seth were those called the sons of God; because it is the wickedness of the men whose daughters were given in marriage to the sons of God, which was great in the earth, and the imagination of the thoughts of whose heart was evil continually, and whom God therefore determined to destroy. From among them Noah was selected, who is a lineal descendant of Seth; therefore, if the children of Cain and Seth are the two characters brought to view in the above-quoted passage, evidently those of Cain are called the sons of God. It is the task of those who take this singular view of the subject to explain why the descendants of Cain should be so greatly preferred to those of Seth that the former are called the sons of God, while the latter are designated as men.

When God had driven Adam and Eve from the hyperborean garden of Paradise, with all its majestic and lovely scenes; when, by the sudden destruction of the perpendicularity of the axis of the earth to the plane of her orbit, the throne of the world was guarded by circumambient icebergs, then was destroyed, "at one fell swoop," that glorious system of internal improvements of which we have spoken in another chapter, and the difficulties of time and space and the resistance of matter were as great to Adam as to any others; and since he had lost his authority, and there were none who would do his bidding, and since he had become the father of a family who were dependent upon him for subsistence, therefore he was compelled to eat bread in the sweat of his face.

It will be remembered that Adam was driven out of Paradise, and afterward the cherubim and the flaming sword were placed to guard its entrance; otherwise, like the Siberian elephant, he too might have been caught and held to this day, a frozen mummy, in the adamantine chains of yet unending ice. God, however, permitted him to "plod his weary way" in search of some more hospitable home. But still he remained within the boundaries of the land of Eden; for, when Cain was banished from the home of his father and the land of his birth, he went eastward of Eden, into the land of Nod.

Adam must have retained his knowledge of the arts and sciences which he brought with him from Paradise; but, being without the means of overcoming the increased natural obstacles to locomotion, he and his descendants were perforce compelled to remain in a fixed locality, and extend themselves as they multiplied, somewhat like the white settlements have done in North America.

As has already been shown, there are many cogent reasons for supposing that part of Eden inhabited by Adam and his antediluvian descendants is identical with the "Atlantis" of the Greek and Roman poets, and that the angry billows of the Atlantic Ocean now ceaselessly surge over the site where their sin and corruption provoked the destruction which overwhelmed them; and it is also apparent that their hyperborean regions, or the blissful land "beyond where the north wind begins to blow," is identical with that part of Eden where Moses locates the garden of Paradise. With these ideas recapitulated, we return to the subject now under consideration.

"When *men* began to multiply, the *sons* of *God* saw the *daughters* of men, that they were fair." There is no mystic meaning or figurative language here, but a plain statement of facts. We have already seen that the parties here brought to view are not the righteous and the wicked, for "all flesh was corrupt;" nor were they the sons of Cain and Seth, because that view would make those of the former a superior race to that of Seth, which is not true in any respect whatever, and we suppose no one will seriously contênd for this conclusion, although the commentators lay down the premises from which it is legitimately deduced.

Who, then, are the parties of whom Moses speaks? When God created the first governing man in his own image and likeness, "Male and female created he them, and blessed them, and said unto them, Be fruitful, multiply, and replenish the earth;" but when he had made Adam, he placed him in the garden to dress it and to keep it, and gave him plenary power to eat of the trees of the garden, except of the tree of the knowledge of good and evil, which is in the midst of the garden. The trees of the garden, we have seen, represent the passions and instincts implanted in Adam, all of which he might freely indulge, except that only which leads to reproduction.

The men of the old governing race came into the world

according to the design of their Creator, and are therefore called the sons of God. Adam, through ambition to be like God in the creation of a race, in violation of a positive prohibition, chose to incur the penalty of the law, the displeasure of his Maker, and propagated his species; hence his children could not, with any degree of propriety, be called the sons of God, but are always spoken of by Moses as "men," or the Adams.

It was not the sons of God who began to multiply at the time spoken of, because for many thousands of years they had multiplied and filled the earth. The language is, "And it came to pass when *men* began to multiply." In the original the word Adam simply means man. When the great king came into the world, he was so far superior to all others that by way of expressing his eminent distinction, he was called *The Man.* Napoleon Bonaparte was *the man* of his day.

The descendants of Adam, being like him, and having been ushered into the world contrary to the express command of the Almighty, were properly called *the* men; therefore, if we render the passage without translation, as we think we may without doing it violence, all doubt, all obscurity, immediately disappears. And it came to pass when the Adams began to multiply, and daughters were born unto them, that the sons of God (the red men) saw the daughters of the Adams, that they were white and beautiful, (for this is the meaning of the word fair,) and they (the red men) took them wives of all which they chose. This practice of miscegenation and corruption of the ways of God had become so wide-spread, not to say universal, that he said, "My spirit shall not always strive with Adam, for that he also is flesh; yet his days shall be an hundred and twenty years."

The days of the red man's life are threescore years and

ten, and if the Adams will indulge in the reproductive act as much as they, I will not interfere with the law established for all reproducing animals, and their lives must be greatly shortened; yet, by reason of their superior physical structure, the days of their lives shall be an hundred and twenty years. We venture here to assert that no debauchee in any age of the world has lived out even this limit, because the law of reproduction is the law of death.

Every one who has observed the effects of misecegenation is aware of the fact that both in the animal and vegetable kingdoms, where the circumstances of production and rearing are favorable, and where the cross is between proximate links in the concatenation of being, the result is an offspring larger and more powerful than either of the parent stocks. The mule is always larger than the ass; and in Kentucky and other places where much attention is paid to the rearing, he is made to grow larger than the horse. By the mixing of doura or sorghum with common broom-corn, we obtain an article far more gigantic in proportions than either of the parent plants; and the same is true of the plant obtained by mixing the common and sea-island cottons. The law of hybridity, which is so unyielding among the lower animals, does not fully obtain among the vegetables; for by long attention to crossing, new standard varieties may be at least partially established.

The cross between inapproximate links in the chain of being, however, are always inferior in every respect to the parent stocks. The mulatto is far inferior physically and morally to either the white man or the negro; but we are not prepared to announce the same result from a first cross, in regard to the offspring of the Indian and the Caucasian. On the contrary, there can be but little doubt that the result, with favorable circumstances for breeding and rearing, would be consistent with the general law, and that the half-breed should be much larger and more powerful than either of the standard races.

What was the consequence of the intermarriage between the sons of God and the daughters of men? It is stated thus by Moses: "There were giants in the earth in those days; and also after that when the sons of God came in unto the daughters of men, and they bare children to them, the same became mighty men, which were of old men of renown." Can Holy Writ or human language make it more clear that the miscegenation of two races is the act which destroyed the order and so corrupted the ways of God, that he determined to destroy the man whom he had created? No such result as the production of giants could, by the operation of any law of nature, by any rational possibility, be obtained by the crossing of the wicked with the righteous.

It is objected that the law of hybridity did not intervene, and that, therefore, the sons of God and the daughters of men could not be of different species; but we have seen that it is not applied to prevent the mixing of the vegetables, deterioration in quality, notwithstanding its greater size, being sufficient to prevent men from destroying to any considerable extent the order of nature in the vegetable kingdom. It is a well-established fact that the mixed races of men everywhere, when carried on for many generations, are inferior to the standard races; and especially when the cross is between the inapproximate white and black races, is physical inferiority most apparent. This, together with the further fact that man is an intelligent moral agent, capable of receiving and appreciating the law, "Thou shalt not commit adultery," is a sufficient reason why the law of hybridity is not applied to men as to the lower animals.

"And God saw that the wickedness of the Adam was great in the earth, and that every imagination of the thoughts of his heart was only evil continually. And it repented the Lord that he had made the Adam on the earth, and it grieved him at his heart. And the Lord said, I will destroy the Adam whom I have created from the face of the earth; both the Adam, and the beast, and the creeping thing, and the fowls of the air, for it repenteth me that I have made them." This is vigorous language, and is used because of the imperfection of our understanding and of our vehicle of thought; and is used to convey the most emphatic and pointed impression of the exceeding wickedness of reproducing contrary to the law of nature; for God commanded everything in the vegetable as well as in the animal kingdom to reproduce after his kind.

It will be observed that the sons of God were not among the living creatures which were doomed to destruction; then, whoever they were, the sin of intermarriage with the daughters of men seems not to have been visited directly upon them.

It would appear from the above that not only had the sons of God misegenated with the daughters of men, but that the beast, and the creeping thing, and the fowls of the air had by the devilish machinations of man destroyed the order in reproduction which God had established; for Moses declares that "God looked upon the earth, and behold it was corrupt; for *all flesh* had corrupted his way upon the earth." Whenever misegenation occurs among the animals it is invariably the result of the interference of man, and that too directly or indirectly by the agency of the white man, who has inherited the desire to create new orders of being from our first parents.

For ages the many species of deer have roamed, in promiscuous herds, the plains of Africa and the wilds of America, where the negro and the Indian have dwelt; but no act of adulteration was ever known among them, while all sorts of crosses are to be found in countries where the white man and mixed races inhabit. The wild cow and the buffalo mix not, neither do the horse and the ass, unrestrained by the dominant race of men. "And God said, The end of all flesh is come before me; for the earth is filled with violence through them; and behold, I will destroy them with the earth."

"But Noah found grace in the eyes of the Lord," and why? Because he "was a just man," that is, his moral conduct was unexceptionable, and he was upright in all his relations with his fellow-men? "He walked with God," or he was devoutly pious; and thus he performed his whole duty toward God and toward his fellow-beings? This might appear to be a sufficient reason why he should have been chosen out of the whole earth; yet it was not enough, for the crowning reason rendered for his election is this, "*he was perfect in his generations.*"

This, according to the rendering of the commentators, is nought but a redundancy, a mere surplusage, which means nothing; for uprightness, the meaning given to the expression, is contained in the declaration that he was "a just man, and walked with God." How could the expression, "he was perfect in his generations," be used with any degree of propriety, if the writer only intended to say that he was upright? Had it been intended for us to understand it according to the vulgar gloss, it should have been written he was perfect in his *generation.* Even with that reading we confess that we could not see why it should have been deemed necessary to have added it to a description of character, as vigorous as our own or any other language could render it, if indeed it could even in that shape be applied to moral conduct.

As we find it written, however, it is exceedingly strange that any one should ever have thought of the explanation which is given to it, and stranger still that the Christian world should have been content with the absurd and violent construction. It is clear that "the veil is still upon their heart when Moses is read."

The writer clearly intended to render, in the passage under consideration, the physical, as he gives us in the other clauses of the description the moral, reasons for the election of Noah. If a man were reading an account of a horse, and came to the words, "and this horse is perfect in his pedigree," what would the world think of the man were he to insist that the meaning of that description was that the horse in question was a gentle, good-disposed animal? And yet his exposition would be as rational; indeed, it would be the very same thing which the commentators do in regard to Moses' description of Noah.

From every point of view we must conclude that when the inspired author asserts that Noah was perfect in his generation, it was simply intended for us to understand that he was purely descended through an unadulterated line from Adam and Eve, without any taint of inferior blood in his veins.

After Noah had been informed of the fact of the coming flood, and had been instructed in regard to the construction of the ark in which he was to save himself and his family, God commanded him, "And of every living thing of all flesh, two of every sort shalt thou bring into the ark to keep them alive with thee; they shall be male and female. Of fowls *after their kind*, and of cattle after their kind, and of every creeping thing of the earth, *after his kind;* two of every sort shall come unto thee to keep them alive."

It will be observed with what precision and point the description "*after his kind*" is added after the enumeration of each variety of living thing. Why is this, or why, after stating that they were to be two of every sort, male and female, was it judged necessary by the writer to add the further description that every pair should be *after his kin*, unless it is intended for us to understand that by "the corruption of all flesh" is meant the general habit of miscegenation, which the Adams had introduced among the animals?

Physical results are produced by physical means; and one of the results of the intermarriage of the sons of God with the daughters of men was the shortening of man's life. This was certainly a physical result. Our own observation teaches us that the mixed races are a short-lived people. Here also we would conclude that the offence which so highly incensed the Almighty was the miscegenation of different species of the genus homo. Spiritual causes produce spiritual effects; but the intermarriage of the sons of God with the daughters of men produced giants. This was not a spiritual, but a physical result; therefore we again conclude, since such crosses both in the animal and vegetable kingdoms produce scions of gigantic growth now, that the offence of the antediluvians was the destruction of the order of nature by the mixing of different species of men and of animals. We also conclude, since there were giants in the earth prior to the time when the wickedness of man became so great, that the first descendants of Cain, who were the children of miscegenation, were giants. "There were giants in the earth in those days; and also after that, when the sons of God came in unto the daughters of men, and they bare children to them."

CHAPTER XXVIII.

THE FLOOD — MOSES AND GEOLOGISTS — MR. HITCHCOCK'S FROG.

"AND, behold, I, even I, do bring a flood of waters upon the earth, to destroy all flesh wherein is the breath of life, from under heaven; and everything that is in the earth shall die." The laws of nature, as they surely and mightily work out the designs of their Author, are here vividly brought to view. We must bear in mind that God effects all his purposes by the use of adequate means; spiritual effects by spiritual causes, and physical results by physical agencies. Spiritual causes could not directly bring on the flood, which was certainly the mightiest physical result which has ever been wrought in our world since its creation; therefore it was produced by the operation of the most powerful physical causes.

In following our author in his narrative, we may be led to introduce the same subject in different connections, but, as already stated in the introduction to this work, we are in search of the truth; and we will, whenever our investigations require us to do so, in order to point an argument, recapitulate or introduce subjects already discussed. We hope, however, to present some new view or idea on all such subjects on every occasion of reintroduction. Whether the course pursued by us is satisfactory to the critics or not, we care not. We write not for them, but for those who would know the truth.

We have represented the earth as symbolized by a human body. All the waters then were gathered into her huge heart, whence by daily pulsations, as may be seen in the ebbing and flowing of the tides at this day, they were driven through deep internal channels or arterial ducts, which were divided and subdivided in their outward course until they were lost in capillary formations at the surface, when, as now, they were taken up by the roots of vegetation and evaporated through the superficial pores of the earth, and then returned in the form of dew. They were then re-collected into rills and rivulets, which united into creeks and rivers like the veins of the human body, and were thus disembogued into the great heart of the world — the one place where the waters were gathered together.

Thus the insensible perspiration, called evaporation, went on by day, and returned in gentle dews by night, to moisten and invigorate the soil. The agency which causes this flux and reflux, as well as the disintegration and recombining of the elements of which the water is composed, is, no doubt, the same active principle of attraction and repulsion which produces the circulation of the blood in man. This agency, in another chapter, we have endeavored to show is electricity.

That the world is not what she always has been is abundantly shown by the geological researches of the present and last centuries. From the granite and old red sandstone, up through all the various formations, to the alluvial and diluvial deposits of the superficial accumulations, God has written, in unmistakable characters, that change and revolution have wrought sad havoc in the constitution of our old world, and that she, like man, is hurrying on to another and still greater change, which will render her forever young, perfect, and vigorous.

The prejudices, the absurd intellectual servitude, and inexplicable imbecility of Christian geologists, have presented a barrier in the investigation of geological truth, which, having been removed, we might now be basking in the noontide splendor of the wisdom of the ages of the past. Is it not exceedingly strange that the learned professors of this recently discovered but noble science, should labor to build up and place it, as it ought to be, in the very foremost ranks of the high branches of learning, and immediately turn round and bend all their energies to battering down the fabric which they are laboring to erect on a solid basis?

The science teaches that the rocks are formed in series, which must have been vast ages in their accretions, and that no fossils are found in the primary proper, or hypozoic rocks. "Life begins to dawn only with the development of the clay-slate group, and to become more abundant as the deposition of the graywacke and silurian proceeds. The earliest forms of vitality are not plants, but animals." The zoöphytes, the molusca, and the crustacea are the forms of life clearly defined which have been discovered in these rocks. We have not the opportunity for consulting authorities, but we believe that they all incline to the opinion that animal life existed in our world before there was vegetation.

It is astonishing that close investigators, such as the geologists must be, should suffer slight appearances to betray them into so violent a conclusion as that just mentioned. Allowing that zoöphytes, molusca, and crustacea are found in the transition rocks, between the primary and secondary formations, and well-defined vegetable fossils are not found until we pass into the limestone which underlies the secondary formations, still, ought not the geologist to look well into the subject before coming to a conclusion so manifestly absurd and irrational?

Is it possible, now, for animal life to be sustained without vegetation? It does not help the matter, to say that the carnivora feed not upon vegetation, for the animate beings upon which they subsist must draw their support from vegetation. The same laws which govern now, in all the departments of nature, must have existed from the beginning. It is the veriest folly to say that animal life must, at this day, be supported by vegetation, but that it was sustained without vegetation, in some age of the world, however remote in the rolling ages of antiquity. The Author of nature is unchangeable, and equally so are all His laws. Hence the low orders of animate being, which are imbedded in the transition rocks, must have been supported by vegetation.

The profound philosopher and inspired historian informs us that the earth was first commanded to bring forth vegetation, and that, too, on the day previous to her introduction into the solar system. He tells us that, on the next day after this latter event, the waters were commanded "to bring forth every living thing which moveth in the waters, and the birds which fly in the air." We understand, as the reader will remember, that a day in the creative week indicates a period of fifty thousand years; therefore vegetation must have grown, matured, and decayed for at least one hundred and twenty-five thousand years, or two and a half geological days, before animate beings proper were called into existence.

In the concatenation of being, the zoöphytes, the molusca, and the crustacea may, with equal propriety, be classed as vegetables or as animate beings, or, rather, they form the connecting link between the vegetable and animal kingdoms. Hence, if these kinds of fossils were found in rocks older, by a hundred thousand years, than those which contain the earliest remains of marsupials and mammals, the fact would not conflict with, but corroborate, the account of the creation given by Moses. The vegetable animals, whose remains are found imbedded in the transition rocks, presuppose the prior existence of vegetation. Vegetation itself must be subsisted on vegetation; hence the fungous growths must have sprung up and decayed through vast ages, before a soil could have been formed in which might grow even the poorer grasses.

The fossils in question are nothing more than the advanced orders of this genus—are the higher links in the fungous chain of being. Let no geologist conclude, therefore, that animal life could, by any possibility, have existed prior to the existence of vegetation. If the vegetation of the epoch under consideration is not impressed upon the rocks, it is because it was of too unsubstantial a character.

The very next rocks above those, or the lowest in the secondary formation, ought to have prevented geologists from falling into so gross and palpable an error; for these are the carboniferous rocks, which proves that vegetation then grew, and for ages had grown, in extraordinary profusion. Christian geologists teach us that animal life existed in our world before vegetation, contrary to reason and contrary to the cosmogony of Moses. Then why should they stultify themselves, and retard the progress of the grand science of geology, by insisting that it affords no proofs of the existence of man prior to the recent formations, or within the last six thousand years, merely because they fancy Moses to have said that Adam was the first man created in the world?

If Moses be authority to them on one point, since these Christian geologists acknowledge the fact of his inspiration, he ought to be on all. If they will not investigate, nor suffer investigation into the antiquity of human fossils, because they vainly imagine the inspired writer as having stated that man has been on this stage of action only about six thousand years, they certainly ought to be careful how they overturn his authority, and do violence to common sense by teaching that animal life existed in the world many ages before vegetation grew.

Had it not been for the pitiable prejudices of these same geologists and would-be defenders of the faith, long since might they have removed the veil from the writings of

Moses, which is still upon their hearts when they read his account of the creation and the fall.

At the island of Guadaloupe the petrifactions of perfect human bodies have been exhumed from solid limestone, said to be of the Devonian series, or of the old red sandstone group, which belongs to the primary, or, more properly, the transition rocks. In the new red sandstone of the valley of the Connecticut River, which is a rock of the middle of the secondary formations, have been found fair impressions of human feet twenty inches in length. On rocks of equal antiquity in Ohio, among many footprints of animals of now living and extinct varieties, it is written, by the finger of God upon these same tables of stone, that the lords of creation were then and there subduing and having "dominion over the fishes of the sea, the fowls of the air, and over every living thing that moveth upon the face of the earth;" for, there too, when those old rocks were soft and plastic earth, the distinct footprints of man were made among those of the wild beasts. In the deep caverns and internal ducts of the earth, in occult fissures, and imbedded in the solid old rocks in all parts of the world, but more particularly examined in the south of France, promiscuously commingled with the fossil remains of extinct and living species of animals, are found the bones of rude earthen vessels from which he ate and drank.

Instead of leading us to admire and adore the power and munificence of the unchangeable Author and Preserver in the past as well as at the present time, the wisdom of the ages written on the rocks has driven the modern philosophers into the folly of infidelity on this and on that hand. The same God who impressed the ten commandments upon the two tables of stone amid the smoke and fire and hoarse thunders of Sinai, has written upon the rocks and the mountains — in the deeply-imbedded fields of coal, the treasures of silver and gold, the heaped-up fossils of extinct and of living species of animals—that this world is immensely old, has been subjected to vast revolutions, and that far back in the retroceding cycles of time, when the colossal mastodon quietly browsed upon the tender buds of the elegant acacia, leisurely ruminated beneath the shade of the towering palm, growing then in the luxuriant plains, where now unending winter shrouds all nature in a winding-sheet of snow, man was then and there subduing and having the dominion over the fish, the fowl, and the beasts. To the same effect we understand Moses to have written in the volume of inspiration.

Why, then, the almost universal attempt to put the God of nature in antagonism with the God of revelation? Why is the scientific lover of truth driven into the rejection of the book of inspiration as a cunningly devised work of man? And why is the unconditional believer in Holy Writ driven into absurd and foolish blundering in the sciences, and into silly, not to say dishonest, apologies for the truth, which God in mercy has revealed to his creature man?

The difficulty all arises from the false gloss of the sacred writings imposed by the wicked priesthood in those dark ages, "which God winked at," and the unaccountable imbecility of the Christian intellect in suffering itself, even in this time of general illumination, still to be led blindly by the traditions of the fathers, into the dark mysticism of the past, to "wrest the Scriptures to their own destruction."

Where do men obtain their authority for asserting that in the sixth chapter of Genesis "the sons of God" means the children of Seth, and that "the daughters of men" are the offspring of Cain? We are bold to assert that such an interpretation is not suggested or even justified by anything in the Bible. Would any man, enjoying the scientific light of the present day, who had never seen or heard of the writings of Moses, on a first reading believe that the author intends for us to understand the days mentioned in the first and second chapters of Genesis to mean twenty-four hours of time, and that from the beginning to the end of the creative week, including the grand Sabbath of Divine rest, was only one hundred and sixty-eight of our small hours? Or, yet again, that the offence of Adam against high heaven was literally and simply only the eating of an apple?

It is humiliating in the extreme to see to what miserable subterfuges Christian philosophers of the present day are driven by the traditional authority of the priesthood of the past. Mr. Hitchcock, an old Christian minister and learned author, in the 31st edition of his deservedly popular work, in attempting to reconcile the grand teachings of geology with the account given of the creation by Moses, winds up his defence of Christianity by boldly declaring to the world that the man who was "learned in all the wisdom of the Egyptians," and who wrote the sublime book of Genesis, under the direct inspiration of the God of nature, was ignorant of the things of which he wrote.

This is a serious charge, look at it as we will. If we profess to communicate facts to an individual, but intentionally keep the understanding of them from him, we are guilty of deep duplicity, and all men will pronounce us dishonest. The charge of ignorance upon Moses is an indirect charge of duplicity upon Him who revealed those facts to Moses. It will not do to say that God did not understand his own laws or the mysteries of nature as brought to light by modern philosophers; therefore let the good man beware, lest the traditions of the ancient priesthood drive him unintentionally to utter words of blasphemy.

Again: the Christian philosopher should be exceedingly cautious how he makes bungling attempts to homologate the truths of science with the traditional interpretations of the

Fathers, lest he should, haply, be found to fight against the truth of God; for how many an honest man, comparing the traditions of the Fathers with the sublime truths of nature, has been driven to the rejection of the grand truths of the Bible!

If, in our geological researches, we are led to conclude that rocks are old, because we find in them the fossil remains of long since extinct species of animals and of vegetables, let us not stultify ourselves and the science of geology by miserable attempts to account for a recent deposit of human remains in the same ancient formation. If the peculiar waters about Guadaloupe will cause the formation of limestone, which may be mistaken by adepts in the science of geology for that belonging to the Devonian system, in one hundred and fifty years, why may not the same rocks be formed elsewhere by the same cause in equally as short a time?

In the secondary rocks are found the fossils of extinct pachydermata, ruminata, and carnivora; and many revolving ages have evidently supervened since their deposition. Vast cycles of ages had consolidated those rocks prior to the expulsion of Adam from Paradise. The traditionary interpretation of the account of the creation by Moses teaches that Adam was the first human being upon the earth, and only about six thousand years ago was he created. The Devonian rocks, or even the limestones of the secondary series, must be many ten times six thousand years old.

Yet, wonder of wonders, two perfect specimens of human bodies, one of which is now in London and the other in Paris, are exhumed from limestone of the transition, or, possibly, of the secondary formation. A great commotion is thereby produced among learned geologists. Two parties are arrayed against each other. The one, with the devilish triumph of infidelity, asserts that this fact proves beyond a doubt the Bible is false; while the other goes deliberately to work to overturn or to hide from view the truth of God as written on the rocks. What say these same geologists in regard to the footprints in the new red sandstone of the valley of the Connecticut?

Mr. Hitchcock informs us that they are not human footprints at all, but that when the old red sandstone was growing, and the new red sandstone was plastic earth, deep in the unfathomable cycles of the past, there was a huge frog, which, by doubling up in some unaccountable way, brought his hind feet immediately in front of his fore feet, so as to make the impressions in question, twenty inches in length, and so exactly resembling the footprints of a giant in walking, both in appearance and in position.

According to your understanding, at least the popular belief, Moses has said that the animals and Adam were made within the same twenty-four hours of time; that if the frog be classed among the living creatures which the waters brought forth on the third day — yet it could not have been made more than seventy-two hours before Adam was made — then of what utility is this singular, not to say ludicrous, frog theory of those old footprints, in defence of the truth of the Mosaic account of the creation? If we ought to believe Moses when he speaks of the creation of Adam, he certainly is worthy of our confidence in regard to the animals; therefore, Mr. Hitchcock's frog could have performed his mysterious doublings but a few hours sooner than Adam could have walked through the valley of the Connecticut. Such paltering with the credulity of the populace might have done very well with the ancient priesthood of Egypt, but certainly it is not becoming in the Christian philosopher of the nineteenth century.

This author, or some other of his class, in speaking of the footprints of animals found on the secondary or tertiary formations near Cincinnati, in Ohio, discourses learnedly to prove therefrom, in the remote period of the earth's plasticity, the existence of the mammoth, the megatherium, and many other mammals now extinct; but, wonderful to tell, intermixed with the others are human footprints, so distinct, so perfect, that even geological audacity dare not assign them to a frog. The author's ingenuity, however, readily informs him that the Indians who formerly inhabited that locality were fond of cutting impressions in the rock, and to them, he has no doubt, we are indebted for the human footprints. Why build a house and immediately tear it down? If the tracks of unknown beasts upon those rocks prove the former existence of species long since extinct, human footprints on the same rocks must prove the coeval existence of man. If the Indians cut the impressions of human feet, who will doubt that they, likewise, cut the concomitant footprints of the supposed extinct animals?

Mr. Hitchcock says: "Sometimes ossiferous caverns have been used by man as a place of habitation, or, more frequently, as a place of sepulture; and hence his bones, as well as fragments of pottery, and other relics of a rude people, are found so mixed with the remains of extinct animals as to lead to the inference that they were deposited during the same period. Indeed, in some of these caverns, in the south of France, it is still believed by some geologists that the remains of men were of contemporaneous deposition with those of the extinct mammalia."

It is strange, beyond our conception, that any people should have been so rude as to have selected as a place of habitation the charnel-house of extinct animals; it is stranger still that they should have been permitted to remain where they died, in their place of habitation; and not less strange, that any people should have searched for those caverns, filled with the bones of extinct monsters and ravenous beasts of the forest, as a most suitable place for the deposition of the remains of their loved lost friends.

Were it not for the traditional belief that Moses has said that men have existed on the earth but six thousand years, who would not conclude that those remains of men were of contemporaneous deposition with those of the extinct mammals with which they are interspersed? If geologists will lay aside this damaging gloss; will honestly read and understand Moses as was intended; will allow that the day of the creative week indicates a geological period of fifty thousand years; that the man who was made in the image and likeness of God, who was created on the evening of the sixth day, male and female, and commanded to multiply and replenish the earth, for many ages had multiplied, lived, and died, and given place to their more vigorous offspring; that not until the earth had become burdened with the teeming millions of her ancient populations, when many species of animals were being exterminated by them, when the necessities of the world required a superior intelligence to rule over them; that then God formed Adam out of the dust of the ground, and breathed into his nostrils the breath of life, and he became a living soul, — if geologists will take this rational view of the subject and honestly investigate it, in a short time they will satisfy themselves and show the world that the remains of the first governing man are found in rocks, at least in tertiary formations, while those of the animal man or Ethiopian will be found as old as the mammalia of the secondary period.

CHAPTER XXIX.

THE FLOOD — THE MEANS USED IN PRODUCING IT — EFFECTS — EXTENT.

"AND, behold, I, even I, do bring a flood of waters upon the earth, to destroy all flesh wherein is the breath of life from under heaven; and everything that is in the earth shall die."

In all the ages which had supervened from "the beginning" to the time when Adam made his advent into the world, it had not rained, but a mist went up and watered the whole face of the ground. If Adam came only six thousand years ago, every geologist will bear us out in the assertion that the world had teemed with animal life long anterior to that era, and that it flourished far more perfectly when there was no rain than it does at the present time.

Astronomers inform us that no clouds are ever discovered floating in the atmosphere of those planets of the solar system whose axes have little or no inclination to the plane of their orbits. The conclusion is irresistible, that the face of the ground in those worlds is watered by the mist which goes up for that purpose. The laws of nature are uniform, and what is true now, here or elsewhere under similar circumstances, has been true at all times and everywhere. Since there was no rain upon the earth in all its primitive ages, therefore there could have been no inclination of its axis to the plane of its orbit; hence there were no extremes of heat and cold, of flood and drought, but one unending spring from pole to pole, and a rich, exuberant soil from the river's banks to the mountain's top, and bounteous plenty all around the circle of the globe.

When the supreme governor of the world, who represented on earth the majesty of the heavens, had fallen from his high estate, and by reason of the intimate connection between the spiritual and physical laws, and as both were now without an executive officer, the perpendicular polarity of the earth was violently destroyed; and then for the first time the voice of an angry God was uttered in hoarse, reverberating thunder. While the vivid lightning, in lurid sheets, fiercely flashed athwart the hitherto serene skies, a black cloud spread from pole to pole, and the rain, descending in a deluge, washed off the loose primitive soil from mountain-top and steep hill-side into the valleys and plains, the poor culprits, driven out from the delightful haunts of Paradise, like timorous deer startled from their cover, fled on through the pitiless pelting of the raging storm, drenched through their goat-skin coats and their blood chilled almost to curdling in their veins by the wintry blasts. On and still on they fled in search of some more hospitable locality.

This is no fancy sketch, but is fully justified by the account of the inspired historian of the events which succeeded the fall. He makes known to us, by the figure of a flaming sword which turns every way to guard the passage, and by the cherubim which represent the fierce winds of the north, that the hyperborean garden was suddenly surrounded by a circumambient wall of ice. We have seen in another place that this result could be brought about only by the sudden destruction of the perpendicular polarity of the earth.

The curse imposed upon the earth for Adam's sake was that "Thorns also and thistles shall it bring forth to thee." It is evident to every observer that thorns and thistles flourish most on alluvial soils; therefore we must understand this curse to mean that the washing rains which were about to descend, would bear the rich soil from elevated to inferior localities, which, being submerged and soaked by the superabundant water, would become hard and impracticable for cultivation, and then, as now, would bring forth thorns and thistles.

This is the only natural means for producing the result named; and since the laws of nature are unchangeable, and since physical causes only produce physical results, therefore washing rains were threatened in the curse. "Thorns also and thistles shall it bring forth to thee." These noxious growths flourish in a troublesome way, on alluvial soils. The sudden and violent destruction of the perpendicular polarity of the axis of the earth to the plane of her orbit, produced such a commotion in our atmosphere, introduced such an abnormal state of things, that all nature was at war with itself, and the hitherto uniform evaporations by day, which were every night returned to the earth in the form of gentle dews, could no longer be governed by the certain and harmonious working of the normal laws; but being partial and irregular, were now and then gathered into thick clouds and descended in furious torrents of rain, destroying the beauty and productiveness of the mountains and hills, and causing an unnatural growth of noxious vegetation in the valleys and the plains. "Thorns also and thistles shall it bring forth to thee."

When the earth was in its upright posture the water flowed without obstruction through its internal channels from the sea to the surface, where it was evaporated, leaving the minerals which it had held in solution in the soil for the support of vegetation; and being reformed, it descended at night in the form of dew to moisten the ground, when it was taken up by capillary tubes, and flowing on, was formed into springs, creeks, and rivers, and was returned to the great reservoir of water, to be again propelled through the same channels, like the circulation of the blood in man.

The water which flowed through the internal ducts kept

them always washed out, for there were no accumulations of loose material or of alluvial matter then, and the salts, alkalies, and other minerals were held in solution until they were borne to the surface and deposited in the soil. When, however, the government of the world passed into the hands of "the prince of the power of the air," and she was violently lurched into a reclining position, the atmosphere and all the surroundings of our world were thereby thrown into confusion. The water was still evaporated, but not being regularly returned to the earth as dew, the firmament was soon surcharged with vapory particles, or, more properly, with the constituent gases of water. The electrical condition by which the water had been evaporated, or, rather, decomposed, being removed, these gases first rushed together into thick clouds, and then descended in torrents of rain.

The soil was washed off, and was borne along, with uprooted trees and dislocated rocks, by the turbid rivers into the ocean; by the tidal throbbings of which this loose material was forced into the internal ducts, and was necessarily deposited at the short turns and outgoing branches of the earth's arteries. For near two thousand years those alluvial deposits were accumulated in the internal channels, so that when "the corruption of all flesh had ripened the world for destruction, those channels were stopped up, and the surging waters finding no outward vent, the earth's crust was rent into fragments, the valleys were upheaved, the hills were blown into atoms, the mountains were upthrown, toppled down, and crushed, and the old surface of the earth was utterly destroyed. "All the fountains of the great deep were broken up, and the windows of heaven were opened. And the rain was upon the earth forty days and forty nights."

When the internal waters gushed out at the rents and fissures made by the mighty throes of nature, they rushed over the face of the ground, so that an immense surface was exposed to evaporation or decomposition by the sun's electricity; therefore a vast accumulation of the constituent gases was gathered up into the atmosphere, and when they were released, they rushed together, and a dense cloud, from pole to pole and from zenith to nadir, spread all around the globe; and at the command of God, the waters came down in floods upon the earth. "And the rain was upon the earth forty days and forty nights."

"And the waters prevailed exceedingly upon the earth, and all the high hills that were under the whole heavens were covered."

This tremendous physical result must have been produced immediately by a corresponding or adequate physical cause; though, indirectly, the moral action of the world's great representative was the baleful power which put this cause in operation. That the cause which finally wrought out the cataclysm was in operation from the time of the fall, in no way vitiates the truth of the declaration that the world was destroyed by water on account of the corruption of the generation then upon the earth; for God, being omniscient, had prepared this destruction for a day and an hour when "the corruption of all flesh" should make the world ripe for destruction.

It has been thought by some that the rain which fell at the time of the flood was the first which had ever fallen on the earth, because it is the first mentioned, and because then the rainbow made its first appearance. We conclude this idea to be incorrect, on the first ground, for the reason that the production of alluvial soil is as clearly evidence of the fall of rain as any declaration could make it. "Thorns also and thistles shall it bring forth to thee."

This announcement renders it morally certain that rain began to fall immediately after Adam's expulsion from the garden of Eden. The additional curse pronounced upon

Cain for murdering his brother, shows that he should fly to a country whose hills and mountains had been denuded of their soil by washing rains, and whose valleys and plains, submerged in the superabundance of the waters which had fallen upon them, and had been poured down upon them from the surrounding uplands, had been converted into swamps and marshes, and therefore, even with much labor, incapable of yielding large crops. "When thou tillest the ground, it shall not henceforth yield unto thee her strength."

The second ground upon which the speculators conclude that the rains at the flood were the first upon the earth, viz., that the rainbow then appeared for the first time, is by no means conclusive; for the rainbow did not appear during the forty days' rain, nor for at least twelve months thereafter. After the flood had subsided, and after Noah had come down from the ark, had built an altar, and offered thereon burnt-offerings, then "God said, I do set my bow in the cloud, and it shall be for a token of a covenant between me and the earth."

Since the rainbow did not appear for some time after the flood, which was brought on partially by the rain of forty consecutive days, therefore the appearance of the rainbow is no evidence that the first rain which fell upon the earth was at the time of the flood. It proves, however, another, and very important fact, namely, until after the flood there had been no partial showers, or sunshine and rain at the same time.

We have seen in the last chapter by what instrumentality the fountains of the great deep were broken up, and that by this means the flood was brought about. It now remains for us to inquire to what extent the waters did actually prevail. We are told that there is no question here, for the declaration that they prevailed fifteen cubits, or nearly thirty feet above the highest mountains, and covered the face of the whole earth, is too broad and emphatic to leave any room to doubt its meaning.

In construing any writing we must give it the meaning which renders it intelligible, consistent with itself, and with well-ascertained extraneous facts; and this rule is applied in the construction of all mere human writings. If one part of a legal document state clearly and emphatically that certain real estate, with all the rights and appurtenances thereunto belonging, is conveyed to a party, and afterward, in the same deed, it is stated that a certain mill-site on said premises is reserved to the grantor, will any court of justice give the mill-site to the party to whom the general estate has been conveyed? Or, if a third party has had a right of way or of water, on the transferred property, "so long time that the memory of man runneth not to the contrary," though no mention is thereof made in the deed of conveyance, yet the courts will so construe the unlimited language that these vested rights of others are not intended to be conveyed. Even oral testimony sometimes may be admitted, to show that the language of a written document, which appears to be general in its application, has, in fact, a limited signification.

Why is this rational, not to say liberal mode of construction extended to all other writings, and ignored, violently rejected, in the reading of the Bible? It does appear that none but professed enemies and disbelievers in its authenticity would contend for the absurd interpetrations which unlearned and bigoted would-be defenders of the faith so strenuously, if not impiously contend for in regard to the books of inspiration.

If the language used by Moses is capable of two modes of construction, the one brings him in continual conflict with himself, with common sense, and with facts clearly established in nature; but the other mode of interpretation shows him to be consistent with himself, consistent with common sense, consistent with the revelations of science — in a word, which presents him as perfect master of the subjects of which he treats, and makes his the grandest and most glorious system of moral, physical, and intellectual learning ever presented for the admiration of man, — it is but just that his pretended friends should adopt the latter mode, and cease to stultify themselves by pretending to be believers in the truth of the writings of the great lawgiver, yet stabbing him in the very house of his friends, and doing all that their weak intellects and vast presumption will enable them to do towards rendering the great philosopher and prophet odious and contemptible?

This is the rule of construction which we have adopted, by which, at least in our judgment, the discrepancies discovered by many in the writings of Moses do not appear, or are easily reconciled. If, for instance, the man made at the close of the sixth day, in the image and likeness of God, who is spoken of in the first chapter of Genesis, be taken for Adam, who was not made until after the grand sabbath had passed, or, at the earliest, in the eighth geological period, if the second be a recapitulation of the first chapter, then to understand the subject, and to reconcile the apparent discrepancies between the same event, is an extremely difficult task; and with the traditional interpretation the same is true of many other passages in Holy Writ.

Without further remark, however, we announce our view of the subject in hand to be that the entire surface of the earth has not at any one time been submerged by water, and it is unfair to so interpret our author. Moses indeed says that the waters covered the face of the whole earth, which might seem to justify a universal application, and for the purposes of the history which he was writing, is literally true; but, in order to ascertain whether we are to understand him as saying that the waters covered the earth from pole to pole and all around its circumference, we must inquire into the moral cause and the physical agencies by which this grand result was produced. We do not intend to be understood to say, with the infidel, that Moses stated what was not true; nor with Mr. Hitchcock, and other tradition-fettered Christians, that the profound philosopher and inspired historian did not understand what he was writing.

What would be thought of the honesty of the man who would insist on construing the whole of the Bible as the commentators do the passage before us? For example, it is positively declared that all flesh was corrupt; yet Noah was found to be a just man, who walked with God; and, although it is said that God had determined to destroy all flesh, and afterward that every living creature wherein is the breath of life was actually destroyed, yet the same author tells us, and in the very same account, that Noah and his family—being eight souls, and two of every living creature upon the face of the earth—were saved; but who would contend, therefore, that Moses has convicted himself of falsehood?

In another place he says that Adam called the woman Eve because she was the mother of all living. Will any one insist that Moses intended to represent Eve as the mother of the monkey, or of any other animal except of the Adamic race, whose history he was then writing? No more are we to understand him as meaning to convey the idea of a universal deluge by the statement, "And the waters prevailed exceedingly upon the earth; and all the high hills that were under the whole heaven were covered;" and common honesty and fairness would compel us, before coming to such a conclusion, to examine the subject thoroughly, both by its internal facts and external surroundings.

The internal circumstances are these:—All flesh had

corrupted the ways of the Almighty, which the author specifically states was brought about through the crime of miscegenation, or by the sons of God intermarrying with the daughters of men, and immediately afterward that all flesh had corrupted His ways. By any fair rule of construction, all flesh, or the lower animals, had corrupted the ways of God, as man had done, by miscegenation. He had commanded all the animals to reproduce after their kind, and the general practice of unnatural crosses had subverted the order which He had established; therefore the destruction of the mixed races of men and of animals was necessary, or the designs of the Omnipotent would have been thwarted, and Adam, not God, would have been the creator of every living animal. But since the Adamic race had been in the world less than two thousand years, notwithstanding their remarkable longevity and fecundity, yet by no possibility could they have filled or spread over the entire surface of the globe, especially as the three-fourths thereof, now under water, was then dry land, and all of it vastly more fertile than now; nor could the crime of miscegenation have extended beyond the limits of the region occupied by the Adams.

The design for bringing on the flood being the destruction of that corruption, would be fully accomplished, if the flood should cover those countries inhabited by the miscegenating men and animals; hence, to submerge the entire surface of the earth was unnecessary. God never performs a superfluous work, therefore Moses intends us to understand him to say that the waters prevailed sufficiently to destroy the corruption of blood from the face of the earth.

Again: we have seen that the flood was brought on by the power of God in the operation of the instrumentalities called the laws of nature. But the waters could, by no natural possibility, prevail over the whole earth, so as to reach a height of fifteen cubits, or near thirty feet above the highest mountains, unless, probably, by the complete expulsion of all the waters from the body of the earth. If all the blood in the human body were expelled therefrom, and retained upon its surface, it might possibly be covered to a depth proportionate to the distance of three miles — the height to which the waters arose in the flood; but to what end would this have been done, and would the God of nature have exercised unnatural power without a purpose? The Adamic and mixed races could not have extended over more than a comparatively small area of country, and since the design of the Almighty was the destruction of that corruption, therefore a universal deluge was unnecessary, and hence, we may fairly infer, was not sent upon the world.

That the mixed races, who were descended from Seth, and the mixed animals, which were about them, were submerged and destroyed by the flood, is abundantly apparent, both from internal and external evidences. Moses has declared the fact in the spirit of revelation, and geology proves that about the time to which he alludes the world was subjected to a wide-spread, watery revolution. The theory of some geologists, of continuous upheaval and subsidence of the islands and continents, will not satisfactorily account for the grand revolution in the earth's crust almost everywhere visible; and Moses alone gives us a rational solution of the mighty problem: "All the fountains of the great deep were broken up."

If the design of the Almighty could be accomplished without the absolute inundation of the entire surface of the earth, and if the universal form of expression used by Moses on this occasion, be employed by him, in conformity with the hyperbolical idiom of the Eastern languages, in regard to this and other facts, to express energetically general but not universal ideas, then may we not, without fear of the charge of infidelity, proceed directly to the investigation of the extraneous facts, which prove that the flood, though general, was by no means universal; though mighty in its operations and grand in its results, yet that the entire surface of the earth was not submerged beneath its turbid waves?

If the whole earth were covered with water at the time mentioned, to the depth of thirty feet above the highest mountains, or three miles above the plains, how were the islands and the Western continent peopled? We are told that the aborigines of America might have reached it in canoes by crossing Behring's Strait, and thence they could have spread out over all the continent; but is this conjecture at all probable?

In the first place, the traditions of all the North American Indians make their fathers to have come from the north-east, and not from the north-west. Again, there is no such people as the American Indian in Asia, in Africa, or in Europe; and it is difficult to imagine how immigration could produce a new race of men, especially as no such result has followed from its settlement by Europeans since its discovery by Columbus. Like begets like in the Western as well as in the Eastern continent; but the aborigines of America are different from all the people of the East in tastes, in pursuits, in personal appearance, in everything which marks animals to be of the same species.

If the canoe conjecture satisfactorily accounts for the original peopling of the Western continent, will it answer to explain how the red man came to be upon the isles of the sea? In the West India Islands, in the Caribbean Sea, in the Atlantic, in the Indian, in the Pacific Oceans, in the South Sea Islands, in the northern zone, wherever there is land, there the red man is found, except only in the Eastern continent and the adjacent islands; and yet the superior white man, never, until within the last few years, has gone beyond the limits of his native continent.

The canoe solution will not explain why the Indians, and they alone, came to be dispersed over so large a portion of the surface of the earth, and we must look for some more rational and satisfactory explanation. It will not do to suppose that the art of navigation since the flood, or in the historic ages, could have been carried to such an extent as to enable navigators to have reached and populated the Western continent and the distant islands of every sea, unless it should have been done by the Phœnicians. Who would seriously conjecture that the inhabitants of the Sandwich and Fejee Islands, or the Esquimaux of the north, are descended from the Phœnicians, within the last two or three thousand years? But if such a proposition might be entertained, the difficulties are by no means removed; and the question still recurs, how were the islands supplied with animal life.

We are still told that all the people of the whole earth spread out from Mount Ararat, and that the islands and the Western continent have been populated by means of boats and canoes. If this solution satisfactorily accounts for the presence of men all over the world, how came the animals in those localities? The wolf, the bear, the panther, the llama, the buffalo, the mammoth, the vast varieties of beasts which roam over the forests of America, many of which are unknown in the Old World; the air thronged with immense flocks of birds and wild fowl, while a thousand varieties of insects and of reptiles swarm and creep through every thicket, swamp, and glen all over the continent and the islands of the seas. And how, we ask, has all this teeming animal life been brought to the Western continent and the widely dispersed islands? If it were the work of man, what was his design for importing, not only to him useless, but vicious animals,—the ravenous beasts, annoying insects and venomous reptiles? To state the hypothesis, it would seem, is sufficient to show its absurdity.

If immigrants from Asia had imported the animals into America and the islands in canoes, we should certainly expect to find none here except the smaller and more useful kinds, instead of the extinct mammoth and megatherium and now existent species, the moose, the sloth, the buffalo, the skunk, the wolf, the bear, the panther; enormous birds of prey, and the mightiest and most deadly serpents known in all the earth. Can we imagine an Indian with his family navigating the watery waste of the Pacific, or ploughing the boisterous waves of the Atlantic in his frail canoe, freighted with such a menagerie as might be collected upon the continent of America, or in any of the islands? No useful animals for domestic purposes are found in any of these localities, but only wild and ravenous beasts and such animals as may be made useful to man by the labors and wiles of the chase.

The canoe or even ship navigation conjecture, will not give a rational solution to the problem before us; wherefore we must search for the truth in some other direction. With the traditional exposition of the Mosaic account of the flood before them, many honest inquirers after truth have right here been driven into quasi, if not into downright infidelity; for the question, unbidden, will continue to present itself, How came men and animals to be on the continent of America, and on the islands of every sea, when first visited by Europeans?

The account which Moses gives of the creation and the flood is therefore flatly denied, or wholly ignored by some, and meanly evaded by others; so that none, no, not one man with common sense or a particle of rational reflection, gives it, or can give to that history (so replete in itself with glorious truth, yet so absurd and inconsistent with itself and stubborn facts, as it is explained by the commentators) his hearty confidence, his firm and unwavering faith. Hence, men who think have been driven to adopt the theory that the work of creation is not limited to time or locality, but that animal being, which evidently springs from the earth, is produced whenever and wherever the circumstances are favorable to such production.

From this stand-point, Dr. Nott and others have concluded that the races of men are some forty-five or fifty in number, and that as many pairs at different times and in different places have sprung into existence in the localities in which they are found—the Indian in America, the Sandwich Islander on his island, the Australian in Australia, and the Esquimaux in the frozen regions of the North—and that the animals got to the various places of their habitations in the same way.

Although this theory is in opposition to revelation, and therefore cannot be true, and although it will not bear thorough scrutiny in the light of reason, and hence must be false, yet all candid men must admit that it is a much more rational view of the subject under consideration than the canoe importation theory of the theologians.

If the account which Moses gives of the creation and the flood be tested by the common-sense rule of construction which is applied to every other writing, the subject of filling the Western continent and the distant islands with living beings will be relieved of very many of the difficulties which have been thrown around it by the traditions of the fathers. "By your traditions ye have made the writings of Moses of none effect."

We have shown the folly of attempting to explain the question, How came men and animals in America and the islands, by the canoe importation conjecture; and the infidel theory of their spontaneous production by the ordinary energies of the earth in its present condition, is fully and satisfactorily answered, and ought to be forever put to rest by the simple fact that, in all the historic ages, not a single animal being has been so produced.

If ignorance and bigotry, if infidelity and presumption could be hushed for awhile, if the veil could be removed from their hearts when Moses is read, and if that great philosopher and inspired historian might be allowed to speak for himself, and to explain his own meaning, much might be known by us which is now considered by the learned to be "hidden mysteries." In this rational view of the inspired writings, and an independent consideration of the facts in nature, we hope to throw some light upon the question, How came men and animals in America and the islands? or, at least, to give impetus to thought in the right direction. All finite subjects are comprehensible by the finite mind, and we are confident that whenever honest investigation is directed to the facts contained in the philosophic and historic writings of Moses, they will be clearly understood, for to this end was he inspired to write them.

CHAPTER XXX.

How the Western Continent and Islands were Peopled — Description of the Ark — The Dove bringing in an Olive Leaf.

HOW were the Western continent and isles of the ocean supplied with animal life?

Since canoe transportation and new creations will not satisfactorily answer this question, we must look for some more rational solution. The world, according to our theory, and, as we think, according to the teaching of Moses, although a great globe, was aptly represented by the human body. The waters were gathered into one place, and the dry ground everywhere else appeared. The sea, then, could not have covered a space of more than six thousand miles in circumference, or some two thousand miles in diameter, if, as we have supposed, it bore the proportion to the size of the earth which the heart does to the body.

No part of the earth was then locked up in ice, and there were no extremes of heat and cold, no pitiless storms to drive back animal life from spreading out from pole to pole, and all around the globe; so that when Adam came, as we have before advanced, the world must have contained many more men and animals than it has had the capacity of supporting since his fall.

The dry ground was crossed only by rivulets and rivers, as the surface of the human body is checkered by external veins. These furnished abundant supplies of water everywhere, but offered no serious obstruction to the diffusion of men and of animals. They had, doubtlessly, spread all over the earth, and, for vast ages before Adam came, had fed upon the luxuriant herbage and luscious fruits, slaked their rising thirst in the limpid waters of the sparkling brooks, lolled beneath the glorious shade of the majestic groves, and basked in the genial sunshine of the happy, rectangular world.

The whole earth was therefore teeming with men and animals when the flood came — when, by the extraordinary surging of "the seas," the waters were forced vehemently into the world's arteries, which had become externally closed, and their granite walls and the adamantine hills were forced upward, and the waters rushed over the surface of the earth. Were the outer extremities of the arteries in a man shut up, and were the blood expelled from the heart into them with sufficient force to burst them, and tear open the overlying flesh, such a body would present a mangled mass which would resemble the map of the world in its present condition.

Notwithstanding the blood would gush out over such a body, and notwithstanding the regions of the heart would be overwhelmed, yet the extremities, the head, the arms, the legs, would not be submerged. Neither was the entire surface of the earth inundated when "all the fountains of the great deep were broken up," and the men and animals on the points left dry were not destroyed. In this way we see no difficulty in accounting for the presence of men and animals in America, and in all the islands of the most distant seas. If there be no other rational view of this subject, then this must be correct.

Many beasts and birds are in the Eastern which are not in the Western world, and many others are in the West which are not in the East. These facts prove that all the animals of the whole earth were not in that country called by Moses "Eden," and by the Greeks and Romans "Atlantis." The more useful animals are all found in the East, while many varieties of beasts and of birds and of reptiles unknown there are discovered in the forests of America.

The ancient land of Eden must have extended over the head and heart of the pristine earth; and when Adam was driven out of the garden at the head, and his return was cut off from thence by icebergs, the body of the earth was still left open to him, and, guided by his superior intelligence, he was led to locate near the sea, or the heart of the world. That was evidently the best, the most fertile, and most pleasant region left to him in the cursed earth.

In that yet comparatively happy land, his descendants, except Cain and his family, who were driven far to the east, into the land of Nod, lived and multiplied and carried on the crime of miscegenation, and of producing the crosses of the inferior animals, until "the corruption of the ways of God" cried to heaven for redress.

When the arteries of the world were bursted, the waters rushed out and prevailed in the regions of the heart, so that they arose to the height of about thirty feet above the highest mountains in the land of Eden or of Atlantis; and every living thing there, except what was in the ark with Noah, was destroyed. The ark, however, was triumphantly borne aloft upon the angry crest of the furiously rushing waters of the flood.

The grand aorta of the world probably arose between where Ireland and the island of Great Britain are, descended through the British Channel and into the straits of Gibraltar, through the Mediterranean Sea, and then deeper into the earth, as it does at this day. When the upper crust was upheaved and torn into fragments by the mighty surging of the pent-up waters, the staunch vessel prepared by Noah, without sail or rudder, and left to the mercy of the winds and the waves, was borne on by the now exposed current of the grand aorta, amid the debris of the crushed and ruined world. On, and still on, the noble bark rode the turbid waves in safety, though nought else could withstand their rage. It passed unscathed the frowning pillars of Hercules, over the seething billows of the Mediterranean, and by a huge wave was lifted far into the interior of Asia, and, at the end of one hundred and fifty days, settled quietly down upon the mountains of Ararat.

Had there not been a vast accumulation of the waters in the region where the ark was driven and tossed, and had there been no depression elsewhere, how could a strong east wind have assuaged them? and why was this stated by Moses to be the means employed for their reduction, unless he intended for us to understand him according to the rational view here taken of the subject? The design of the flood was the destruction of the miscegenated men and animals in Eden, therefore the submergence of the entire surface of the globe was unnecessary, and hence it was not accomplished.

The mixed race of men sprung from Cain and his Indian wives are not included among those who were doomed to destruction, for they were neither the sons of God or a pure race, nor were theirs the daughters of men or of the Adams. When he declared his punishment to be greater than he could bear, although no mitigation thereof was granted him, yet the promise was given of exemption from personal violence, which, we have seen, extended to his mixed offspring, was so understood by him, and was still in full force. "Whosoever, therefore, shall kill Cain, vengeance shall be taken upon him seven-fold."

Since the miscegenated race of Cain had been expressly permitted by the Almighty, and that too for nearly two thousand years, and since no allusion whatever is made to Cain or his descendants in the description of the moral cause of the flood, therefore they cannot be included, except by implication, among those who were devoted to destruction. The presumption would be violent, and cannot be indulged, unless something can be found in the writings of Moses, our only authority on the subject, upon which it may be rationally based; hence we confidently conclude that the descendants of Cain were not involved in the wide-spread destruction of the flood.

One great object of the advent of Adam, a fundamental principle for the government of the world, was that he should prevent the extermination of the various orders of being which God had established. If all the animals were not in the country were Noah was, and if a pair of every species upon the whole earth were not taken into the ark — which is rendered utterly impossible by the dimensions —

then God, being unchangeable, whose purposes are the same yesterday, to day, and forever, would not send the destruction of the flood upon numberless species and whole genera of the unoffending creatures which he had made.

The intermarriage of the sons of God or the red men with the daughters of men was the crying sin of the world; hence, clearly, the former would not be taken by Noah into the ark. Yet since they were spread all over the earth, since their mission was not accomplished, or the fact would have been alluded to by Moses; since they had bruised the heel of the seed of the woman by their agency in bringing on the flood, and the subsequent ills to the sons of Adam which have grown out of that event; and since the seed of the woman must bruise the head of the serpent or of the red race, therefore the latter could not then be destroyed. For all these, and many other strong reasons, we conclude again that the flood, though general, was not universal.

From a rational point of view all of Asia could not have been submerged, because the Mongolian race or the descendants of Cain, whose authoritative history extends far beyond the flood, are still there. All of America was not under the waters, because the pure-blooded red man—not one specimen of whom can be found in the Eastern continent—has always been here; nor were the islands overwhelmed, because the Indians could never have reached them in their canoes, with the wild beasts and venomous reptiles which are now upon them.

The Pacific Ocean has never been subject to that tremendous commotion which so prevails in the Atlantic. This shows that however the heart of the sick man may contract and wildly surge, as in the Atlantic, yet the weakened throbbings of arterial circulation only are exhibited in the Pacific. This of itself, were there no other existent facts, would lead us to the conclusion that the eastern portion of

Asia and the western part of America, and possibly the whole intervening space, were not under the water at the time when Noah went into the ark.

It is probable that while Eden, Atlantis, or that part of the globe lying between the western coasts of Europe and Africa and eastern shore of America, possibly including much of both continents, were covered by the waters of the flood, the opposite hemisphere was dry land; and that when by the strong east wind the accumulated waters were driven out of the Atlantic, they spread out to the west, and then, and not until then, was the Pacific formed.

The presence of the negro in Africa is a strong reason in favor of the supposition that all of that country was not submerged; yet since he is treated in every other connection as an animal, just as the orang-outang and gorilla are, so may he have been treated in this place. There are, however, stronger reasons for concluding that all of Africa, as well as of Asia and America, was not under the waters at that time; as the presence there of enormous wild beasts, carnivora, and herbivora, and mighty and venomous serpents.

The ark was five hundred and fifty feet long, nearly ninety-two feet wide, and three stories high. The upper story, we may suppose, was used as the storehouse, and for the accommodation of Noah and his family; the second was assigned to the graminivora, and the third to the carnivora and the reptiles. This floor was, no doubt, divided into compartments, so as to keep the animals from destroying each other. The same must have also been true of the second, or the smaller and weaker species of the graminivorous animals, during the five months in which the ark was tossed by the boisterous waves of the flood, would certainly have been trampled to death by the larger and stronger kinds.

In the upper story might have been stored immense quantities of grain and hay for the support of the animals which lived on that kind of food; but upon what were the carnivora supported for the twelve months which they spent in the ark? Had the largest varieties of the graminivorous animals been in the ark, even the vast stores of vegetable matter, which was no doubt gathered in the ark by Noah, might have been exhausted, and famine and death would have made the ark a terrible charnel-house.

If it be rational to conclude that sufficient stores might have been placed in the ark for a twelvemonth's supply for all the animals which live on vegetable matter, yet how could the carnivora have been supported? It will not do to say that they were miraculously sustained; for natural, physical means were employed to save them from destruction by the flood, and ample provisions were made for the support of Noah and his family. "Of every clean beast thou shalt take to thee by sevens."

The offal of these clean beasts, or those of them which were used by Noah, might be sufficient to support some of the smaller carnivora, but would by no means be enough to feed them all. The fowls of the air were taken by sevens, yet their superfluous numbers would have failed to satiate the ravenous appetites of all the carnivora. The food which Noah was commanded to store in the ark for himself, and for the animals, must have meant vegetable supplies; therefore the larger and more destructive carnivora could not have been in the ark; and, hence, all of Africa was not covered by the water.

The larger kind of animals, as the elephant and the rhinoceros, the lion and the tiger, the anaconda and the boa-constrictor, have never been found in Europe, or any part of the world inhabited by the Caucasian race; except possibly along the borders, where they have approached those countries occupied by Mongolians and Africans. If those animals were in the ark, is it not a little singular that they have never been found in countries which appear evidently to have been submerged, and where history clearly proves the descendants of Noah to have inhabited? Everything goes to show that all of the earth has not been under water at the same time since the creation of animate beings upon its surface.

It is just as evident that there was, about the time of Noah, a wide-spread, a general, an universal watery revolution; and since no human beings like them have ever been met with, therefore he and his family were the only individuals of that race who were saved from the flood. Every living thing in all the land of Eden or Atlantis, where the race of Adam inhabited, except what was in the ark, was destroyed; for the waters prevailed one hundred and fifty days before they began to assuage, and Noah did not venture from his place of safety, neither let out the animals which were with him, until a whole year and nine days had passed. It is equally clear that, notwithstanding the general language employed by Moses, yet the entire surface of the earth was not all this time under water. "But even unto this day, when Moses is read, the veil is upon their heart."

We need not make too much allowance for the idiom of the language in which Moses wrote, nor yet for the peculiarity of the people for whom he wrote; because, if one of our own people lived in the valley of the Mississippi, and that river overflow his banks, the man thus surrounded and shut in from the world, in afterwards describing his situation, would use the expression, "The whole face of the earth was covered with water." In any part of the country, when a very heavy rain is described, we hear it said continually that "the whole face of the earth was covered with water." This mode of expression, we presume, is used by us as similar language was used by Moses to convey the idea of an extraordinary amount of superficial water; and therefore we need not puzzle ourselves on that score, or stultify the account of the flood, by attaching an extreme meaning to a form of expression so generally employed by ourselves to convey a general but not a universal idea.

Had the entire surface of the earth been submerged for a whole year under salt water, all the vegetation of the whole earth would certainly have been destroyed, and a new creation of grass, of herbs, and of trees would have been absolutely necessary. Had this been the case, would not Moses have mentioned the fact? No difficulty whatever is raised by him on this subject, and we presume that none existed. It will not do to say that vegetation was miraculously preserved under the water, for it would have been just as easy for Omnipotence to have preserved animal life in the same way; but since the latter was cared for by the use of adequate means, therefore all vegetation which remained so long a time under water was then, as it would be now, utterly destroyed.

Too much water is as certain death to vegetation as is too much heat. We are told, however, that the occasion of which we are speaking was an extraordinary one, and the necessities of the case absolutely demanded the miraculous preservation of vegetation under the waters. In every other instance, when Moses wishes us to understand that a miracle is wrought, or when something is done contrary to the ordinary working of the laws of nature, he not only tells the facts, but minutely describes all the attendant circumstances. In this instance, however, where it is supposed that a most stupendous miracle is wrought, our author makes no mention of it, not even the slightest allusion to it; hence no miracle of the kind was wrought.

Preparation was for years going on for the preservation of animal life, and Noah took his family, and the animals, and a sufficient amount of food for a year's supply, into the ark, and in this way escaped a watery death. Vegetation is as surely destroyed by water as is animal life; and yet no mention is made by Moses of any effort by Noah to preserve the seeds even of the most useful grains, much less of the trees of the forest.

At the termination of the flood, we find that, instead of vegetation being preserved by Noah in the ark, the dove found the trees growing, and brought to Noah an olive leaf, not dead nor fallen off, but plucked from the tree; therefore the trees were kept alive and growing through the flood; but since they could not live so long as twelve months under water, therefore the flood could not have been all this while upon the surface of the earth.

After the tempestuous waters of the flood had driven and tossed the ark for five months, the mightiest wave of the lacerated heart of the world lifted it, with its living freight, far into the interior of Asia, and, retroceding, left her upon the mountains of Ararat. It is impossible for us to conceive how the idea has become so wide-spread in Christendom, that the ark was floating above those mountains, and that, the waters abating, she settled down upon them.

Moses says that "the waters prevailed upon the earth an hundred and fifty days, and after the hundred and fifty days the waters were abated; and the ark rested in the seventh month, on the seventeenth day of the month, upon the mountains of Ararat." The flood came on the seventeenth day of the second month, just five months previous to the time when the ark was stranded in Western Asia. Five months, of thirty days each, are one hundred and fifty days; therefore, when the ark rested on the mountains of Ararat, the waters were at their highest, for not until after that were the waters abated.

There is nothing whatever in the text requiring us to

understand that the ark rested on the top of the mountains. We speak of a man living in the mountains, and correctly, too, although we know that he lives in a beautiful little valley on some mountain stream, while the mountains rise on every side to an immense height above his residence. A man tells you that he killed a grizzly bear on the Rocky Mountains, but, in detailing the circumstances of the event, he informs you that the killing was actually accomplished in one of the deepest gorges of the range. Shall we do violence to the language of Moses, if we conclude that the ark was driven up to, and into, a valley on some stream running through the mountains of Ararat?

No mention is made of Noah and his family, and of the animals which were with them in the ark, coming down from a high mountain after they had left the ark; but, by every fair rule of construction, we must understand that, where the ark rested, there Noah built the altar, and there the promise was given that the world should no more be destroyed by a watery revolution. The mountains of Ararat, the Ural, and the Himalayan chains, it would seem, were that boundary where Omnipotence had said to the rushing flood, "Thus far shalt thou come, and here thy proud waves shalt be stayed;" and on the crest of the mightiest billow the ark was borne up and rested among or on the high grounds near the mountains of Ararat.

For five long months, or one hundred and fifty days, Noah, shut up in the ark, was driven and tossed by the furious waves of the Atlantic and the Mediterranean, not yet brought within their bounds, or relieved of the overcharge of waters, which afterwards flowed off to fill up recent depressions and newly excavated beds, where are now the oceans, gulfs, and seas. It is not strange that his mind had been so exercised by his terrible voyage, and by the grand revolution then going on in the earth, that, for at least two months after the ark "rested upon the mountains of Ararat," he did not dare even to open the window of the ark.

When, finally, he did so, and looked out, the tops of the mountains were seen. We must not conclude, from this, that the waters were still surrounding and covering all of the mountains except their tops, but just what Moses says, that those within the ark saw the tops of the mountains. We cannot conceive how the waters, which had been abating for some two months, had gone down only a few feet, and that in forty days thereafter Noah should have expected them to have been entirely removed, as he certainly did, or he would not have sent out for the purpose of ascertaining the fact.

The window was a small aperture, and, as a matter of course, was placed as high in the wall of the ark, or as far from the water as might be, and when it was opened, those within could not see through the thick wall except straight before them. All that is proven by the tops of the mountains being seen is that the ark was in their neighborhood, and when Noah opened the window and looked up through it, he could see only the tops of the mountains. "A window shalt thou make to the ark, and in a cubit shalt thou finish it above." This would seem to indicate that the window was either in the top, or near the top of the ark, and that it was only two feet square.

The dash of the waters, which bore the ark out to the mountains of Ararat, did not remain long there, or did not extend far beyond where the ark rested; because the raven which was sent out by Noah evidently went into or beyond the mountains, and there remained until its mate was released from confinement. From this time until the animals were all released was several, certainly more than two, weeks, during which time the raven would undoubtedly have perished, had it not found dry ground and grain or fruit for its support.

You say that the dove which was at first sent out about the same time with the raven, found not where to rest its feet, and therefore came back to Noah, and was taken in by him. We suppose that the dove, on this first tour of discovery, flew westward over the wide watery waste, where lately the ark had been driven in its trackless career, and consequently found nothing upon which to rest, and, when worn out in the fruitless search for such an object, it naturally enough returned to the ark.

Had it flown eastward, it might surely have found a resting-place, for the tops of the mountains had been seen for several days at least previous to this fruitless search for a resting-place. Seven days later it went out, and not only found dry ground, but an olive-tree with leaves growing upon it. It is clear, therefore, that the dove did not go in the same direction, when it went out the second time, that it had gone the first.

These facts prove unmistakably that, even in the neighborhood of the ark, the flood had not remained on the land all the time that Noah was in the ark; indeed, that the water could not have continued for any considerable length of time over the country about that locality. But since a part of the earth was not under the water during the whole time of Noah's stay in the ark, therefore the entire surface of the earth need not necessarily be submerged at all. If all of the earth were not covered, then the animals and the men in the localities which were exempt would not be destroyed. The descendants of Noah certainly have occupied the western part of Asia, the northern part of Africa, and all of Europe; but it cannot be proven from history that they were ever in any other part of the world until within a very recent period.

Very different races of men have always inhabited Asia, Africa, and America from those who have dwelt in Europe. Many animals are found in the former places which were never known in the latter; therefore these diverse races were not descended from Noah—all the animals were not in the ark; hence the whole face of the earth was not covered by the waters of the flood; but the men and animals in America and the islands, as well as in Asia and Africa, remained in those localities through the flood, and their offspring have remained on them up to the present time.

It remains for us now to inquire into the geological effects produced in the earth's crust by this grand watery revolution, and to show the erroneous views of geologists in regard to the handwriting of God upon the rocks, or, rather, that there is no difficulty in reconciling the Mosaic cosmogony with geological learning.

CHAPTER XXXI.

THE COSMOGONY OF MOSES COMPARED WITH THE FACTS OF GEOLOGY—THE EARTH WHEN A CRUST—FORMATION OF ROCKS—THE THREE STAGES IN THE LIFE OF MAN COMPARED WITH THE THREE REVOLUTIONS IN THE EARTH.

IN the development of the sciences, it has ever been the case that men have formed parties; one of which have insisted that the discovered truths of science prove the Bible to be false, and the other that the sciences are contrary to the Bible, and therefore they are untrue. Time and further investigation have shown the blind wickedness of the one, and the stupid folly of the other, so far that in all of the sciences there has been a homologation, how bungling soever it may have been, except only in the grand science of geology; and in regard to this we believe that the truth of God in science, and in revelation, is destined to a more lucid vindication than in any which have preceded.

Already the folly of construing Moses as having asserted that the works of creation began only six thousand years ago has been seen, acknowledged, and abandoned by all persons of respectable intelligence, though the authority of Moses may suffer never so much. The voice of astronomy was not understood, or not heeded by the Caucasian race until within a very recent period; but now its teachings are received by all. No question is now raised between it and the Bible; but it is considered as powerfully illustrative of the beauty and glory of the works of nature, and of revelation. So all the sciences, except geology, are now found to be the handmaidens of religion, and exponents of the natural, as well as of the revealed laws of God. It is known that geology contains truth, and in its further progress it certainly will be found more powerfully to corroborate and illustrate revelation than anything that has gone before.

The friends as well as the enemies of the Bible have agreed in the reading of the handwriting of God upon the rocks, to arrange them, according to age, into primary, secondary, and tertiary formations, and the alluvial and diluvial, or recent accumulations. It is most generally thought by geologists that the granitic and other hypozoic rocks, or, as they are denominated by some, the plutonic rocks, are of igneous formation; hence, all conclude that in the first ages of the world neither vegetation nor animal life could have existed in our earth. Moses has told us that for the first two days and a part of the third the world was in a formative state, and that towards the close of the third day, or geological period, vegetation began to grow. According to our view, one of those days indicates a geological period of fifty thousand years, which would give over a hundred thousand years for the formation of plutonic rocks, or two hundred thousand for the formation of all the rocks beneath the series in which are found the remains of the vertebrated fishes and fowls; and two hundred and fifty thousand years before we meet with the evidence of mammalia, and three hundred thousand years until the highest order of men is met with which were upon the earth before Adam came.

The plutonic rocks form the base upon which rest all the others, and are the foundation of the earth's crust. The geologists therefore conclude that our world was once in an incandescent state — a conclusion to which, if we subscribe, it must be with the express reservation that we do not admit the truth of their corollary to the proposition that the interior of the earth is and has always been a molten mass of liquid fire. It will be remembered that, according to our views, there is no natural heat in the matter of which this or any other world is composed; that heat as well as light is the result of electrical action; that the sun is the great source of electricity to the solar system; and that the Almighty Builder, having established conduction between that centre and outside matter, by this means formed the worlds, drew them into orbits, and holds them there, to do his bidding and accomplish his designs.

It is only when a current of electricity meets with opposition, or with matter which does not permit its free passage, that it gives off heat and light. The longer matter is subjected to the action of electricity the more perfectly will it admit of conduction; therefore, we may rationally conclude that, when a section of chaotic matter is first bisected, it will offer less facility to electrical conduction than the matter which has been organized into a world; and hence the heat and light must be much more intense in the world while forming than after it has become organized.

In this view, since the comets are worlds in process of formation, and are composed of matter recently brought under the influence of the solar electricity, we would expect the solar light and heat to be far more intense at the comets than at any of the organized worlds, however near the sun; and we should therefore expect them to become incandescent, which the observations of astronomers lead them to believe is actually the case. Since our world, like all others, must have passed through the comet state, and while the matter of which it is composed was very much diffused, and yet offered much more resistance to the free passage of the electric current than now, then the heat must have been proportionally great; and although it may have been at an immense distance from the source of light and heat, yet we would expect the heat in the formative world to have been extremely intense; and the geologists inform us that the primitive, or plutonic rocks give unmistakable evidence of igneous origin.

Now, for our world to have been so heated as indicated by those rocks, in its present position in the solar system, and with its present surroundings, and then to have been cooled down so as to have formed a crust upon which vegetable and animal life might exist — aye, so that its poles should become locked up in unending icebergs — when viewed in the calm light of reason, seems to us to be a wild chimera, utterly unworthy of serious consideration, much more of earnest confidence as a philosophical theory. That our world has been in an incandescent state is perfectly evident to the most superficial scholar; then the question forces itself upon the inquirer after the truth, How was the earth brought into the condition of a molten mass? and, How was it cooled down to its present temperature?

Since the laws of nature are as unchangeable as their Author, had the earth, in its present position and relationship, ever been so highly heated, how could it possibly have cooled down? If the solar rays, through a series of years or of ages, had continued to increase the heat of the earth, notwithstanding its free radiation, until it became a molten mass, then it would be incomprehensible how the heat could ever have been decreased, or why it should not have continued to increase so long as the earth remained in the same relationship to the sun.

It is indisputably true that the earth has been vastly hotter than it is now, even to incandescence; therefore it would appear that her relationship to the source of heat has undergone some very great, if not radical, revolution. Is not the account of this change given by Moses satisfactory —incomparably more so than any other explanation which has ever been suggested? He informs us that our world was at first created as a part of the great chaotic mass of the material universe; that from that mass Omniscience designed the formation of worlds and vast systems of worlds; that the first act in their organization was to cause the universal agent to circulate or move, and electric light flashed into the dark abysm; that by the same agency matter was bisected and caused to revolve upon axes, so as to divide the light from darkness; that for ages they flew through space, alternately attracted to and repelled from various points, until the magnetic condition was established in the different worlds, when they were introduced into their respective systems, and thus the times and the seasons were fixed for them, and thus were they prepared to sustain the vegetable and animate beings for which they were designed.

The plutonic rocks, forming the basis of our world's crust, and apparently composing her entire internal structure, proves beyond doubt her former incandescence. This fact has not yet been satisfactorily accounted for, nor can any rational solution to the grand problem be given, except that contained in the account of the creation, by Moses. From this we understand that our world and, by consequence, all others pass through the comet or incandescent state before being introduced into their respective positions in the systems of the worlds to which each belongs.

According to the arrangement of the inspired philosopher, the first geological cycle would extend through the geological periods, denominated by him the first, second, and third days of the creative week. The formations of those ages are called by modern geologists primary rocks. On the third day of the creative week the earth was commanded to bring forth all manner of vegetation, which continued to be the only kind of life upon the globe until the fifth day of the creative week, when the waters were commanded to bring forth abundantly the fishes of the sea and the fowls of the air. On the sixth day the earth was commanded to bring forth every living creature which moveth upon the face of the earth; and at last, towards the close of the period, God created the man in his image and likeness, and rested through a geological period of fifty thousand years; and after this, how long we are not informed, he created Adam.

Geologists have adopted the same order in their classification of the rocks and their arrangement of geological periods, without any reference whatever to the learning of the profound philosopher and inspired writer of the history of the creation. The primary rocks were formed on the first and second days; those of the transition on the third; those of the secondary formation on the fourth and fifth — the carboniferous depositions having been made when the earth was introduced into the solar system. The rocks of the tertiary formation were consolidated on the sixth and the seventh days, and all the intervening time up to the fall of Adam; and from the fall to the present time have been deposited the recent accumulations.

We should expect the evidences of the action of heat to diminish as the transition series rise, and we should expect also some traces of the existence of vegetation,—in the secondary formations the carboniferous depositions and the fossil remains of fish and fowl, and in the tertiary the remains of all kind of animals, including man. These occult truths, promulgated by Moses more than three thousand years ago, are proven to be wonderfully correct, and are made manifest by the researches of modern geologists. That the earlier vegetable fossils are confined principally to ferns and plants of aquatic origin, and the scarcity of the fossils of birds, and indeed of all the animals in all the formations until we come to the recent accumulations, is owing to the quiet which then prevailed in the earth; "for the Lord God had not caused it to rain upon the earth, and there was not a man to till the ground." The earth was cursed for Adam's sake, and that curse is described in such a manner as to show us that a great geological revolution then occurred; and we actually perceive a wonderful increase of fossils in the latter part of the tertiary and through the recent formations.

In the peaceful periods of the world there are comparatively but few fossiliferous remains either of vegetables or of animals; because then there were no violent geological agencies acting upon the earth's crust. There was no rain then to sweep timber and animals from mountains and from hills into the valleys and the plains, and to cover them with alluvial earth — to be preserved as fossil evidences of their former existence; and consequently in the early rocks we find only the fossils of fishes and vegetation, which, however, proves accurately that the order of creation was understood and described by Moses.

Before proceeding further, we must, in a work like this, cope with another question which legitimately comes up in this connection, that is by what agency are the rocks formed? In answering this question we beg the reader to remember our postulate, laid down in a previous part of this work, that in all nature there are no two causes which will produce the same result; and therefore, when we ascertain that a certain cause will work out a certain result, we may rest satisfied that similar results are always produced by the same cause.

We have attempted to prove that electricity is the only agency by which mind acts upon matter; and the formation of the rocks is no exception to the rule. If it can be shown that one rock is or may be formed by electricity, then all rocks are formed by the same means.

"The recent experiments of Mr. Robert Weare Fox, of Great Britain, show that clay subjected to a long voltaic action becomes laminated, so as to resemble clay-slate in its structure. Very probably an electric agency is essential in those cases where heat and water seem to produce the effect, and that these causes operate chiefly by exalting the electricities and giving mobility to the particles." (Hitchcock's Geo., 25th ed., 291.)

We see here that the geologists are convinced from actual experiment that clay-slate, at least, is formed by the action of electricity; and we believe they all admit that the formation of the crystaline rocks is the result of galvanic action. The conglomerate rocks and the sandstones are said to be held together by the chemical affinity between their particles; but we have seen that all attraction and repulsion among the particles of matter everywhere are effected by electricity; therefore those rocks also are formed by electrical agency.

If there be any exception to the proposition that the rocks are formed by the action of electricity, it must be in the case of the igneous rocks. We have seen, however, that heat is the result of electricity; therefore we confidently conclude that all the rocks are formed by electrical agency.

It is pretty well agreed among scholars that in all cases of petrifications electricity is the principal, if not the only agency. M. Alcide D'Orbigny says, (vol. 1, p. 56,) "In many instances galvanism and electro-magnetism are concerned in petrification; especially where the organic substance is converted into crystaline matter. The juxtaposition of mineral matters forms galvanic combination, which produce the requisite currents." This view is now entertained by most if not all writers on the subject.

We must look still further into the geological views, brought out by the sacred historian, before dismissing this branch of our subject. In the last chapter we have seen that this writer brings to view the same order in the classification of the geological formations as that adopted and followed by modern geologists, that is, the primary, secondary, and tertiary formations, and alluvial or recent accumulations.

These rocks, it would seem, should always be found in this order: the alluvial deposits on the surface, the tertiary rocks just beneath, the secondary below these, and the primary underlying all and resting upon their granite base or foundation of the earth's crust. This, however, is not always the case, for sometimes we find granite and other plutonic rocks at the surface, and, in many instances, the order of the rocks entirely reversed, or in utter confusion and disorderly juxtaposition.

Geologists have concluded from these circumstances, and

from the deposition of animal remains in different formations, that there have been various geological revolutions in the earth's crust. Mr. Hitchcock, who believes that "death was introduced into the world as a *prospective* result of man's apostasy," thinks that there have been four, possibly five, geological revolutions in our earth.

He says "dykes and veins frequently cross one another; and in such cases the one that is cut off is regarded as the oldest. By this rule it may be shown that granite has been erupted at no less than four different epochs." Again, "If we take only the larger groups of animals and plants, whose almost entire distinctness from one another has been established beyond all doubt, we shall still, at least, have five nearly complete organic revolutions on the globe, viz.: 1st. The existing species; 2d. Those in the tertiary strata; 3d. Those in the cretaceous and oolitic systems; 4th. Those in the upper red sandstone group; and, 5th. Those below the new red sandstone. Comparative anatomy teaches us that animals and plants in these different groups would not have lived in the same physical circumstances. Geology shows that some of the less perfect organisms are found in the newer formations." "M. Alcide D'Orbigny corroborates Hugh Miller in the declaration that the progress of the race," that is, of fishes, "as a whole, though it still retains not a few of the higher forms, has been a progress, not of development, but of degradation," and they assert that the same is true of the mollusk.

We have made these references to distinguished geologists, in the first place, to show that the evidences of geological epochs are too palpable to escape the observation of any; and, in the second place, that the order of the strata is so frequently reversed and in confusion as to lead these, as well as other geologists, to the conclusion that there have been four or five different grand geological revolutions or fundamental upheavals at the beginning of as many epochs; and, finally, we have made these extracts from Mr. Hitchcock to show how foolishly inconsistent, not to say inexcusably absurd, he, a profound investigator of nature, and all that class of writers are in the fruitless effort to prove that they understand the science of geology, and that its teachings are not contrary to the traditional interpretation of the Mosaic account of the creation. This author, as noticed in another place, blunders so far as to inform us that Moses did not understand the subjects upon which he wrote.

Nevertheless, there have been different geological epochs, each embracing vast cycles of ages; and in the last chapter, we have endeavored to show that our author not only understood these truths, but that when the science of geology has been perfectly developed, then the veil will be removed from their hearts when Moses is read, when it must be apparent how unnecessary have been, we will not say the dishonest, but puny and ridiculous defences of his cosmogony. "He was learned in all the wisdom of the Egyptians," and was therefore so rich in the knowledge which had come down from beyond the flood, that he was above comparison, the superior to those of our time who beg for him the indulgence of the Christian public, and who excuse his supposed blundering in the sciences on the score of his pitiable ignorance, and that, too, after he had been inspired by Omniscience to write about them.

Man, whose body represents the world, has his three periods of life. The infant grows up into youth; he then acquires the strength and vigor of manhood, which rapidly passes away, and the man is in his third stage of life or old age, which will be soon crowned by weakness and decay, and the man departs from the stage of action. The three geological periods of the world answer to these stages in the life of man; and as he passes almost imperceptibly from one to another, so it appears that the world has glided from one geological period into another.

As in infancy man is weak and helpless, so we have seen that the world was in the beginning without soil or productiveness; and this was the time of the growth of her bones or of the formation of the hypozoic rocks. As in manhood we are strong and vigorous, so in the mediaeval ages the world was covered with a rich and exuberant soil, and was gloriously clad in luxuriant crops of grass, and herbs, and vast forests of noble timber. This was the time of the formation of the transition and secondary rocks or the vegetable epoch.

In the glory and vigor of vegetable growth, when possibly it covered the earth more richly than it has done since, and as the youth, when rejoicing in the very zenith of young vitality, passes the age of puberty, so the earth, when robed with the immense, to us incomprehensible, comet growth of vegetation, was introduced into the solar system.

Then the earth underwent that grand geological revolution which forms the base of the secondary formations. The change of temperature and surroundings of the comet and the world in its fixed orbit around the sun, was so powerful that vegetation was almost if not entirely killed, and being thrown down, was formed into the immeasurable fields of anthracite and bituminous coal. After this revolution had been wrought, vegetation, from the seeds upon the earth, began to grow again, and from the now rich soil soon she was covered with luxuriant swards of vegetation, and with the majestic forests of the secondary or animal period. Vegetation, removed suddenly from the hot-house and exposed to the vicissitudes of the open air and the unmitigated rays of the sun, will die; a sudden removal from regular sunlight to shade is equally fatal to vegetable life. The change from the comet to the orderly world-state must have been as great as the instances here mentioned, therefore the comet vegetation must have died, and hence the deposition of the coal measures of the carboniferous ages.

As in old age a dim eye, gray and falling hair, a dry and shrivelled skin, sapless joints, and diminished body, with accumulated diseases, bowing in decay, indicate speedy dissolution, so the confused commingling of the geological strata, deeply imbedded forests, the waters wide-spread over much the largest portion of the earth's surface, heavy rains sweeping the soil from the mountain sides and hilly slopes, cutting deep gulches and broad ravines, and miserably scarring the whole surface of the globe; parching drouths wilting, withering, destroying vegetation on the deflowered, impoverished soil; the angry flashes of lightning, with hoarsely muttering thunders; the volcano heaving up mighty masses of liquid fire, and the earthquake causing the earth to reel to and fro like one affected with the palsy of old age; all nature warring with itself, indicate that the cataclysm is passed and the ecpyrosis is now at hand; that the close of the last geological period is upon us, and that a new series of ages must now begin. What though the world may continue for a thousand years, it is but as one day in geology, which in the peaceful and quiet ages of the world would scarcely leave its impress on the rocks.

Moses and the prophets knew better than we the vast extent of time which God employs to work out his mighty designs; and in view of the imperfection of our judgment and the weakness of our comprehension, and to aid us, in these last times, in the development of the truth in the light of science, we are assured, by more than one inspired writer, that "A thousand years is as one day with the Lord."

It is a strange fact that none but the Christian and the Jew, who alone have the true philosophy of the creation, should be the only people anywhere, or at any time, who hold to the absurdity that the world, now evidently decaying and hurrying on to speedy dissolution, is of such ephemeral existence as to have continued but for six thousand years, or six lives of such perverse creatures as was Adam after the fall, and his descendants; for the antediluvians lived near a thousand years; but "the veil is upon their heart, even unto this day, when Moses is read." All other people, except these guardians of revealed truth, contemplate the world as having existed through countless ages of hoary antiquity.

In Syncellus' account of an old Egyptian Chronographan, after assigning an eternity of existence to Vulcan, it claims a period of time for the reign of the kings of Egypt, from Sol the son of Vulcan to the thirtieth Tanite dynasty, of about forty-two thousand years. The Chinese claim that their nationality has stood for sixty thousand years. The Etruscans and the Persians considered the world vastly old; they numbered the years in the epochs of the past by hundreds of thousands. The Chaldeans, according to their own record, had been observing the stars for 473,000 years, when Alexander the Great was in Asia.

Moses is not singular in assigning different epochs to the world, which he calls days, for all the ancient philosophers did the same thing. He did not tell us, in round numbers, the years embraced in an epoch, yet we think that he has placed the key to that number in our hands, if we will search for it in the code of laws and ceremonies which he gave to the Jews.

The Arabians, Pythagoras, Strabo, and other ancient philosophers, variously estimated the periods, or full cycles of time, at from 120,000 to 360,000 years; and according to the deduction which we have heretofore made, the astronomical day is 50,000 years, and therefore the creative week is 350,000 years, that being a complete cycle of time; and yet the year in prophetic time being 360 days, therefore the true time should be 360,000 years.

The history of nations, the learning of the philosophers, the handwriting of God upon the rocks, all, all proclaim the gigantic folly of the Christian theory that the world is but six thousand years old. This theory, it is contended, is the theory of Moses; but, if we have done only partial justice to this subject in our former discussion, it is evident to the reader that there is not a word in the writings of the inspired philosopher to found or even to justify such a theory, and that it rests entirely upon the traditional exposition of that author for its support.

Had Moses said that the ending of one and the beginning of another were the first period, instead of saying that the evening and the morning were the first day, no one would ever have thought of the six thousand years' theory. We hope that we have made it clear that a day of twenty-four hours could not, by any possibility, have been meant by him in the account of the creation; for upon this mistaken view rests the mistaken theory. "But the veil is upon their hearts, even unto this day, when Moses is read."

Having shown, as we hope, to the satisfaction of the unprejudiced reader, that our author was learned in the wisdom of the ages; having exhibited the points of agreement between him and other ancient philosophers in regard to the periods of time, and that there is no material issue in respect to the duration of those periods; and having also brought to view the points upon which he and modern geologists coincide in opinion, it still remains for us to examine the subject of geological revolution a little further in the light of reason and revelation.

"In the same day were all the fountains of the great deep broken up." We must keep before us the fact of the internal circulation of the waters through all the body of the earth, like the circulation of the blood in the body of a man; and that the arteries had been stopped up by the material which the heavy rains had washed from the surface, and which had been borne by the rivers or veins into the sea or heart for nearly two thousand years, or from the time of the fall to the flood. During all this time stratified rocks were being formed within the interior channels, and in the valleys and beds of rivers, creeks, and low places on the surface of the earth, by the deposition of clay, lime, sand, and vegetable matter; and we might therefore expect to find stratified rocks, cretaceous formations of the metals, veins, and vegetable matter through the earth's crust, above, below, and in the rocks of the most ancient formation.

When all the fountains of the great deep were broken up, the earth's crust was upheaved and torn to fragments, as the human body would be were all its arteries suddenly and violently burst open. In that grand geological revolution of the earth's crust all around the world's great heart, the one place into which the waters had been gathered, and from whence they pulsated to the extremities of the earth, must have been entirely crushed and hurled up with as much force and violence as would have followed had a mighty magazine of powder been laid in the interior channels, and exploded by a spark of electricity.

In such an explosion it is evident that most of the earth's crust would be confusedly upheaved; that the hills would be turned out of their place; the mountains would be torn open; deep fissures would be made; grand precipices would be formed; the waters would rush out, and, covering all the low places, prevail in all the regions near the sea, to the depth of thirty feet above the highest mountains. Removed from this locality and towards the extremities, the upheaval would not be so violent nor general, and many high points would not be submerged; and we actually find Asia and

Africa inhabited by men and animals which could not have been in the ark; and America and the islands, which could not possibly have had any previous communication with the Eastern continent, were inhabited by men and animals when first visited by navigators from Europe, the stage of action upon which was discharged the living freight of Noah's ark.

In this general upheaval and crushing of the earth's crust, the plutonic rocks were thrown to the surface; the secondary and tertiary rocks were hurled up and tumbled down among those older formations; and animal and vegetable remains falling into the apertures made by the bursting of the internal channels, when the waters subsided, or rather were reduced to their present order, the geological formations were left in that state of reversion and confusion in which we now find them—plutonic rocks at the surface, tertiary rocks on the granitic base; and again secondary formations underlie all; and yet again the rocks of all ages commingled in utter and inexplicable confusion.

The vast forests, labyrinthine jungles, and heavy swards of rich vegetation of the antediluvial world were confusedly hurled into the apertures and low places, and thus were formed those coal measures called lignite, and thus the confusion was produced in the older formations of anthracite and bitumen.

Many of the stratifications of the rocks, especially those of the cretaceous and oolitic systems, are evidently depositions from water. We have intimated that all deposits, through all the pristine ages of the world, were made at the surface or at the termination of the internal channels. We may rationally conclude that large deposits were made, and all kinds of stratified rocks were formed in the internal channels during the disturbed era from the fall to the flood.

At the time of the general upheaval, when all the fountains of the great deep were broken up, these formations were upheaved, thrown down, and left in their present position. The course and position of drift show how tremendous must have been the upheaval towards the head or north pole, and what a mighty external current must have set in from that direction towards the region of the heart. Although, after this general wreck of the earth's crust, we would expect, as is actually the case, that the waters would flow down and submerge most of the southern hemisphere, especially towards that pole, yet we ought not to look for the evidences there, of the violent geological revolution, which are everywhere so abundant in the north.

Since the free and uninterrupted flow of electricity around the earth has been destroyed by the obliquity of the earth's axis, many subsidiary and local circuits have been established, as proven by magnetic beds and magnetic mountains. When these currents are interfered with, or the chain of conduction is slightly fractured, the most intense heat known in art or in nature results; and by this means coal measures deeply imbedded in the ruptured ducts, where once flowed the internal waters, are set on fire, and the wonderful phenomena of the earthquake are produced, or, finding vent through the upper crust, all the grand and majestic scenes of the volcano are exhibited.

If there be no external aperture, and if the raging fires within can effect none, the molten rocks must be forced off through the earth's arteries still left open, and into crevasses and fissures which were not closed up at the time of the general unheaval, and present to the geologist the appearance of dykes and veins of metals and of granite and hypozoic rocks through the secondary and tertiary formations. By the flowing of the waters through the world's arteries—into which all kinds of substances were forced by the palpitation of the sea and deposited in them, and in the grand upheaval at the time of the flood sections of them being cut off and not filled with other matter — was formed the caverns of the earth, in some of which are found the remains of men and animals.

Most of these animals, as well as the lignite depositions of vegetable matter, were no doubt made at the time of the mighty geological revolution, when men and animals and rocks and trees were upheaved and plunged down into the very bowels of the earth. Many more of those collections were also made during the unquiet ages, from the fall to the flood, in the way which we have suggested. But let not the geologist therefore conclude that no depositions of human remains were made in the peaceful ages, deep in the vast revolving cycles of time, long anterior to the advent of Adam. If human petrifactions are discovered in the upper secondary, or in tertiary rocks; if human footprints are found upon them, let him not stultify himself and damage the sublime science, which he represents, by foolish conjectures in regard to how those bodies were *recently* petrified, and those footprints were *recently* made.

We would be pleased to investigate these subjects fully, but our increasing pages admonish us not to dwell here; nor do we deem it necessary, since our object is to suggest general ideas, and not to write a special treatise on any of the sciences. We have been led into these, as we think, rational views of the laws of the mind and of matter in following our author, but we leave details to adepts in the various sciences, believing that they will do ample justice to their respective subjects.

With due deference, however, we would right here suggest to the geologist, that if he will examine the science from our stand-point, we feel thoroughly satisfied that he will be able to reconcile many of the difficulties which are looked upon as insurmountable, are called "hidden mysteries," and so slurred over, and even those geological facts which are accounted for, he will find may be much more satisfactorily explained from ours than from his point of view.

Moses speaks of but three occasions in the world's history in which there could, by any possibility, be marks of general violent revolution impressed upon the rocks; and these are, at the time when the world was introduced into the solar system, at the time when she lost her perpendicular polarity, and at the time when "all the fountains of the great deep were broken up," and thorough geological investigation will certainly prove that there have been no more.

CHAPTER XXXII.

RECAPITULATION—"THY KINGDOM COME," &C.—ANSWER TO THE QUESTION, "WAY DID GOD PERMIT THE PROPAGATION OF THE ADAMIC RACE?"—NECESSITY FOR THE ADVENT OF CHRIST.

HAVING taken a cursory view of the creation; of the laws of nature, as brought to light by Moses; of their subversion, or interruption by the rebellious conduct of the world's great representative; of the effect of Adam's conduct upon the physical condition and government of the world, as well as of the hopeless moral degradation into which his race is plunged,—we have seen how perfectly the will of God was done in the earth through all the pre-Adamic ages; and how, in the time of the innocency of the world's great monarch, the vegetable kingdom continued to flourish more vigorously than formerly, and all the animals, subserving the objects for which they had been designed, freely indulging in all the passions and appetites which God had implanted in them, and enjoying happiness to the full extent of their capacities. All the laws of nature were in beauteous harmony then, working out the great designs of the world's Creator; while Adam, as the sole sovereign of all the earth, sat gloriously enthroned at the head of the globe, the vicegerent of God, clothed with ample powers for the purpose as God, morally, physically, and intellectually governing the world.

His will was the law of the world. He was the monarch of all the earth. None rebelled against his authority; none disputed his divine right to rule. He gave law to all, and, being perfectly qualified and adapted for the sole sovereignty and the exercise of God-like power on earth, his own will was the "law unto himself." He freely indulged without restraint in the gratification of every passion, appetite, and desire of his nature, except only the one passion represented by the tree which grew in the midst of the garden. The gratification of the desire prompted by that passion was spoken of as the eating of the fruit of the tree of the knowledge of good and evil; and Adam was solemnly warned by his Maker, "In the day thou eatest thereof, thou shalt surely die." The act of reproduction, we think we have proven, is the cause, the only cause, of death. The passion indulged by Adam would not only cause his own and the death of all his procreating race, but would bring wild disorder and hopeless confusion into the world; because it would introduce upon the stage of action more than one being indued with all the high ambitions appropriate to sole sovereignty.

In solitary grandeur Adam governed the world for ages, how long accurately we know not, but until Omniscience decided that it was not good for him longer to be alone, and he then made a woman and gave her to be with Adam as a companion. He imbued her with tastes and capacities which would qualify her to enter into and to appreciate his designs for the development of the moral, intellectual, and physical condition of the teeming millions of his subjects, and for the improvement of his great kingdom, the world.

We have seen that the spirit of evil having entered into the most gifted and most trusted of the servants of Adam; that, by reason of his superior intelligence, he persuaded the woman from the path of duty, and that Adam, consenting to her folly, and partaking of her crime, dethroned himself, and cursed the world with physical obliquity, and with a race of beings, every individual of which, possessing a nature like his own, could not be satisfied with anything short of universal sovereignty.

Adam was then the wilful author of envy, jealousy, strife, confusion, hatred, malice, and murder in this world, because each individual of his abnormal race looks upon every other as a rival and an enemy—as an intruder into the world which he conceives should be all his own. Not only was this state of warfare between the individuals of the new race the unavoidable condition of their being, but the old governing men, heretofore the willing subjects of Adam's authority, seeing that he had fallen from his godlike position of solitary majesty, and had placed himself as the propagator of a race among the mortals of the earth—the proud old race therefore refused longer to be governed by him, utterly spurning the idea of submission to his descendants. "I will put enmity between thee and the woman, and between thy seed and her seed." The animal man, and the entire animal creation, obeying their natural instincts of allegiance to their old masters, the red men, rebelled against or fled from the new and vicious race, and have steadily refused submission to them until this day, except when compelled thereto by superior force or superior intelligence.

It was not through ignorance that Adam became the

author of this confusion and this terrible state of warfare; for "*he* was not deceived, but the *woman* being deceived, was in the transgression." Even then a merciful God discovered a plan by which he might save a race which had been ushered into the world contrary to his designs, and radically subversive of the peace, harmony, and order which he had established. "The seed of the woman shall bruise the serpent's head."

There could be no peaceful subordination of a race to one of their own number, because every individual of that race must consider himself the equal of every other individual of the same race; hence, when the necessities of the world required that it be brought under the control of one will, the Almighty created a man for that purpose, who was so evidently superior to all other beings in the world, in personal appearance, and moral and intellectual endowments, so separate and distinct from all others, that there could be no grounds, no, not the shadow of a temptation or of a suspicion of partiality towards any living creature. Such a one, clothed with the power of God, and installed as his vicegerent on the throne of the world, might be bowed to and served by the proudest individual of the proudest race, without any abasement or loss of self-respect.

But let the spell once be broken, let the fact be made known that such a mighty sovereign has lost the divine right by which he ruled; let it be understood that he has rebelled against the supreme authority, and forfeited the confidence of his God—has become subject to death, like the multitude of his subjects—and who doubts that, under these circumstances, there would be a spontaneous uprising among them, and that the fallen monarch would be dethroned, disrobed of all power—would be contemned by his former subjects, who would either put him to death or drive him into exile.

This latter result did actually follow as a consequence of the unhappy fall of Adam, as that event is described by Moses. With his guilty partner, he was driven from his palatial garden. His own perverted nature, as well as the impassable physical barrier, must ever prevent his return thither; but he was still permitted to stop and settle in a distant part of the land of Eden. There, weighed down with a sense of his guilt and disgrace, he toiled on with miserable forebodings, certain of the fact that he would fall a victim to the grim monster death before the expiration of the day of a thousand years.

The wretched condition of the Adamic race, with its unsatisfied desires; of vaulting ambitions doomed to disappointment; of hard labor and unrequited toil; of strifes within and wars without; of envy, jealousy, hatred, malice, love unreturned, covetousness, theft, murder, incest, all unnatural desires and miserable appetites; with a morbid love of life, and ever reminded by sickness, sorrow, pain, and the death of all things that they, too, at last must surely die, for the fiat has gone forth, "dust thou art, and unto dust shalt thou return"—is the horrid legacy left by Adam to his miserably wretched race. Yet, "God so loved the world that he gave his only-begotten Son, that whosoever believeth in him should not perish, but have everlasting life."

Let us now return to the point from which we started. We set out with the design of ascertaining, as far as we might do, the meaning of the petitions in the Lord's Prayer, "Thy kingdom come; thy will be done on earth as it is in heaven." If, in our investigations into the grand mysteries brought to light by the inspired philosophy of Moses, we have done anything towards the development of the truth, if we have made any progress towards the establishment of a stand-point, from which, by a rational view of the laws of mind and of matter, we may obtain a glimpse at what the kingdom of God was while Adam reigned in Paradise, and how the divine will was then fully accomplished by all his creatures, so far have we gone towards ascertaining what is meant by those petitions; for what Omnipotence first designed to do he will most assuredly accomplish at last.

There was no rivalry, no strife, no envy, no jealousy, no warfare, no murder, no conflict of interests, no sickness, no sorrow, no pain in all the wide dominion of Adam in his reign of innocency; but all was done according to the will of God, and peace and harmony brooded over all; and all, in obedience to the law of their being, when their allotted time came, quietly, and without protracted pain or fear, passed through their mortal change. How different was the scene when the unbidden race of Adam was thrust upon the stage of action!

Adam was made to be immortal, and therefore the love of life was the strongest passion of his soul; so that when he sinned and became subject to the law of death, had there been nothing else to mar his peace of mind, yet the fear of death was a living terror which must ever make him miserable. The race of abnormal beings, whom, in disregard of the express will of his God, he forced into the world, inherited all his woe, and, on account of their actual conflict with each other, were of necessity in a much more wretched condition than the fallen monarch himself.

What conflicts, what ineradicable inconsistencies and warring passions are there in the character of the descendants of Adam! History deals with this wretched, restless race alone—except in rare instances, where it takes cognizance of those nations sprung from this and the serpent race; and what a tissue of disappointed ambitions, of pestilence, of famine, of war, of robbery, of murder, of rape, of rapine, and of an apparent design on the part of every individual of the abnormal race to over-reach, to circumvent, to crush, to ruin, to annihilate utterly, every other individual of the same race! Cruelty, not only toward our own race, but toward all of God's creatures, is the first manifestation of the infant mind, sure to be educed by the least opposition to our perverted will.

History is continually repeating itself in regard to the warfare forever being waged in the soul, even on the subject of our devotions. It is impossible for the loftiest intellect, even of the pure Adamic race, to keep always before it the idea of abstract spiritual existence. On account of the love of physical power, and of the pomp and pageantry of royal authority; notwithstanding the envy, jealousy, and hatred, which our race has ever borne its rulers while living, yet when dead and no longer to be feared as rulers, or hated as superiors, thousands have ever been ready to elevate them to still higher honors, to apotheosize and worship them as tutelary gods; hence, idolatry made its appearance in the earliest historic ages, and has continued, notwithstanding the introduction of Christianity, among the highest types of the Adamic race even down to our own time.

It is true that a great system of philosophy has grown up from and has been nourished into strength by Christianity. It is true that this philosophy has led to the discovery of the powers of electricity and of electro-magnetism; that it has shown us some faint glimmerings of animal magnetism, or rather of electro-magnetism in its application to and between living animals; yet we have advanced so far beyond the starting-point, have soared so immeasurably above the loftiest conceptions of our fathers, that the Christianity which was just the thing for them is contemptible in the light of the mighty rationality of the present age, and is therefore to be uprooted, thrown down, and consigned with the rubbish of the past to the pages of history, as have been other antiquated systems and exploded theories.

That there is such a thing as animal magnetism, and that

it is to some extent under the control of the intelligence in man is evident; but how this is done is the great philosophical question which is presented for investigation. Instead, however, of approaching the subject in the light of reason, and endeavoring to unfold the sure laws connected with it by honest intellectual efforts, a moon-struck progressionist flies off in a fit of transcendentalism into the mystic fields of nothingness, and calls his vacant discoveries a system or ism, to which his moon-struck followers prefixed his name. Mesmerism soon grows into biology, which matures into clairvoyance; and as noxious weeds are ever of most rapid growth, so no time is lost till from the root of clairvoyance the philosophy of the table, the monomania of modern spiritualism, ripens into wide-mouthed infidelity and vulgar blasphemy.

Already we see "the mediums," in imitation of the ancient priesthoods of paganism, establishing one system for themselves, while they present a very different theory for the faith and practice of their ignorant followers. The former worship the all-pervading spirits in everything, but more particularly in themselves; while they induce their dupes to worship the spirits of their dead friends at the shrine of the table — a duty which most devoutly they perform.

The table-worshippers are agreed upon the subject of devotion to the table, but they call on different gods. Some call on Andrew Jackson and Henry Clay; some on George Washington and Daniel Webster; some on Napoleon Bonaparte and Abe Lincoln; and others on divers spirits "black, white, and gray;" but no two seem to have selected the same gods, nor any one of them to have determined to make any one of these deities supreme; for this is the very thing which has driven them from the worship of the true and only God.

There is nothing more revolting to the feelings of the

proud and ambitious race of Adam than submission to any authority whatever; but absolute submission to and dependence upon an individual will, even though it be that of the only-begotten Son of God is too galling, and our proud nature will not bear it. Let the table-worshippers pause for one moment, and ponder the words of wisdom which came to the children of men in tones of thunder from Sinai's burning crest:

"Thou shalt have no other gods before me. Thou shalt not make unto thee any graven image, or any likeness of anything that is in heaven above, or that is in the earth beneath, or that is in the water under the earth: thou shalt not bow down thyself to them, nor serve them: for I the Lord thy God am a jealous God, visiting the iniquity of the fathers upon the children unto the third and fourth generation of them that hate me; and showing mercy unto thousands of them that love me, and keep my commandments."

Our race has never been quiet, never happy, never peaceable. With intellect capable of vastly more elevated views than the old governing race, which, uncontaminated by contact with the white man, has no idea of the existence of any god except that of the Great Spirit; and yet with a love of pomp and material power inherited from Adam, in whom these instincts were implanted in order that he might not cloy in the discharge of the royal prerogatives and duties of the office of grand sovereign of all the earth, our race is ever aspiring to the intellectual, and yet held down by their love of materiality to the level of the animal man. They have ever been the most elevated and the most degraded of earthly beings.

Among this race are the scholar, the philosopher, the poet, the orator, the discoverer, and cultivator of the arts and sciences; among these too are the murderer, the thief, the worshipper of gold and of silver and their own fellow-beings, and the destroyer of the order of God by miscegenation; and these extremes and inconsistencies are warring continually in the breast of each unfortunate individual of the abnormal race. The mind of the Adams' is in terrible conflict with itself. We admire truth and right, and yet our action is false, our life is all wrong.

With these strange inconsistencies inherited from our great progenitor, who was created good, and pure, and upright; and who, by his own volition, introduced a race of beings into the world with all his lofty aspirations for sole sovereignty and high supremacy, and the utter impossibility of gratifying them; all the passions were converted into evil, and brought into full play so soon as the second man came upon the stage, for we are informed that he murdered in a fit of jealousy the third, who was his own brother.

Who is astonished at the incompatibilities of our nature, or could expect the race to have been other than one of idolaters, hating and seeking the destruction of their rulers, aye, of all their fellow-beings while living, yet ready to adore and worship them as gods when dead? With the Indian we worship intellectuality, we adore spirit; with the negro we prostrate ourselves to stocks and stones, and grovel at the shrine of silver and of gold; and thus all that is within us is at war with ourselves, so that it is hard for us to conceive how the devils can be more miserable than we.

Some one says it is strange that a good and merciful Being would have made us thus. Let us repeat here that God did not so make us, for all that he made was good; but Adam, who was made perfect and exalted high over all, aspiring to become the author of a race superior to all those whom God had made, introduced this unhappy state of things.

We came upon the stage of action contrary to the known will of heaven, in defiance of "the God in whom we live, and move, and have our being." Then how can any rational man for one moment entertain a thought of charging him with being the author of our woes?

It is true that we came into being without our knowledge or consent; but it is also true that we are here contrary to the Almighty Will, clearly announced; therefore if we wish to fix the cause of our wretchedness and the responsibility of ameliorating our condition, it certainly must rest upon him who was not deceived, but wilfully and wickedly became our procreator; let no man, therefore, charge God with being the author of our sufferings.

It is said that since He is boundless in goodness and mercy, He ought to have prevented the propagation of such a miserable race by the exertion of His power. At what time could He have exercised such power? The strongest passion in the soul of Adam was the love of life; then would it have been an act of mercy towards him had the Almighty struck him down while pleading for his life? Would not that have savored more of the vengeful tyrant than of an offended but kind and indulgent father?

When Adam had lost his innocency and his high sovereignty he was a vagabond in the earth, and the sole hope of solace in his declining years was, that he might raise up a numerous offspring, whom he still would have the right to control, and whose affections he might expect to retain. Would it have been a merciful dispensation towards Adam had the children of his hope all died in infancy? What man, even at this day, when the world is full of men, rejoices in that mercy which removes all of his infant children from his arms?

Is there a man of the pure lineage of Adam, in all the wide earth, who has never felt a desire to have an offspring? Would you deem it a mercy for your children all to die in infancy? If Abraham and Isaac and Jacob, if all men in all ages have considered it a great mercy to be blessed with children, was it not a greater mercy to Adam to bless him with children? Then it would have been a terrible curse upon Adam, had he not been permitted to raise children. At no time would it have been considered a merciful dispensation had the race been prevented or cut off.

Then, if we would demand relief from the ills of life of any one, as a matter of right, it must be of Adam; but he is long since dead; yet the ills of which he was the author remain, and are continually increasing. "I, the Lord thy God, am a jealous God, visiting the iniquity of the fathers upon the children to the third and fourth generation." "We are conceived in sin and brought forth in iniquity," but shall the Immaculate be responsible for our sinful being? We came into the world in contravention of the express command of God, and shall he be charged with being the author of all our ills?

The responsibility of our being rests with Adam, and his is the obligation to relieve us of our woes; but, even when living, his was a puny arm of flesh, too weak to remove the burden of depravity from our nature, too short to reach the waters in the wells of salvation. He could not save himself, then how could he save others?

Since we could not be saved by an arm of flesh, and since the angels, who are finite spirits, could not sympathize in the trials, temptations, and weaknesses of our material nature, nor atone for the infinite offence of Adam, any more than they could have accomplished the design for which he was originally intended; and since we were forced into the world contrary to the divine will, and had no claims even upon His ordinary providence, as all other races of men and of animals have; since, in a word, "we were without hope and without God in the world," we, of all beings, were most miserable.

In this hopeless condition, in this time of dire necessity, the second person in the adorable Trinity, the Logos of God, proposed to clothe himself in flesh, that he might condemn sin in the flesh, that he might become a propitiation for sin, that he might become subject to the law, and die the just for the unjust. What wondrous love is this, that the Son of God should voluntarily become allied to the accursed race, should take upon himself the load of our original sin, the burden of our individual transgression, and willingly become subject to the violated law! "The seed of the woman shall bruise the head of the serpent" was the promise of hope given our guilty parents, even in the day of their transgression, which was more definitely repeated by the prophets in various ways and at divers times.

When Jacob blessed his sons, he said that "the sceptre shall not depart from Judah, nor a law-giver from between his feet, till Shiloh come." Moses says, "The Lord thy God will raise up unto thee a prophet from the midst of thee, of thy brethren, like unto me: unto him ye shall hearken." Isaiah very boldly says, "Unto us a child is born; unto us a son is given; and the government shall be upon his shoulder; and his name shall be called Wonderful, Counsellor, the Prince of Peace, the Mighty God, the Everlasting Father."

About seven hundred years after Isaiah's time, the above and concurrent prophecies began to be fulfilled, by the appearance of the man Christ Jesus, with such wonderful accuracy as to appear to be, not the foretelling of future events, but the faithful records of present occurrences. Therefore we are assured that what is yet unfulfilled will be fully accomplished in the end.

"In this was manifested the great love of God towards us, because that God sent his only-begotten Son into the world, that we might live through him." We have seen that the descendants of Adam were an unbidden race, as much so as the mule and other miscegenated animals, and that, therefore, no provision was made for them in the economy of nature; and yet, after Adam had become a procreator, God, of his infinite mercy, extended his providential care over the new race, as over other races of men and the animals. Nevertheless, inheriting the faculties, instincts, and ambitions of Adam, with an uncontrollable aspiration for that immortality which the procreator had forfeited, and the fear of death forever tormenting him, the language of the heart of each individual of the abnormal race is, "O wretched man that I am, who shall deliver me from the body of this death?"

When the combined wailings of a hopelessly helpless race reached the sublime courts of the Merciful Sovereign of the universe, he determined upon a plan by which he might be just, and yet the justifier of sinners. The plan was, merely to carry out his original design for the establishment of a theocratic government in the world, by the building up of a peculiar people from the children of the Adams. "For when we were yet without strength, in due time Christ died for the ungodly."

We have assumed, and hope that we have made it appear to the reader, that Adam came into the world to govern the teeming millions of the old races of the red and black men; and we have seen that order and harmony prevailed from the poles all around the globe; and that the resources of the earth were probably more largely developed then than at any prior or subsequent period; that the ruler of the world transgressed the law of his being by becoming the procreator of our race, and thus brought death upon himself and all his descendants; that they were naturally like him, ambitious of universal sovereignty, therefore that each looked upon every other as the rival of himself, and, hence, envy, jealousy, hatred, strife, and confusion were introduced into the world by the act of our fore-parents. Adam transgressed the law in the act of becoming our progenitor, brought himself under the curse of the law, and so death passed upon all his race; for all in him have sinned.

We have seen that enmity should naturally exist between the races of the beguiled and the beguiler, between the seed of the woman and the seed of the serpent; that a state of warfare should exist between them, until the latter should finally be exterminated; hence, we conclude that the Indian must finally disappear from the face of the earth, crushed and destroyed by the white man, or the seed of the woman.

We have seen that Cain was permitted to become the progenitor of a mixed race, from whom, we suppose, have sprung the race of Asiatics called Mongolians.

The presence of the arts and sciences, their idolatrous worship and superstitions, as well as their traditions, all go to prove that the Mexican and South American Indians were not pure blooded, as in North America, but were, in all probability, at least to some extent, mixed with the Asiatics or descendants of Cain.

Canaan was cursed because he misecegenated with a woman of the lowest race of human beings, or a negress; as Cain had previously been cursed for taking to wife an Indian woman. Although a race was permitted to grow up from the illicit intercourse of Canaan and this inferior woman, yet it must necessarily be stamped with inferiority, for a servant of servants should he ever be. This was not fulfilled in those of his children who settled in Palestine, for, although they were a grossly sensual people, the Phœnicians were among the most civilized of the ancients. They then could not have been descended from the inferior or servile race.

Canaan, then, besides his Caucasian wife, from whom his historic family sprang, must have had a negro concubine, from whom was descended the race upon whom Noah pronounced the curse of servility. From the fact that no mention is made of this race in history, we suppose that Canaan, in order to prevent the curse from being fulfilled, and to hide from his eyes the living mementos of his guilt, as we have seen men do in our own day, removed this miscegenated family far from the borders of their superior brethren.

Although the course which he took is not pointed out by history, yet the existence of the mulatto or Malay race shows that he took them to the extreme south of Asia. But how are we to account for the presence of this race in the islands of the Indian Ocean, adjacent to the south of Asia? "And unto Eber were born two sons: the name of the one was Peleg; for in his days was the earth divided."

By the dividing of the earth, what are we to understand? That boundary lines between the nations were then drawn, and portions of the earth assigned to the three sons of Noah? This will not do; for if this were the case, no attention was paid to the division. Somehow or other it has gotten into the heads of many Christians that Asia was settled by the children of Shem, Africa by those of Ham, while those of Japheth went into Europe; but since Moses says no such thing, we are unable to ascertain upon what authority the belief is founded.

It is true that Moses says, "By these," or the sons of Japheth, "were the isles of the Gentiles divided in their lands;" which, according to the received opinion, may mean the Archipelago and the Grecian islands. He is much more explicit in locating the families of Shem and Ham, and he expressly sets forth the fact that they all settled in the south-western part of Asia, between the Euphrates, and in Europe and Africa. There most of both families remained, and were the actors in the scenes of sacred history.

If one family of the sons of Mizraim went into Egypt,

they bore with them no marks of inferiority, no more than did their brethren whom they left in Asia. If Assyria were a Shemitic nationality, yet is it certain, from the testimony of Moses, that it was founded by Nimrod, the grandson of Ham. It appears from the writings of this author that at least the children of Shem and of Ham settled together in western Asia; while from profane history we learn that the Phœnicians and Egyptians, children of Ham, emigrated to and peopled the Grecian islands wholly or in part, and certainly that civilization, with the arts and sciences, were taken there by them.

These facts, it would seem, should settle the question in regard to the event commemorated by the name of the great-grandson of Shem, so far as to satisfy us that it could not possibly have been, according to popular belief, the apportionment of Asia, Africa, and Europe among the sons of Noah. Not being able at this time to investigate the subject satisfactorily to ourself, we will merely suggest, as a probable conjecture, inasmuch as we believe that the Malayans or mulatto race sprang from Canaan's illicit intercourse with a negress, and inasmuch as this race is found in the extreme south of Asia and the adjacent islands—that that division of the earth commemorated by this man's name was a large depression of country between Asia and Africa, by which means—and points of land being left above water—the Malayans got into the islands.

The mixed races, especially the Mongolians, have the capacity for appreciating the arts and sciences, and are men "to till the ground," or who will cultivate the soil, while the pure-blooded Indian will not adopt the arts of civilization, nor will he be coerced, nor submit to any restraint whatever upon his personal liberty. He will not bow his proud neck in toil, nor soil his lordly hands with any labor save what is absolutely necessary to give him the "dominion over the fish of the sea, the fowl of the air, and over every living creature." It would therefore seem that he must pass away; for in the present impoverished state of the soil, its meagre productions, and its crowded and increasing populations, he who will not work must steal, or perish for the want of food; hence it appears that the Adamic and mixed races must usurp the place of the old governing race.

When the purposes of God and her necessities required that the world be brought under imperial government, no individual could be found in all the earth suitable to be placed at its head. It would have been an unmitigated curse to have taken one of the fishing, fowling, hunting nomads from the pastimes of his fathers, to compel him to remain in the garden of Eden, and to devote his whole time to governmental affairs. All the pomp and pageantry of unlimited power would have possessed no charms for him. If a suitable person of that race could have been found, or if one had been specially gifted for the purpose, who would willingly have taken the government upon his shoulder, would his fellow-men, the men of his own race, have submitted cheerfully to his arbitrary will, his despotic authority?

Again: to have taken an individual of this race, with the instincts which he inherited from his fathers, and to have compelled him to devote himself exclusively to government, to philosophy, to the arts and sciences, to agriculture and commerce, would have been a thousand times worse than death to him—would have made him a maniac, or driven him to take refuge from the onerous tasks of his position by the commission of suicide. Then, to meet the emergencies in the case, God made a man out of the dust of the ground, and breathed into his nostrils the breath of life, and he became a living intelligence, with all the adaptations requisite to sole universal sovereignty.

If the old red race would not submit to one of their own

number, and if it were necessary for the peace and well-being of the world, then, that a new man should be created for its government, how utterly hopeless the supposition that any individual of the abnormal race should be found who could rule the restless, ambitious, aspiring sons of Adam, and how pressing the necessity for an extraordinary personage to arise who could bring order out of chaos, who could control the angry passions of the tumultuous multitudes, and bring the lost upon salvable grounds!

The red men were here in obedience to the command of God, to multiply and replenish the earth; while the white man came in contravention of his expressed will. "In the day thou eatest thereof thou shalt surely die."

The red man, satisfied with the control of his own family, and with the rich provisions of nature, rich in the herb and in the fruits of spontaneous growth, and rich in the fish, fowl, and living creature which he had the unrestrained right to use at will, and the free and full indulgence of all his appetites and passions — that natural man lived on in happiness and perfect contentment, without an annoying thought of the future till the time of his change came, when, without pain, he quietly lay down and died, and his undefiled spirit returned to the God who had given it.

How different is the case with the white man! Inheriting all the instincts of other animals, with the lofty intellect and towering ambition of gods, with envy, hatred, jealousy, malice, revenge, every unholy desire and evil purpose indulged to satisfy the promptings of the flesh; a consciousness within, ever thundering to the soul, all this is wrong, wrong morally, wrong physically, wrong every way; he is most unhappy. Immortality is lost, sovereignty is lost beyond the hope of recovery; in these indulgences, therefore, he must be supremely wretched.

Ambitious to be the sole monarch of the world, he is

a cringing, fawning slave to those in power; panting for immortality, he grovels after the things of time and sense; with an intellect capable of grasping the sublime truths of nature, and the exalted attributes of nature's God, he bows to senseless sticks and stones, and worships gods of silver and of gold. Possessing a high appreciation of the intellectual and the moral, he lives in ignorance and vice. He greedily drinks in the intoxicating draughts of sensuality, of folly, of wickedness. Yet he admires virtue, wisdom, and goodness. He is a god, a demon, a man, a brute; at war with himself, at war with nature, at war with his God.

"For I delight in the law of God after the inward man: but I see another law in my members warring against the law of my mind, and bringing me into captivity to the law of sin which is in my members. O wretched man that I am! who shall deliver me from the body of this death?"

CHAPTER XXXIII.

THE DIFFERENT FORMS OF GOVERNMENT NOTICED — DEATH SENT AS A BLESSING UPON ADAM — OUR DESIRE FOR IMMORTALITY — HOW CAN THE SONS OF ADAM BECOME THE SONS OF GOD? — CHRIST THE SECOND ADAM — DIFFERENCE BETWEEN ADAM AND HIS DESCENDANTS — THE DOCTRINE OF ELECTION — OFFICE OF THE SECOND ADAM.

IN answering the question with which our last chapter closes, we will endeavor to elucidate more fully some views taken in the previous pages of this work. There was no possible chance for the ambition of the Adamic race to be satisfied in this world. While there was but one individual of this race, and no fear of death before him, he might be happy here, for everything was here to make him so. But when more than one came upon the stage of action, happiness was out of the question; for there was no universal empire with which to satisfy the cravings of his ambitious nature; and had all his rivals been removed, and had the coveted boon of supremacy been bestowed upon one individual of the abnormal race, yet the constant fear of death would have tormented him out of all hopes of happiness.

The natural result of the seduction of Eve by a man of the old governing race was that they should hate each other; for such is the result of moral turpitude even to this day. That there should be enmity between the old and the new races was equally unavoidable; for the proud red man could scarcely bow to the lord of the whole earth, when he was clothed with the power of God, and as God governed the world, then certainly he would not submit to the authority of any individual of a numerous race of mortals, much more sinful, and therefore more wretched than it were possible for him to be.

The sons of Adam, with their towering ambition, deemed themselves justly entitled to the inheritance of all the rights and prerogatives once enjoyed by the father of the race. They claimed the absolute control of the red and black men, and of the entire animal kingdom; hence, not only was there enmity between the two domineering races, but a state of warfare was initiated then, and has continued, and must continue until the last unadulterated Indian has fallen a victim before the onward march of Caucasian civilization of Caucasian ambition, and of Caucasian justice. "The seed of the woman shall bruise the serpent's head."

The white man gains nothing towards securing that high supremacy, for which his soul pants, by the absence of the red man. On the contrary, having usurped the place of the ancient race, each one desires the sole sovereignty, and looks upon every other as a rival; wherefore there is no hope of peace in the world.

Every one feels and acknowledges the necessity for government, to restrain the angry passions of men, and yet all hate authority in the hands of another, and chafe under restraint. From this cause has sprung the many vain efforts in Caucasian countries to establish and maintain republican governments, than which a greater absurdity has never been attempted by our deluded race. For such a government to succeed, it is not only necessary for each individual to be the equal of every other in the eye of the law, but that each should be willing for every other to be his equal in fact, which, we have seen, is impossible in the very constitution of our abnormal race. Therefore, from this standpoint, as well as in the light of history, we see the utter folly of attempting this form of government among people of our wretched, restless race.

Aristocracy, for the same reasons, is impossible as a lasting institution. No form of government can ever secure the great object for which it is intended, that is, peace and harmony among its subjects; yet no doubt the very best form of human government is the despotic, or a government by one will backed by sufficient power to restrain, by coercion, the angry and contending passions of the multitude.

Even in such a government, however, there can be no happy individual. The monarch who has tasted of despotic power, thereby has all his innate desires for universal sovereignty aroused; and this vaulting ambition doomed to disappointment, with the fear of death ever before his eyes, renders him miserable. The knowledge that the king is made of the same clay; has derived his being from the same origin with themselves, and their own petty rivalries with each other — their jealousies, disappointments and mortified ambition — render all his subjects wretched.

It is certain, then, that all kinds of government are oppressive to us, make us unhappy; yet our opposing ambitions render it absolutely necessary for us to be governed. O wretched men that we are, "who shall deliver us from the body of this death?"

View our situation as we may, as individuals we "have no hope," and are miserable; as communities we are "without God in the world," and are therefore thrice wretched; nor can we help ourselves. There is no help in an arm of flesh. God only can raise us up from our miserable estate, place us on salvable ground, and give us a reasonable hope of happiness in the future. He, foreseeing all the wretchedness which would be accumulated upon our race, solemnly warned Adam against its propagation, "In the day thou eatest thereof thou shalt surely die;" yet in the plenitude of his goodness and mercy, even in the day of Adam's transgression, he determined to save the abnormal race by the power of his own right arm.

We are too gross to be governed by spiritual agencies alone; too proud to be governed by one of an inferior race; too envious to be governed by one of our own; too perverse to live without government; each individual too ambitious to be satisfied with less than the sovereignty of a world; too intellectual to be wholly ignorant of the existence of a God, and that we are in some way responsible to him, yet too ignorant to comprehend his attributes and worship him directly as the great intelligence of the world; therefore, to meet these and a thousand other conflicting circumstances in our miserable situation, a merciful God determined to send his own Son into the world, "that whosoever believeth in him should not perish, but have everlasting life."

With the natural desires, passions, and perversities of

our nature, it is evident that we must be at enmity not only with each other — with all animate nature, which refuses to be subject to our will, with the earth, which will not yield us her strength without much labor — but also with God himself. The questions are ever recurring to the mind, Why has he made me thus? Why are not the circumstances with which I am surrounded of a pleasant character? Why is not the world peaceful, quiet, harmonious? Why am I born but to die? Or why, O why was I or the world created at all?

God is not the author of misery or of confusion; and we hope that we have in these pages made it apparent, from a rational point of view, how sin entered the world by Adam and death by sin, and how through him and his descendants all the difficulties of which you complain were brought about; wherefore, in order to their removal and the salvation of our race, it is necessary not only to uproot our inordinate ambition and consequent jealousy, envy, and hatred towards each other, but to crush out of our minds enmity towards the God of the universe; "because the carnal mind is enmity against God: for it is not subject to the law of God, neither indeed can be."

Had there been no sin in the world, a new man might have been made of the dust of the ground, and ushered into the world for the purpose of governing and ameliorating its condition, as was done when Adam came; but would our ambitious race, with all of its perverted passions, have submitted to such an one, however comely in appearance or preeminent in intellect?

Again: had God commanded the earth to bring forth a body, as he did that of Adam, had breathed into his nostrils the breath of life, and had placed him upon the throne of the world, such an one in no possible way could have become a saviour of the Adamic race. Being wholly unallied to us, not being tempted as we are, he could not assume our sins, could not make an atonement for them; and, not being "touched with the feelings of our infirmities," he could not make due allowance therefor; and hence, instead of being a merciful ruler, securing the happiness of his subjects, he would have been an unrelenting despot,—ruling in justice and truth, but without that compassion which our perverted nature stands so much in need of, and thus the abnormal race would have been rendered still more miserable.

Had such an individual lived holy as an angel, of what benefit could it have been to us? It would not have been an example for us to have emulated, because, not being of like passions with ourselves, we might have admired the purity of his character and life, and envied him for his preeminency, but we certainly would have hated God more vehemently for making him more fortunate than ourselves. God, however, sent his own Son in the likeness of our sinful flesh, that he might condemn sin in the flesh.

Christ took not upon him the nature of angels, but the form of a servant, that he might teach purity by example as well as by precept; that from him the proud and ambitious might learn humility; that the vicious might learn virtue; that the wicked might learn righteousness; that the reasonableness of the law might be vindicated, and that all men might be left without excuse.

It was necessary for the accomplishment of the designs of the Almighty, that a being should come into the world superior to all the sons of Adam, that our proud nature might be brought to submit to him as our king. He must have assumed our nature and "brother to our souls become," that he might have the feelings of our infirmities; and he must be tempted in all points as we are, that he might be our prophet, and teach us the ways of life.

He must voluntarily submit himself to the law of death, though he should commit no offence against the law of life, in order that he might become our sacrifice and our priest. By the creative fiat of Jehovah all these requirements were fully met.

"The Holy Ghost came upon a virgin of Israel, and the power of the Highest overshadowed her; therefore that holy thing which was born of her is called the Son of God." This was as much a creation as if God had commanded the earth to bring forth the body, and had breathed into his nostrils the breath of life; and he was justly called the Son of God, because he had no man for his father.

He, however, was made of a woman, made under the law, and was therefore flesh of our flesh and bone of our bone. He is the Son of God, and yet he is our brother. He was subject to like passions with ourselves. He was tempted in all points as we are; could be touched with the feelings of our infirmities. He was a man of sorrow and acquainted with grief; and as the Son of God he commanded, and the warring elements obeyed his voice. He had power to lay down his own life, and he had the power to take it again.

"Great indeed is the mystery of godliness; God was manifest in the flesh, reconciling the world unto himself." Jesus was the Son of man, born of a woman, born under the law, of the house of David, of the seed of Abraham; and "He came in the likeness of sinful flesh, and for sin condemned sin in the flesh." He was the Son of God, conceived by a virgin of the Holy Ghost, inspired by Deity; for God himself breathed into his nostrils the breath of life, and he assumed the likeness of his Father, and "bore the express image of his glory."

When he was baptized of John in Jordan, the Holy Ghost descended in the likeness of a dove and brooded over him, and a voice from heaven declared, in the hearing of all the people, "This is my beloved Son, in whom I am well pleased." He was therefore very God and very man. He was bone of our bone and flesh of our flesh; yet, "In the beginning he was the Word, and the Word was with God, and the Word was God. The same was in the beginning with God. All things were made by him; and without him was not anything made that was made. In him was life; and the life was the light of men."

"He came to be a propitiation for our sins, and not for ours only, but for the sins of the whole world." God himself declared him to be "a high priest forever after the order of Melchizedek"—that is, there was none like him going before, and none like him could ever follow after him. Other high priests inherit their office and transmit it to their descendants, but the office of Christ is without beginning of days or end of years. They yearly offer the blood of bullocks and of lambs for themselves and for all the people; but this man, who knew no sin, offered his own life once upon the altar of sacrifice as an atonement for the sins of the whole world, and then entering the sanctum sanctorum of the universe sat down upon the throne at the right hand of the Father, to show his wounds and plead the merits of his blood for all the lost descendants of Adam's miserable race.

Therefore, as by the offence of one, judgment came upon all men to condemnation, even so by the righteousness of one, the free gift came upon all men unto justification of life. "For as in Adam all die, even so in Christ shall all be made alive." "And so it is written, The first man Adam" (not the first man, but the first who was called Adam,) "was made a living soul; the last Adam was made a quickening spirit."

When Adam transgressed the law of his being and became the procreator of a race, he brought himself under the universal law that whatever reproduces must die; and having become the propagator of a race of mortals of an ambitious, restless, perverse, and desperately wicked nature, God in mercy to Adam, lest he should put forth his hand and take the fruit of the tree of life, and eat and live forever, or, in simple language, should repent of his folly, abandon his crime, and should be forgiven, and should therefore live through all future time the miserable witness of the wickedness, the folly, the bloody crimes of the ambitious, restless, dying wretches whom he had cursed with being; hence, God in mercy drove him out of Paradise, and left him to pay the death penalty of the law which he had chosen to violate.

Notwithstanding that the death of our race is the terrible result of sin, yet it was sent in mercy to Adam, aye, and to his race; for who could imagine any other hell so intolerable as an eternity of such a life as that which we live here? We have all seen individuals to whom death came as a friendly relief; but let us suppose that Adam had been permitted to take and eat the fruit of the tree of life, and had lived through all the six thousand rolling years which have transpired since his fall; had been the eye-witness of all the wars, murders, thefts, robberies, adulteries, incests, famines, sickness, sorrow, pain, and death, which have made up all the history of his race, and who could imagine a being more miserable than Adam would have been?

That the law of reproduction should be the law of death, was ordained in mercy; and in great mercy it was allowed to operate upon Adam and his race. We can understand this; we can readily perceive how terrible a thing it would be for all the lost race of Adam to live always; and yet the fear of death, the love of immortality, is the living, goading anxiety of every son and daughter of the abnormal race. We know that it is not best for us to live, yet, oh! how we fear to die.

No man is happy in his present situation, but hopes — by the acquisition of more wealth, of higher political station, of personal influence, of oratorical celebrity, of literary distinction, of military renown,—that he will better his condition, that he will improve the circumstances with which he is surrounded, that he will add to himself those things which are necessary to perfect his happiness, and that with himself, at least, all will be well in the future. He knows, however, how utterly preposterous it is for all others to expect happiness in this life.

With all the vigor and tenacity of our souls, we love the future of our present life; and notwithstanding time flies with the speed of thought, yet, short as is the space allotted us, we press towards the future, in which we expect to be so much more happy than we now are. We contemn the present, we despise and loathe the circumstances with which we are surrounded, still hoping against hope, against the light of experience, against our better informed judgments, that we shall be happy in the future. Nevertheless, the happy future keeps ever just before us, and we remain still in possession of the miserable present.

We are wretched now, we are miserable here, and yet we desire with all the energies of our nature to live on; we wish to stay here, still foolishly hoping that all will be well in the future; and yet full well we know that the future of happiness can never come to us in our present mode of existence. In hope we live, in hope we make all our efforts; without hope the present would be intolerable; and yet we know that our hopes can never be realized.

How could we be more miserable, than we are, in this living death? "O wretched man that I am, who shall deliver me from the body of this death?" "I thank God, through our Lord Jesus Christ," for in him is brought to view a reasonable hope of life and salvation to our lost and ruined race. "The wages of sin is death; but the gift of God is eternal life through Jesus Christ our Lord."

We have seen that Adam was made pure and good and highly intellectual, and was sent into the world to be its sovereign; and that since he was made to be immortal, the love of life and sole sovereignty was so deeply implanted in his nature, that happiness without them was utterly impossible. He evidently understood the great law that whatever reproduces must die, and was solemnly warned against its infraction in the figurative language, "In the day thou eatest thereof thou shalt surely die."

We have seen that the woman whom God gave to be with Adam was persuaded by one of his servants, a red man, that she might become the mother of a race of like superiority with herself and Adam; "for," said he, "God doth know that in the day ye eat thereof your eyes shall be opened, and ye shall be as gods, knowing good and evil." The devil never uttered a more fearful truth than this, although his purpose was only to deceive; for, whereas, they had only known good; after they had eaten the forbidden fruit, they and the race sprung from them have known evil, and that continually; so that they, better than any other creatures, knew good and evil, because theirs was the knowledge derived from actual experience.

We have seen that the men of the old red race, who multiplied and replenished the earth in obedience to the command of their Creator, were called the sons of God, while the descendants of Adam were called men or the Adams, because they had been ushered into the world contrary to the expressed will of the Almighty, and they were therefore "strangers and aliens" to the household of God, "having no hope, and being without God in the world;" that this law, when violated by Adam, was no longer insisted upon, and that which was a mortal sin in Adam was not even rebuked in his descendants; nevertheless, "Death hath reigned over them from Adam to Christ, who had not sinned after the similitude of Adam's transgression."

We have seen that the rebellion of the world's great king against the authority of high heaven, not only imposed death and misery upon the race whom he chose to propagate, as the unavoidable condition of their being, but transferred the government of the world to him who is called "the prince of the power of the air and the prince of this world;" and that the earth was cursed by the destruction of the perpendicular polarity of its axis, and thus all nature suffered in the fall of Adam. "*For the creature was made subject to vanity, not willingly, but by reason of him who hath subjected the same* IN HOPE." "For we know that the whole creation groaneth and travaileth in pain together until now."

We have concluded that since the race of Adam was thrust unbidden into the world, they have not, as his other creatures, the right to claim even his ordinary providence; and yet "God so loved the world that he gave his only-begotten Son, that whosoever believeth in him should not perish, but have everlasting life."

It now remains for us to show how we, who are by nature strangers and foreigners to the household of God, have received "the power to become the sons of God." "They which are the children of the flesh, these are not the children of God; but the children of the promise are counted for the seed." "So, then, they that are in the flesh cannot please God." "For if ye live after the flesh, ye shall die." "Because the carnal mind is enmity against God; for it is not subject to the law of God, neither, indeed, can be." "As in Adam all die, even so in Christ shall all be made alive."

These, and many other scriptures which might be cited, prove that all who die in Adam, and that are strangers and aliens from God, are the children of the flesh, and not children of God; and yet, in the days of Noah, there was a class of beings in the world who were called the sons of God. The crying sin for which the world was destroyed by the flood of waters was the fact of the Adams giving their daughters in marriage to the sons of God.

The anger of God was kindled, not against the sons of God for this intermarriage, but against the Adams, whose daughters they took to wife. The offspring of these intermarriages were children of the flesh; for, instead of being called the sons of God, as their fathers were, it is not only said that they were giants, but that they became mighty men, or Adams.

The Mongolian, or mixed race of Cain, whom he brought up from the daughters of the sons of God, and the Malay or mixed race whom we have concluded were reared by Canaan and a negress, are the descendants of Adam; not perfect in their generations, it is true, but yet descendants of Adam. From these mixed races could not spring that seed which must bruise the serpent's head, because enmity, which was the result of the fall, should exist between the seed of the woman, or the Adams, and the seed of the serpent; therefore, where these two seeds were amalgamated, it would be impossible for the one to bruise the other's head, or for that other to bruise his heel.

The mixed races, or the Mongolians and Malayans, have never been a warlike people; but the unadulterated red men, as well as the white race, have ever been not only warlike, but wherever they have met, they have been deadly enemies and uncompromising belligerents. If, therefore, the declaration that the seed of the woman should bruise the serpent's head, in the twofold sense in which we have taken it; that is, that the Adams, or white men, should exterminate the serpents, or red men, and from the Adamic race should arise a mighty Prince, who should restore all things as they were before the fall — then there was an absolute necessity for the general destruction of the giants, or mixed descendants of Seth.

Noah, however, was found to be perfect in *his generations*, and he was saved from death by the flood, and through him the pure race of Adam was preserved. Christ, in order that he might be the second Adam, in order that he might be the restorer, and that he might be the king, not only of the inferior races, but that he might be supreme over all, must needs be perfect in his generations. This could not be, were he, in any way the most remote, connected with or descended from the negro race.

Were the people of the United States to ask for a king to rule over them, notwithstanding the monomania on the subject of the unity of the races, and the wide-mouthed professions of love and sympathy for "our unfortunate black brother;" yet it is doubtful whether the most devout worshipper of the black god would be willing to receive a mulatto, or an individual in whom there was the least taint of negro blood, to be the perpetual ruler of this country. Fanaticism might induce us to submit to a man of mixed blood, but will the most ultra fanatic deliberately seek to make the children of a negro the superiors, the rulers of his own through perpetual generations?

On the contrary, we are so jealous on this subject that we could find none among the millions of pure-blooded white men in America whom we consider good enough to be elevated so greatly above ourselves, but more especially whose children we willingly would assist in constituting the hereditary lords and sovereigns of our own; and if anarchy, misrule, and oppression should goad the people of this country into a change of their form of government, we may expect that they will choose a king from some of the royal families of Europe.

Moreover, to test fully your feelings in regard to the equality, or, rather, the superiority of one race over another, do not ask what you would do yourself, but suppose that you have a daughter, beautiful in person, accomplished in mind, amiable in disposition, every way lovely, and such as you would have her to be, would you look among the sable sons of Africa for a partner for your child? Would not every feeling within you revolt at the thought of giving her to the embraces of a man known to have the most remote taint of negro blood in his veins?

It is the voice of nature thundering to your mind and conscience that miscegenation is a terrible crime against the order which God has established — a proclamation to you, individually, of that great fundamental law, "Let every creature multiply after his kind." If, however, the Indian and the negro are descended from Adam and Eve, it is but right that their more fortunate white brethren should bring the unfortunates up by giving their daughters in marriage to the sons of negroes and Indians, and by taking wives for their sons from among Indian and negro women.

No sane man will thus voluntarily curse his posterity with that inferiority which invariably attaches to the mixed races. Then reason, and the interior voice of nature, as well as revelation, all proclaim the plurality of the races, the crime of miscegenation, and the impossibility of a man of mixed blood having the capacity for ruling the highest type of men. Hence we must conclude that the man Christ Jesus, who came into the world not only to restore the dominion which Adam lost, but also to build up a kingdom from the abnormal race itself, must be perfect in his generations, or purely descended, through Noah, from Adam and Eve.

Moreover, to assure us of this fact, — being supposed to be the son of David, — his lineage from Adam is carefully preserved and transmitted to us. Thamar, the mother of Phares, through whom the royal family of Israel descended, was a Canaanitish woman; a proof, if additional evidence were necessary, that the descendants even of Canaan, against whom the curse of inferiority was directed — at least those of them who inhabited Palestine — were of the pure blood of the white man, or Adam. The virgin Mary was of the tribe of Levi, of the family of the priests, of whose perfect lineage there could be no doubt; and they were descended from Ham, as well as from Shem, for the wife of Levi was a Canaanitish woman. We have no evidence that the genealogy of Christ in any way comes down through Japheth. The latter, however, is the dominant, if not the superior, family at this day; so that we may safely conclude that these families may have produced varieties of the Adamic or white race; but by no possibility could the sons of Noah have been the creators of the three standard races of men.

History deals with the families of each, and they are and have ever been white men. Ancient history, both sacred and profane, introduces for its characters the children of Shem and Ham; and if any mention is made of the children of Japheth, it is only the rude barbarians who inhabited Greece and Rome when the descendants of Ham colonized those countries, and planted there the arts and sciences which they had brought from their native land. It is only in comparatively modern times that the Scandinavian hordes have poured down from northern Europe and become historic characters.

Even in this view, had not Canaan been the father of the mixed, and therefore inferior, race of the Malayans, yet the curse of Noah has been fully verified. If these northern hordes be the descendants of Japheth, of which we suppose there can be no doubt, have they not taken possession of and dwelt in the tents of Shem, and have they not been served by the people of Southern Europe and Northern Africa, countries settled by Phœnicians, whom we know to have been the children of Ham, and of his son, Canaan?

Nevertheless, Christ Jesus is perfect in his generations, as Noah was, and consequently is perfectly competent in this view to be the ruler of nations. Since, however, our race is so ambitious, so averse to submission to any authority of an equal, hence, he who was born of our race, was conceived by the virgin, by the power of the Highest, and was therefore the only son of God of the Adamic race.

He alone, of all the Adams' posterity, came into the world in obedience to the commands, and in conformity with the preordination of the Almighty. All others were forced in upon his providence, on which account he is called the second Adam. The first Adam was the son of God, and came into the world to be its supreme ruler, but having failed, through disobedience, it was necessary that the second Adam come to accomplish his mission.

The government of a peaceful, quiet, and happy world, such as it was when the first Adam came, was not laid upon his shoulder; but a world of warfare, where every evil passion ran riot, where all was lost, ruined, was the inheritance of the second Adam, and he must first restore order, peace, subordination, before he could fully inaugurate his government. In order to do this, the demands of the violated law must be satisfied, and a peculiar people must be raised up from the abnormal race.

"The carnal mind is enmity against God; for it is not subject to the law of God, neither, indeed, can be." This enmity must be overcome, which could not be effected but by making the children of the flesh the children of God. When we have been made children of the Most High, and not till then, are we in a position to receive instruction from him necessary to qualify us to fill the exalted positions to which we aspire, without which we can never be happy, and which will be the inheritance of the children of God.

The question comes up, here, How can the children of the flesh become the heirs of God and joint heirs with the Lord Jesus Christ? "Verily, verily, I say unto thee, except a man be born again, he cannot see the kingdom of God." This divine declaration shows that we are not the sons of God, that we are aliens and foreigners to his household. In order, therefore, that we become his children, it is absolutely necessary that we be born again.

Had we been his children naturally, in other words, had we come into the world in obedience to his command, would it not be singular to say "Ye must be born again," and that without regeneration no individual of the Adamic race can see the kingdom of God? Nevertheless, we are the children of Adam, procreated in disobedience of the known will of God, with the avowed intention of rivalry with him; for the inducement offered by the serpent was this: "For God doth know that in the day ye eat thereof . . . ye shall be as gods."

We are not only miserable because we have inherited from our first parents the high ambition for sole sovereignty and immortality, which in the very nature of things cannot be gratified, but because we have inherited also the carnal mind, which is enmity against God; wherefore "we are without hope, and without God in the world." Then, "Marvel not that I said unto thee, Ye must be born again. That which is born of the flesh is flesh, and that which is born of the Spirit is spirit."

The abnormal race have been born of the flesh, and therefore of the flesh reap corruption, or, being reproduced and reproducing again, they must be subject to the universal law that whatever reproduces must die, and like must beget like in every sense of the word; therefore the love of immortality and of royal authority, which were bestowed on Adam for the wisest and noblest purposes, have been by him transmitted to all his race. The gratification of these desires, or the means of their gratification, he could not transmit to his children, because he forfeited both the one and the other in the very act of becoming our father.

It is clear, then, that the children of Adam are not, neither can they become, the children of God, except they be adopted by him. "Nicodemus saith unto him, How can a man be born when he is old? can he enter the second time into his mother's womb, and be born?" The question of Nicodemus is still a great mystery; yet it is certain that except a man be born of the Spirit and water, he cannot enter the kingdom of heaven.

Since flesh and blood cannot inherit the kingdom of God, and since we are the carnal children of carnal Adam, therefore we must be regenerated, and born of water and the Spirit, before we can become spiritually minded; we must be adopted into the family of God, then we can have the right to claim him as our father.

How could this be, since we are flesh and blood, and at bitter enmity against God, who is a spirit of such immaculate purity that he cannot look upon sin or rebellion against his authority with the least degree of allowance? Our gross, contaminated nature cannot come in direct contact with the transcendent intelligence of the universe; "for no man may see God and live;" "because God, out of Christ, is a consuming fire."

He created Adam pure and holy and good, and for a particular purpose, which he could not accomplish if he became a procreator. In violation of an express command, he did propagate his species; hence, notwithstanding God is our Creator and our Judge, yet we are not his children, and have no claims whatever, not even upon his general providence. Nevertheless, of his boundless mercy and infinite goodness, he ordained a plan whereby we might be saved from our hopeless wretchedness.

He sent his Son in the likeness of sinful flesh, who should condemn sin in the flesh, and who should stand as a daysman between God and man. He was appointed our Judge, who "was tempted in all points as we are, and who could be touched with the feelings of our infirmities."

We cannot come directly to God; yet we may approach his Son, for he assumed our material nature that, through him and by him, our sins might be forgiven, and we might receive the power to become the sons of God. "Unto us a child is born, and unto us a son is given," and the same is the "Everlasting Father." "Through him we receive the spirit of adoption, whereby we cry, Abba, Father."

As "the first man Adam" is our natural father, "in whom we all die," so "the second Adam is the Lord from glory," in whom we may all live, and through whom we have access to the throne of the heavenly grace, and are made the children of the Most High. For "if any man be in Christ, he is a *new* creature," no more "a stranger and foreigner, but a fellow-citizen with the saints and of the house of God." "There is therefore now no condemnation to them which are in Christ Jesus, who walk not after the flesh, but after the Spirit."

"For we know that the whole creation groaneth and travaileth in pain together until now. And not only they, but ourselves also, which have the first-fruits of the Spirit, even we ourselves groan within ourselves, waiting for the adoption, to wit, the redemption of our bodies." Then, although we may have been regenerated and born again, and are the children of God by adoption, yet "we have not apprehended, but we press forward that we may apprehend, and we groan within ourselves for the" full "adoption, to wit, the redemption of our bodies."

Had we been made to die as the red man was; in other words, had Adam been made to reproduce, and therefore subject to the law of death, and had his disobedience brought upon himself and his race what is termed "moral and spiritual death," (if the language conveys any idea, and if we understand it,) then, when we had been received into the family of God, we should have been contented. The desire, however, of the immortality of the body, inherited from Adam, who was made to be immortal, both soul and body, renders it necessary to our happiness that we live forever in our dual nature.

Christ came into the world to purchase back our bodies from death. When "he was crucified, dead and buried, and rose again on the third day," then were fulfilled all the prophecies which refer to him as our prophet and our priest, and the resurrection of the bodies of the pure-blooded and, possibly, of the miscegenated descendants of Adam was secured. "For as in Adam all die, even so in Christ shall all be made alive."

"Now, if Christ be preached that he rose from the dead, how say some among you that there is no resurrection of the dead?" "If in this life only we have hope in Christ, we are of all men most miserable. But now is Christ risen from the dead, and become the first-fruits of them that slept. For since by man came death, by man came also the resurrection of the dead."

We may have been adopted as the children of God, yet we have not the full assurance of that adoption until the redemption of the body is accomplished, that is, until we have passed through the change necessary to satisfy the law violated by Adam, and our bodies are raised to immortality through the merits of the second Adam. When we have attained to the redemption of our bodies, "then shall we see clearly, and know even as we are known," and then will hope be merged in fruition, and we shall be "heirs of God, and joint heirs with the Lord Jesus Christ."

"There is no other name given under heaven whereby men may be saved, except that of the Lord Jesus." Through him we may be regenerated; we may be born again; we may be adopted into the household of God; and through him we may attain to the resurrection of our bodies. He is the incarnation of Deity, for the purpose of reconciling the Adams to God.

He, as the great captain of our salvation, assumed our sinful nature, and by fulfilling the law and satisfying all its requirements, vindicated its reasonableness, and left us without excuse. How often is God charged with having made us with passions and instincts which render it impossible for us to keep the laws? If Adam sinned, why was not he alone punished, and his descendants left to stand upon their own merits? Or why was such a test of obedience imposed upon him that he could not resist the temptation to its violation?

We have seen that Adam could not have been made different from what he was, otherwise he could not have filled the high station which he came into the world to occupy. We have seen that God, in mercy to his lonely, isolated condition, made a woman, gave her to be with Adam as a companion, but solemnly warned him against the act of procreation; and that the woman, in the face of this warning, suffered herself to be drawn away from the path of virtue, not for the purpose of gratifying a resistless passion, but to the end that she might become the mother of a race superior to all the races which God had made; that Adam was not deceived, but having consented to the folly of the woman, was wilfully the author of all our misery and all our sufferings; of all our sickness, sorrow, pain, and death.

The second Adam came into the world to undo what was thus so fearfully done amiss by the first Adam. He did not come a pure, new creation from the hands of his Father, as the first Adam had done, but was born of our sinful race, yet was he conceived by a virgin of the Holy Ghost. He was the son of Adam, and he was the only-begotten son of God; indeed, the only son of God of this entire race, except the first Adam, and those who are adopted into his family through the merits and intercessions of the second Adam.

He was not only tempted, as the first Adam was, but he was tempted in all points as we are, yet without sin. The lust of power and the pride of life were appealed to, but the Son of man resisted them all. He was buffetted, spat upon, and evil entreated in a thousand ways. He was scourged and imprisoned; he was numbered with the transgressors; his name was cast out as evil; and, finally, he was put to the most cruel and ignominious death which the malice of devils could invent; yet, "as the sheep before her shearers is dumb, so he opened not his mouth."

By a thought, he could have prevented all of these indignities; by a word, he could have destroyed his persecutors; but he submitted to all, for, had he not suffered on, how could we have been saved? Had he not submitted, how should we have learned humility? Had he not died, how could we have attained to the redemption of the body, to wit, the resurrection of the dead?

He came to reconcile the world to God, which could be accomplished only by his suffering and death; but now the justice of God towards man is so clearly vindicated, that we are left wholly without excuse. Adam was made a free agent, and he chose death rather than life; we, being like him, are also free agents, and we may choose between life and death as freely as did Adam.

The difference in the condition of Adam and his race is this, that the former was pure, and holy, and good, and must have voluntarily sinned before he could die; while we are "conceived in sin, and brought forth in iniquity," and naturally subject to the law of death; but if we will accept of Christ as our prophet, priest, and king, we shall attain unto immortality, and an inheritance incorruptible, and that shall not fade away.

If we shall choose life, then shall we be chosen to be the sons of God, then shall we be elected, then shall we be regenerated, then shall we be adopted into the household of our Heavenly Father, and all our desires having been chastened and brought into subordination to his will, we shall have them fully gratified, as fully as those of Adam were when he was assured of immortality, and held in his hands the government of the world. We shall occupy a more desirable position than he, for having passed through our change from death unto life, our immortality, as his did, will not depend upon any contingency whatever; but being his glorified sons, "we shall be heirs of God, and joint heirs with the Lord Jesus Christ."

We are all the children of Adam, the children of the flesh, and enemies to God; but he, of his abundant mercy, sees proper to adopt from among us into his family such as obey him, and by the power of his Holy Spirit he brings them into covenant relations with himself. Others, who harden their hearts and stiffen their necks, he leaves to themselves, who work out, with greediness, their own destruction.

"What shall we say then? Is there any unrighteousness with God? God forbid. For he saith to Moses, 'I will have mercy on whom I will have mercy, and I will have compassion on whom I will have compassion.' So, then, it is not of him that willeth, nor of him that runneth, but of God that showeth mercy. For the scripture saith unto Pharaoh, Even for this same purpose have I raised thee up, that I might shew my power in thee, and that my name might be declared through all the earth. Therefore hath he mercy on whom he will have mercy, and whom he will he hardeneth."

If we go to an orphan asylum, and select one of its inmates, and adopt her as our own child, raise and educate her as such, and make her the heir to our whole estate, all must agree that this is a great mercy to the poor orphan whom we have adopted; but who will charge us with injustice towards those orphans whom we passed by, or who will insist that because we are pleased to adopt one, that therefore we are bound to adopt all the inmates of the asylum?

We are the orphans whom our father Adam has left in this great lazar-house—the heirs of penury, of want, of misery, and of death. Without money and without price, God, through the death and resurrection of his Son, has freely restored us all to that immortality which was forfeited by Adam. "For as in Adam all die, even so in Christ shall all be made alive." If his goodness and mercy lead him to select from us such as shall become heirs of salvation, what offence is that to those whom he does not elect, whom he does not adopt into his family?

He, being omniscient, will adopt those only whom he foreknows will be the heirs of salvation. "For whom he did foreknow he also did predestinate to be conformed to the image of his Son, that he might be the first-born among many brethren. Moreover, whom he did predestinate, them he also called; and whom he called, them he also justified; and whom he justified, them he also glorified."

Nevertheless, the plan of salvation is as broad in its application as the misery wrought by the fall. Not only shall all rise again to immortality — some to reign with Christ, and the others to go away into that perdition prepared for the devil and his angels — but the ample commission is, "Go into all the world, and preach my gospel to every creature; and he that believeth and is baptized [or maketh a public confession that Christ is the Son of God] shall be saved; and he that believeth not shall be damned." The offer of salvation is free to all, and since we are free agents, we all may accept or reject it; therefore, "thou art inexcusable, O man! whoever thou art;" and if thou art lost, thou canst not lay the blame to the charge of thy God, nor yet of Adam.

CHAPTER XXXIV.

THE FIRST AND SECOND ADVENT — THE FAITH OF THE CHRISTIAN — THE FAITH OF THE JEW — BOTH TAUGHT IN THE BIBLE — MISAPPLICATION OF PROPHECY.

THE original design of the Almighty in sending Adam into the world was that he might be the sole sovereign of the world, and that he might consolidate all the tribes and families then upon the earth into one vast kingdom, which, as vicegerent of God, he should govern in a manner similar to the government of the hierarchy of the heavens. Since Adam failed in the performance of his duties, and by his voluntary act introduced a condition of things which rendered it impossible for him to effect the object of his mission; and since the race over whom he came to rule was representatively active in the introduction of the new and superior race; and since the enmity between them, and the ambition of the latter and the pride of the former would forever preclude the possibility of subordination and peace and quiet among either race—therefore, it became necessary for the second Adam to come into the world, to accomplish the will of his Heavenly Father, and to establish his kingdom on earth, as he had first intended.

Moreover, because the old red race has well-nigh passed off the stage of action before the onward march of the restless, usurping race of Adam; since these "are children of the flesh," and since "the carnal mind is enmity against God, not subject to the law of God, neither indeed can be," therefore they must be adopted and be made the children of God before his kingdom could come, before his will could be done on earth as it is done in heaven.

The divine majesty was manifested in the flesh. He was born of a woman, and labored and suffered among the children of men. He died in obedience to the law, was buried, and in the power of God arose again on the third day. He showed himself to his disciples, proved to them that he was not a spirit merely, in the resemblance of manhood, but that he was "clothed upon" with the identical body in which they had known him. When all was finished, and the evidence of his death and the resurrection of his body were fully established, then, in the presence of about five hundred witnesses, he ascended up to his God and to our God, and a cloud received him out of their sight.

What must have been the anguish and disappointment of the disciples, who had followed him in all his travels, and who had firmly believed he was the promised Messiah who should have restored the throne of David in more than its primitive glory, when they saw him smitten, stricken of God, and afflicted, and unresistingly led to execution, and when they saw him taken from the cross, dead, and buried?

They were seized with amazement. They were frightened

from their faith in the garden of Gethsemane; for though he had time and again foretold these events, yet they could not believe that the Son of God could suffer. When all was finished, when they saw their Master evidently dead, they were scattered, like sheep without a shepherd, over the mountains of Israel. They wandered about without purpose; but finding no comfort for the loss of their head, no palliative for the anguish, the mortification of their misplaced confidence, they came together on the third day to condole with each other of their great bereavement and their unutterable disappointment.

They said to one another, "The chief priests and our rulers have delivered him to be condemned to death, and have crucified him. But we trusted it had been he which should have redeemed Israel; and, besides all this, to-day is the third day since all these things were done." "Then Jesus, presenting himself to them, said unto them, O fools, and slow of heart to believe all that the prophets have spoken! Ought not Christ to have suffered these things, and to enter into his glory?"

When the disciples were assured of the fact that he had really risen from the dead, "they asked of him, saying, Lord, wilt thou at this time restore again the kingdom to Israel? And he said unto them, It is not for you to know the times nor the seasons which the Father hath put in his own power."

It is apparent that not only the Scribes and Pharisees looked for Messiah to come in the character of a mighty conqueror, to establish in great pomp the regal authority of his father David, but even the chosen apostles, who had followed him through all his pilgrimage, still believed, after his death and resurrection, that his mission here was to establish then a universal temporal empire, which should be as permanent as the everlasting hills. No doubt this was the kind of kingdom of which they understood him to speak in all his teachings while he remained with them, else why should they have contended about who should be the greatest in the kingdom of God? else, why should the sons of Zebedee have requested that they might sit on his right hand and on his left, when he should come into his kingdom, or ascend the throne of his father David?

There is a large class of prophecies which indicate pointedly that the power of Christ should be what we term temporal power, or a government symbolized by the reign of David. The doctors of the law had seized upon these, and had wholly ignored that other class of prophecies which speak of it only as a spiritual kingdom, wherein he would rule only by moral suasion, and in which his only sceptre should be love.

They remembered that he should take the government upon his shoulder, that he was to be "the Prince of Peace. Of the increase of his government and peace there shall be no end, upon the throne of David, and upon his kingdom, to order it, and to establish it with judgment and with peace from henceforth even forever." Nevertheless, they were oblivious to the fact that he should be "despised and rejected of men; a man of sorrows, and acquainted with grief; that he should be wounded for our transgressions, bruised for our iniquities; and that by his stripes we should be healed." They forgot the prophecy which says, "He was taken from prison and from judgment, and who shall declare his generation? for he was cut off out of the land of the living." Neither did they remember that "he should make his grave with the wicked and with the rich in his death."

He taught his disciples from the first that it was necessary for Christ to suffer many things, and to be crucified by the Jews; that his mission in the world at that time was to establish his spiritual kingdom; that is, to put in operation the means for bringing many sons unto God, and thus to prepare the way for finally establishing the throne of David, or the universal empire of the second Adam.

Their minds, however, were not fully impressed with this view of the subject until he had risen from the dead, and had commissioned them to "go into all the world and preach my gospel to every creature; and he that believeth and is baptized shall be saved, and he that believeth not shall be damned." After that, and when they had seen him received up into heaven, they perceived the import of the prophecies which spoke of "the sufferings of Christ," and lost sight of those which speak of "the glory which should follow;" and thus the broad issue between the Christians and the Jews was made up, and has continued to this day.

When the prophets foretold the restoration of Israel and the throne of David, the Jews would not understand them to mean more than the gathering together of the twelve tribes of the sons of Jacob, and the re-establishment of the authority of the son of Jesse over them, as it was in the days of Solomon; no, not even when they declared that God had given to his Christ "the heathen for an inheritance, and the uttermost parts of the earth for a possession."

Though after his resurrection he succeeded in impressing the minds of the apostles with the truth that they were to preach repentance, faith, and baptism, the forgiveness of sins, regeneration, and adoption into the family of God; yet they believed that they were sent but to the lost sheep of the house of Israel; for it was only after a vision and an express command from heaven that Peter could be induced to go into the house of that devout man Cornelius, and preach the gospel to him and his, because he was not of the circumcision. When the vessel was let down from heaven filled with all manner of four-footed beasts and creeping things, and the language of the vision was "Arise, Peter, kill and eat," the reply of the chief of the apostles was, "not so, Lord, for I have never eaten anything that is common or unclean."

The broad extent of the commission, "Go into all the world and preach my gospel to every creature," was not thoroughly comprehended by the apostles even after all this. Not until after the subject was grasped by the expansive intellect of the great apostle of the Gentiles, who had been brought up at the feet of Gamaliel, and was thoroughly taught in the law and the prophets, was it clearly understood by the twelve witnesses themselves, that the middle wall of partition was utterly broken down and removed; and that henceforth there should be no difference between the Jew and the Gentile, the bond and the free; but that all men everywhere were now called upon to repent and to be baptized for the remission of their sins; and that it was just as necessary for the Jew as for the barbarian to be regenerated and adopted into the family of God.

No doubt the apostles, especially Paul, understood that after the Adamic race had been made the children of God by adoption, and a people had thus been prepared for the establishment of a theocracy, then Christ would come the second time, with power and might, to establish the throne of his father, David, and to govern the world as God governs the heavens. The learned apostle on one occasion was caught up to the third heavens and saw unutterable things; things which it was unlawful for him to make known on account of the ignorance of men.

Had Paul revealed to us what he saw at the time referred to, we suppose we should not now be under the necessity of making an argument to prove that the class of prophecies concerning Messiah, which are believed by the Jews, are as true as those believed by the Christians; but perhaps it is just as necessary for our good that the veil should have been upon our heart, as that it should have been upon that of the Jew.

Had the Christian world been all the while confidently looking forward to the establishment of the temporal power of their Master, "the unlearned and the unstable would have wrested" this truth "to their own destruction." How could they have been instructed in the doctrine of regeneration, of humility, of faith in the atonement, of repentance and right living, had their minds been always fixed on the grandeur and magnificence of the universal empire, which should be established by their once despised but now risen and glorified Lord? Nevertheless, if we will look at the subject in the light of reason and unprejudiced construction, we shall see that the Scriptures which describe the temporal authority of Messiah, are as pointed and as clear as those which refer to his spiritual kingdom.

The Christian thinks it worse than Bœtian stupidity in the Jew not to perceive that their own prophets have represented that Christ should come in the flesh and suffer meekness, to teach us humility; that he should come, as a prophet and priest, to secure the regeneration of the children of the flesh, to establish his kingdom in their hearts and make them spiritual, that they might receive the power to be called the sons of God.

The Jew considers it a strange delusion in the Christian to believe that He who should be called Wonderful, Counsellor, the Mighty God, the Everlasting Father, the Prince of Peace, of the increase of whose government there should be no end, should ever be stricken, smitten of God, and forsaken; that He should be crucified in the company of thieves and buried as any other mortal man.

The Christian looks upon the Jews as being absurdly bigoted, self-conceited, and wilfully blind to the truth. He feels absolutely certain that "the veil is upon their heart, even unto this day, when Moses" and their own prophets are "read;" and he believes that since they had the oracles of God committed to them, and yet rejected and murdered Him who was sent of heaven to sit upon the throne of David, therefore they are justly given over to hardness of heart, "to believe a lie, that they may be damned." Hence it has come to be orthodox Christianity to despise the Jew as a reprobate, and to hate him for his thrift; but we forget that He in whom we trust said to the Canaanitish woman, "I am sent to the lost sheep of the house of Israel; is it meet to take the bread of the children and give it to dogs?"

The Jew considers the Christian to be contemptibly superstitious, inasmuch as they worship as God a man who was executed as a felon near two thousand years ago. He deems them unpardonably presumptuous, for that they take upon themselves to understand Moses and the Hebrew prophets better than he who has Abraham to his father; that they, being Gentiles, and therefore strangers and aliens from the commonwealth of Israel, should thrust themselves into the place of the lawyer and the doctor, and assume the office of expounders of the laws of his fathers to him who is native and "to the manner born." Thus, it is not strange that unmitigated hate has existed between the Jew and the Christian for near two thousand years, without the most remote prospect of a reconciliation under the present dispensation.

It certainly is wrong for the Jews to refuse to have the man Christ Jesus to reign over them. It was wrong for them not to receive him when he first made his advent into the world. Oh, how fearfully wrong to take him, who had done no evil, from prison and from judgment and to deliver him into the hands of the executioner, and that too in the very face of the most graphic description of the scenes in which they were actors by their prophets! However, it was thus necessary for Christ to suffer, and this offence must needs have come. But woe unto those by whom it came; it had been better for them that a millstone had been tied about their necks and they had been drowned in the midst of the sea, and far better that they had never been born.

Had it not been thus; had Christ, who was a Jew according to the flesh, been universally received by the Jews, then the Gentiles might have excused themselves by saying that this was a Jewish religion, and was not therefore of any binding force upon them. Now, however, since he was rejected by the Jews, to whom he came, the Gentiles devoutly received him, and claim the Christian religion as their own system.

Knowing that Christ has come into the world, and has died that we might live; that he ascended up to his God and to our God, to advocate the merits of his blood for the remission of our sins; that through him the children of the flesh, or the Adams, may be made the children of God by adoption, they believe that his offices have all been filled, and that although he was very God and very man, for the purpose of bringing us into covenant relations with God, henceforth he is but God with us.

The Jews are still looking for the wonderful character combining the manhood with the attributes of the godhead to come into the world; for they know that Jesus of Nazareth has not ascended, or occupied the throne of his father David; which must be accomplished, or, as they believe, Moses and the prophets were false witnesses of the glory and grandeur of the reign of Messiah.

It will not do to say that the prophets described the celestial authority, because there he is God, and his kingdom is from everlasting to everlasting; and it is a great confusion of ideas to make Israel to mean heaven, and the throne of David to signify the high empyrean of the eternal Father. Therefore the construction placed upon these prophecies by the Jews is correct, or their true meaning has not yet been apprehended.

Jesus Christ was despised and rejected of men; he was a man of sorrow and acquainted with grief; and he was so poor that he not only had not where to lay his head, but was reduced to the necessity of performing a miracle in order to pay his tribute to Cæsar. He was a prisoner at the bar of Pontius Pilate, and from thence he was led forth and executed as a common malefactor. How does this comport with the exalted majesty of him who should "come in power and great glory," and should occupy the throne of David until all powers and principalities were put under him?

We conclude that, though the Jews were wrong in not understanding the prophecies which foretell that Christ must first come in humility and weakness, in order to secure the means for the adoption of the abnormal race of the Adams, yet that it is equally wrong in the Christian to lose sight of those prophecies which portray, in glowing colors, the temporal power of Christ, which certainly have not yet been fulfilled, nor is it possible that they should be unless he shall come again into the world; and, it may be, that this mistake of Christians may prove still more fatal to them than the blind unbelief of the Jews did to that devoted people.

The Jews are now confidently looking for the advent of Messiah; but the Christians believe that he has already come and fulfilled all his mission here, and that henceforth he sits at the right hand of the majesty of the heavens as God ruling in the affairs of men.

If the Christian faith be correct, what becomes of the prophecies already mentioned, and many others to which we may hereafter refer? That God has created and sustains all things; that he is a jealous God, and rules in the heavens;

that he is justly entitled to the homage of every creature in heaven and in earth, are facts made known to us by Moses and the prophets in plain language; then is it reasonable to suppose that they would teach us the same truths by representing heaven as Israel, and the eternal throne of God as the throne of David?

We are ready to admit that heavenly things are compared to earthly things, when it is necessary to enable us to comprehend the heavenly; but inasmuch as the idea is universal that God rules in the heavens, and inasmuch as the object of Moses and the prophets was to impress upon us a knowledge of the true God, to teach us of his attributes and how we might worship him aright, is it at all reasonable to suppose that Isaiah and the later prophets would have taught us the same truths by the figure of a little kingdom on earth and the throne of a man?

We may be told that the prophecies here alluded to are intended to show us how intimately the godhead and the manhood are united in the person of Christ; but if this be the only view which we are to take of the subject, we are again led into a hopeless confusion of ideas.

Was the incarnation of the Son of God for the salvation of the heavens? or was it in order that this world might be redeemed from the curse of the law? Has the world not only been placed in as good, but in a better condition by the second Adam, than it was in before the transgression of the first Adam? And is there no further necessity for the God-man to intercede for us with the Father?

If all the offices of Christ, the incarnate Son of God, have been filled by him, there can be no further necessity for his dual character, and we should now respect him merely as man, or we should adore him only as God. If all who died in Adam have been already made alive in Christ; if the spirit of adoption, whereby we cry, "Abba, Father," has been received into the heart of every son and daughter of Adam; if the kingdom has been restored to Israel, and if the son of David has been placed upon his throne; if the world has been restored to the condition of bliss in which it was before the fall of Adam; if all these things have been accomplished, then has Christ completed the work assigned him, and "then," says Paul, "cometh the end, when he shall have delivered up the kingdom to God, even the Father." But we do know that these things have not been done; wherefore we must still look for the man Christ Jesus to come among us, to establish the throne of David forever, and to bring into our miserable world more than the blessedness of the Adamic ages.

The unbelieving Jew, whom we consider accursed of God, believes all of the Old Testament prophecies in regard to the temporal or earthly glory of Messiah; and from the rivers to the ends of the earth this peculiar people are anxiously looking for the Prince of peace to come and restore the kingdom of Israel, and to establish the throne of David forever.

The Christian, however, who believes that Jesus was the Christ,—that he has come into the world, has suffered the just for the unjust, to secure the adoption into the household of God both of the Jew and of the Gentile,—not only ignores those prophecies, but utterly refuses credence to the emphatic declarations of him whom they call Lord, and of the witnesses whom he chose out of the world to bear record concerning him.

"And when he had spoken these things, while they," the five hundred witnesses, "beheld, he was taken up; and a cloud received him out of their sight. And while they looked steadfastly towards heaven as he went up, behold, two men stood by them in white apparel; which also said, Ye men of Galilee, why stand ye gazing up into heaven?

this same Jesus, which is taken up from you into heaven, shall so come in like manner as ye have seen him go into heaven."

After discoursing of the scenes which should transpire in the last days, Christ himself says (Mark): "And then shall they see the Son of man coming in the clouds, with great power and glory." He says the same in Luke; and in John he says: "And if I go and prepare a place for you, I will come again and receive you unto myself, that where I am, there ye may be also." In Matthew he says: "And then shall appear the sign of the Son of man coming in the clouds of heaven, with power and great glory."

If these, and many other New Testament Scriptures, were taken in connection with the writings of Moses and the prophets, where they speak of Messiah coming as a prince and a ruler, then might the Christian as well as the Jew be now looking for the advent of Immanuel. Therefore, "what I say unto one, I say unto all, Watch, for in a day and an hour when you do not expect, the Son of man will come." The Christian, however, does not look forward to a second coming of the Son of man, but only that "Christ shall come as God, to judge the world in righteousness."

Before fixing down irrevocably on this conclusion, does it not become us, who are not of the circumcision, to have sufficient regard to the opinions of the doctors of the law — who are of the seed of Abraham, and heirs of the covenant — to give the subject of the temporal power of Christ a thorough investigation in the light of reason? If the Jewish rabbi of all ages and every clime, have looked, and still look for Messiah to establish the throne of David, which is a temporal authority, ought we to treat the subject lightly?

If the Jews made a fatal mistake in ignoring the prophecies referring to the spiritual kingdom and first advent of Christ — notwithstanding the fact that they were the children of promise, to whom was committed the oracles of God—ought we not, who are aliens and strangers from the commonwealth of Israel, to be very cautious how we heartily and presumptuously reject the stronger, plainer, more pointed prophecies in regard to his temporal kingdom, in which all Israel believes, lest haply, we who have been made the favored recipients of the later dispensation, be found fighting against Christ in the day in which he shall "come in the clouds of heaven, with power and great glory"? Is it not possible that such an attitude of unbelief might prove more fatal to us than that of the Scribes and Pharisees did to them—as fatal as that of the antediluvians in the preaching of Noah did to them.

Jesus himself has said, "I came not to destroy, but to fulfil the law. Heaven and earth may pass away, but not one jot nor one tittle shall pass from the law until all be fulfilled."

Some one says the New Testament Scriptures above allude not to a second coming of Christ in his dual character, and that the judgment which he will then dispense will be only in the character of God, the eternal majesty. We have already shown that if this view were correct, then those prophecies which refer to his temporal power and glory, to fulfil which, as well as others, he assumed our sinful nature, have utterly failed.

Again: what does John mean in the apocalyptic vision, when, after stating that Satan should be bound and cast into the bottomless pit, and shut up and sealed, that he might deceive the nations no more until a thousand years were fulfilled, he says: "And I saw thrones, and they sat upon them, and judgment was given unto them; and I saw the souls of them that were beheaded for the witness of Jesus, and for the word of God, and which had not worshipped the beast, neither his image, neither had received his mark upon their foreheads, or in their hands; and they lived and reigned with Christ a thousand years?"

And again he says, "Blessed and holy is he that hath part in the first resurrection; on such the second death hath no power, but they shall be priests of God and of his Christ, and reign with him a thousand years." When "the Lion of the tribe of Judah, the root of David," had prevailed, the spirits of the redeemed "sung a new song, saying, Thou art worthy to take the book and open the seals thereof; for thou wast slain and hast redeemed us by thy blood out of every kindred, and nation, and tongue, and people; and made us kings and priests; and *we shall reign on the earth*." Paul says, "If we have received the spirit of adoption, then the Spirit itself beareth witness with our spirit that we are the children of God; and if children, then heirs, heirs of God and joint heirs with Christ." Hence he concludes that, although "it does not yet appear what we shall be, yet when he comes in his kingdom we shall be like unto him;" for he has secured our adoption into the family of God, and he is our elder brother.

From all this, and very many other passages in the New Testament, it seems equally as clear that the Christian should expect Christ to come the second time in power to establish his temporal kingdom, as that the Jew should confidently look for a similar glorious advent of Messiah, from the declarations of the prophets. The prophecies are just as vital, and should have as much binding force upon the Christian as upon the Jew; and the old prophecies concerning the temporal kingdom of Messiah, and the New Testament Scriptures which speak of his coming the second time in power and great glory, must refer to the same grand consummation; wherefore the Christian has cumulative evidence to the effect that Christ will come the second time, and that his mission then will be to establish the throne of David forever.

The Jews reject Jesus as the Christ because they will not understand the prophecies in regard to the humiliation of the first coming of Messiah; yet they look, without doubt, for the Christ to come speedily, for the purpose of assuming the royal prerogatives of a mighty monarch, a character in which also he was certainly expected by Moses and the prophets.

The Christians think exceedingly strange that the Jews should not understand the prophecies which show how absolutely necessary it was for Christ to come into the world, and be despised and rejected of men, to suffer and satisfy all the requirements of the law, to the end that we might receive the spirit of adoption, whereby we cry, "Abba, Father." Yet Christian ministers may be found who ridicule the idea of a second advent, who treat with scorn and contempt the proposition that Christ must come again for the fulfilment of unaccomplished prophecies in the Old and New Testaments, for the verification of the declarations of Moses and the prophets, and of himself, and of his chosen apostles.

Faith is made the condition of salvation. "He that believeth and is baptized shall be saved; but he that believeth not shall be damned." Then the Christian, it would seem, should be the heir of the kingdom; but is he really so? He says that he believes that Jesus is the Christ of God; and in this faith he has been baptized. Nevertheless, he does not believe him when he declares that he will again come into the world as a judge and a ruler. Does he then honor him whom he calls Lord? Can a man believe him to be the Son of God, and yet discredit the declarations which he made?

Christ is either false or true. If true, he must be so in all things. He cannot be partly false and partly true. Neither can any one partly believe in Christ and partly disbelieve him. "He that believeth and is baptized shall be saved, and he that believeth not shall be damned."

When "Christ shall come the second time without sin unto salvation;" when he shall come, not in humility, but "in power and great glory;" when "the heavens and the earth shall pass away with a great noise, and the elements shall melt with fervent heat;" and when the new heavens and the new earth shall be created, and the throne of David shall be established forever, the faith of the Jew places him in a situation to receive Immanuel heartily, and to say fervently, "Hosanna to the son of David; blessed is he that cometh in the name of the Lord."

But is the more highly favored Christian, who does not expect Christ to establish a temporal kingdom in the world, prepared so to receive him when he comes as shall become the children of the kingdom? "What I say unto one, I say unto all, Watch, for in a day and an hour when you do not expect, the Son of Man will come."

CHAPTER XXXV.

THE FIRST AND SECOND ADVENT, CONTINUED — THE PROPHECIES IN RELATION TO THE FIRST HAVE BEEN FULFILLED — WHO WILL BE CHRIST'S SUBJECTS IN HIS REIGN OF POWER? — HOW CAN THIS EARTH BE MADE THE ABODE OF PEACE? — "BUT THE DAY OF THE LORD SHALL COME AS A THIEF IN THE NIGHT" — THE NEW JERUSALEM.

FROM what has been said in the last chapter, it is hoped that the patient student, if not the ordinary reader, will perceive both from Old and New Testament Scriptures that the Son of man must come again into the world to fulfil the prophecies, and to carry out the original designs of Omnipotence in regard to the government of the world. When he shall "descend with a shout, with the voice of the archangel and with the trump of God, the dead in Christ shall rise first, and we who remain shall be changed in the twinkling of an eye," and be caught up to meet him in the air, where we shall remain with him while the work of the new creation is being accomplished.

Then the temporal kingdom of the Messiah will be established "in power and great glory," in which shall dwell righteousness and true holiness; and all that was lost in Adam shall be fully recovered in Christ. As Adam reigned in the world prior to the fall, so must Christ reign after the restoration. Then, and not till then, will be answered the prayer, "Thy kingdom come; thy will be done on earth as it is in heaven." Then "the sword shall be beaten into the ploughshare, and the spear into the pruning-hook, and the nations shall learn war no more." Then shall the "Prince of peace" sit upon the throne of his father David, and reign in the power of God a thousand years.

Who will be his subjects? and how can this earth be made the abode of peace and happiness, so that "nothing shall hurt in all the holy mountain," and bounteous plenty and undisturbed contentment pervade the universal empire of the world? The first of these questions is plainly and fully answered in many passages of the New Testament.

When Christ comes, he will be attended by the saints who have been murdered for the witness of Jesus; by the hundred and forty-four thousand of Israel; and by an innumerable company of those who have washed their robes and made them white in the blood of the Lamb; who have come up through great tribulation from every kindred, nation, and tongue. His retinue shall be composed of all the righteous of the race of Adam who have fallen victims to the effects of sin, but shall be then resurrected by the power of God; and those who remain, being suddenly changed, shall be added to the mighty concourse of the subject-followers of the great king.

Instead of Adam reigning in Paradise, surrounded by the multiplying, reproducing, and therefore dying servants whom he had chosen from the tribes of his subjects, the old red race; the Son of man shall sit upon the throne of universal majesty, highly exalted in the city of the New Jerusalem; and shall govern the world in power and great glory, while his high empyrean is surrounded by his happy servitors, the saints of all ages who have been regenerated and adopted from the family of the Adams' into the household of God; whose mortal bodies having passed through the mystic change have been resurrected to immortality.

How superlatively beatific must be that kingdom whose capital city shall be most magnificent in structure; and within whose jasper walls sickness, sorrow, pain, and death can never enter; and where unsatisfied desire can never be known. The balm of Gilead will be there, and the great Physician — who, when in the world establishing his spiritual kingdom, though poor and despised, gave sight to the blind; opened the deaf ear; gave speech to the dumb; healed the halt, the maimed, and all manner of diseases among the people; aye, restored the dying and the dead to life and health, and even called Lazarus from his grave — will be there.

He will be as merciful, as kind, as powerful, when he comes in his kingdom, as he was in the days of his humility; then disease, and pain, and death cannot exist among the servitors around his throne, the inhabiters of the holy city; and, no doubt, if any mortal thing could pass the shining gates and enter the golden paved streets within the burnished walls of that place of sublime beatitude, such mortal would immediately become immortal, for death can never gain admittance into that stronghold of the King of Life.

God is not the God of the dead, but of the living; and the mission of his Son is to save the dying and restore the dead to life; to accomplish which, "He once tasted death for every man," wherefore death can no more come near him. Death, however, still riots in the world, and will still dispute the sway of the King of Life, even after he has sat down on the throne of David in the beloved city.

"For he must reign till he hath put all enemies under his feet. The last enemy that shall be destroyed is Death. For he (the Father) hath put all things under his (the Son's) feet. But when he (the Father) saith all things are put under him (the Son), it is manifest that he (Death) is excepted, which did put all things under him (Death). And when all things shall be subdued unto him (the Son), then shall the Son also himself be subject unto him (the Father) that put all things under him (the Son), that God may be all in all."

"For as in Adam all die, even so in Christ shall all be made alive. But every man in his own order; Christ the first fruits, afterwards they that are Christ's at his coming. Then cometh the end when he shall have delivered up the kingdom to God, even the Father; when he (Christ) shall have put down all rule, and all authority, and power." Where is the scene to which reference is here made? Is it in the heavens or in the earth?

It must be evident to every one that the earth, and the earth alone, is meant; for the declaration, that "as in Adam all die, even so in Christ shall all be made alive," renders the meaning of the apostle indisputable. There can by no possibility be any connection between the transgression of Adam and the death of the inhabiters of other spheres. Adam was a finite being, and his authority, though embracing the entire earth, could not extend beyond its confines, nor his conduct affect the condition of beings in other worlds.

The angels died not in Adam, wherefore they are not made alive in Christ; hence the scene described by Paul in the above quotations is in the earth, and cannot, by any rational implication, extend beyond the earth. There is no death in heaven; there is no enemy there; neither can all things there be subdued under him; for there he is the word of God, by whom all things were created, and his authority is from eternity to eternity. Hence, as before, the scene described above is not heaven, but the earth; the things spoken of are of the earth; and the authority, and power, and rule which Christ shall put down, are evidently of the earth.

To spiritualize the above language, as in the manner of some, that is, to give it application only to the spiritual kingdom of Christ, would render it a meaningless jargon of about equal value with "a sounding brass, or a tinkling cymbal;" therefore we conclude that the apostle, in the spirit of prophetic vision, mounted far beyond the temporal sufferings of Christ and of his members to the glory which should follow in the establishment of his earthly empire. On and still on the prophetic ken extended, to the close of that grand cycle of ages denominated by the old prophets, "from everlasting to everlasting," and the highly favored apostle saw when the last great enemy, Death, was subdued under the mighty king, whom he then beheld delivering the temporal authority of the world to the Father, since its government had never been entirely assimilated to the hierarchy of the heavens, "that God may be all in all."

"But the day of the Lord will come as a thief in the night; in the which the heavens shall pass away with a great noise, and the elements shall melt with fervent heat;

the earth also and the works that are therein shall be burned up." In this, and other parallel passages of Holy Writ, is described the grandest, the most sublime of all the revolutions in nature, so vast, so mighty, so sublime in itself, so magnificent, so glorious in its result that inspiration speaks of it as a new creation.

As no effect is produced without the use of adequate means; as physical causes alone accomplish physical ends; and as the result here described is powerfully physical, therefore its cause must be adequate and physical; and the character of this work will not permit us to slur it over without investigation, in the easy, unphilosophical, not to say stupid way of calling it one of "the hidden mysteries."

It may be as well, however, to notice the fact that many persons make the last quoted passages refer to the final scene in the world's history — the last grand act in the eventful drama of human affairs and of earthly interest. A little thought, it would seem, ought to dispel this error. Reference is evidently made to the closing up of the present order of things, of unsatisfied desires and physical suffering; but it refers also to the ushering in of a grand epoch of peace, of quiet, of happy conditions of the Divine government, in which the will of God shall "be done on earth as it is done in heaven," as we hope to make fully appear before we have done.

In the former pages of this work we have attempted to show that since Adam was a physical as well as a spiritual being — that inasmuch as he held in his hands the physical and spiritual control of the world — therefore when he fell, it was by sinning against the physical and spiritual laws; and hence that both his spiritual and physical authority were delivered to the adverse spirit, who had prevailed against him, and who is called the "prince of the power of the air and the prince of this world."

If the physical laws, as well as the spiritual condition of the world were perverted by the fall of Adam, then the physical condition of happiness in the world as well as spiritual redemption, must be recovered by Christ, else the sure word of prophecy will fail, else the Scriptures cannot be fulfilled, and the holy men who were inspired to write them will be found false witnesses of God. Since these things *must be so*, let us inquire by what means the earth may be restored to a better condition even than that in which it existed prior to the fall.

To accomplish this glorious result has been the work of God ever since the fearful fall of Adam, which slowly, according to human estimation, yet surely tends to final and triumphant success. To redeem the fallen race, to adopt the children of the flesh into the household of God, to build up a spiritual kingdom on earth, in which the Son of God might reign as his Father rules in the heavens, was the object of the former advent of Messiah into the world. When he comes the second time it will be to sit upon the throne of David, and to wield the sceptre of the world until all enemies, even Death himself, are subdued under him.

The converse of the means used by the adversary in bringing physical suffering and ruin into the world, must be those employed by Omnipotence in bringing about the restoration. Then in the fulness of time we would conclude that God will cause the magnetic influence of that benign heaven, which formerly held the world in her upright posture, again to be fastened upon her, when her perpendicular polarity and all her happy conditions, prior to the fall, must be fully restored.

The mighty revolution in nature, which is denominated the new creation, will not be gradual and gentle, but sudden and violent; for "the day of the Lord will come as a thief in the night; in the which the heavens shall pass away with a great noise, and the elements shall melt with fervent heat; the earth also and the works that are therein shall be burned up."

When the earth was thrown down from her perpendicular posture, the equal days and nights were destroyed; the hitherto even temperature of climate was changed into the extremes of heat and cold, so that Paradise was suddenly surrounded by inaccessible icebergs, and the fertile regions of the equator were converted into arid wastes by the torrid rays of a vertical sun and the inauspicious winds of the tropics. The placid current of electricity from the sun was so interrupted by that grand revolution, that the regular evaporation of water by day and the descent of dews by night were almost entirely prevented.

By the irregular evaporations, which were formed into clouds, and then converted into water by flashes of excited electricity, so that the rains descended occasionally as now, until the fulness of time when the fountains of the great deep were broken up, and the rain pouring down in torrents for forty days and forty nights, the great revolution of the earth by water was accomplished. So, in like manner, if the earth were suddenly thrown back into her perpendicular position, the results predicted by the prophets might be expected.

When the fountains of the great deep were broken up, the internal channels or arteries not already so filled were engorged with the vast amount of vegetable matter which had accumulated upon the surface through the mighty cycles of time from the third day of the grand creative week down to the time of the cataclysm. Since then, the greater part of any remaining sections of arteries and internal apertures of the earth, by the continual washing of the rains, have been filled up with vegetable matter.

In the revolutions at the time of the introduction of the

earth into the solar system, at the time of the flood, and by the continuous accumulations since the latter event, have been formed the vast anthracite and bituminous coal fields through all the interior of the earth, as extensive in proportion to the body of the globe, in all probability, as the arterial and other cavities to the human body. The waters which once circulated freely through the interior of the earth, as the blood circulates in the healthy body of a man, have been forced out upon the surface, and their internal places being filled with combustible matter, it would seem that ample means were prepared for the grand conflagration of the world's ecpyrosis.

Were the earth suddenly thrown back to her perpendicular position, the current of electricity which flows from the sun around our globe, permeating the whole body of the earth, magnetizing a mountain of iron here, and setting on fire a coal field there, (thus producing a volcano,) instead of passing around the earth in spiral curves, diverging from the equator towards the poles, as at present, would pass in parallel circles around and through the earth, from pole to pole, as in the pre-Adamic and innocent ages.

New chains of conduction must be formed, which must, of necessity, be different from those of present conduction. If the current of electricity be obstructed, as is rational to suppose, in its new passage through non-conducting combustible matter, ignition must occur; hence, from a rational view of the subject, we must conclude that, if the earth were suddenly thrown back to a perpendicular position, the electricity from the sun, passing in unusual directions, would set on fire instantaneously all the vast coal fields through all the extensive channels where once flowed the waters of the whole earth.

If a human body were depleted of all its blood, and if all the arteries, veins, and internal cavities were filled up with highly inflammable matter, and if a spark of electricity be thrown into that body so as to set it on fire, the burning body would present a miniature representation of the grand conflagration of the world.

Malachi says, "For behold the day cometh that shall burn as an oven;" and again, "Who may abide the day of His coming, and who shall stand when he appeareth; for he is like a refiner's fire."

Joel says, "I will show wonders in the heavens and in the earth, blood and fire and pillars of smoke. The sun shall be turned into darkness, and the moon into blood, before the great and terrible day of the Lord come."

Matthew says, "Immediately after the tribulation of those days shall the sun be darkened, and the moon shall not give her light, and the stars shall fall from heaven, and the powers of the heavens shall be shaken; and then shall appear the sign of the Son of man in heaven; and then shall the earth mourn, and they shall see the Son of man coming in the clouds of heaven, with power and great glory. And he shall send his angels with a great sound of a trumpet, and they shall gather his elect from the four winds, from one end of heaven to the other."

Mark says, "But in those days, after that tribulation, the sun shall be darkened, and the moon shall not give her light, and the stars of heaven shall fall, and the powers that are in heaven shall be shaken. And then shall they see the Son of man coming in the clouds, with great power and glory."

Luke says, "And there shall be signs in the sun, and in the moon, and in the stars; and upon earth distress of nations, with perplexity; the sea and the waves roaring; men's hearts failing them for fear, and for looking after those things which are coming on the earth; for the power of heaven shall be shaken. And then shall they see the Son of man coming in a cloud, with power and great glory."

Is it possible that these and parallel Scriptures have no meaning at all, or, if any, that it lies in some mystic spiritualization, more difficult of comprehension than the heights of eternity or the depths of infinity? Unless we are hopelessly infatuated with the traditional follies of the old commentators, let us take a rational view of the subject, when it must appear that the grandest and most sublime physical revolution which has ever come upon our earth is foretold in these passages.

When all the anthracitic and bituminous substances in the earth, from its centre to its circumference, are at once set on fire, the imagination fails to picture the terrific grandeur of the awful scene. We may conclude, from what Peter says, that there will be such an explosion as never has been heard upon our earth — as will shake her to her centre — and the smoke mounting up will darken the heavens, when the internal fires shall have burned to the surface; "for," says he, "the heavens shall pass away with a great noise, and the elements shall melt with fervent heat."

The elemental metals — the gold, the silver, the precious stones which have been largely accumulated by the action of water in the bowels of the earth — will be melted, sublimated, and thrown to the surface, separated from all impurities; "for He that shall come is as a refiner's fire;" and he shall purify the gold until it shall be "transparent like glass."

As the coal fields are consumed, the former arteries and internal veins of the earth, by that means and by the ejection of the metals, will be completely opened up through all the body of the earth, and the melted, sublimated minerals and metals will be driven out upon the surface by the internal "fervent heat."

As the largest arteries in the human body which come directly to the surface are in the head or temples, so we may conclude it is with his great prototype, the world; and in that case the sublimated metals would be thrown up the grand aorta to the north pole, or the head of the world, in greater abundance than elsewhere; and where the artery or river parts into four heads at the surface, there should be a vast deposit of fine gold and precious stones.

If our investigations in the former part of this work led us to conclude correctly that the north pole, or head of the world, is the place where Paradise was located; that is, the garden which God planted, where Adam reigned and fell — whence he was driven by his offended Maker, as Lucifer was from the high heaven; that on account of the inclination of the earth's axis, it was bound up in adamantine chains of yet unending winter — then, as the elephant which was released in a state of perfect preservation from the icebergs of Siberia, in the current century, may we not rationally suppose that the lovely garden where Adam lived and reigned, and where God visited him as a father visits his son, stands untouched by the hand of time, even at the present day; and that if the earth be brought back to an upright position as suddenly as it was thrown down, then, when the world is on fire, and all that part of it which has been stained with violence and blood and miscegenation, the head or north pole will be thawing into pleasantness; and that the first throbbings of the great artery which passes up into her temple and parts into four heads in the garden of Eden will throw out vast amounts of gold and precious stones? The precious stones will be deposited in large quantities there, and the liquid gold flowing through the pleasant walks of the garden, the former capital of the world, and cooling there, the streets of the city whose Maker and Builder is God will have all its pavements of solid gold.

Furthermore, if the waters of the river of life immediately flow out through the reopened channel, may not the very trees which grew in the garden before sin entered, be warmed and moistened into renewed and vigorous life, so that all the lovely scenes which surrounded Adam in the days of his innocency and happiness, may stand more grandly glorious than ever; while the same tree of life which is in the midst of the garden, will droop beneath the burden of its luscious, unplucked fruit, upon which last rested the longing eyes of Adam when he was driven from the sacred haunts of Paradise?

It is possible, however, that the old tradition and the glowing dreams of the ancient poets in regard to the blissful hyperborean regions, and the speculations of modern scientific explorers of an open sea at the north pole, may be correct; and the rapid circulation of accumulated electricity about the pole may make eternal spring even within the circumambient walls of ice. In this case, the sweet groves of Paradise, rendered still more grand and glorious by the perennial growth of six thousand years, since the flight of Adam, may cluster with majestic trees and embowering vines, while gentle breezes, redolent of virgin flowers and luscious fruits, may render the heaven-favored retreat a place where even a God might deign to fix his seat of power and glory.

But to return. During the burning up of the old earth (for that part of the globe which we can visit is the only earth to us), the gold and the precious stones, we may suppose, will be thrown up through the grand aorta to the head of the world in such profuse abundance that they will constitute the only building material in all the regions of Paradise. It may be that the sublimated precious stones will be upheaved to the height of fifteen hundred miles about the pole, and at the distance of seven hundred and fifty miles on every side from that centre where now stands a wall of ice, and that being there condensed and solidified, they will form the jasper walls of the New Jerusalem which John saw in the apocalyptic vision.

It may be that Adam designed the building of the holy city, and, in his long and quiet reign over the world, that he collected much material for this purpose; but having sinned, he was expelled from the garden, and that, with all other grand designs which he had formed for future accomplishment, fell to the ground, or, rather, were reserved to be performed by the second Adam. David had it in his heart to build the temple at Jerusalem, and gathered together great store of building material; but because he was a man of blood, therefore he was not permitted to erect the edifice. His son Solomon was inspired with wisdom for the great enterprise, and he, almost without an effort, obtained everything necessary which had not been accumulated by his father, and he built that house which was the glory of his kingdom and the wonder of the nations. Everything in the Jewish religion and about the temple was typical; then was not the temple itself a type, and did it not represent the holy city which John saw "descending out of heaven from God"?

He saw the New Jerusalem descending out of heaven, but did not see it ascending; wherefore we must understand that it shall be located, not in heaven, as is vainly supposed by some, but on the earth. When John saw that city, she had "the glory of God; and her light was like unto a stone most precious, even like a jasper stone, clear as crystal, and had a wall great and high, and had twelve gates, and at the gates twelve angels, and names written thereon, which are the names of the twelve tribes of the children of Israel.

"On the east three gates, on the north three gates, on the south three gates, and on the west three gates. And the wall of the city had twelve foundations, and in them the names of the apostles of the Lamb. And he that talked with me had a golden reed to measure the city and the gates thereof, and the wall thereof. And the city lieth four square, and the length is as large as the breadth; and he measured the city with the reed twelve thousand furlongs. The length and the breadth and the height of it are equal; and he measured the wall thereof a hundred and forty and four cubits, according to the measure of a man, that is, of the angel.

"And the building of the wall of it was of jasper, and the city was pure gold, like unto clear glass. And the foundations of the wall of the city were garnished with all manner of precious stones. The first foundation was jasper, the second sapphire, the third chalcedony, the fourth an emerald, the fifth sardonyx, the sixth sardius, the seventh chrysolite, the eighth beryl, the ninth a topaz, the tenth a chrysoprasus, the eleventh a jacinth, the twelfth an amethyst. And the twelve gates were twelve pearls; every gate was of one pearl; and the streets of the city were pure gold, as it were transparent glass.

"And I saw no temple therein; for the Lord God Almighty and the Lamb are the temple of it. And the city had no need of the sun, neither of the moon to shine in it; for the glory of God did lighten it, and the Lamb is the light thereof." How grand, how magnificent, how gloriously beautiful the city here described! Grand in its proportions, magnificent in its structure, and gloriously beautiful in the priceless richness of its precious materials!

This city, or the pattern of it, came down out of heaven, and was established on the earth as her great capital city. It will be builded on "a great and high mountain," for in such a locality was it shown to the prophetic apostle. "And the light of the city was like unto a stone most precious, even like a jasper stone, clear as crystal."

If there be a great and high mountain at the north pole, answering, as we suppose, to the head of a human being;

and if the holy city be built upon its crest, as the temple was built upon the top of Mount Zion, surrounded with a jasper wall one hundred and forty-four cubits, or two hundred and sixty feet in thickness, twelve thousand furlongs, or fifteen hundred miles in height and length; it is evident that if the earth revolve upon her axis perpendicularly to the plane of her orbit, no light of the sun or moon could ever reach within its walls; and hence John tells us that there is no need of the sun nor of the moon in that city, but that "the light thereof is like a jasper stone, clear as crystal." The New Jerusalem, then, will be lighted by pure, original light, which, with the clearness and brightness of the sun, will shine upon its own streets, and, like the sun, it will be brilliantly luminous to all of the earth where it is visible, and to the distant worlds upon which it will shine.

May not this original light, to some extent, exist at the north pole at the present time as manifested in the occasional splendid displays of the aurora borealis? If so, then the existence of an open sea, and the beatific hyperborean regions of the poets, at the north pole and their cause are at once and satisfactorily explained.

CHAPTER XXXVI.

Description of the New Jerusalem — Where Situated — Its Inhabitants — Ezekiel and John.

WE have anticipated in our last chapter, and must now return. We have seen that the heat which shall dissolve the elements will be internal, and will be produced by the burning out of the vast fields of anthracite and bituminous coal deposited through all the arteries and interior veins of the world. While this intense heat is raging, the water will be vaporized and driven out with that "great noise in the which the heavens shall pass away." The melted metals will also escape from the secret places in the bowels of the earth, and, in coming to the surface and flowing down ravines and the old beds of creeks and rivers, will so line them as forever to preclude all danger of abrasion from the flowing of the waters.

We have already seen what an extraordinary flow of gold there will be to the north pole, or head of the world, up that channel, through which the waters of the river of life will course, after the new earth is created; wherefore we may conclude that the channel of that river, at least, will be lined with massive refined gold, whatever metals may line other streams.

While the elements are melted with fervent heat, many depressions will be made; the rugged mountains, crags, and hills will be melted down; and as the coal fields become exhausted, and as the internal heat subsides, the atmosphere will be cooled, the vapory particles will be reduced to water and again returned to the earth. It will not descend in the form of rain, but be distilled like the heavy dews.

This process will facilitate the cooling down of the earth. The condensation of the water and the falling of the mist will continue until the internal fires are extinguished, and all the waters of the rivers and oceans have been returned to the earth. If, however, all of the waters shall re-descend which now cover three-fourths of the surface of the globe, what will become of them? For John says, "And I saw a new heaven and a new earth; for the first heaven and the first earth were passed away; and there was no more sea."

In this respect the new earth will be different from the old earth, even while it yet maintained its upright posture; inasmuch as "the waters were gathered together into one place," which God in the creation called sea; in the new earth, however, there will be "no more sea." Nothing in Holy Writ would indicate any abatement in the quantity of water pertaining to the earth, but there are many passages which show that there will then be water. John says, "And he (that is, the angel) shewed me a pure river of water of life, clear as crystal, proceeding out of the throne of God and of the Lamb."

Moreover, it is a law in physics that nothing can be destroyed. Matter may be caused to assume many different forms. Compounds may be resolved into their simples, but if left free they will be re-compounded again; for the same law which combined them at first, will reunite the elements in the same proportions and form the same compounds whenever those elements are brought into juxtaposition.

By the action of fire or electricity water may be decomposed, resolved into its constituent gases, yet not one particle of them can be annihilated; but so soon as the disturbing electricity or heat is withdrawn, the normal electricities will force them together again in the form of water. Hence we conclude that the quantity of water belonging to the earth will not be diminished, not even to the extent of a single pint, by the grand ecpyrosis at the new creation. Nevertheless there will be "no more sea;" how then will the waters be disposed of in the new earth?

The arteries and internal veins of the earth will be thoroughly burned out, and the metals and precious stones, all the elements contained within them "melted with fervent heat," will be driven out and thrown to the surface. The depressions which now form the beds of lakes, gulfs, seas, and oceans will be upheaved; and the cooling down of the surface while the fire still rages within, will cause much larger internal cavities than were at the old creation. So that from a rational point of view there can be no more superficial sea, but all the waters will be gathered into the interior of the earth, thus rendering still more perfect the resemblance between the earth and the human body.

The waters of the channels, which answer to the veins in man, will flow out upon the surface for the use of man and beast, then sinking will be disembogued into the great internal sea, by whose ceaseless motion they will be driven out again. The waters will be pulsated back and forth in the body, as indicated by the tidal throbbings in the sea at the present day; except that, uninfluenced by the winds or other disturbing causes, the flux and reflux of the waters will be as regular as the circulation of the blood in a healthy human body.

The whole face of the new earth will present a smooth but undulating surface. All the rich vegetable mould now lying in deep morasses and the bottom of the seas will then be upheaved, and present a dry and inexhaustible soil. Grand and glorious mountains and lovely hills here and there, with rich and fertile sides, will dot the whole face of the earth. A thousand rills, and brooks, and rivulets, and rivers will meander through towering forests and ambrosial bowers; while a rich carpet of vernal green, variegated with sweet flowers of a thousand hues, will spread out in every direction; and luscious fruits, from pole to pole and through all the year, depend from every fruitful bough of tree and vine. Oh! the earth will be a paradise then, an empire over which even the Son of God may delight to reign.

The heavens will also be renewed; for John says, "And I saw a new heaven and a new earth." We see the necessity for the renovation of the earth, and we have attempted to show how that revolution will be effected; but how can a new heaven be created so as to take the place of the old one; to what end and by what means will this grand revolution be accomplished? for God always uses adequate means by which to effect his designs, and all things are done for adequate reasons, whether or not we can fathom them.

The earth will be the same in material and position in the solar system, and the new creation in regard to it will consist in a grand geological revolution wrought out by the mighty agency of fire, and for the purpose of converting the present miserable world into the abode of happiness. The heavens, however, are pure, and good, and blest, and need not be renovated to make them more blissful. We cannot perceive either from prophecy or by the light of reason, why or by what means they may be newly created; therefore we conclude that the "new heaven" which John saw does not mean the holy place where the throne of God and the angels are, but merely the visible heaven above us.

Since the revelation under discussion, as well as all others, is intended for our instruction, and is evidently descriptive of the grand scenes which will then be transpiring upon the earth; and since Moses places the creation of the sun, moon, and stars on the fourth day of the creative week — that being the time when the earth was introduced into the solar system, and the time when to the earth the heavenly bodies appeared to be ushered into being — we conclude that the old heavens will pass away, and the new heavens will be created only in appearance from the earth. We have seen that "the great noise" and the "fervent heat" of which Peter speaks, pertains to the mighty change which will then be wrought in the earth; now let us see if the creation of the new heavens which John and the prophets saw, has not reference to the same terrestrial revolution.

Suppose that an astronomer be taking observations upon the heavens, when the earth is suddenly thrown into an upright position, that is, when the north pole is thrown back 23½ degrees, so that the earth will revolve upon her axis exactly in the plane of her orbit, would not the heavens be new to him?

Further, the atmosphere will be dissolved by the "fervent heat," and when its constituent gases, oxygen and nitrogen, are recombined, all vicious exhalations and noxious gases will have been removed from the firmament, and, as a consequence, the heavenly bodies will appear through the pure and perfect medium of the new world's atmosphere so much more grand and glorious than through the vitiated and murky air which now surrounds us, that the most devoted astrologer would fail to recognize the constellations, or point out the place of the most noted star. "And I saw a new heaven and a new earth; for the first heaven and the first earth had passed away; and there was no more sea."

It does appear that the whole scene depicted by the apocalyptic writer pertains to the earth, and that heaven is referred to merely to show how vastly different in appearance will be even the external surroundings of the new earth. The last clause of the above quoted sentence, it would seem, should settle the question definitely that the ecpyrosis will be a geological and not an astronomical revolution.

After the great burning is finished, after the first heaven and the first earth have passed away, and the new heaven and the new earth have been created, then John saw the holy city on a great and a high mountain, which descended from God out of heaven. It will be fifteen hundred miles long, fifteen hundred miles wide, and fifteen hundred miles high. Its walls of jasper stone will be two hundred and sixty-four feet in thickness. We have seen that no light of the sun or moon can penetrate those walls. John tells us there is no need of such external light, "for," says he, "God Almighty and the Lamb are the light thereof;" but lest we might be deceived, and conclude that God in this or any other instance effects physical ends without the use of physical means, John gives us to understand that the light corruscated from the jasper walls upon the golden streets and mansions of the beloved city. Nothing is done without the use of adequate means.

The exact dimensions of the city are given, as well as the height and thickness of its walls, and the material of which it will be constructed. It will have twelve foundations of precious stones, and twelve gates of pearl; and we must understand that the foundations spoken of each extends from one of the gates to another, and so around the city. From the foundations upward, to the height of fifteen hundred miles, the walls will be built of jasper stone, two hundred and sixty-four feet thick.

We are informed, also, that the streets of the city will be of gold, and that the city itself will be built of fine gold. We are told that there will be the great white throne of God and of the Lamb within the city, and clearly, that there will be twelve other thrones, upon which the twelve apostles will sit, judging the twelve tribes of Israel. "Do ye not know that the saints shall judge the world?" It therefore appears that there will be other judicial thrones within the city than those of the apostles and the great white throne of the Lamb.

In the Revelation, John gives us the proportions of the city, the material of which it is constructed, its walls, its streets, and the city itself. He mentions particularly at least thirteen thrones; and in his evangelical work he reports Christ as having said, "In my Father's house are many mansions. I go to prepare a place for you, that where I am, there ye may be also."

That there must be large provision made for the adopted is evident from the fact that John saw, besides the hundred and forty and four thousand who had been sealed of the tribes of Israel, an innumerable host of every nation and kindred and tongue, who had washed their robes and made them white in the blood of the Lamb, and who are before the throne of God, and serve him day and night in his temple. A mansion for each of the saints will be prepared in the house of God.

If the description of the holy city be a material fact in part, it must be so throughout. If one part be taken literally and the other figuratively, there is an end to all rational inquiry into its meaning. We must not so garble the sacred record. John certainly intended to represent the New Jerusalem as a material city to give us its exact literal dimensions.

"And he that talked with me had a golden reed to measure the city, and the gates thereof, and the wall thereof. And the city lieth four square, and the length is as large as the breadth; and he measured the city with the reed, twelve thousand furlongs. The length, and the breadth, and the height of it are equal. And he measured the wall thereof, an hundred forty and four cubits, according to *the measure of a man, that is, of the angel.*"

The last clause of the last sentence fixes the construction to be literal as to the measurements of the city, and hence, according to all rules for logical, aye, of fair construction, we must take John's description of the New Jerusalem in a literal sense. But if it be taken literally, the city which John saw is the material capital of the world, situated on a great and a high mountain; and it would appear to be a legitimate subject of inquiry for us to try to look into its internal structure.

Is not the phraseology, "In my Father's house are many mansions," rather peculiar, and does it not require explanation to render it intelligible? The word house signifies "a place constructed for the protection of goods, of animals, and for the residence of man;" while the word mansion means "an edifice for the residence of man." The former has the larger, the more comprehensive meaning, while the latter, though more restricted in signification, yet ordinarily carries with it the idea of greater dignity.

In aristocratic countries the lord to whom the estate belongs dwells in a mansion; but his tenants live in houses. The citizens of so-called republics need not, however, go to foreign lands for the illustration here presented; for the *parvenue* aristocrats of our democracies are far more pretentious than the lords of the ancient nobility.

Whenever the words house and mansion are used in the same connection, the latter always conveys the more enlarged idea; and we venture to say that in no other instance, than that now under consideration, is the thought expressed in the English language of a mansion being erected inside of a house.

We presume that this singular expression has not attracted special attention, because it has been received as a figure; but if it would not be good in a literal sense, it cannot possibly be good as a figure. Can a mansion, aye, can many mansions be built in a house? We have seen that in the ordinary use of language this is impossible. Usually the expression is taken figuratively, that is, "my Father's house" is considered the spiritual or intellectual heavens; but in that case what shall we make of it? How can mansions for the abode of the resurrected saints be erected in those heavens?

"In my Father's house are many mansions" is all literal or all figurative. The resurrected saints are material beings. After Christ had risen from the dead, he said to his disciples, "Behold my hands and feet, that it is myself; handle me, and see; for a spirit hath not flesh and bones, as ye see me have." "For if we believe that Jesus died and rose again, even so them also which sleep in Jesus will God bring with him." Therefore the resurrected saints will have "flesh and bones," or will be material beings, and must be accommodated with material abodes. "In my Father's house are many mansions. I go to prepare a place for you."

We understand by "my Father's house" that the holy city, the New Jerusalem, is meant. No other city has ever been described which could with propriety be called a "house;" but this one, whose walls are as tall as they are long, has all the proportions of the most glorious house ever presented for the contemplation of the human intellect. It is fifteen hundred miles long and fifteen hundred miles wide, therefore it has the capacity for containing very many magnificent mansions.

Our only means for looking into the internal structure of the beloved city, besides the few hints given us by John, is to draw deductions analogically from the temple of Solomon and other divinely authorized buildings. It will be observed that these were parallelograms, but divided into three separate compartments of the same dimensions, and perfect squares.

The main building of the temple was forty feet wide and one hundred and twenty feet long. It was divided into three equal sections—the oracle forty feet square and forty feet high, the holy place, or the place of the altar, forty feet square and twenty feet high, and the court where the worshippers assembled, on the floor of the temple, which, like the other compartments, was forty feet square. The porch on the east end of the temple was as wide as the main building, or forty feet, and extended to the front twenty feet. The chambers on the sides of the building were ten, twelve, and fourteen feet, one story above another, showing a diminution in the walls of the house as they ascended. The temple with the chambers was sixty feet wide, without the porch was one hundred and twenty feet long, and it was one hundred and twenty feet high. The porch was adorned with the pillars Boaz and Jachin, or (Beauty and Strength,) and should have been finished by the erection of a third, representing Wisdom; but this could not be, because that pillar was broken, where it was cast, in the clay grounds between Succoth and Zeradatha; a loss, which some of our readers are aware, could not be repaired.

The tabernacle which Moses constructed in the wilderness was built with a view to the same proportions; it having been about sixty feet long, sixty feet high, and twenty feet wide. The first deduction which we make is that divinely authorized buildings are perfect squares; then these squares are multiplied by the mystic number three, giving the parallelograms of the temple and the tabernacle. To the temple was added the half square of the porch, for ornament. From these facts, and those given us by John, we may possibly be able to form a probable conjecture of the internal structure of the holy city.

The "Holy of holies" in the temple was forty feet long, forty feet wide, and forty feet high, or a cube; and John tells us that the walls of the New Jerusalem form a cube of fifteen hundred miles. If that city shall be to the new earth what the oracle was to the earth, then, as we shall hereafter see, it will give us a clue to what will be the dimensions of the new earth. At the present, however, we have to do with the city itself.

If we divide the city into three equal parts, we shall have three parallelograms in the proportions of the temple and of the tabernacle—that is, each of the parallelograms will be composed of three squares of five hundred miles, which gives us nine such squares in the city, or the sacred number multiplied by itself. As in the Jewish economy, the mystic number seven multiplied by itself gives us a round period of time, so also the sacred number three times three gives the full square of the holy city.

Moreover, the front of the temple should have been ornamented with the three pillars of Wisdom, Beauty, and Strength. The first, through the wickedness of man, was wanting; but when the New Jerusalem shall be constructed, there will be no sin; and accordingly John tells us that the front of the city will be adorned with three gates of pearl. There will be, however, four such fronts, making the gates correspond in number with the twelve tribes of Israel, and the foundations of the wall with the twelve apostles.

The "sanctum sanctorum" was in the west end of the temple; wherefore, according to strict analogy, the great white throne of God and of the Lamb, which John saw, should be in the western extremity of the city. But since the former could not be approached except from the east, and since the city will be entered as well from the west, therefore the analogy cannot in this respect be pursued. Equal facility will be offered for entering the city from the north and south as from the east and west; hence it would appear that the throne of the King of kings should be established in the centre, or ninth square, of the city.

There will be no more necessity for the oracle into which the high priest entered once a year to make offerings for himself and all the people. Since the veil is broken down, that compartment, as well as the one in the east, may be appropriated to the use of worshippers. Since the daily sacrifice will have ceased, it would seem that the throne of God and of the Lamb should be erected in the place where the great altar stood.

In this way we may dispose of the central parallelogram running from east to west, or three of the great squares, embracing one-third of the city. The north and the south present similar fronts to the east and west, and for the same reasons the great white throne would be established on the central square of the central north and south parallelogram.

Thus, He who once bore the cross upon which He was ignominiously put to death, will be highly exalted upon the mighty throne erected in the centre of the grand cross of the holy city.

The great white throne will, we may suppose, present four similar fronts; since that is the case with the walls of the city on the east, west, north, and south. The proper front of the throne, however, will be to the east. Besides the five squares which make the grand cross, there are four others in the four corners of the city, which go to make up the grand sacred square and add to the glory of the great King. Each square of the city will contain 250,000 square miles, which multiplied by nine will give 2,250,000, the number of square miles within the jasper walls of the city, the pattern of which John saw descending from God out of heaven.

To the model of the great throne no clue is given, unless it be the mercy-seat, over which brooded the two cherubim, whose wings met in the middle and touched the walls on either side. Nevertheless, it is a great throne, and, according to our deductions, it stands in the centre of the grand cross and of the beloved city. It fronts north and south, east and west, and must be ascended by steps on all sides.

Out of the throne proceeds a pure river of water of life, clear as crystal. "In the midst of the street of it, and on either side of the river, was there the tree of life, which bare twelve manner of fruits, and yielded her fruit every month: and the leaves of the tree were for the healing of the nations." "And I saw, as it were, a sea of glass mingled with fire; and them that had gotten the victory over the beast, and over his image, and over his mark, and over the number of his name, stand on the sea of glass, having the harps of God." Thus the surroundings of the throne are described by John.

In the elaborate description of the restored Israel, and

of the New Jerusalem by Ezekiel, we can see no discrepancy when compared with that of John; and it must be evident, to every one who will take the trouble to examine them, that the two prophets spoke of the same great events. The admeasurement of Ezekiel being multiplied by ten, the city which he saw, will give the dimensions of the New Jerusalem as seen by John. It may be that the former saw not more of the city than a square of one hundred and fifty miles; yet it is clear that he saw the grand cross and the sanctuary which is in its centre.

If we understand the proper mode of calculating the admeasurement of Ezekiel, the oblation for the holy ground is fifty miles square, and the sanctuary in its centre is five miles square, which, multiplied by ten, would make the house which shall be built for the "Prince" fifty miles square, in the midst of a square of five hundred miles, or the entire central square of nine squares of five hundred miles in the New Jerusalem which John saw. In regard to the dimensions of the latter, there can be no doubt, for the apocalyptic writer positively tells us that the admeasurement of the angel in that case was the same as that of a man.

After giving a minute description of the sanctuary, Ezekiel says, "Then he" (the revealing angel) "brought me back by the way of the gate of the outward sanctuary which looketh towards the east; and it was shut." We have already concluded that the great white throne which John saw has four equal fronts, yet the principal front should be that towards the east. Why, then, should Ezekiel find the principal gate at this front shut? Let him explain the mystery.

"Then said the Lord unto me, This gate shall be shut; it shall not be opened, and no man shall enter in by it; because the Lord, the God of Israel, hath entered in by it; therefore it shall be shut. It is for the Prince; the Prince he shall sit in it to eat bread before the Lord; he shall enter by the way of the porch of that gate, and shall go out by the way of the same."

The Prince here spoken of is evidently the same as he who is called by John the "Lamb of God;" and that the sanctuary of Ezekiel is identical with the throne of God and of the Lamb is proven by the fact that the "Lord" and the "Prince" alone might enter at the east gate. The princes of Israel could not enter the oracle of Solomon; hence the vision of Ezekiel could not refer to the literal restoration of the Jews to Palestine.

John saw the New Jerusalem on "a great and high mountain;" and Ezekiel tells us that the house of the Prince, which is in the centre of the city, is built upon the top of the mountain. "This is the law of the house; upon the top of the whole limit thereof shall be most holy." According to our understanding of the measurements of this prophet, this space is fifty miles, or, being multiplied by ten, to make it correspond with the literal admeasurement of John, it is, as before, five hundred miles square, or the ninth part of the grand square of the New Jerusalem.

The house in the centre of this square, by John called the throne of God and the Lamb, is a square, as we understand it, of fifty miles, and, analogically, it must be fifty miles high. We suppose that, like the city itself, it is entered by three gates on the east, three gates on the north, three gates on the south, three gates on the west, for easy access from all parts of the city; yet, as we have seen, the grand gate in the centre of the eastern wall is closed, and is opened only for the ingress and egress of the mighty Prince who reigns over the holy city.

The palace extending twenty-five miles east, west, north, and south from the centre, there will remain of the most holy square two hundred and twenty-five miles in all directions. We may suppose that the "sea of glass mingled with fire," or the magnificent courts of the palace, so beautiful and so grandly glorious that it was represented by John as a sea of glass mingled with fire, will extend towards the four fronts to the distance of fifty miles.

Upon this space, "having the harps of God, stand those who have gotten the victory over the beast, and over his image, and over his mark, and over the number of his name. And they sing the song of Moses, the servant of God, and the song of the Lamb, saying, Great and marvellous are thy works, Lord God Almighty; just and true are thy ways, thou King of saints." These Ezekiel represents as the singers in the temple of the tribe of Levi.

The remaining space of the most holy square, being one hundred and seventy-five miles to the east, west, north, and south, we may suppose to be filled up with royal mansions, in which dwell the singers, and others of his highly favored servants whom the great King has chosen to serve him continually in his holy temple.

John says, however, that he saw no temple in the holy city; but "the great white throne of God and of the Lamb," no doubt, within the palace, to the less lucid vision of other prophets, appeared to be and is called the sanctuary and the temple. In the centre of the divine palace is erected the throne upon which the son of David shall sit and reign forever. That centre is exactly at the north pole, and, as we have seen before, at the centre of the garden where Adam lived and reigned over the world prior to his fall.

There the river parted into four heads to water the garden of Paradise, and there "the waters of the river of life, clear as crystal, shall proceed out of the throne of God and of the Lamb." "Afterward," says Ezekiel, "he brought me unto the door of the house; and behold! waters issued from under the threshold of the house eastward; for the forefront of the house stood towards the east, and the waters came down from under the right side of the house, at the south side of the altar," or, as John would say, of the throne.

"Then brought he me out of the way of the gate northward, and led me about the way without unto the outer gate by the way that looketh eastward; and behold! there ran out waters on the right side." The house, then, fronts, at least, to the north and east, and the waters of the river, though passing out at the east front, yet they flow out at the south end of that front.

As the veins in the top of the human head are quite small, but by rapid aggregation soon form the great jugular vein which pours the blood from the brain to the heart, so the waters flow out from under the throne, and are speedily united, and form the river of life. "And when the man that had the line in his hand went forth eastward [that is, outside of and beyond the wall of the house], he measured a thousand cubits, and he brought me through the waters; the waters were to the ankles. Again he measured a thousand, and brought me through the waters; the waters were to the knees. Again he measured a thousand, and brought me through; the waters were to the loins. Afterwards he measured a thousand, and it was a river that I could not pass over; for the waters were risen — waters to swim in — a river that could not be passed over."

If the palace be fifty miles square, then the waters run from the throne to the east front, and beyond that twenty miles, before they become "a river that could not be passed over" without swimming. After the river passes beyond the walls of the city, it runs down in the exterior plain and disembogues into the internal sea, just as the blood of the head and brain, after being united into one channel, flows externally down the neck, and plunging into the chest, is emptied into the heart."

John says, "In the midst of the street of it," (that is, of the city) "and on either side of the river was there the tree of life, which bare twelve manner of fruits, and yielded her fruit every month; and the leaves of the tree were for the healing of the nations." Ezekiel says, "And by the river upon the bank thereof, on this side and on that side, shall grow all trees for meat, whose leaf shall not fade, neither shall the fruit thereof be consumed; it shall bring forth new fruit according to his months, because their waters they issued out of the sanctuary; and the fruit thereof shall be for meat, and the leaf thereof for medicine."

In the midst of the garden of Eden was the tree of life, and John saw the same growing in the midst of the Holy Jerusalem; therefore, as we have concluded before, the capital of the new created earth will be precisely where the garden of Eden was. As it was watered by the waters coming up the world's aorta, so the beloved city will be gladdened by the rippling waters of the river of life, or the world's great jugular vein.

We have seen that it is possible that the trees which grew in Paradise might be preserved through the cataclysm and the ecpyrosis, and that the identical groves which God planted in the garden of Eden, which bore ambrosial fruits, and the same clustering vines which yielded the nectar which Adam enjoyed when king of the world, will grow in the courts along the golden paved streets of the New Jerusalem. With an additional growth of six thousand years, how magnificently grand and glorious will be those groves! They will no doubt have attained proportions corresponding with the extent and lofty height of the grand capital and the walls of the city.

As the river of the water of life runs through the palace,

so we may expect at least the tree of life will grow within its royal precincts, as well as on that space in front of the palace, by John likened to a sea of glass mingled with fire. In all the remaining front of the most holy square of one hundred and seventy-five miles in extent, many glorious mansions will rise among the towering groves and embowering vines. They will be for the residence of the highly favored saints who are admitted to service in the palace and about the throne of the universal King.

The four squares, east and west, north and south, each of five hundred miles, will be assigned to the residence of the hundred and forty and four thousand of the sealed of the tribes of Israel. Over them the twelve apostles will rule. Reuben, Judah, and Levi shall occupy the square to the north ; Joseph, Benjamin, and Dan, the square to the east ; Simeon, Issachar, and Zebulun, the square to the south ; Gad, Asher, and Naphtali will occupy the square to the west. This information we derive from Ezekiel, but to which of these different squares the different apostles will be assigned we are not informed.

The square of five hundred miles will be divided into three equal parallelograms, fronting to the centre and running back to the walls. Each of these parallelograms will be one hundred and sixty-six and two-thirds miles wide by five hundred in length. The thrones of the apostles should be erected on the front of the section of the city over which each of them reigns.

In the centre of the front of the parallelogram will stand the apostolic palace, probably seven miles square and seven miles high in a square of fifty miles. These palaces will be constructed in the mode of the grand palace of the great King. The square of fifty miles, watered, as is all the city, by branches of the river of life, overshadowed by the ancient groves of Paradise, in which rise the mansions of those who serve around the apostolic thrones, will present a corresponding yet a dissimilar appearance to the palace and the exterior grounds of the most holy square.

The remaining spaces to the right and left of the apostolic palaces will form squares of fifty-eight by fifty miles. These, we may suppose, will each be divided into three parallelograms, fronting towards the great throne twenty-seven miles, running back to the extent of the apostolic square, or fifty miles.

These parallelograms have a palace of probably five miles square resembling the apostolic palace, to which they are subordinate. The next section of the larger parallelogram is divided into seventy-two sections, each containing a palace and its surroundings; twelve of which are subject to one of the thrones to the right or left of the throne of the apostle. These subdivisions continue until each of the parallelograms is divided into twelve thousand sections, all subordinate to the apostle, whose allegiance is due directly to the King of kings.

Thus the four squares to the right and left, and to the front and rear of the central square, which form the grand cross, will each be divided into twelve parallelograms, five hundred miles long and one hundred and sixty-six and two-thirds miles wide; each assigned to the twelve thousand of the sealed of each of the twelve tribes of Israel. One of the apostles shall reign over each of these tribal sections of twelve thousand kings, and all shall cast their crowns at the foot of the great throne at the centre of the cross.

The four squares of five hundred miles each, in the four corners of the city, will be assigned to that host which no man could number, of every nation, kindred, and tongue. In these squares there will be an equal number of thrones, or "a hundred forty and four thousand thrones; therefore there will be, at the least, two hundred and eighty-eight thousand thrones subject to the great throne. All the ministers of all these kings, and all the hosts of the servitors of the great king who inhabit the central square, and serve the King of kings both day and night, will make the "hosts of the holy city" truly "innumerable."

Behold the city, with two hundred and eighty palaces, built upon the model of the great palace, besides the unnumbered mansions of the subjects and ministers of those who sit upon those thrones, and all, both palaces and mansions, constructed of fine gold and precious stones! Is it not a place where a God may dwell? Is it not a capital worthy of the Son of God?

The mansions constructed after the pattern of the temple of Solomon, vastly larger in their proportions near the great throne, and diminishing in size as they increase in numbers towards the outer walls of the city, will be built of the same precious material as the palaces, and the very meanest building within those jasper walls, embracing 2,250,000 square miles, will, no doubt, be equal to the temple at Jerusalem in size and structure, and as far surpassing that house in the splendor of material as fine gold excels the cedars of Lebanon and the stones which Solomon's workmen hewed in the mountains. The gates of the city are pearls, and the streets are paved with gold. The mind of man cannot conceive the grandeur, the beauty, the glory of the New Jerusalem, rendered more sublimely magnificent by the ancient sweet groves of Paradise, planted by the hand of God, and nourished by the waters of the river of life, which permeates every street and lane in all that mighty city. There the saints of all ages live and reign, and no mortal thing can ever enter the pearly gates of the city, for God and the Lamb are the light and life of it. Magnificently grand and glorious will be the capital of the new earth.

"And the nations of them which are saved shall walk in

the light of it; and the kings of the earth do bring their glory and honor into it. And the gates of it shall not be shut at all by day; for there shall be no night there. And they shall bring the glory and honor of the nations into it." This proves, if proof be wanted, that there will still be nations after the first resurrection; that they will have kings to rule over them, who shall bring their glory and honor into the New Jerusalem; which, therefore, will be upon the new earth and her great capital city.

With the lights before us, let us inquire what will be the condition of "the new earth wherein dwelleth righteousness." When Christ shall have restored all things, and is seated upon the throne of David, the government of the whole world is laid upon his shoulder, when he shall wield the sceptre of universal sovereignty once held but afterwards lost by Adam, then more than Adamic blessedness will be restored to the world.

As we have seen before, the new earth will be much larger in superficial extent than it now is. There will then be no disturbing cause to impede the easy and regular flow of the solar electricity, and therefore no partial or spasmodic evaporations; but a general decomposition of water by day, and a regular recombination of its component gases and the descent of the resultant dews by night, as was the case in the ages of the world's perfection and innocency. Hence there will be no more rains to wash off the soil, nor abrasions by the water-courses, so that the rich earth will grow richer still by every crop of vegetation decaying and remaining where it grows.

There will then be no parching drouths, no hurtful rains, no extremes of heat and cold, no suffocating calms nor furious winds, no turbid waters overflowing their prescribed channels, nor strife nor hindrance in all the laws of nature; because He sits upon his highly exalted throne and controls the destinies of the world, who, even in the days of his weakness, commanded the tempest-tossed ocean, "Peace, be still," and the roaring winds were hushed, the seething billows were smoothed as a sea of glass, in obedience to his potent voice.

A luxuriant sward of rich grasses, and of sweet and succulent herbage in every direction, will enable the contented animals to feast without effort and be satisfied. All the grains and useful plants will spontaneously, or with little care, yield through all the year from the bosom of the rich and bounteous earth. The tall pine will wave its graceful plumes high in the gentle zephyrs, which will softly whisper, "Peace on earth, good-will to men." The gigantic oak will proudly rear its stately boughs in vigorous strength far above every surrounding forest, fit emblem of the exalted majesty of all the earth. The vine-clad hills and mountain-tops will be glorious to behold. Rich orange groves, the graceful palm, and every cognate tree pleasant to the sight and good for food, dwarfed specimens of which are now seen only in the tropics, or laboriously cultivated in the temperate zones, will then most perfectly flourish in every dell and valley and extended plain from pole to pole, and all around the circle of the globe. Sweetly murmuring brooks and sparkling rills will in mellow music flow along their gold and silver channels, through every forest, rich grove, and leafy bower. This is the new earth which shall be inherited by the saints; nor have we drawn an overwrought, but the faint, feeble outlines of a picture of what the earth new created will be; for "as it is written, eye hath not seen, nor ear heard, neither have entered into the heart of man, the things which God hath prepared for them that love him."

CHAPTER XXXVII.

The Ecpyrosis — The New Earth — Its Inhabitants — Man made Immortal again through the Resurrection — Reproduction, consequent Death in the New Earth.

TO what end will the earth be remodelled, enlarged; have all her hidden treasures exposed to the light, all the disorders in her nature healed, the wealth of soil of the ages of the past brought to the surface, and consequent unbounded supplies of vegetable production all over the earth, unless there shall be material beings here to use, to appreciate, and to enjoy these vast material supplies, this boundless beauty of physical perfection?

Our great high priest has said, "Blessed are the meek; for they shall inherit the earth;" truly not now, but when the kingdom of God shall come, and when his will shall be done on earth as it is done in heaven. Those who are meek and lowly now shall be highly exalted then; those who are poor and needy now for Christ's sake, shall then abound in wealth; they that are "least among men shall be great when the kingdom of God shall come."

How can these things be, since the just as well as the unjust must die? "Jesus said unto her, I am the resurrection and the life; he that believeth in me, though he were dead, yet shall he live." "Now if Christ be preached that he rose from the dead, how say some among you that there is no resurrection of the dead?" "If the dead rise not, then is not Christ raised; and if Christ be not raised, your faith is vain; ye are yet in your sins. But now is Christ risen from the dead, and become the first fruits of them that slept. For since by man came death, by man came also the resurrection of the dead. For as in Adam all die, even so in Christ shall all be made alive."

The testimony of the twelve apostles and of the five hundred disciples proves, if human evidence can prove a fact, that Christ, who was crucified, dead, and buried, did arise and come forth from the grave on the third day; that he showed himself openly to his disciples, talked with them, ate with them, and in his true body ascended up to heaven in their presence. They were not deceived as to these facts; they either occurred just as they are related, or the five hundred entered into a conspiracy to deceive the world in regard to the most momentous facts ever brought before the minds of men; and therefore are utterly unworthy of confidence on any and all subjects.

It might be possible for the twelve apostles, though illiterate fishermen, to combine to palm off a deception on mankind; but the fact of the resurrection of Christ is proven by five hundred men and women; and we venture to say that if the story of the resurrection was an invention, it is the only instance in the history of our race where so many men and women testified to the same falsehood, and not one out of the number ever betrayed the villany. The fact of the resurrection is clearly proven by the sacred record; it is strongly corroborated by concurrent profane history; in a word, there is no fact in history more satisfactorily proven than that of the death and resurrection of Christ. "But if the spirit of him that raised up Jesus from the dead dwell in you, he that raised up Christ from the dead shall also quicken your mortal bodies by his Spirit that dwelleth in you."

Moreover, if it be clearly proven that one individual of the race of Adam has been raised from the dead, the question, it would appear, should be definitely settled that every one of that race may be also raised from the dead. Is it not strange, then, that so many should doubt, that so few should fully and confidently believe that when these bodies of ours are laid in the dark, cold grave, they shall ever be warmed again into life? The tree which is cut down and buried puts forth a sprout, and the tree arises again in newness of life; so the body which is sown in corruption will germinate itself into renewed and incorruptible being.

We believe as firmly that such a Roman as Julius Cæsar lived as that we live ourselves, or that the sun will rise in the east on each recurring morning. Do we believe as surely that these bodies, after being dead, shall rise again? We know that the sun will rise every morning, because we have seen it do so all our lives; but the fact that such a man as Julius Cæsar flourished in Rome a short time before the Christian era, is not more clearly and fully proven, nor by better and more reliable authority, than the fact of the resurrection of the man Christ Jesus. If he certainly did rise from the dead, it would be irrational stupidity to doubt that we who have just such bodies as his shall also rise.

What is there difficult of belief in the resurrection? It is mysterious how the grain of corn which is buried should germinate into life and produce other corn; yet we can easily believe the fact, because it is patent to our senses; but if the resurrection of the body is made palpable to the reason, shall we hesitate to believe in its truth? It is to us wonderful that the earth should have been compelled to bring forth the first animals, yet all will admit the truth of the proposition.

We see that animals exist only as they are reproduced by other animals; then, if we reason no higher than our experience would go, we must conclude that they have been reproducing forever; but if we search for the primary causes of things, if we weigh things nicely in the scales of rationality, we must perceive that animal life, which depends on circumstances for every moment of its being, could not be self-existent, and therefore not eternal. If the first animals had a beginning, which must have been so from the necessity of the case, how was it?

The naturalist will readily believe that the fungus growths of vegetables, and some of the molluscous growths in the animal kingdom, even now are produced by a favorable combination of circumstances in the operation of the natural laws. He reasons that if the lowest orders of vegetable and animal being may be thus produced now, then, when the circumstances were still more favorable, higher types of both kinds of life may have been originated in the same way.

If, however, the earth may be energized into the production of some animal bodies, it may have produced the first pairs of all animals,—since there must have been first pairs of animals; and since neither reason nor experience has ever suggested any other means for the original production of the animals, therefore the conclusion is irresistible that all vegetable and animal existence was originally brought into being by the vital energies of the earth; that is, that the laws of nature, by which reproduction is now nourished, at some period in the world's history were vigorous enough to bring forth a spontaneous production of vegetable and animal life.

Nevertheless, the question is not left to the uncertain deductions of reason; for Moses tells us that God commanded the earth, and she brought forth the grass, the herb, the tree; that he commanded the waters, and they brought forth the fish and the fowl; and in the fulness of time he commanded the earth, and she brought forth all kinds of animal life, including that of man. The question is settled; and all are agreed that the power of the universal intelligence is sufficient to create the body and organize the life of man from the earth without parents; but when the body has been organized, when it has been inhabited by a rational soul, may not the same power reorganize the body, though dead and disorganized?

Would it be more wonderful, or would it require a greater exertion of power, to recreate the body of Adam than was necessary in the first place to form it? It is legitimate to conclude that the earth may be brought into a condition when, at the command of Omnipotence, the dead bodies of men will be reorganized, and their spirits will return and reoccupy the tenements which decay had driven them to abandon. "But some man will say, How are the dead raised up? and with what body do they come? Thou fool, that which thou sowest is not quickened except it die; and that which thou sowest, thou sowest not that body that shall be, but bare grain; but God giveth it a body as it hath pleased him, and to every seed his own body."

"So also is the resurrection of the dead. It is sown in corruption, it is raised in incorruption; it is sown in dishonor, it is raised in glory; it is sown in weakness, it is raised in power; it is sown a natural body, it is raised a spiritual body." Upon this last declaration many have made shipwreck.

It is said that all bodies are material; that materiality cannot be converted into spirit; therefore, to say "a spiritual body," is to say that there is no body whatever; and by this kind of sophistry some persons high in church authority fritter away the doctrine of the resurrection until it means nothing.

The body is not the body which is raised, and yet it is the same. It is not the same, because "whereas it is sown in corruption, it is raised in incorruption; whereas it was sown in dishonor, it is raised in glory; whereas it was sown in weakness, it is raised in power;" and yet it is the very same; for it is our mortal body which shall be quickened by the Spirit of the Most High.

We know nothing of the resurrection except what is taught us by the illustrious example given us by the Son of man, who died upon the cross, was buried, and who rose again on the third day, and thus became the High Priest as well as the all-sufficient sacrifice of our religion, and King of all the earth.

"And as they thus spake, Jesus himself stood in the midst of them, and saith unto them, Peace be unto you. But they were terrified and affrighted, and supposed that they had seen a spirit. And he said unto them, Why are ye troubled? and why do thoughts arise in your hearts? Behold my hands and my feet, that it is I myself: handle me, and see; for a spirit hath not flesh and bones, as ye see me have." "Then saith he to Thomas, Reach hither thy finger, and behold my hands; and reach hither thy hand, and thrust it into my side; and be not faithless, but believing."

This is the resurrected spiritual body of Jesus; yet could we have stronger and more pointed proof of its materiality, or of its identity with the body which had been nailed to the cross, which had been pierced by the Roman soldier, which was evidently dead and buried? He was the representative of the entire race, and since he died in obedience to the law of our being, so also must we die. As he arose from the dead, so also will we, in the fulness of time, arise from the dead. As his spiritual body was a material body, and the very same which was crucified, so also must ours be the same as those in which we now live.

Without pursuing the subject, we shall assume the fact as proven that the meek of this and of the former ages, who shall have part in the first resurrection, will inherit the earth; but being kings and priests, and having come up through great tribulation from every nation, kindred, and tongue, "are fitly joined together in a holy temple," are "made one in Christ;" therefore they cannot, with any propriety, be called the nations of the earth. If we be adopted into the family of God, then are we his children; if children, then heirs—"heirs of God, and joint heirs with Christ."

Christ is a king and a priest, and all the adopted and redeemed will also be "kings and priests unto God." How can they be kings without kingdoms? and how can there be kingdoms without subjects? "Blessed and holy is he that hath part in the first resurrection: on such the second death hath no power, but they shall be priests of God and of Christ, and shall reign with him a thousand years." All, then, who have part in the first resurrection shall be made kings, exalted upon thrones, and have sceptres given to them; but to what end? Are the insignia of royalty to be bestowed upon the resurrected saints without any corresponding authority?

To place a diadem upon one's head, a sceptre in his hand, the royal robes of a king upon his person, to induct him into the seat of majesty, and then tell him he must be content with these baubles—that there is no kingdom for him to govern, no subjects to do obeisance to his authority—would be intolerable mockery. Such promotion would not be highly prized or greatly sought after by men in this present life. Then can it be imagined, for one moment, that the glittering prize, held out as the inheritance which shall endure through eternal ages to those who are adopted into the household of God, will prove to be nothing but empty show and high-sounding titles?

The Saviour said to the apostles: "And I appoint unto you a kingdom, as my Father hath appointed unto me; that ye may eat and drink at my table in my kingdom, and sit on thrones, judging the twelve tribes of Israel." Paul says: "Know ye not that the saints shall judge the world?" "And I saw thrones," says John, "and they sat upon them, and judgment was given to them; and they lived and reigned with Christ a thousand years."

Are we to believe that these and many other parallel passages mean nothing, and that the apostles and saints of all ages, for whom the Son of God has suffered and died, who washed their robes and made them white in the blood of the Lamb — for whose redemption the power of Omnipotence is exerted — shall all the celestial powers unite to save the sons of men, that they may be made show kings, such as the Lears and Macbeths, who "strut their brief hour upon the stage," and then pass off into the stern realities of life? Shall the passion for high sovereignty which we have inherited from Adam, and which was bestowed upon him for the noblest purposes, be flattered and encouraged in us by the hope held out to us of being made kings in the after life; and when the promise is realized, will it be naught but vain pageantry?

God is not mocked, neither will he deceive any man; and the fruition, instead of falling short, will go beyond our expectations; "for eye hath not seen, ear hath not heard, neither hath it entered into the heart of man to conceive of the things which God has in reservation for those who love his appearing." The saints will certainly be kings; those kings must have kingdoms; those kingdoms must have subjects; hence there must be other inhabitants where they dwell besides themselves. Those inhabitants shall constitute the nations of the new earth, and those kings shall rule over them, and bring the honor and the glory thereof into the holy city, and lay them down at the foot of the great white throne of God and of the Lamb.

Moreover, the waters of the river of life shall flow out from beneath the throne, and the leaves of the tree of life shall be for the healing of the nations. When Christ shall come again, "all things shall be put under him; for he must reign until he has put all enemies under his feet. The last enemy that shall be destroyed is death. When this last enemy is destroyed, then shall the Son also himself be subject unto him that put all things under him, that God may be all in all." There shall be death, then, in that kingdom where Christ shall reign a thousand years, at the end of which time this last enemy shall be crushed.

Death, however, cannot affect the resurrected saints; for nothing dies, or can die, except that which reproduces. "It is sown a natural body; it is raised a spiritual body." Every perfect natural body, whether vegetable or animal, is reproductive; but spirit is not reproductive; therefore, the effect of death and the grave is to remove the desire and the capacity for reproduction; hence, the body is no longer natural, but spiritual, or non-reproducing.

"And Jesus answering, said unto them, The children of this world marry and are given in marriage; but they which shall be counted worthy to obtain that world and the resurrection from the dead, neither marry nor are given in marriage; neither can they die any more; for they are equal unto the angels, and are the children of God, being the children of the resurrection."

Nothing in the question of the Sadducees seems to call forth an answer in regard to the duration of the life which shall follow the resurrection; but they believed that if there were a resurrection, they must marry and be given in marriage. Christ informed them that they neither marry nor are given in marriage: that is, do not reproduce, and, therefore, they cannot die any more. The carnal mind, which is enmity against God, which is not subject to the law of God, neither, indeed, can be, is certainly the same which drove Adam from the garden of Eden, and brought death upon himself and all his race. Philoprogenitiveness can be wholly removed from the Adams only by death and the resurrection.

"When they shall rise from the dead, they are as the angels in heaven;" they cannot die, neither can they suffer from any disease; but the leaves of the tree of life are for the healing of the nations, who, therefore, must be subject to the law of death, and hence must be a multiplying people. Not only so, but they are also liable to sin. The resurrected saints shall be priests as well as kings. Now, the office of a priest is to make intercession with God for the sins of the people.

In further and incontestible proof of the fact that a sinful, multiplying, dying race of men will exist in the new earth, is the grand finale in human affairs as described by John. After Christ and his saints shall have reigned in the new earth a thousand years, in uninterrupted peace and prosperity, then Satan, who has all this time been kept in prison, will be "loosed for a little season, and shall go out to deceive the nations which are in the four quarters of the earth, Gog and Magog, to gather them to battle; the number of whom is as the sand of the sea."

All this, and much more, shows that the earth, during the reign of Christ, will be inhabited by men and by animals as at the present time. How will they get there? Will they be created as at the first, or will they be borne beyond the ecpyrosis as they were preserved through the cataclysm? The former hypothesis will not do, for the new creation of all animate nature, immediately after its destruction, would seem to indicate that there was something wrong in the former creation, and that the design was to improve upon it.

Again: if the vegetable and animal kingdoms were to be wholly destroyed, and a new creation were placed upon the new earth, the prophets would surely have seen so mighty a result, and they would as surely have intimated the same to us. If this were the case, the object for which Christ came into the world could not be accomplished. He came to be the prophet, priest, and king of the lost race of Adam. In the first two offices he has already appeared; and now he must come as the king, not of a new race of beings, but of the children of Adam, who have been new created and made the children of God.

"Behold, I show you a mystery; we shall not all sleep, but we shall all be changed, in a moment, in the twinkling of an eye, at the last trump;" "and the dead in Christ shall rise first; then we, which are alive and remain, shall be caught up together with them in the clouds, to meet the Lord in the air." It would seem, then, that the question is placed beyond doubt, if Paul be taken as authority, the race of Adam will be preserved through the destruction by fire, for many passages show that immediately after the descent of Christ, and while he remains in the air, the burning will occur.

There has been no law violated, no offence against God has ever existed in any of his creatures on earth, except in the white or Adamic race; that is, no constitutional offence, an offence which works a corruption of blood; therefore, if this race pass alive beyond the ecpyrosis, that grace which is sufficient to save them from all their sins will certainly be sufficient to bring every living creature into the happy new earth.

Since Noah outlived the flood by building an ark, which floated upon the bosom of the waters for five months, and furnished him a home for a whole year; and since God accomplishes all his designs by the use of adequate means; therefore we must expect that if men and beasts and birds and fishes are kept alive through the destruction by fire, it will be done by natural and physical means.

"For, behold, the day cometh that shall burn as an oven; and all the proud, yea, and all that do wickedly, shall be stubble; and the day that cometh shall burn them up, saith the Lord of hosts, that it shall leave them neither root nor branch. But unto you that fear my name shall the Sun of righteousness arise with healing in his wings; and ye shall go forth, and grow up as calves of the stall. And ye shall tread down the wicked; for they shall be ashes under the soles of your feet in the day that I shall do this, saith the Lord of hosts."

We have seen that many points on the earth's surface were not submerged by the flood, and that the men and animals on the continents and islands were there saved from destruction by water; so we may conclude that, although the elements shall melt with fervent heat, yet there may be points, and, in a rational view of the subject, there must be points, where animal and vegetable life will be preserved.

The heat will be much more intense at the equator or in the adjacent regions, for there, whether superficially or deeply imbedded in the earth, the greatest deposits of coal must be formed, and there the internal fires will burn most furiously. All living animals will instinctively flee towards the cooler regions of the poles. In this way, it is possible that much animal life may be preserved.

The inventive mind for years has been greatly exercised on the subject of ærial navigation; and although the grand problem has not been fully and satisfactorily solved, yet we may expect that the avistor, or ærial vessel, will yet be manœuvred in the upper air with equal ease and accuracy and far more grace than the ocean steamer in a smooth and capacious bay.

The ark, however, was fitted with neither sail nor rudder; but Noah, having stowed in its hull an ample supply of food, after having taken in the last pair of animals, closed in himself and the living freight, committed the fortunes of all living creatures to the sole guidance of Providence, in the boisterous winds and tempestuous waves of the upheaving flood. So, in like manner, if the ærial vessels were properly constructed, with a view to the carrying of provisions, and left, as the ark was, without any attempt to control its motions, even with the present amount of knowledge of navigating the air, we can see no serious difficulty in preserving animal life through the ecpyrosis.

Any number of avistors might be constructed and held in readiness, or, if it were the design of the Almighty that one man be selected to save life from the fire, as Noah did from the water, might not a vast ærial ark be built to preserve a much larger amount of animal life than was borne over the flood by the ark of Noah? We can see nothing which would seriously militate against such an hypothesis.

It would seem that one or both of the above means might serve in that great emergency. Reason indicates the former, or that there will be points on the earth where vegetable and animal life will not be consumed in the general burning; and revelation shows that the avistor, or some such means, will be employed in the saving at least of human life. "For this we say unto you by the word of the Lord, that we which are alive and remain unto the coming of the Lord shall not prevent them which are asleep. For the Lord himself shall descend from heaven with a shout, with the voice of the archangel, and with the trump of God; and the dead in Christ shall rise first; then we which are alive and remain shall be caught up together with them in the clouds."

In the parallel passage before quoted, it is stated that we shall be changed first; but in what will the change consist? Will we be changed in all respects, so as to be exactly like those who have part in the first resurrection? This would be the suspension of a great fundamental law of the unchanging God, namely, that whatever reproduces or is reproduced must die.

We can perceive no necessity for the performance of so stupendous a miracle, — a miracle which would effect the entire subversion of the law; and hence we expect no such miracle to be wrought. The change, although it may be inconceivably great, can by no means, as we think, extend so far as to render us absolutely immortal without passing through the gates of death.

By the change, our constitutional imperfections and inherited physical defects will be removed; our mental infirmities will be cured; but, wonder of wonders! all our moral obliquities will be separated from us as far as the east is from the west. Envy, jealousy, hatred, malice, covetousness, all evil desires and wicked inclinations shall be removed from our nature, and we shall be the children of God in that sense which is designed by our holy religion; because we shall serve the Lord Christ in his blessed kingdom. Notwithstanding, since we shall continue to be a reproducing race, though without offence, we must still be subject to the law of death; for it is unchanging and unchangeably fixed that whatever reproduces must die.

"We have also a more sure word of prophecy; whereunto ye do well that ye take heed, as unto a light that shineth in a dark place, until the day dawn, and the day-star arise in your hearts: knowing this first, that no prophecy of the Scripture is of any private interpretation. For the prophecy came not in old time by the will of man: but holy men of God spake as they were moved by the Holy Ghost."

After giving the then future history of the nations up to our own time, as the facts have proven to be correct, Daniel says, "And in the days of these kings," or of the governments as they now exist, "shall the God of heaven set up a kingdom, which shall never be destroyed; and the kingdom shall not be left to other people, but it shall break in pieces and consume all these kingdoms; and *it* shall stand forever."

Again he says, "I saw in the night visions, and, behold, one like unto the Son of man came with the clouds of heaven, and came to the Ancient of days, and they brought him near before him. And there was given him dominion, and glory, and a kingdom, that all people, and nations, and languages should serve him: his dominion is an everlasting dominion, which shall not pass away, and his kingdom that which shall not be destroyed."

"And the kingdom and dominion, and the greatness of the kingdom under the whole heaven, shall be given to the people of the saints of the Most High, whose kingdom is an everlasting kingdom, and all dominions shall serve and obey him." "How great are his signs, and mighty are his wonders! his kingdom is an everlasting kingdom, and his dominion is from generation to generation."

Hence it would appear that the thrones of the people of the saints will be subordinate to that of the Most High, which shall endure from generation to generation. This description renders it certain that this dominion cannot be established in heaven or among immortals, but upon the earth and over a multiplying and dying race — immortal rulers, but dying subjects.

Isaiah says, "For, behold, I create new heavens and a new earth: and the former shall not be remembered, nor come into mind. But be ye glad and rejoice forever in that which I create: for, behold, I create Jerusalem a rejoicing, and her people a joy. And I will rejoice in Jerusalem, and joy in my people: and the voice of weeping shall be no more heard in her, nor the noise of crying. There shall be no more thence an infant of days, nor an old man that hath not filled his days: for the child shall die an hundred years old; but the sinner being an hundred years old shall be accursed.

"And they shall build houses and inhabit them; and they shall plant vineyards, and eat the fruit of them. They shall not build, and another inhabit; they shall not plant, and another eat: for as the days of a tree are the days of my people, and mine elect shall long enjoy the work of their hands. They shall not labor in vain, nor bring forth for trouble; for they are the seed of the blessed of the Lord, and their offspring with them. And it shall come to pass, that before they call, I will answer; and while they are yet speaking, I will hear." "For as the new heavens and the new earth, which I will make, shall remain before me, saith the Lord, so shall your seed and your name remain."

It abundantly appears, from this and other prophecies, that children shall be born, and that men shall die after the new heavens and the earth shall have been created, and that the time of the gathering of the tribes of Israel is not until Christ the king shall come in his kingdom. "In that day shall Israel be the third with Egypt and with Assyria, even a blessing in the land, whom the Lord of hosts shall bless, saying, Blessed be Egypt, my people, and Assyria, the work of my hands, and Israel mine inheritance." We must look, therefore, for the restoration of other nationalities than that of Israel; and if, as we suppose and have attempted to show, Israel will not be restored until after the creation of the new earth, the others must be restored at the same time, and there will be many nationalities in the kingdom of Christ and his saints.

"But of that day and hour knoweth no man, no, not the angels of heaven, but my Father only. But as the days of Noah were, so shall also the coming of the Son of man be. For as in the days that were before the flood they were eating and drinking, marrying and giving in marriage, until the day that Noah entered into the ark, and knew not until the flood came, and took them all away; so shall also the coming of the Son of man be. Then shall two be in the field; the one shall be taken, and the other left. Two women shall be grinding at the mill; the one shall be taken, and the other left."

It would appear from this, and parallel passages, that at least a part of those who shall remain alive are to be saved from the fire, as Noah was from the flood; but there is this marked difference, — that whereas Noah saved himself and his entire family in the ark, at the coming of the Son of man, the faith of the father will not save the son, the faith of the daughter will not save the mother, but in both cases the one shall be taken and the other left.

In this way the whole world will be sifted, and those will be chosen whose hearts and lives are right in the sight of God; and they with all the animals shall be saved by flight to the higher and cooler latitudes; or more probably, after their change, the sons and daughters of the race of Adam may ascend, as we have already suggested, in avistors, or ærial arks. It is possible that in the change such a knowledge of the laws of nature will be imparted to them as to enable them to ascend through the air without the intervention of any visible means, other than is used by us in moving from point to point upon the surface of the earth, or in leaping obstacles, or up into the air.

The point, however, which we particularly wish to make, and to urge upon the reader, is the simple fact that there will be a multiplying and dying race of men in the new earth as there was before and during the happy reign of Adam, and before he, by sin, brought death upon himself. We hope that we have made this fact clear in the light of revelation by the passage cited, or at least that enough has been said to enable the honest inquirer after truth to pursue the subject to a satisfactory conclusion. If so, we are ready to investigate and to understand the form of government, the political position of the denizens of the new earth.

We are plainly informed that Christ shall reign from generation to generation. Again: we are told that the saints, those who have come up through great tribulation, and have washed their robes and made them white in the blood of the Lamb, shall reign with him a thousand years. Christ's kingdom is to be an universal empire; and as we have seen, it is to be upon the earth; but the meek, or the saints, shall inherit the earth, and they shall govern the nations, at least the twelve apostles shall sit upon twelve thrones and judge the twelve tribes of Israel. Therefore the universal empire of the world will be divided and subdivided into kingdoms and sub-kingdoms, into royal provinces and sub-provinces, and into municipalities, and over each of these, the smallest as well as the largest, a sceptered saint, invested with regal dignities and sovereign authority, shall reign. Each will owe fealty to the king next in authority above him; and he to his superior; and so on up to the highest; and all shall bow at the throne of the King of kings, and all will pay willing allegiance to the universal Lord, the mighty Prince of peace. The feudal system, with its king and dukes, and lords of manors, gives us the best idea of this involution of sovereignties of these many, many kingdoms which will compose the grand empire of Christ.

We may judge from present indications that most of the pure-blooded Indians who are on the earth when the ecpyrosis comes will be in the southern hemisphere. If we bear in mind the analogy which we have all along drawn between the human body and the world, the southern hemisphere represents the lower extremities, in which the internal ducts and cavities were small, and in which coal deposits must be very limited compared with those of the northern hemisphere.

Then, whatever may be the means used for preserving the

elect of the Adamic race, we would conclude that the red men, or so many of them as shall be chosen, together with the animals of that region, will be kept alive by fleeing towards the south pole. The red man will not entirely escape the curse which was inflicted upon his race by that representative man who tempted Eve to her fall. "Cursed art thou above all cattle." Isaiah, after describing the blessed state of the new earth, says, "And dust shalt be the serpent's meat;" thus showing that he who is more subtle than all the beasts of the field, will be in the new earth; and that the curse, at least in part, has clung to the race even through the world's grand ecpyrosis.

The figure made use of by Isaiah is strongly representative of deep humiliation. The degradation of the Indian or serpent race will consist in this, that the tribal form of government, or rather savage freedom so much loved by that ancient race, must be forever given up, and they must be brought under the rule of the saint-kings of the hated race of Adam.

In that kingdom none but immortals will hold authority. Those who have lived in hope — have died in the faith, have come up through great tribulation, have washed their robes and made them white in the blood of the Lamb — they, resurrected, shall be kings and priests unto God, and shall reign in the holy city, and on the mountains, and they shall rule over the people and nations and kindreds and tongues all over the luxuriant and happy earth.

The curse which Adam inflicted upon the world being removed, all vegetable and animal beings will flourish as when Adam reigned in Paradise. All of the children of the flesh, or of Adam, who are preserved through the ecpyrosis, shall be redeemed from the abnormal relationship in which we now stand in the Divine economy; for we shall all be adopted into the household of God. Nations, at the coming of Christ, shall be born in a day, or, as Paul expresses it, be changed in a moment, in the twinkling of an eye.

All inherited diseases and constitutional defects will be removed by the change which shall pass over the denizens of the world; yet the law, that whatever reproduces must die, is immutable; and though they be long-lived as "the trees," yet God hath said, "In the day thou eatest thereof," or reproducest, "thou shalt surely die;" therefore, the people of the new earth may live out a day, or a thousand years, as did the antediluvians, but still they must die; for "the child shall die an hundred years old."

That there will be sin in the new earth is proven by the priestly office of the rulers of the people; but the fact is placed beyond a peradventure, by the declaration of Isaiah, that "the sinner of an hundred years old shall be accursed." That the people will have the capacity to do wickedly, and that they will actually sin, is proven by the fact that after a thousand years' imprisonment the Devil will be released a little season, in which he will deceive the nations of the earth, and induce them to rise in mighty rebellion against the government of the universal King.

CHAPTER XXXVIII.

THE "ANCIENT OF DAYS"—"ONE LIKE UNTO THE SON OF MAN"—THE PRAYER "THY KINGDOM COME," &c., NOW FULLY ANSWERED.

WE must remark upon one or two other points and we have done. "One like unto the Son of man came unto the Ancient of days." We have used this passage in another connection; but the question, Who are these characters — the one like unto the Son of man and the Ancient of days? comes up for solution, and we are unwilling "to call it Jacob, and go on."

We believe that the older commentators understand them to be Christ and the everlasting Father. Some late writers, however, have thought that the Ancient of days represents the fifth in the series of governments, the one like unto the Son of man being Christ; but a still later writer makes the one like unto the Son of man, who received dominion and a kingdom from the Ancient of days, to represent the sixth and final human government, as brought to light in the vision of Daniel.

That the Ancient of days cannot mean the eternal Father is evident from the fact that such a representation would be a gross violation of the second commandment. Daniel, as the prophet of the Most High, could not have represented the mighty God as an old man, whose garments were white as snow, "and the hair of his head was like the pure wool."

"Thou shalt not make unto thee any graven image, nor any likeness of anything that is in heaven above, or that is in the earth beneath, or that is in the water under the earth: thou shalt not bow down thyself to them, nor serve them: for I the Lord thy God am a jealous God, visiting the iniquity of the fathers upon the children unto the third and fourth generation of them that hate me, and showing mercy unto thousands of them that love me, and keep my commandments."

If Daniel intended the likeness of the old man whom he calls the Ancient of days to be a representation of Deity, he certainly presented the picture to be worshipped; therefore, he was not only a wilful, flagrant violator of the law, but a teacher of idolatry. This violent supposition would make that highly-favored prophet a wolf in sheep's clothing — the devil in robes of light — with greater ability to lead the people astray on this subject than any other man, because his zeal for the pure worship of the true God induced him, literally, "to brave the lion in his den."

How nearly would Daniel's old man, with curly hair, clothed in white robes, and seated on a chariot-throne of fire, resemble the Jupiter Olympus of the Greeks, and the Jupiter Tonans of the Romans? No other writer in the Bible attempts to give us a picture of the Universal Intelligence; hence, we would conclude that it is doing great injustice to this prophet to understand him as representing the Omnipotent as the Ancient of days.

Again: in the parallel vision of Nebuchadnezzar (for both this and that of Daniel were in regard to the then future governments of the world), the fifth kingdom is represented by the feet of the image, which were composed of iron and clay; and the sixth is represented by the little stone cut out of the mountain without hands, which smote the image upon his feet, and broke in pieces the iron and the clay, the brass, the silver and the gold, the materials of which the image was formed; and the stone became a great mountain, and filled the whole earth.

If the Ancient of days, in the vision of Daniel, represents the Deity, what shall we say of the corresponding objects, the iron and the clay of the feet of the image of Nebuchadnezzar? If the iron and clay in the feet of the latter represent a partly spiritual and partly temporal government, which, as well as all human governments whatever, shall be broken to pieces by the little stone cut out of the mountain, it would seem that the Ancient of days should foreshadow the same thing.

The first four objects in the vision of Daniel refer to the same governments as the first four in the image of Nebuchadnezzar. Nearly all the commentators are agreed, no doubt correctly, that the little stone in one vision signifies the church, and the one like unto the Son of man in the other means Christ. If the two visions indicate the same things in the first, second, third, fourth, and sixth representations, without controversy they must agree in the fifth objects. A rational view of the subject renders it perfectly clear that the vision of Daniel is a re-exhibition of the facts brought out in that of Nebuchadnezzar, the former enlarging and elucidating the features presented less distinctly in the latter vision.

If, therefore, the iron and the clay in the feet of the image represent the Church of Rome, so also must the Ancient of days in the vision of Daniel. If the iron and the clay represent the union of church and state throughout Christendom, then the Ancient of days represents the universal union of church and state. If the Ancient of days in the one vision means, as some contend, the government of the United States of America, then the iron and the clay in the other must mean the United States.

The first four governments are purely of human invention; and the fifth also, in the vision of Nebuchadnezzar as explained by Daniel, is a human government mixed with another element. That element, as explained in the prophet's own vision, is the power of the saints. It seems that this power existed, though not in force, during the reign of the ten kings represented by the ten horns of the fourth beast, and that the government represented by the eleventh horn, which came up and before which three horns fell, made war with the saints, and prevailed against them until the Ancient of days came, when judgment was given to them. Hence we conclude that the fifth object in the one vision and in the other, represents human government as it exists in Christian countries at the present day, largely directed as it is by the influence of the Christian churches.

"And in the days of those kings" (represented by the ten

toes of the image, and of the ten horns, and of the other horn of the fourth beast) "shall the God of heaven set up a kingdom which shall never be destroyed." This is the explanation of the little stone, or sixth object, in the vision of Nebuchadnezzar, and must be identical with the sixth object, or the one like unto the Son of man in the vision of Daniel.

In the one vision, the stone crushes the image representing human government, and the God of heaven sets up a kingdom which shall never be destroyed; and in the other, the one like unto the Son of man is presented before the Ancient of days, or the representative of civil and ecclesiastical institutions, and receives "dominion, and glory, and a kingdom, that all people, nations, and languages should serve him; his dominion is an everlasting dominion, which shall not pass away, and his kingdom that which shall not be destroyed."

Instead, therefore, of limiting the fifth representation in the former vision to a single church, we should, no doubt, understand it to symbolize all Christian governments in these last days, because in all the people are governed by ecclesiastical law and ecclesiastical influence, as well as by state authority. The fifth object in the vision of Nebuchadnezzar brings to view the idea only of the union of church and state; while the corresponding representation in the vision of Daniel sets forth the same, and the additional idea of individuality called the Ancient of days.

We have seen how preposterous is the interpretation which would make the Ancient of days to mean the eternal Father; then who is this venerable, this august, this majestic character, whose garment was white as snow, and the hair of whose head was like pure wool; whose throne was like the fiery flame, and his wheels as burning fire? It might be possible that this exalted character is used merely as the ideal of the improved governments of Christendom; but it is not at all probable. If the Son of man means an individual, so also must the Ancient of days signify an individual; but if so, what individual was meant?

It was not Messiah, because he is the one like unto the Son of man, who came to the Ancient of days and received the dominion, the glory, and the kingdom which were taken from the latter. Since the individual represented by the Ancient of days cannot be the first Adam who wilfully forfeited all authority and all claims to dominion then and forever; nor the second Adam, who, by the fulfilment of the law, won back an everlasting kingdom which shall never be removed; then who is this Ancient of days who shall deliver up the dominion into the hands of the one like unto the Son of man? Unless we can answer the question from the Scriptures, it must forever remain one of the "hidden mysteries."

"And it came to pass, that the beggar died, and was carried by the angels into Abraham's bosom: the rich man also died, and was buried; and in hell he lifted up his eyes, being in torments, and seeth Abraham afar off, and Lazarus in his bosom. And he cried and said, 'Father Abraham, have mercy on me, and send Lazarus, that he may dip the tip of his finger in water, and cool my tongue; for I am tormented in this flame.' But Abraham said, 'Son, remember that thou in thy lifetime receivedst thy good things, and likewise Lazarus evil things: but now he is comforted, and thou art tormented.'

"And besides all this, between us and you there is a great gulf fixed: so that they which would pass from hence to you cannot; neither can they pass to us, that would come from thence. Then he said, 'I pray thee therefore, father, that thou wouldest send him to my father's house: for I have five brethren; that he may testify unto them, lest they also come into this place of torment.' Abraham saith unto him, 'They have Moses and the prophets; let them hear them.'

And he said, 'Nay, father Abraham: but if one went unto them from the dead, they will repent.' And he said unto him, 'If they hear not Moses and the prophets, neither will they be persuaded, though one rose from the dead.'"

From this account of our Saviour it would appear that the disembodied spirits of the righteous go to some intermediate place between this stage of action and heaven; where they are comforted, and where they enjoy the company of the patriarchs and prophets; of the good who have gone before, and of the saints of all ages. It would also seem that Abraham is the chief personage there, because that he is the father of the faithful; and the place itself, because it is the receptacle of the faithful or of Abraham's spiritual children, is called in the above account Abraham's bosom.

"And Jesus said unto him" (the thief), "Verily, I say unto thee, to-day shalt thou be with me in Paradise." Lazarus went to Abraham's bosom, and Christ and the redeemed thief went to Paradise. There is no intimation anywhere in the Bible of more than one intermediate place of rest for the spirits of the just between the earth and the heavens; then it is evident that Abraham's bosom and Paradise are but different names for the same place.

Moreover, we have already seen that Paradise is the garden of Eden; hence, may we not conclude that Abraham's bosom is the Paradise from which Adam and Eve were driven out, which was surrounded by a physical barrier to prevent their physical return? The spirits of the faithful do go to that beatific place, and there Enoch and Moses and Elias have gone; and Abraham, the friend of God and the father of the faithful, presides over the happy hosts.

Those justified spirits are our ministering angels, and therefore they are still connected with the affairs of men, and Abraham controls the spiritual interests of the world. If these facts and deductions be correct, then the Ancient of days in the vision of Daniel must be Abraham; and when the Prince of peace shall come in his kingdom, he will not only crush out all the political institutions of the world, but Abraham shall yield up his authority as the father of the faithful into the hands of him who hath redeemed the world to himself, and who henceforth shall be King of kings and Lord of lords, and exercise all dominion, both spiritual and temporal, over all the earth forever and forever.

The sixth and last object in the visions of Nebuchadnezzar and of Daniel—which represented all human government to the end of the world—being, in the former, a little stone cut out of the mountain without hands, which smote the iron and clay of the feet and crushed the image to powder, and grew and increased until it filled the whole earth; and in the latter vision being "the one like unto the Son of man, whom they brought near before the Ancient of days, and to whom was given dominion, and glory, and a kingdom, that all people, nations, and languages should serve him"—evidently allude to the coming of a mighty power, which has not yet been established, and whose conditions can only be complied with by the introduction of divine power into the governments of the world.

Daniel says that the one like unto the Son of man "came with the clouds of heaven," which is the identical language used by our Saviour himself, and all his apostles, in describing the second coming of Christ to establish his final kingdom here; therefore, the sixth object in each of the visions under consideration refers to the establishment on earth of the theocratic government of Messiah.

Daniel says, "His dominion is an everlasting dominion, which shall not pass away, and his kingdom that which shall not be destroyed." John says, "Blessed and holy is he that hath part in the first resurrection; on such the second death shall have no power: they shall be priests of

God and of Christ, and shall reign with him a thousand years.".

According to the commonly received interpretation of these prophecies, they are at issue, and incompatible with each other; but in reality, as we will see in the end, there is no difference between them, except, perhaps, that the later prophets saw more clearly as to the duration of the mighty kingdom. Nevertheless, Daniel might have said, with propriety, of the permanent government of "the one like unto the Son of man," which he, with Isaiah, saw increasing gloriously through the grand procession of the ages in the mighty cycles rolling down amidst the mystic evolutions of the future, that "His dominion is an everlasting dominion, which shall not pass away, and his kingdom that which shall not be destroyed."

John, however, fixes the time of the duration of the kingdom of Christ on earth at "a thousand years." It is believed that all Christians are agreed that this period of time is to be taken literally; upon what grounds, and for what good reasons, we confess that we are unable to perceive. Nowhere else, in all the prophecies, is literal time in the future given; then why should any one suppose that so violent a departure would be made from the invariable rule for writing and construing prophetic time in this isolated instance?

All are agreed that "time, times, and the dividing of time," and "time, times and a half," in the writings of Daniel, and "for a time, and times, and half a time," in Revelation, signify three years and a half, not of ordinary, but of prophetic time, in which each day represents one of our years. In the prophetic month are thirty days, in the year twelve months, then in the prophetic year are three hundred and sixty days; so that "time, times, and half a time" indicate one thousand two hundred and sixty years.

The seventy weeks in Daniel indicate four hundred and ninety years; the five months in Revelation are one hundred and fifty years. The thousand three hundred and five and thirty days, and a thousand two hundred and ninety days in Daniel, and the forty-two months and the thousand two hundred and threescore days in Revelation, mean respectively 1335 years, 1290 years, and 1260 years. But why multiply references? for in all these, and many other places, it is established beyond a doubt that a day in prophetic time is taken for a year.

Is it not passing strange, then, how the idea has become so widely prevalent that in a solitary instance John should have departed from the otherwise unbending rule for the writing and construction of prophetic time? How twelve hundred and sixty days in one chapter should mean twelve hundred and sixty years, and one thousand years in another chapter of the same book should mean but a thousand years, and that, too, without any notice whatever by the author of any difference in the mode of construction, would be one of the greatest enigmas with which we have ever met in the art of communicating thought by written language; and, unless there is some reason potent and unavoidable, we shall reject the absurd, vulgar gloss, though the traditions of all the Fathers be against us.

John tells us that Satan shall be bound a thousand years, and that the saints shall reign with Christ a thousand years; therefore the time here spoken of by him refers to immortal beings; an epoch, according to Isaiah, in which the child shall die being an hundred years old, and the lives of men shall be like the lives of trees, which now grow from generation to generation. Who will contend that the prophets would make a day mean a year in the historic ages of the present race of ephemeral men, and in the very same connection that he should use plain language, making a year stand for a year in regard to that time in which immortals are the actors? A few moments' reflection will satisfy any one that the thousand years in which the saints will reign with Christ should be so construed as to be placed at least on as high ground as that on which all prophetic time referring to the past and the present is placed.

We have seen that in the grand historic visions of Daniel and of John a day means a year, a week means seven years, a month thirty years; and there can be no departure from this rule of construction without notice of the variance either in the text or the context. Therefore, when John speaks of an epoch in the world's history, in which the actors are immortals, he cannot intend to express by "a thousand years" less than one thousand years of days or 360,000 years.

We hope that it was made apparent in the former part of this work that a thousand years are but as one day with the Lord; and this is the inferior day in divine computation, used only in connection with the history of our race. If this rule be applied in the construction of the time under consideration, that is, by ascertaining the number of days in 360,000 years, which is done by multiplying by 360 the number of days in one year, we obtain 129,600,000 days. If each of these days be taken for 1000 years, we shall have 129,600,000,000 years adumbrated in the thousand years of Christ's reign on earth — an eternity to our comprehension, a duration to which the prophets might well refer as being from everlasting to everlasting.

As we have the sure word of prophecy for the former term; since 360,000 years seem to be a period of time worthy of the efforts of the Son of man for the establishment of his kingdom; since it would be sufficient time for developing and perfecting the operations of nature; since it would be one full year of human superior, or of divine inferior time, therefore we are content, for the present at least, to treat the subject in this light.

It would be irrational to suppose that the mighty efforts of God, which have been made for the redemption of the world, extending, as they have, through six days or six thousand years, would be made to secure the triumph of his designs for a single day of one thousand years. Shall the devil reign six thousand years? and shall Christ, the anointed of God, reign but one thousand years?

Adam lived out almost such a day, even after he had violated the law of life; and shall the resurrected and immortal Adam, whose mission is to put all things, even death, under his feet, reign in the redeemed and recreated earth no longer than the old and sinning Adam lived in the old and cursed earth? We repeat it, that by no rational construction nor logical deduction can we arrive at the conclusion that Christ with his saints shall reign in the new earth less than 360,000 years.

Here we may remark, as we have done before, that the Arabians, Pythagoras, Strabo, and other old philosophers, who, no doubt, drew their information from the Egyptians, the Chaldeans, and other such sources of the learning of a deeper antiquity, fixed full periods of time at from 120,000 to 360,000 years. This would suggest the curious inquiries, did not the learned associations of the ancient priesthood preserve some traces of the true order and mode of the creation? and was not geology, a science which has but recently been revived among us, understood by them much more perfectly than it is now by our most learned professors? or, still more probably, that both of these conclusions are correct? There is an astonishing coincidence in the profound teachings of modern geology, the learning of the ancient philosophers, and the cosmogony of Moses, in the reading of the footprints of the ages of the past and the future grand procession of the mighty cycles of time, as brought to view in the apocalyptic visions of Daniel and of John.

The saints shall reign with Christ in the new earth a thousand years of prophetic time, which is really not less than 360,000 years. This will be a Sabbath of rest for the weary earth, a glorious epoch for the dominion of the Son of man. The new earth will be restored to more than her pristine beauty; her exuberance of soil and luxuriance of production will far surpass the old earth, even prior to the fall of Adam. There will be "no more sea," and its surface will be greatly enlarged beyond its present limits, will be covered everywhere with the richest grass and herbage, with bountiful harvests of grain and every kind of tree, bearing luscious fruits to supply the wants of men and beasts.

What untold millions may live and flourish and be happy then, with every want and every desire gratified as soon as they arise! The polarity of the earth will be rectified; the days and nights will be equal from pole to pole through all the year; the seasons will only slightly vary, as the earth passes from the perihelion to the aphelion of her orbit. There will be no extremes of heat and cold; there will be no rains nor drouths, because the flow of electricity will be uninterrupted, and no angry flashing of the lightning, but the regular evaporations by day will be recompounded and descend in due by night. No extraordinary exhalations of noxious vapors from stagnant waters or rapidly decaying vegetation can exist; so that there can be no such thing as malarious sickness in all the earth.

By reason of the purity of the atmosphere, the heavens will be new; the days will be glorious by the bright shining of the sun; the nights will be beauteous by the clearness of the moon and stars, and by the rich corruscations of light from the holy city. It is not strange that the lives of the reproducing men of that grand epoch should be as the lives of the trees, and that children should die being an hundred years old.

Oh, this will then be a glorious world! The Son of man will be highly exalted upon the great white throne in the midst of the New Jerusalem, surrounded by the most highly favored of the saints as his ministers of the realm and servants of his will; while others of the resurrected saints will be enthroned as kings and priests in the states and provinces of the world, and will all go regularly up to the holy city to bear their allegiance and lay the glory of the nations at the foot of the throne of the great King. "And there were great voices in heaven, saying, The kingdoms of this world are become the kingdoms of our Lord, and of his Christ; and he shall reign forever and ever."

So far as we have gone in establishing a rational view of the condition of the world prior to the fall, and of the present abnormal state of things, so far have we proceeded in ascertaining what it must be in the future. What God first designed in regard to our world, he will certainly accomplish in the end. All moral evils must be removed. All physical ills must be cured. This, and this alone, can satisfy the conditions of prophecy and the demands of reason. Then let us here close devoutly, as we began, with the petitions, "Thy kingdom come; Thy will be done on earth, as it is done in heaven."

THE END.

CPSIA information can be obtained
at www.ICGtesting.com
Printed in the USA
LVHW032001130323
741532LV00002B/374

9 783382 119843